Seating Arrangements

Seating Arrangements

Maggie Shipstead

W F HOWES LTD

This large print edition published in 2012 by
W F Howes Ltd
Unit 4, Rearsby Business Park, Gaddesby Lane,
Rearsby, Leicester LE7 4YH

1 3 5 7 9 10 8 6 4 2

First published in the United Kingdom in 2012
by Blue Door

A CIP catalogue record for this book is available
from the British Library

ISBN 978 1 47120 178 3

Typeset by Palimpsest Book Production Limited,
Falkirk, Stirlingshire
Printed and bound in Great Britain
by MPG Books Ltd, Bodmin, Cornwall

To my parents, Patrick and Susan,
pillars of everything

The river bears no empty bottles, sandwich papers,
Silk handkerchiefs, cardboard boxes, cigarette ends
Or other testimony of summer nights. The nymphs are
  departed.
And their friends, the loitering heirs of City directors;
Departed, have left no addresses.

T. S. ELIOT, *The Waste Land*

CONTENTS

THURSDAY

FRIDAY

SATURDAY

THURSDAY

CHAPTER 1

THE CASTLE OF THE MAIDENS

By Sunday the wedding would be over, and for that Winn Van Meter was grateful. It was Thursday. He woke early, alone in his Connecticut house, a few late stars still burning above the treetops. His wife and two daughters were already on Waskeke, in the island house, and as he came swimming up out of sleep, he thought of them in their beds there: Biddy keeping to her side, his daughters' hair fanned over their pillows. But first he thought of a different girl (or barely thought of her – she was a bubble bursting on the surface of a dream) who was also asleep on Waskeke. She would be in one of the brass guest beds up on the third floor, under the eaves; she was one of his daughter's bridesmaids.

Most mornings, Winn's entries into the waking world were prompt, his torso canting up from the sheets like the mast of a righted sailboat, but on this day he turned off his alarm clock before it could ring and stretched his limbs out to the bed's four corners. The room was silent, purple, and dim. By nature, he disapproved of lying around. Lost time could not be regained nor missed mornings

3

stored up for later use. Each day was a platform for accomplishment. Up with the sun, he had told his daughters when they were children, whipping off their covers with a flourish and exposing them lying curled like shrimp on their mattresses. Now Daphne was a bride (a pregnant bride, no point in pretending otherwise) and Livia, her younger sister, the maid of honor. The girls and their mother were spending the whole week on the island with an ever-multiplying bunch of brides-maids and relatives and future in-laws, but he had decided he could not manage so much time away from work. Which was true enough. A whole week on the matrimonial front lines would be intoler-able, and furthermore, he had no wish to confirm that the bank would rumble on without him, his absence scarcely noticed except by the pin-striped young sharks who had begun circling his desk with growing determination.

He switched on the lamp. The windows went black, the room yellow. His jaundiced reflection erased the stars and trees, and he felt a twinge of regret at how lamplight obliterated the predawn world, turning it not into day but night. Still, he prided himself on being a practical person, not a poetic soul vulnerable to starlight and sleep fuzz, and he reached for his glasses and swung his feet to the floor. Before going to bed he had laid out his traveling clothes, and when he emerged from the shower, freshly shaven and smelling of bay rum, he dressed efficiently and trotted downstairs, flipping on more lights as he went. He had packed Biddy's Grand Cherokee the night before, fitting everything together with geometric precision: all the items forgotten and requested by the women, plus bags and boxes of groceries, clothes for himself, and sundry wedding odds and ends. While the coffee brewed, he went outside with the inventory he was keeping on a yellow legal pad and began his final check. He rifled through a row of grocery bags in the backseat and opened the driver's door to check for his phone charger, his road atlas – even though he could drive the route with his eyes closed – and a roll of quarters, crossing each off the list in turn. Garment bags and duffels stuffed to fatness made a bulwark in the back, and he had to stand on tiptoe and lean into the narrow pocket of air between them and the roof to confirm the presence in the middle of it all of a glossy white box the size of a child's coffin that held Daphne's wedding dress.

'Don't forget the dress, Daddy,' the answering machine had warned in his daughter's voice the previous night. 'Here, Mom wants to say something.'

'Don't forget the dress, Winn,' said Biddy.

'I won't forget the damn dress,' Winn had told the plastic box.

He crossed 'Dress' off the list and slammed the back hatch. Birds were calling, and yellow light bled through the morning haze, touching the grassy undulations and low stone wall of his neighbor's estate. Strolling down the driveway to retrieve his newspaper from a puddle, he noticed a few stones that had fallen from the wall onto the shoulder of the road, and he crossed over to restore them, shaking droplets from the *Journal*'s plastic sack as he went. The hollow sound of stone on stone was pleasant, and when the repair was done, he stood for a minute stretching his back and admiring the neat Yankee face of his house. Nothing flashy and new would ever tempt him away from this quiet neighborhood inhabited by quality people; the houses might be large, but they were tastefully shrouded by trees, and many, like his, were full of thin carpets and creaking, aristocratic floors.

His Connecticut house was home, and his house on Waskeke was also home but a home that was familiar without losing its novelty, the way he imagined he might feel about a long-term mistress. Waskeke was the great refuge of his life, where his family was most sturdy and harmonious. To have all these people, these wedding guests, invading his private domain rankled him, though he could scarcely have forbidden Daphne from marrying on the island. She would have argued that the island was her island, too, and she would have said Waskeke's pleasures should be shared. He wished that the ferry could take him back into a world where the girls were still children and just the four of them would be on Waskeke. The problem was not that he wasn't pleased for Daphne (he was) or that he did not appreciate the ceremonial importance of handing her into another man's keeping (he did). He would carry out his role gladly, but the weekend, now surveyed from its near edge, felt daunting, not a straightforward exercise in familial peacekeeping and obligatory cheer but a treacherous puzzle, full of opportunities for the wrong thing to be said or done.

He drove north along leafy roads, past brick and clapboard towns stacked on hillsides above crowded harbors. The morning was bright and yellow, the car scented with coffee and a trace of Biddy's perfume. Freight trains slid across trestle bridges; distant jetties reached like arms into the sea. Pale rainbows of sunlight turned circles across the windshield. For Winn, the difficulty of reaching Waskeke was part of its appeal. Unless forced by pressures of time or family, he never flew. The slowness of the drive and ferry crossing made the journey more meaningful, the island more remote. Back when the girls were young and querulous and prone to carsickness, the drive was an annual catastrophe, beset by traffic jams, mix-ups about ferry reservations, malevolent highway patrolmen, and Biddy's inevitable realization after hours on the road that she had forgotten the keys to the house or medication for one of the girls or Winn's tennis racquet. Winn had glowered and barked and driven with the grim urgency of a mad coachman galloping them all to hell, all the while knowing that the misery of the trip would sweeten the moment of arrival, that when he crossed the threshold of his house, he would be as grateful as a pilgrim passing through the gates of the Celestial City.

Arriving at the ferry dock an hour early, exactly as planned, he waited in a line of cars at a gangway that led to nothing: open water and Waskeke somewhere over the horizon. Idly, he rolled down the window and watched gulls promenade on the wharves. The harbor had a carnival smell of popcorn and fried clams. When he was a child, for a week in the summer his father would leave the chauffeur at home in Boston and drive Winn down to the Cape himself (such a novelty to see his father behind the wheel of a car). The ferry back then was the old-fashioned, open-decked kind that you had to drive onto backward, and Winn had thrilled at the precarious process even though his father, who might have played up the drama, reversed the car up the narrow ramp with indifferent expertise. They had owned a small place on Waskeke, nothing grand like the Boston house, just a cottage on the edge of a marsh where the fishing was good. But the cottage had been sold when Winn was at Harvard and torn down sometime later to make room for a big new house that belonged to someone else.

The ferry docked with loud clanging and winching and off-loaded a flood of people and vehicles. Some were islanders on mainland shopping expeditions, but most were tourists headed home. Winn was pleased to see them go even if more were always arriving. A worker in navy blue coveralls waved him up the gangway into the briny, iron-smelling hold, and another pointed him into a narrow alley between two lumber trucks. He checked twice to be sure the Cherokee was locked and then climbed to the top deck to observe the leaving, which was as it always was – first the ship's whistle and then the slow recession of the harbor's jumbled, shingled buildings and the boat basin's forest of naked masts. Birds and their shadows skimmed the white-caps. Though he never wished to indulge in nostalgia, Winn would not have been surprised to see shades of himself stretching down the railing: the boy beside his father, the collegian nipping from a flask passed among his friends, the bachelor with a series of dimly recalled women, the honey-mooner, the young father holding one small girl and then two. He had been eight when his father first brought him across, and now he was fifty-nine. A phantom armada of memory ships chugged around him, crewed by his outgrown selves. But the water, as he stared down over the rail, looked like all other water; he might have been anywhere, on the Bering Strait or the river Styx. Without fail, every time he was out on the ocean, the same vision came to him: of himself lost overboard, floundering at the top of that unholy depth.

As the crossing always had the same beginning, so, after two hours, it always had the same end

– a gray strip of land separating the blue from the blue, then lighthouses, steeples, docks, jetties reaching for their mainland twins. There was a little lighthouse at the mouth of the harbor where by tradition passengers on outbound ferries tossed pennies off the side. Livia had said as a child that the sea floor there must look like the scales of a fish, and, ever since, the same thought had come to Winn as he passed the lighthouse: a huge copper fish slumbering below, one bulbous eye opening to follow the ferry's turning propellers. They docked, and as he drove down the ramp into the bustling maze of narrow streets that led out of Waskeke Town, he hummed to himself, relishing solid land.

A battered mailbox labeled 'VAN METER' with adhesive letters stood at the entrance to his driveway. The narrow dirt track was edged by tall evergreen trees, and he drove up it with mounting excitement, the trees waving him on until he emerged into sunlight. Atop a grassy lump, not quite a hill, that rose like a monk's tonsure from an encirclement of trees, the house stood tall and narrow, its gray shingles and simple facade speaking of modesty, comfort, and Waskeke's Quaker past. Above the red front door a carved quarterboard read 'PROPER DEWS,' the name he had given the house upon its purchase. The pun was labored, he knew, but it had been the best he could come up with, and he had needed to replace the board left by the previous owner – 'SANDS OF THYME' – a name Winn disdained as nonsensical, given that no herb garden had existed on the property before he planted one. The house had been his for twenty years, since Livia was a baby, and over those twenty summers, time and repetition had elevated it from a simple dwelling to something more, a sacred monolith over which his summer sky somersaulted again and again. He parked the car near the back door and gazed up at the neat procession of windows, their panes black with reflected trees.

Something about the place seemed different. He could not have said what. The gutters, shutters, and gables were all intact, all trimmed with fresh white paint. The hydrangeas were not yet flowering but the peonies were, fat blooms of pink and white. He suspected he was projecting some strange aura onto the house because he knew Biddy, Daphne, and Livia were inside with all the bridesmaids and God only knew what other vestal keepers of the wedding flame. As he sat there, listening to the engine tick its way to quiet, a shard of his nearly forgotten dream punctured the pleasure of his arrival. He might have been in the car, or he might have been back in his bed, or he might have been running one finger down a woman's spine. He tried to push the dream away, but it would not go. He wiped his glasses with his shirt and flipped down the rearview mirror to look at himself. The sight of his face was a comfort, even the chin someone had once called weak. He arranged his features into an expression of patriarchal calm and tried to memorize how it felt – this was how he wanted to look for the next three days. Extracting the dress box and leaving the rest, Winn went around to the side door and let himself in, almost tripping over an explosion of tropical flowers that erupted from a crystal vase on the floor just across the threshold.

'Biddy,' he called into the quiet, 'can we find a better place for these flowers?'

'Oh,' came his wife's voice from somewhere above. 'Hi. No, leave them there.'

He let the screen door slam behind him – even though, years before, he had affixed a now-yellowed card to the door that said 'do NOT slam' – and stepped around the flowers. He set the dress box down on the floor and grimaced at a pile of sandy and unfamiliar shoes. He matched them in pairs and lined them up along the baseboard. Down the hallway of white wainscoting was a bright rectangle of kitchen light. To his right, the back stairs bent tightly upward, and to his left was a coat closet. Inside he found the usual reassuring line of raincoats and jumble of tennis racquets and beach sandals, but on the top shelf, shoved in with a faded collection of baseball caps and canvas fishing hats, a cluster of gift bags overflowed with tissue paper and ribbon.

'Biddy! What are all these bags in the closet here?'

Again Biddy's voice floated down from on high. 'Bridesmaids' gifts. Leave them alone, Winn.'

'But let me look first,' said someone close behind and just above him. 'Daphne said they're good.'

Winn turned around, unprepared to see her so soon. 'Hello, Agatha!' he said, sounding too jovial.

Agatha came down a few steps and leaned to kiss his proffered cheek. Her collarbones and dark nook of cleavage dipped down and floated back up again. He caught a musky scent, heavy like a man's cologne, and underneath it the smell of cigarette smoke. She always smelled like smoke even though he had never seen her in the act. She must still sneak around like a teenager, sitting on windowsills, dangling her cigarettes out pushed-back screens. Winn had known few women he would describe as bombshells, but from the undulant contours of her body to her air of careless, practiced dishevelment, Agatha was an authentic specimen. She wore assemblages of thin garments that might have been nightclothes – lace-edged dresses with torn hems, drawstring pants that sat below her hipbones, flimsy cotton shorts – clothing that answered the requirements of decency while still conveying an impression of nakedness. She piled up her hair with bobby pins and odd pieces of ribbon or elastic, and she was always rooting through her purse for something or other and tossing out an alluring potpourri of lipsticks, lighters, crumpled receipts, and bits of broken jewelry.

'How are you?' she asked in her slow way, sounding like she had just woken up. She was wearing a short dress of gauzy white layers that he found oddly bridal. 'Welcome to the madhouse.'

'I'm very well.' Winn took a step backward, and something poked his thigh. A bird of paradise from the flower arrangement. 'Is it a madhouse?'

'It's fun – if you like girls. You're outnumbered.' She counted on her fingers. 'Three bridesmaids including me. Plus Daphne and Livia. Your wife and her sister. Am I missing anyone? No. That makes it seven to one.'

'Celeste is staying here?'

'Biddy didn't tell you?'

'Maybe she did and I forgot.'

'Sorry, Charlie. Plus the coordinator is in and out all the time. We did a dry run with the hairstylist this morning. Daphne wants everything kept simple, thank God. One time I was in a wedding where they did our hair with tendrils dangling down everywhere like dead vines. Makeup practice is tomorrow, and what else? Manicures? There's something with the dress, too, making room for baby probably. I'm sure I'm forgetting something. Anyway, lucky you.'

'Lucky me,' Winn said. He rubbed his chin and wondered how much all that was costing him. He wondered, too, how she could be so calm while he felt jumpy as a marionette. She, after all, had been the one to take his hand at Daphne's engagement party, and he had been struggling to keep her from his thoughts ever since. Truthfully, he had been struggling to keep her from his thoughts for years, but the party was the first time she had shown any interest. He didn't flatter himself – he had seen her around enough men to know flirtation was, for her, an impersonal reflex, and sex appeal was something she rained down on the world indiscriminately, like a leaflet campaign. And nothing had happened. Not really. Only an interlocking of fingers under the privacy of the tablecloth, but still the touch had shocked him. And she had been the one to take the seat next to him, to find his hand where it was resting on his knee and pull it toward her.

Agatha gazed down at him, her head tilted to one side, almost to her shoulder. 'Anyway, I've been sent to get the dress.'

'Right!' He pivoted to pick up the white box and held it out. 'All yours.'

She hefted it. 'It's heavier than I expected.'

'I'm told a pregnant bride requires scaffolding.'

She laughed, a single syllable that stuck in her throat, less an expression of mirth than a bit of punctuation, a flattering sort of ellipsis. She hitched her chin and rolled her eyes up toward the second floor. 'I should take this to Daphne.'

He said Okay! and Bye! as though ending a telephone call and watched her disappear around the bend of the stairs. He'd known Agatha since she was fourteen and Daphne's first roommate at Deerfield, and though she must be twenty-seven now, he couldn't shake his idea of her as a Lolita. His attraction still embarrassed him as much as

15

when it had revolved around her field hockey skirt. She had been a lackluster athlete; probably she had played only because she knew she looked spectacular in skirt and kneesocks, loping down the field with her hair in two messy braids. Did she even remember taking his hand? She had been tipsy at the party, everyone had been, and at the time he had panicked because, after all these years, she *knew*, perhaps had always known. But, that night, lying awake and thinking of her bare knee under the back of his hand, her palm against his, he found he was relieved; now the chips would fall where they may.

Stepping around the flowers, he shut the coat closet and walked down the hall to the kitchen. As children, Winn's daughters had run through the house upon first arrival each summer to remind themselves of all its singularities and unearth relics of their own brief pasts. They made joyful reunions with the canvas sofas, the insides of closets, the views from all the windows, the books on fish and plants and birds, the bowls of sea glass, the wooden whale sending up its flat, wooden spout on the wall above Winn and Biddy's bed, the flower patch where the sundial lay half concealed beneath black-eyed Susans, the splintery planks of the outdoor shower. The kitchen cupboards were thrown open so the cutting boards and bottles of olive oil might be greeted and the enormous black lobster pot marveled over. The hammock was swung in and the garage door

16

heaved up to reveal, through cirrus whirls of dust, an upside-down canoe on sawhorses and the ancient Land Rover they kept on the island. The girls would converge on Winn and clamor at him until he unbolted and pulled open the hatch to the widow's walk so they could stand on top of the house and look out over the island.

But sometime during their teens, they had stopped caring whether everything was as they remembered and moved swiftly and directly to their rooms to arrange their clothes and toiletries. Little blasts of squabbling percussed the walls as they vied for territory in their shared bathroom. Winn had taken up the job of walking around the house to inspect all the nooks and crannies. He breathed lungfuls of salt and mildew and tipped frames back to center with one finger. He opened all the closets. He tested the hammock. He walked blindly through the spiderwebs in the dark garage.

This time on his rounds downstairs he found that everywhere he looked there were more *things* than there should have been, more *stuff*, and yet for all the women in the house and all their feminine appurtenances, no one came down to greet him. He went out to the car and brought in the luggage and groceries. Leaving the duffels at the foot of the back stairs, he carried the groceries into the kitchen and pushed aside a layer of magazines to make room on the counter. Makeup pencils and brushes were everywhere, abandoned helter-skelter as though by the fleeing beauticians of Pompeii. He walked around collecting them and then set them upright in an empty coffee mug. He straightened the magazines into piles. From the sink he extracted an object his daughters had taught him was an eyelash curler. A round brass ship's clock ticked at the top of a bookshelf, its arrow-tipped hands and Roman numerals insisting it was four thirty. He looked at his watch. Not yet one. He pressed his fingers into a puddle of face powder spilled on the dining table and walked them across the varnished top, leaving a trail of flesh-colored prints that he immediately wiped up with a sponge. Even in his study, his cloister of masculine peace and quiet, he found a nail file and the top half of a bikini on his desk.

He was holding the bikini top by its strings and examining it (it was white with red polka dots, the fabric worn thin, the straps looped in a messy knot instead of a bow; he wondered if Agatha's were the breasts that had last filled its cups and if she could have left it on purpose) when a movement out the window caught his eye. From the side of the house a slope of grass rambled down to the trees, interrupted here by a pair of stray pines with a hammock strung between them and there by a badminton net and there by his vegetable garden, wrapped in flimsy green fencing to deter the deer. After years of taking a bearable tribute from around the edges, the deer seemed to have grown in numbers or appetite, and the previous summer, the family had arrived to find all Winn's herbs and

18

vegetables eaten down to nubs. He had gone out at once and bought a roll of green plastic mesh and strung it savagely around his plants. The fence was unsightly – Livia said the garden looked like a duck blind – and still the yield was a disappointment. Some condition of soil or climate had stunted the plants into spindly bearers of flaccid leaves and runty fruit. Biddy had broken the news to him over the phone, bridesmaids squealing in the background. 'I'm afraid you don't have much of a harvest,' she said.

'Is it the deer?' he had asked.

'No, everything's just a little on the sickly side.'

'Why?'

'Oh, Winn, I'm not a botanist,' she had said, sighing.

Livia was lying in the hammock. Blue shade fell over her bare legs and arms, and she had twisted her hair into a dark rope and pulled it around her head and across her neck. A book lay open on her stomach, the breeze ruffling the pages. Her hands were pressed flat against her face. That was the motion that had attracted his attention: the lifting of her hands from the book. She was very still; he did not think she was crying. After a long time she dropped her hands to her clavicle and stared up into the branches. Winn's softer emotions came upon him rarely, as unexpected visitations from a place he could not guess at. He reached out and touched the window. Flat on her back in the cool shadows, Livia looked like a funeral statue. He knuckled three quick beats on the window and then again, harder, but she didn't turn her head. His powdery fingerprints ghosted the glass. He wiped them away. He thought he would go out and see her, but a stampeding sound came from above, and when he emerged, it was to a kitchen full of women.

'Hello, dear,' he said, pecking Biddy on the cheek.

'I want to leave those flowers there so I don't forget to take them to the Duffs' hotel later,' she said.

'I don't know how you'd forget them. I thought I was in the Amazon.'

'After the wedding I'll remember things again. Until then you'll have to step around the flowers.'

He went around stamping cheeks with his businesslike kisses: first Daphne and then Biddy's sister Celeste where she stood beside the refrigerator fishing an olive out of a jar with her index finger. Agatha and the other bridesmaids were lolling against the counter, and he kissed each of them, saying, 'Agatha, hello again, Piper, Dominique.'

'How was the trip?' asked Biddy.

'Easy. I got an early start. The crossing was smooth.'

Celeste thrust a half-filled tumbler into his hand and clinked it with her own. Three olives drifted around the bottom. 'You don't have any martini glasses,' she said. 'Other than that, everything has been fabulous.'

Setting the glass on a stack of magazines, he said, 'Is the sun over the yardarm already?' He seldom drank hard liquor anymore, especially not in the middle of the day, but if he reminded Celeste of this, she would want to know for the umpteenth time why not, and he was in no mood to explain that it had to do with his headaches and not at all with any judgment of those who daily embalmed their innards from the moment the sun inched past its apex to the hour when their feet tipped them onto whatever couch or bed was handiest.

'Depends on where you keep your yardarm,' she said. Her smile was localized to her lips and their immediate region. Biddy had explained that Celeste had gotten carried away with wrinkle injections, but the effect was still eerie.

Winn frowned and turned to the bridesmaids. 'Having a good time, girls?'

'Yes,' came the chorus from the bridesmaids, who had settled with Daphne in a languid clump against the sink. Like Daphne, Agatha and Piper were blond and short. Dominique was tall and dark, a menhir looming over them. She was the child of two Coptic doctors from Cairo and had spent most of her breaks from Deerfield with the Van Meters. Her face was symmetrical but severe, a smooth half dome of forehead descending to steeply arched eyebrows, a nose with a bump in its middle, and a wide mouth that drooped slightly at the corners in an expression of not unattractive mournfulness. Muscle left over from her days as

21

a swimmer armored her shoulders and back. Her hair, which was not quite crimped and African but also not smooth in the way of some Arabs', was cut very short. He hadn't seen her for a few years. After college in Michigan she had flown off to Europe (France? Belgium?) to become a chef. He liked Dominique; he respected her physical strength and her skill with food, but he had never understood her friendship with Daphne, who took no interest in sports or cooking and who seemed diaphanous and flighty beside her.

Dominique pointed one long finger out the window. 'Your garden is looking a little peaky,' she said.

'So Biddy told me. I haven't gone out to take a look at it yet.'

'Were you having problems with the deer?'

'Terrible. They're glorified goats, those things. But Biddy doesn't think they're the culprit this time.'

'Yeah, I didn't see much nibbling, except around the edges. And I looked for aphid holes and that sort of thing but didn't see enough to explain why it all looks so sad. Maybe the soil is too acidic.'

'Could be.'

'Did you do the planting?'

'The first time, eight or nine years ago, but a local couple does the basic caretaking when we're not here. Maybe they tried something different. I hope if they wanted to experiment they wouldn't do it in my garden.'

Dominique nodded and looked away as though concealing disdain for people who did not tend their own vegetable gardens.

'I'm so psyched for the wedding,' Piper announced out of the blue and in a high chirp, which was her way. She and Daphne had met at Princeton, and Winn knew her less well than the others. Always in motion, propelled along by a brittle, birdlike pep, she seemed a tireless font of chipper enthusiasm. She was pale as bone and dwelt beneath a voluminous haystack of white blond hair, her glacial eyes and red-lipsticked lips adrift in all the whiteness like a face drawn by a child. Her eyebrows were barely discernible, her nose small and sharp. Some men found her powerfully attractive, Winn knew, but she left him cold. Her looks were ethereal and a little strange, but Agatha's were concrete, radiant, tactile; her limbs could almost be felt just by looking at them. Daphne fell somewhere in the middle. They were three shades of woman arrayed side by side like the bewildering, smiling boxes of hair dye in the supermarket.

'It's beautiful here,' Agatha said, letting her head fall onto Piper's shoulder. A male friend of Daphne's had, years ago, in a moment of drunken gossip, implied that Agatha was a closeted prude – *There's no engine*, he'd said. *You hit the gas and nothing happens* – but Winn had trouble believing something so disappointing could be true.

'Thanks for bringing my dress, Daddy,' Daphne said.

'Yes,' he said to Agatha. 'Waskeke is the way the world should be.' He was staring at her too intently and looked away, at Biddy, who was rummaging through the grocery bags. With a grunt, Daphne pushed off from the sink, waddled across the kitchen, and plopped into a Windsor chair behind Winn. 'Daphne,' he said, turning, 'are you feeling all right?'

'I feel fine,' she said.

'Why did you make that noise?'

'Because I'm seven months pregnant, Daddy.'

He asked for and received a full briefing on the status of the weekend. Where was Greyson? At the hotel with his groomsmen, Daphne said. His parents? They would be arriving around five. The head count for that night's party, a dinner Winn would be preparing, was seventeen. The get-together would be a casual thing, with lobsters, a chance for everyone to enjoy the island before they had to get serious about matrimony, a sort of pre-rehearsal-dinner dinner. Had Biddy confirmed the lobsters? She had.

Winn nodded. 'All right,' he said. 'Well, then good.'

'By the way,' Daphne said, 'Mr Duff is allergic to shellfish.'

Winn fixed her with a look. 'Why didn't you tell me sooner?'

'It's no big deal. Just buy a tuna steak, too.'

'Are you going to call him Mr Duff after you're married?' asked Celeste.

'I have a hard time addressing him as Dicky,' said Daphne gravely. 'He says to call him Dad, but most of the time I don't call him anything.'

Biddy said, 'Everyone calls him Dicky. It's his name. He won't think it's odd for you to call him by his name. You're being ridiculous.'

'Re-dicky-ulous,' said Dominique, and the women laughed.

'Where's Livia?' Winn asked, even though he knew.

'Around here somewhere,' said Daphne. 'Hating me. You know, I really think her dress is pretty. I really do. I wanted to set her off from the other bridesmaids, which is a nice thing, isn't it? She's just being contrary. It's a green dress. That's all. She says it's the exact shade of envy and everyone already thinks she's jealous even though she's not, but it's not the color of envy. It's more of a viridian.'

'Too late to change it,' said Biddy.

The moment of welcome faded into a lull. The staring half circle of female faces made Winn uneasy. With a loud, contented sigh, he turned to look out the window. Daphne held her hands out to Dominique and was heaved to her feet. 'Ladies,' she said, beckoning to her bridesmaids. They wandered off, their voices drifting through the house like the calls of distant birds.

'Nice trip?' Celeste asked, having lost track of the earlier part of the conversation.

'Couldn't have been smoother,' he said.

'You must have gotten up at the crack of dawn.'

25

'Just before.'

'Drink up there, Winnifred.' She picked up his glass and handed it to him again with a wink. 'You deserve it.'

'If you insist.' He touched his lips to the liquid. Gin.

The house was L shaped, with a planked deck filling the crook and extending out over the grass. Through the kitchen's French doors, Winn saw Livia walk up the lawn and onto the deck. She wore an old pair of gray shorts, and her legs were thinner than he had ever seen them. When she came through the doors and into the kitchen, a push of salt air came with her.

'Oh, Dad,' she said. 'Hi.'

She made no move to embrace or kiss him. In the hammock, she had appeared sepulchral and blue, but that must have been a trick of the shade because she looked fine now, a bit pale but fine. She turned away, chewing the side of her thumbnail.

'Hi, roomie,' Celeste said.

'You two are bunking together?' Winn said. Biddy must have sprung the arrangement on Livia, otherwise he would have already gotten an earful.

'Yes,' said Livia in a neutral voice, inspecting her hand. The nails were bitten to nothing, and the flesh around them was torn and raw.

Celeste jiggled her glass enticingly. 'Can I get you a drink?'

'No, thanks.'

'Moral support for Daphne?' Celeste asked. 'Poor thing not having a drink at her own wedding. I don't know what I would have done without a drink or two during my weddings.'

'Let alone your marriages,' Biddy said.

'Only you,' Celeste said, swatting Biddy's flat backside, 'could say to that to me.'

'Daphne can have a glass of champagne,' Livia said. 'She's seven months. It's fine.'

Celeste sipped. 'Is it? Shows what I know.'

'Maybe I will have a drink,' Livia said. 'I'll get it myself.'

'How is Cooper?' Winn asked Celeste. 'Still in the picture?' He reached out to touch Livia's hair as she moved away.

'He's fine. He's sailing in the Seychelles. He wanted to come but he couldn't.'

Livia took a bottle of wine from the refrigerator and picked at the foil. 'Do you think he'll be number five?'

'I'm getting out of the marriage business.' Celeste raised her glass as though someone had made a toast. 'Though I'll admit all this is making me sentimental. Nothing beats being a bride. Oh well. Days gone by. I'll have to live vicariously through my nieces.'

Livia threw the foil into the garbage. 'Don't look at me.'

'Oh, sweetheart, it was his loss. There are so many fish in the sea. You're only nineteen.'

'I'm twenty-one.'

'You are? Well, then, you're an old maid.'

Livia put a corkscrew to the bottle and twisted it. Winn watched the curl of silver disappear. Her fingers wrapped so tightly around the bottle that her bones stood out under her skin. Winn wanted to tell her she didn't need to squeeze so hard, wringing the bottle's neck like she was. He remembered once watching her shatter an ice cream cone in her hand, crying out in surprise at the cold shards of waffle. 'I forgot I was holding it,' she had said. 'I was thinking of something else.' Why Livia always had to be so forceful, straining when she didn't need to, was beyond him, but he held his tongue. She clamped the bottle between her knees and pulled until it exclaimed over the loss of its cork.

CHAPTER 2

THE WATER BEARER

Before he became a father, Winn had assumed he would have sons. He had expected Daphne to be a boy, had lain with his ear against Biddy's pregnant belly and heard male voices echoing down from future lacrosse games and ski trips. He saw a small blue blazer with brass buttons, short hair combed away from a straight part, himself teaching a boy to tie a necktie. He would drive his son to Harvard when the time came and help him carry his bags through the Yard, would greet his son's roommates and their fathers with hearty handshakes. His son would join the Ophidian Club, and Winn would attend the initiation dinner and drink with the boy who would live his life over again, affirming its correctness at every juncture.

When the screaming ham hock the doctor pulled from between Biddy's legs turned out to be unmistakably female, all crevices and puffiness, he felt a deep and essential surprise, not only that the child brewing in his wife those nine months was a girl but that he, Winn, possessed the seeds of a feminine anything. Inside the tangled pipes of his testicular factory there existed, beyond all reason, women. Watching Biddy and Daphne nestle together in the hospital bed, he realized he had been mistaken to think that pregnancy and birth had something to do with him. He had imagined that by impregnating this woman he had ensured she would deliver a son who would go forth and someday impregnate another woman who would, in turn, have a son, and so on and so forth down the Van Meter line into the misty future. But now, instead, there was this girl-child who would grow breasts and take another man's name and sprout new branches on an unknown family tree and do all sorts of traitorous things a son would not do. The shifting and swelling of Biddy's boyish body into a collection of spheroids, the quiet communion she lavished on her belly, her new status with her sisters and her covey of friends – all this should have told him he was standing at the threshold of a club that would not have him. Even though women held out their arms and exclaimed, 'You're going to be a faaa-ther!' he suspected they had seen him all along for what he was: the adjunct, the contributor of additional reporting, the lame duck about to be displaced from the center of his wife's affections. The surprise should not have been that he had a daughter but that any boys were ever born at all.

When, five years later, Biddy announced she was pregnant for the second time, Winn assumed from

the first that the baby would be a girl. The deck
was stacked; the game was rigged. Daphne was so
staunchly female that the possibility of his and
Biddy's genes being put back in the tumbler and
coming out a boy seemed too small to bother with.
Biddy gave him the news in bed in the morning,
and he kissed her once, hard, and said, 'Well!'
before going downstairs to sit behind the *Journal*
and think about a vasectomy. He was at the kitchen
table, staring sightlessly at the pages when he
heard the rustling, tinkling sound that announced
Daphne. She slid into a chair and sat eating red
grapes out of a plastic bag. She wore a piece of
crenellated, bejeweled plastic in her hair, and a
cloud of pink gauze stood up where her skirt bent
against the back of the chair.

'Good morning, Daphne. Going to dance class
today?'

'No. That's on Wednesday.'

'Isn't that a dance skirt you're wearing?'

'My tutu? I just threw this on.'

Winn stared at her. She looked back at him and
fingered one of the strands of plastic beads that
garlanded her neck. Somehow in her infancy she
had absorbed a set of phrases and mannerisms
that Biddy called breezy and Winn called absurd
but that, in any event, had her swanning through
preschool like an aging socialite. They left her once
with Biddy's eldest sister, Tabitha, and went to
Turks and Caicos for a week, hoping Tabitha's son
Dryden would get her to dirty her knees a little.

31

Instead, they returned to find Dryden draped in baubles and Daphne arranging clips in his hair.

'Dryden,' Biddy said, 'you look awfully dressed up for this time of day.'

The boy released a sigh of weary sophistication. He fluttered his blue-dusted eyelids and spread his fingers against his chest. 'Oh, this? This is nothing. The good stuff's in the safe.'

To Winn, Daphne was a foreign being, a sort of mystic, a snake charmer or a charismatic preacher, an ambassador from a distant frontier of experience. The academic knowledge that she was the product of his body was not enough to forge a true belief; he felt no instantaneous, involuntary recognition of her as flesh and blood. Not for lack of trying, either. He had changed her diapers and held her while she cried in the night and spooned gloopy food into her mouth, and certainly he loved her, but she only became more and more strange to him as she got older, and his love for her gave him no comfort but instead made him alarmingly porous, full of hidden passageways that let in feelings of yearning and exclusion. Sitting behind the paper, he imagined with trepidation a house populated by two Daphnes, a Biddy, and only one Winn.

'Daddy,' came the piping voice from across the table, 'am I a princess?'

'No,' Winn said. 'You're a very nice little girl.'

'Will I be a princess someday?'

Winn bent the top of the newspaper down and looked over it. 'It depends on whom you marry.'

'What does that mean?'

'Well, there are two ways for a woman to become a princess. Either she's born one, or she marries a prince or, I think, a grand duke – although I'm not sure those exist anymore. You see, Daphne, many countries that used to have princesses don't anymore because they've abolished their monarchies, and an aristocracy doesn't make sense without a monarchy. Austria, for example, got rid of all that business after the First World War. Hereditary systems like that aren't fair, you see, and they breed resentment among the lower classes. Anyway, the long and short of it is, since you weren't born a princess, you would need to marry a prince, and there aren't very many of those around.'

Reproachfully, she ate a grape and then wiped her fingers one at a time on a napkin. He returned to reading.

'Daddy.'

'What?'

'Am I *your* princess?'

'Christ, Daphne.'

'What?'

'You sound like a kid on TV.'

'Why?'

'Because you're full of treacle.'

'What's treacle?'

'Something that's too sweet. It gives you a stomachache.'

She nodded, accepting this. 'But,' she pressed on, 'am I your princess?'

'To the best of my knowledge, I don't have any princesses. What I do have is a little girl without any dignity.'

'What's dignity?'

'Dignity is behaving the way you're supposed to so people respect you.'

'Do princesses have dignity?'

'Some do.'

'Which ones?'

'I don't know. Maybe Grace Kelly.'

'Who is she?'

'She was a princess. First she was an actress. Then she married a prince and became a princess. In Monaco. She was killed in a car accident.'

'What's Monaco?'

'A place in Europe.'

Daphne took a moment to absorb and then asked, 'Am I your princess?'

'We've just been through this,' Winn said, exasperated.

She looked like she was trying to decide whether her interests would be better served by smiling or crying. 'I want to be your princess,' she said, teetering toward tears. Daphne was an accomplished crier, plaintive and capable of great stamina. For a girl so physically delicate and soft in voice, she was unexpectedly stalwart in her emotions. Her tears were purposeful, as were her smiles and pouts. Biddy called her Lady Macbeth.

Ducking back behind his paper, Winn did what

was necessary. 'All right,' he said. 'Daphne, you are my princess.'

'Really?'

'Absolutely.'

Daphne nodded and ate a grape. Then she cocked her head to one side. 'Am I your *fairy* princess?'

Biddy, when Winn went looking for her, was getting out of the shower. Through the closed door he heard the water shut off and the rattle of the shower curtain. She was humming something to herself. He thought it might be 'Amazing Grace.' Knocking once, he pushed open the door, releasing a cloud of steam. Her bare body, flushed from the shower, was so close he could feel the heat coming off her back and small, neat buttocks. A foggy oval wiped on the mirror framed her breasts and belly button, the dark badge of hair below, his tight face hovering over her shoulder. After fall stripped away her summer tan, her skin tended toward a certain sallowness, but the hot water had turned her chest and legs a rosy pink. Already, her breasts looked swollen. A white towel was wrapped around her head. Her reflection smiled at him. *Biddy*, he had planned to say, *maybe one is enough.* He would suggest they sit down and make a pros and cons list. He was holding a yellow legal pad and a blue pen and had already thought of cons to counter all possible pros.

'What is it?' she asked, her smile draining away. He wondered if she had already guessed that he had trailed her to this warm, foggy room to argue her baby away from her. She had some lotion in her hand, and he watched her rub it on her sides and stomach, across stretch marks from Daphne that were only visible in the pale months. 'Winn?' she asked. 'What?'

'What was that you were just humming?' he asked.

'"Unchained Melody,"' she said.

'Oh.'

'And?'

'And what?'

She took another towel and wrapped it around herself, tucking in the end beneath her armpit. 'What else?'

'Nothing important.'

'What's that for?' She pointed at the legal pad.

'I needed to take some notes.'

'About what?'

'A work thing.'

She turned to the mirror and asked, almost casually, 'Are you excited about the baby?'

Winn was silent.

'Are you?' Biddy prodded.

'Yes,' Winn said. 'No.'

'No, you're not excited?' She and Daphne had the same way of wrinkling their foreheads when their plans went awry. 'What were you going to say when you came in here?'

He tapped the legal pad against his thigh. 'I'm not sure.'

'Winn, out with it.'

'Fine. I was thinking about saying we shouldn't jump into anything. We didn't exactly plan this.'

'We always said we would have two.'

'We hadn't talked about it in years. Maybe four years.'

'No, we talked about it last year. On Waskeke. At the bar in the Enderby. You said you'd like to try for a son.'

'We'd been drinking, and that was still a year ago.'

'I didn't think it was empty talk. We always said we'd have two. I understood our plan was for two. We always said so.'

'I thought . . . I *assumed*, apparently incorrectly, that we'd both cooled on the idea.'

'You should have said if you'd changed your mind.'

'You should have said you wanted another one.'

'Let me ask you this, if you could know right now that it's a boy, would we be having this conversation? Would you have made one of your lists? That's what you have there, isn't it?'

He hid the pad behind his back and soldiered on. 'I didn't know you'd gone off the pill,' he said. 'Did you do it on purpose?'

She rummaged in a drawer. 'I forgot for a week. I know you don't like to be surprised, but I thought we wanted this. I thought if it happens, it happens. I didn't realize you had changed your mind. You should have said something.'

'I didn't know I had to. I didn't realize I had

given tacit approval to conceive a child at the time of your choosing.'

He stepped back in time to remove himself from the path of the slamming door. The bath began to run. Biddy's sisters said that Biddy was drawn to water in times of need because she was an Aquarius. Winn put no stock in astrology – the whole concept was embarrassing – but he admitted that his wife's passion for baths, showers, lakes, rivers, ponds, swimming pools, and the ocean was a powerful force. Biddy descended from a line of people who were at once remarkably unlucky and extraordinarily fortunate in their encounters with the sea. Since a grandfather many greats ago had managed to catch hold of a dangling line after being swept by a wave from the deck of the *Mayflower* and be dragged back aboard, her forebears had been dumped into the ocean one after the other and then, while thousands around them perished, been plucked again from the waves. A grandaunt had survived the sinking of the *Titanic*; a distant cousin crossed eight hundred miles of angry Southern Ocean in a lifeboat with Ernest Shackleton; her father's cruiser was sunk at Guadalcanal, and he saved not only himself but three others from shark-infested waters. The grandaunt's photograph, a grainy enlargement of a small girl wrapped in a blanket and looking very alone on the deck of the *Carpathia* without her nanny (who had gone to the bottom of the Atlantic) hung in their front hallway.

Whatever the root of Biddy's affinity for water,

as long as Winn had known her, she had been able to submerge herself and come out, if not entirely healed, at least calmed, her mood rubbed smooth. But he could not have anticipated that she would emerge from this particular bath and find him where he had settled with the newspaper in his favorite chair and announce that she was going to have a water birth for this baby.

'A what?'

'A water birth. You give birth in a tub of warm water. There's a hospital in France that specializes in it. We're going there.'

Winn felt an 'absolutely not' pushing its way up his throat. He had married Biddy partly because she was not given to outlandish ideas, and he felt betrayed. But the rafters of the doghouse hung low over his head. 'Sounds like some kind of hippie thing to me,' he said.

'I've done research. Candace McInnisee did it for her youngest, and she swears by it.'

'You did research before you knew you were pregnant?'

'We always said we would have two, Winn. And since you're not the one giving birth, I don't see why you should mind where it happens.'

Winn lifted his paper and let it fall, a white flag spreading on the floor in marital surrender. He held out his arms. She came close, leaned to kiss him on the forehead, and slipped away before he could embrace her.

★   ★   ★

39

Livia was born in France in a tub full of water, and she, like Biddy, had spent the years since her birth returning, whenever possible, to an aqueous state. She had once come home from a fruitful day in the fourth grade and declared that she was a thalassomaniac and a hydromaniac while Biddy was only a hydromaniac, which was true. Biddy's love of water did not extend past the substance itself, whereas Livia loved all water but especially the ocean and its inhabitants. During her time at Deerfield, she had baffled Winn by organizing a Save the Cetaceans society and by spending her summers on Arctic islands helping researchers count walruses or on sailboats monitoring dolphin behavior in the Hebrides. She had passionately wished to join the crew of a vessel that interfered with Japanese whaling ships, but Biddy had managed to convince her that she would be more helpful elsewhere. Now she was studying biology at Harvard with plans for a Ph.D. afterward. She had made it clear to Winn that she thought his ocean-provoked existential horror was a bit of willful silliness. From the age of eleven, she had insisted on getting and maintaining her scuba certification and was always after Winn to do the same, though the idea held no appeal for him. He had snorkeled a few times and once swam by accident out over the lip of a reef, where the colorful orgy of waving, flitting life dropped into blackness. He felt like he had taken a casual glance out the window of a skyscraper and seen, instead of yellow taxis and human specks crawling along the sidewalks, only a chasm.

Winn had expected Livia's passion for the ocean to fade away like her other childhood enthusiasms (volcanoes, rock collecting), but a vein of Neptunian ardor had persisted in the thickening stuff of her adult self. She spotted seals and dolphins that no one else noticed, and she was on constant watch for whales. A stray plume of spray was enough to get her hopes up, and after she had stopped and peered into the distance long enough to be convinced no tail or rolling back was going to show itself, she would blush and fall silent, seeming to suffer a sort of professional embarrassment. She claimed she would be happy to spend her life on tiny research vessels or in cramped submersibles, poking cameras and microphones into the depths as though the ocean might issue a statement explaining itself. His selkie daughter. How Livia could feel at home in a world so obviously hostile was beyond him, as was her willingness to lavish so much love on animals indifferent to her existence.

Daphne was the simpler of his daughters to get along with but also the more obscure. By the time she finished college, she seemed to have shed the serpentine guile of her infant self, or else her manipulations had grown so advanced as to conceal themselves entirely. He couldn't be sure. A smoked mirror of sweetness and serenity hid Daphne's inner workings, but Livia lived out in the open, blatantly so, the emotional equivalent of a streaker. Livia's problem was a susceptibility to strong feelings, and her strongest feelings these days were about a boy, Teddy Fenn, who had thrown her over. She had seen too many movies; she did not understand that love was a choice, entered and exited by free will and with careful consideration, not a random thunderbolt sent from above. He had told her so, but she would not listen. She was angry at the world in general and Winn in particular, so he was angry with her in return. In the interest of familial peace, he would try to put everything aside for the wedding, and perhaps Waskeke would exert a healing influence, bring her back to herself.

He needed to buy more groceries for dinner and to deliver Biddy's lunatic flowers to the Enderby, where the Duffs were staying. With the aim of forging an alliance, he sought out Livia to see if she would come along. She was in the bathtub.

'It's after two,' he said through the door, 'so the sooner we go the better.'

'Where's Celeste?' Livia asked.

'Up on the roof.'

'Communing with the vodka gods?'

'And with your mother.'

A splash. 'Give me a minute.'

They rattled back down the driveway in the old Land Rover, the Duffs' flowers blooming up from between Livia's knees like a Roman candle.

'What do you say we take the scenic route?' Winn said, pausing at the road.

She shrugged. 'I thought we were in a hurry.'

Only to get out of the house, he thought. In the hour since his arrival, he had managed to offend Biddy by suggesting that all the test runs with makeup and hair and such were an extravagance and also to walk in on Agatha in the downstairs bathroom. He hadn't seen anything, only her surprised face and bare thighs (the gauzy white dress concealed their crux) and a wad of toilet paper clutched in her hand, nor had he said anything, which made the situation worse. He had closed the door – not slammed it but closed it quietly and deliberately – before fleeing up to the widow's walk to tell Biddy he was going to the market.

The day was warm and unusually still. Split-rail fences and a thickety layer of brush hemmed in the road. The interior of the island was occupied mostly by scrublands called the Moors, low hills with sharp, rusty vegetation and bony, crooked trees, like a piece of the Serengeti delivered to the wrong address. On the ocean side, shingled houses were scattered among scrub pines, cranberry bogs, and marshes. They drove past the undulating, sand-trapped meadow belonging to the Pequod Golf Club, its ovoid greens marching off like footprints left by an elephant. Distant golfers bent and flexed, launching unseen balls into the blue air.

'Heard anything about the Pequod?' Livia asked.

'No, not yet,' Winn said, trying to sound cheerful. 'I'll have to call up Jack Fenn and get the latest.'

Livia let her head tip back until she was staring up at the Rover's ceiling. 'Would it be so bad not to join? You already belong to a thousand clubs. You hardly even go to half of them. I don't see why belonging to the Pequod is so essential.'

'It's not *essential*. Nothing is *essential*. I think we'll all enjoy the membership, that's all.'

'Can you leave the Fenns out of it at least?'

'Unfortunately, no. Look, they're not my favorites, either, but Fenn and I go back long before you and Teddy were even born. We have a relationship that has nothing to do with you.'

'Not to mention Fee,' Livia said snidely, refer-ring to Jack's wife, Teddy's mother, who was an ex-girlfriend of Winn's.

'Ancient history,' said Winn. As a consequence of its selectivity, his world was sometimes too small. 'No need to bring it up. Nothing to do with the Pequod.'

'No one besides you even golfs,' Livia said to the ceiling.

'There's a gym there, and a bar. They have nice events – dances, silent auctions, theme parties. You'll like it.'

She let her head roll in his direction. 'I do *love* silent auctions.'

'Don't be sarcastic, Livia. It isn't ladylike.'

For three summers Winn had languished on a secrecy-shrouded wait list for membership in the

Pequod. For three summers he had kept bitter evening vigils on the widow's walk, staring out at what he could see of the course from the house: only a scrap of the tenth hole, but that bit of grass was the gateway to a verdant male haven and confessional. In the decades he had been coming to the island, he had always thought of membership as something obtainable but deliberately left for later. So it was to his bafflement that he had pulled all available strings and schmoozed all relevant parties, including the Fenns, and still he found himself relegated to guest status. He had an excellent track record with clubs. Though no club could equal the pleasures of his college club, the Ophidian – a brotherhood of such importance that he wrote one Christmas newsletter exclusively for its members and another for the remainder of the Van Meter family's acquaintance – he had joined other clubs, in New York and in Boston, one in London, all places where he could drop in for dinner and feel welcome and sit in a leather chair and read newspapers hinged on long wooden sticks. He belonged to more specialized clubs, too, for the purposes of swimming or golf or racquet sports, and none had ever hesitated to accept him as a member. But Jack Fenn was on the Pequod's membership committee and Fee Fenn was on the social committee, and, truth be told, Winn never knew where he stood with them, if bygones were bygones or not.

To change the mood, he reached over and patted

Livia's bony knee. 'So,' he said, playing jolly, 'the big day!'

'It's not my big day.'

'Don't be sour. Your day will come.'

She moved her leg irritably, and the flowers trembled. 'I wouldn't mind if everyone would stop telling me that. I'll either get married or I won't. I'm not jealous. I'm looking forward to this weekend being over. End of story.'

'That's not quite the spirit, Livia.' Yearn as he might for the end of the wedding hoopla, Winn knew he must ride in front of the troops, sword raised, toward a successful event. 'Especially from the maid of honor. You're in charge of honor.'

He meant it as a joke, but she said, grimly, 'I thought you weren't impressed with my honor.'

He refrained from answering. They passed a marshy pond crowded with cattails and bulrushes.

'Look at the egret,' she said.

Winn glimpsed a tall, slender shape and a flash of white wings. 'It's a heron,' he said.

'No, it's an egret. Egrets are white. Herons aren't.'

'Well,' said Winn in a voice that signaled he was being kind but not sincere. 'All right.'

In town, the traffic was slow, and without a breeze the car was warm. Livia shifted the flowers, and some greenery tickled Winn's hand. He pushed it away. Livia sighed and rested her elbow on the window's edge. 'All these people. Too many people.'

'Hopefully they're not all wedding guests,' he said.

She snorted. 'Do you have any idea what it's like to share a room with Celeste?'

'I think I can imagine.'

'After the lights are out, I hear ice cubes rattling around. Then she tries to get me to girl talk with her and whispers questions about my love life until she falls asleep, which is when she starts snoring. You can't imagine. She sounds like someone trying to vacuum up a mud puddle.'

Many times in the past, over holidays or vacation weekends, Winn had been kept awake by Celeste's industrial rumble from several rooms away, but he said, 'Buck up, pal. I'd appreciate if you'd contribute by being nice to your aunt.'

'I contribute. I contribute in lots of ways. I'm the maid of honor. I'm a servant to the pregnant queen. Why do I also have to be a companion to the drunken aunt?'

'Celeste has had some rough breaks along the way. The charitable thing would be to cut her some slack.'

'She's a gargoyle.'

'She's a ruin.'

'Of her own making. I can't get away from her. She's everywhere with her martinis and her stories. She's like, "Roomie, did I tell you about the time my third husband ran off to Bolivia with my best friend's daughter? You don't know heartbreak until your third husband has run off to Bolivia with your best friend's daughter." That *clink-clink, clink-clink, clink-clink* that lets you know she's coming – it's like the shark music in *Jaws*.'

47

'Be thankful you weren't around for that divorce, the Bolivian one. That was a dogfight.'

'I don't think a divorce that happened twenty-something years ago is an excuse for her to be a complete mess.'

'What do you propose we do?' Winn said. 'Should we put her in a burlap sack and push her off the ferry?'

'The sack is probably overkill.'

'If she wants to get drunk and say the wrong thing, then that's what she's going to do. And as much as we'd like for her not to exist, she does. Death, taxes, and family, Livia.'

The farm might have been the end of the earth. A thin seam of ocean sealed its fields to the sky, all of it coppered by the sun. The water's surface, choppy and striated with light, was beautiful, but Livia liked to think about what was teeming underneath: phytoplankton, of course, stripers, bluefish, bonito, maybe tuna, certainly fish larvae and fry, worms and mollusks in the sea floor. Pelicans diving to fill up their huge mouths. Seals. Perhaps a whale, although they were rare around Waskeke. In previous centuries, the islanders had hunted sperm whales and right whales almost to extinction, and Livia suspected the animals still picked up bad vibes from the surrounding waters.

The older she got, the more claustrophobic she felt within her family. Her father's desire to join clubs had once seemed perfectly normal but now struck her as grasping and embarrassing. He seemed to believe his various clubhouses, stuffy old buildings full of stuffy old people, were bunkers that would shelter him from the fallout of ordinary life, protect him like the green fence out in the yard was supposed to keep his precious vegetables safe from the menacing deer. Teddy had felt a similar skepticism about his own family, and she had imagined that together they could forge a new freedom, make lives of their own, but then he had left her, an outcome she could not accept. She kept turning the breakup around and around in her mind like a Rubik's cube, unable to puzzle out what had driven him off. She had never been so happy as she was with him. He had been happy, too – she was sure of it.

'For Christ's sake,' her father said, waiting for an old lady to maneuver her Cadillac out of a parking space in the market's gravel lot.

The market building, towering over a clump of greenhouses, resembled an enormous, gray-shingled schoolhouse. Livia got out first and walked ahead. Inside, the market was airy and cool and smelled of field dirt, tomatoes, cold meat, and cellophane. Her father caught up with her, peering over his glasses at a list he'd written on a napkin. 'Corn, tomatoes, lettuce, I brought cocktail onions from home, we need pickles, we'll get shrimp at the seafood place, we'll get smoked salmon at the seafood place, something-not-shellfish for Dicky, lobsters are being delivered, then bread, cheese, et cetera, et cetera. You get the corn first, please, Livia.'

'How much?'

'We've got seventeen for dinner, so why don't you get twenty ears.'

'Do you have a cauldron to cook it all in?'

Tilting his chin down, he gave her one of his trademark *looks*, half smiling, steely eyed.

'Okay,' she said. 'Never mind. No problem.'

She found a cart and was steering it toward a tasseled mountain of corn when she saw Jack Fenn and his daughter Meg standing beside the refrigerated shelves of fresh herbs. Even from the back they were easy to identify because they, like Teddy, were redheads. Six months had passed since she'd last seen Jack, since before the breakup, but he looked the same, like Teddy but older. He wore a blue shirt with the collar undone, and he was handsome in a rough, shaggy-dog way, with full lips and thick marigold hair that was long enough to cover the tops of his ears. He was holding Meg's hand, a market basket over the crook of his other arm. Meg was a tall girl, a woman really, and she was dressed with perfect neatness, like a child in a school uniform: oxford shirt, webbed belt, broomstick legs poking out of Bermuda shorts and into a set of ankle braces, beneath which her long feet in gray sneakers nosed each other like a pair of kissing trout. Her hair was in a French braid, exposing the hearing aids she wore in each ear, and her face might have been pretty if not for the wide, crooked mouth that slanted open, revealing teeth and darkness. Jack asked her something – Livia could not hear what – and she replied with a round, deep burst of sound like four or five words spoken all on top of one another. Shoppers looked up from their lettuces and bell peppers. Jack set down his basket and reached for a bag of baby carrots, still holding her hand.

Livia turned to find her father. He was holding a tomato in front of his nose and frowning at it. With as much stealth as she could muster, she abandoned her cart and slunk toward him, her back to the Fenns. Catching sight of her, he said loudly, 'Livia, would you find me some black peppercorns?' Grasping his arm, she tried to turn him toward the door, but he stood as though hammered into the floor. 'What are you doing?' he said. 'I need tomatoes.'

'Can we just go? I'm not feeling well.'

That was true enough. Her desperation had become a sort of nausea. His eyes lit with worry, and he glanced once at her belly as though she were suddenly Daphne and pregnant and the object of great concern and pillow plumping. But Meg Fenn let loose another blast of her foghorn voice, and he looked up.

'Fenn!' Winn called boisterously over Livia's head. 'Jack Fenn!'

Jack lifted a hand and walked in their direction with Meg shuffling beside him, her trout feet tumbling over each other.

'Winn,' Jack said. 'Hello, Livia.' He leaned in to kiss her cheek, and she felt the corner of her mouth spasm. She prayed she would not cry. Her father's hand twitched toward Meg and then veered back and froze into a signpost pointing at Jack. Jack set down his basket and allowed Winn to pump his broad paw. Livia put her arms lightly around Meg, who stood very still to receive her embrace. 'I like your belt,' Livia said. She noticed the girl was wearing lip gloss and remembered once seeing Teddy's mother applying it, holding Meg's chin in her hand.

Jack turned his green eyes on Livia, Teddy's eyes, and she blushed, conscious of her thinness. 'How are you?' he asked.

At the same moment, her father, radiating a sudden vigor, said, 'Can you believe the traffic today?'

'I'm fine,' Livia said.

'Absolute pandemonium,' Winn said in answer to his own question.

Tripped up, they all hesitated, and gradually discomfort saturated the air as though puffed from an atomizer. The cause, Livia knew, would not be named or alluded to, not here beside the tomatoes or anywhere else where her father and Teddy's father happened to be at the same time. Her father would rather die than acknowledge in Jack Fenn's presence that, for five short weeks, the two of them had shared an embryonic grandchild. Nor had Livia ever spoken with Jack about her pregnancy.

The last time she had seen him was in a different life, back before she had gotten knocked up, when Teddy was still her boyfriend.

'Have you been out on the links yet?' Winn asked Jack, a note of ingratiating fellowship creeping into his voice. His body was taut, humming with too much enthusiasm. The possibility occurred to Livia that he wasn't even thinking about her but only about the golf club.

'Just once,' Jack said.

'Good!' Winn said. 'Good! Glad to hear it.'

Meg spoke, addressing Winn. 'You like golf?' she asked, vowels dwarfing her sticky, guttural *k* and *g* sounds. Livia had explained to her father a thousand times that Meg could understand him, but still he froze whenever he had to communicate with her. He stared, neck straining forward, pupils moving over her face in a rapid search for comprehension, and then he gave up and examined his wristwatch.

Meg repeated herself, louder, and Winn looked helplessly at Livia. With an apologetic glance at Jack, Livia translated. 'She said, "You like golf?"'

'Oh. I do. Very much,' Winn told Livia.

Jack lifted his daughter's hand and kissed it. Meg's eyes and her wide mouth closed, making her face look, in its moment of repose, normal.

'Do *you* like golf?' Livia asked Meg, and Meg laughed like a honking goose.

'Say,' Winn said to Jack, 'I heard somewhere that you're involved in the bluffs project.'

'Unfortunately.'

Winn chuckled. 'Fenn versus nature.'

'The lighthouse is set to be moved next summer,' Jack said. 'But that's the easy part.' He went on about some scheme to shore up a disappearing beach with drainage pipes and to reinforce crumbling bluffs with rebar, concrete, and wire baskets of rocks called gabions. A line of expensive houses sat atop the cliffs, and every year their owners paid a foot or so of lawn in taxes to the wind and rain, the brink creeping slowly closer to their cedar porches.

'I hate to say it,' Winn said, 'but those houses are goners. Five years and they're in the drink.'

Livia saw an Atlantis of gray-shingled houses, weather vanes spinning in the currents beneath a white foam sky, fish at the windows and in the attics, the shadow of a whale sweeping over the roofs like the shadow of an airplane. She marveled at the two of them, chattering on like this. Her father claimed things had been awkward with the Fenns since his college years, when he had belonged to the Ophidian and Jack, a legacy, had not been invited to join. Then Winn had slept with Jack's wife (long before Jack met her, but still), and Livia had slept with Jack's son. Then Teddy had broken her heart. She had sacrificed their child. What could be more intimate? Probably she should be grateful the conversation was only about rebar and property values even if something in her was longing for them to acknowledge, just once, what had happened. Not likely. Even when she and Teddy were still together, relations between the families had been less than comfortable. The few times both sets of parents came together for dinners in Cambridge they had all bravely skated the hours away on a thin crust of chitchat.

Jack shook his head. 'I have to say I hope you're wrong, Winn. That wouldn't do the island any good.'

Winn raised a finger. 'But you didn't build there, did you? No sense taking that kind of risk when you're finally getting your own place. Rent on the bluffs, buy on the flat.'

'I don't know — we considered building there. Of course, we're still renting. The new house won't be livable until the end of the summer. Even that's not for sure. How is your family? The wedding's soon, isn't it?'

'Saturday,' Livia said.

'Just a small affair,' Winn said. 'Mostly family.' He touched his chin. Livia guessed he was worried Jack would feel slighted.

Jack said, 'Remind me of the groom's name.'

'Greyson Duff,' said Winn. 'It's a fine match. We're all very pleased.'

'Congratulations,' said Meg, and Jack kissed her hand again.

Livia was astonished to feel her father's fingers clasp her own, once, quickly, and then release. The touch was something between a caress and a pinch. She could not remember the last time he had held her hand. 'Thank you,' she said to Meg.

'How is Teddy?' Winn asked.

Heat crept into Livia's face. She willed herself to hold her gaze steady, not to fold her arms. Jack smiled. He had always been kind to her. 'He's fine,' Jack said. 'In fact, he's made a very big decision.' Livia braced herself, though she did not know for what.

'Oh?' said Winn.

Winn wished he had gotten more of an opportunity to probe Fenn about the Pequod, but the man had stonewalled him as usual and then dropped the news about Teddy into the conversation like a meat cleaver. Teddy had joined the army. A chip off the old block – Fenn had done two tours in Vietnam. His time in the army was something people always mentioned about him, that and Meg. Now they would talk about Teddy, too, how he had traded Harvard for Iraq, and everyone would feel sorry for Jack and Fee because they must be *so worried* but thank heavens they had such stalwart spirits. Teddy's decision seemed rash and odd to Winn, but at least it would take him far from Livia. Let the Fenns do as they pleased. Let them cultivate their moral superiority the way some people grew enormous, prizewinning pumpkins or watermelons that were, when you came down to it, really just freaks.

The damp fragrance of corn silk and the dusty,

acidic smell of tomatoes overpowered the perfume of the Duffs' flowers, which shuddered and bobbed between Livia's knees. Leaving her in the car, Winn popped into the seafood store, and once he was back in the car, he found he wasn't sure where he wanted to go. After hesitating long enough at a stop sign to draw the indignant horn of the driver behind him, he turned left.

'Aren't we going to the Enderby?' Livia asked. She had not spoken since they parted ways with the Fenns in the market.

'First we're going to take a look at this house of Fenn's,' he said, choosing to ignore her petulant tone.

'Seriously? What if someone's there?'

'Is it a crime to visit our friends' house?'

'I can't believe Teddy joined the army.' She said 'army' as though it were the name of another woman.

'Well,' said Winn, 'the apple doesn't fall far from the tree. Jack is the same way, always having to showboat. That family has a holier-than-thou streak a mile wide. Just between you and me, I've never cared for it. He uses that girl like a shield.'

'Meg?' Livia said. 'I think they'd probably prefer she was normal.'

'We all make sacrifices,' Winn went on, 'but they expect everyone to praise theirs all the time. This army thing seems excessive. Why not the navy? Why not the air force? Coast guard? No, the Fenns have to make a show out of humility. Teddy should have gone to West Point if he wanted to go this route.'

'I don't think this was the plan from the beginning. Not that I know anything, apparently.'

'I don't see why he has to be a grunt like his father.'

'Wasn't Jack drafted?'

'Yes, but he handled it in a very odd way. He could have deferred. Men like Greyson have it figured out. Greyson gives up the little things, little luxuries. He doesn't overdo it. He'll be good for Daphne that way.'

'I don't think being selectively cheap is the same thing as enlisting.'

'So you're on the Fenns' side now?'

'I wish you hadn't mentioned Teddy.'

'I was being polite. Better to hear the news from Jack, anyway. Now you won't be caught off guard.'

'You can't go around asking about Teddy like he's just another person, Dad.'

'He *is* just another person, Livia. He should be, anyway.'

'Well, he's not!'

'Ah,' Winn said, 'here we are.'

In his opinion, the finest houses on the island were marked by dented mailboxes and rutted driveways. Only a chimney or maybe a widow's walk should be visible from the road. Jack Fenn's house, however, was a blatant, dazzling Oz set against the blue horizon of Waskeke Sound. Privet plants wrapped in burlap stood in wooden boxes at regular intervals along the road like blindfolded prisoners, holes already dug and waiting for them in the rich-looking soil. After a few years, they would merge into a hedge and provide a semblance of privacy, but the driveway was needlessly wide, a blinding avenue of broken quahog shells that unspooled in a graceful S curve up to the house, where one offshoot led to a garage and the other to the front door, making a loop around a flagpole. To one side of the house, confined by an infant hedge of its own and a cage of dark green chain-link, a mountain of red clay waited to be spread and rolled into a tennis court. Yet another nascent hedge encircled an empty, freshly poured swimming pool and the wooden bones of a pool house.

Winn turned in between two glossy black post lanterns, crunching on the shells. The flagpole at the top of the driveway was the nautical style, a yardarm across a mast, and stood in an oval of dirt. No flags were flying, but the cords were ready, their clips dinging against the metal pole, waiting to hoist the colors when the Fenns were in residence. The windows still bore the manufacturer's decals. Part of the ground floor had been covered with new, lemony shingles, stark against the tar paper. Two years might pass before they faded to the desirable gray, and until then the house would be a bright imposition on the subtle landscape. The beginnings of a yard – paving stones, sacks of cement, a heap of mulch – loitered in the broad expanse of dirt that would one day be a lawn.

Tarpaulins covered bales of shingles on one side of the driveway. The roof was a steep landscape of peaks, dormers, and gables, all sheathed in new cedar shake that shone in the sun. Brick chimneys crowned with terra-cotta pots pointed at the sky. Above the whole mess presided the bright copper sails of the three-masted clipper ship Fenn had chosen for his weather vane. Winn's weather vane was a man alone in a rowboat.

'Anyway,' Livia said, 'Greyson's sacrifices are completely superficial. They're not any kind of real loss. They're just symbolic of loss. You know, like giving up chocolate for Lent or rending garments or something. At least what Teddy's doing is genuinely hard.'

'Would you look at the size of this place,' said Winn. 'I'm surprised. Jack comes from a fine old family. This is . . . it's showy.'

Construction debris was strewn around: rolls of wire, crumpled wrappers, twine, tape, pipes, buckets crusted with cements and sealants. Two beige portable toilets stood a discreet distance away. 'The house is poorly designed,' he said, pointing up through the windshield. 'It must be a swamp up on that roof after a big rain. You see? I can pick out at least two spots where water will pool. They'll have leaks. They probably already do. Shake is tricky. If you don't cover the nail holes properly, you get leaks.'

'Fine,' said Livia. 'The Fenns have made a mockery of roofs. They join the army just to bug you, and they design their houses to really get under your skin.'

'You disagree?'

'I don't want Jack Fenn to drive up and find us sitting here staring at his house.'

'It's a ridiculous house. I'm telling you. Look at that roof. Millions of dollars just to have leaks.'

'Dad, people like living by the ocean. Why shouldn't they have a nice house if they want?'

'So you think people should have everything they want even if what they want is an ostentatious eyesore?'

'I don't think it's an eyesore.'

'This house is an eyesore.'

'I don't know – to each his own. We could have built a house like this if we wanted to, right? It's just not our style.'

Leaning forward with his chest pressed to the steering wheel, craning to see the roof, Winn was gratified by Livia's use of 'our,' that she was including herself in his aesthetic of quality, longevity, and simplicity. Since their childhood he had told his daughters he was going to give away all his money before he died, and they should make or marry their own if money was what they wanted. Better that than letting them feel the same disappointment he had after his parents died, when he discovered his inheritance was little more than untenable expectations. He had done well enough, but he was thankful for the way a certain degree of gentle dilapidation could be made to suggest old wealth. Shabbiness of necessity was easily disguised as modesty and thrift. Not that having a simple, hard-won summerhouse instead of this castle by the sea would qualify him as shabby by most standards.

'Right?' Livia persisted. 'We just do things differently. You aren't a fancy house kind of guy.'

'What do they need such a big house for?' he said. 'Is Teddy going to have a thousand children?'

Livia drew the Duffs' flowers up onto her lap. 'That's the last thing I want to think about, assuming he lives long enough to have children.'

'Don't be dramatic. He'll be fine. Anyway, the girl's not going to have any.'

'I can't even wrap my head around . . . what if I was his only chance?'

The premise, simple enough on its surface, gave way beneath Winn's consideration, dropping him into a feminine thicket of improbable hypotheses and garbled cause and effect. He clapped her knee. 'Now, listen. I don't want you thinking this army business has anything to do with you.' He drove around the oval and back down the driveway. Livia was obscured by pink and orange flowers and curls of green, leafy things, a tiger in the grass.

'What if Teddy and I get back together?' she said.

'I don't think that's very likely.'

'Thanks a lot!'

'Do you think you're going to get back together?'

'I don't know. I'm just saying.' She pulled the

vase even closer to herself. 'What would you have done if I had been born like Meg Fenn?'

'I don't know. I suppose I would have gotten used to it.'

'Really?'

'I think when something like that happens you rise to the occasion.' In truth, Winn could not imagine holding the hand of his grown daughter as she bellowed beside a pyramid of tomatoes.

'If Daphne had been born like that, would you have had another child?'

'I couldn't say.'

'Would you have wished you had never had children?'

'This is a silly conversation.'

At the Enderby, Livia jumped out with the flowers and took them inside. When she returned, she looked naked without her portable jungle, and the car felt empty.

After he'd parked in front of the house, Winn said, 'Tell your mother I'll be in in a minute.' Livia took two of the grocery bags and went inside, and Winn walked along the driveway past the garage and down a path shaded by trees and padded with a russet layer of pine needles. Unseen birds burst into a chorus of jabbering laughter as he passed. He paused beside his garden, peering through the deer fence in consternation. Dominique had chosen the right word: sad. The plants were all smaller than they should have been and drooped on rubbery stems: dwarfish melons, bloodless tomatoes, cucumbers that had not come up at all. There were some acceptable-looking green beans, but he saw no sign of the chervil or hyssop he had requested. Mint, which would grow in the crater left by a nuclear blast, was the only thing flourishing. The idea occurred to him that the caretakers could be sabotaging his little agricultural oasis, mistreating the soil or planting in adverse weather conditions. Poking his fingers through the fence, he rubbed a few leaves of mint together and walked away, farther into the trees. He held his fingers to his nose and sniffed the weed's sharp, sweet smell.

He walked until he could no longer see the house, and then he looped back, coming to the edge of a dense clump of trees and brush and spotting, through the branches, Agatha sunning herself on the grass near the house. She was lying on a blue and white towel, and he recognized her polka-dotted bikini as the one from his study. She must have gone in there to retrieve it. Perhaps she had left him something else, a hair clip or a scarf. The afternoon sun was dropping lower in the sky, and a serrated front of tree shade advanced across the grass toward her bare toes. Daphne came out the French doors from the kitchen and crossed the deck and then the lawn, carrying a towel. She wore a black bikini, her huge, naked belly protruding brazenly between the two halves. Piper followed, turning to shut the doors behind her and giving Winn a view of wishbone thighs and a derriere so nonexistent that the blue fabric of her bathing suit hung in flaccid wrinkles. As Daphne shook out her towel, Agatha reached up and patted the side of her bare leg in a friendly way. Piper settled crossed-legged on the grass, her face obscured by massive sunglasses like ski goggles. Daphne eased herself down so her feet were facing Winn and the hummock of her pregnancy hid the top half of her body. Her shadow, humped like a camel, drew a smooth, dark curve over Agatha's flat stomach and golden hipbones.

Watching them, he became aware of the elasticity of his lungs, the hard ridges of tree roots pressing into his feet, the muscular, rippling action of swallowing. His heart raced with stealth and vitality. That was another man's house, another man's daughter and her friends. He was a stranger, a prowler, a hunter, a wood dweller excluded from their world. The girls' obliviousness transformed them, although he couldn't pinpoint how. He couldn't decide if they seemed more innocent when left to themselves, or more unabashedly sensual. Or were they unreal, like mermaids caught basking on a rock? They were only sitting – but there was *something* about them. Daphne, distorted by pregnancy, could not be reconciled with the little girl he remembered. Piper sat erect and unmoving, a sphinx. Agatha was lying on her back with her knees bent, and she moved her legs in a slow rhythm, bumping her thighs together and then letting them fall apart. A narrow strip of polka-dotted material concealed her crotch, and it tightened and slackened as she moved her legs, lifting slightly.

Close in his ear, a voice said, 'Boo!'

CHAPTER 3

SEATING ARRANGEMENTS

Biddy stood with her hands on the edge of the kitchen table, leaning over a slew of guest lists, place cards, and seating charts. She felt like a general planning an offensive. Beside her, Dominique, faithful aide-de-camp, mirrored her posture.

'What if,' Dominique said, switching two cards, 'we move these like this. Situation neutralized.'

'No,' said Biddy, 'because then I've got exes sitting at the same table. Here.' She touched the paper.

'They wouldn't be okay?'

'It's not ideal.'

Dominique tapped her lips with one long finger and considered. Biddy, seized by affection, patted her on the back. She missed Dominique, especially during the holidays, when she had been a household fixture all through high school and college, Cairo being so far away. Dominique had been the sort of worldly kid who sought out the company of adults and who, at fourteen, had considered herself all grown up. When she stayed with the Van Meters, she behaved more like Daphne's indulgent aunt than her friend and spent most of her time helping Winn in the kitchen and running errands with Biddy while Livia, little duckling, followed wherever she went and Daphne lay indolently in front of the television. Agatha had spent a few holidays with them, too, but her presence was less comfortable. Biddy was always finding cigarette butts in the flower beds and catching Winn staring and waking up to the sound of Agatha laughing and drunkenly thumping the walls while the others shushed her and tried to convey her to bed. Once Biddy had gotten up and flipped on the light at the top of the stairs, surprising them – Daphne, Dominique, Livia, and Agatha – like a family of possums in the sudden brightness. Agatha was lying on her side and inexplicably clinging to the balusters while Dominique worked to pry her fingers loose and Livia and Daphne grasped her ankles to keep her from kicking.

'What if,' Dominique said, pointing at the seating chart, 'we move him to the leftovers table?'

'Yes,' said Biddy. 'Perfect. But I feel bad calling them leftovers.'

Dominique pushed the place card across the table with the authority of a croupier. *Le mélange,* then.' She stood back and looked at Biddy, her long eyebrows kinked and her long, sad mouth pulled quizzically to one side. 'How are you? I mean – really.'

Biddy was so surprised by the question that her

eyes began to water. 'I'm fine,' she said, fussing with the cards to indicate the unimportance of her tears. 'I'm great. I'm so happy for Daphne – I want everything to go well.'

'Of course you do,' said Dominique. 'This is an insane amount of work. You're handling it like a champ.'

Biddy was forced to take a tissue from the box on the counter. She never wore mascara, but she dabbed carefully nonetheless, coming up under her lashes the way she remembered her mother doing. To be seen, really looked at, the way Dominique had fixed on her, was unsettling. Her family barely noticed her, but she couldn't blame them: she had changed so little over the years that people were never reminded to reconsider her. 'It *is* a lot of work,' she said. 'It really is.' Making the confession gave her a small thrill, and she went on, feeling her way. 'And sometimes it feels like a natural conclusion to raising a daughter, that you run yourself ragged to make this one day as perfect as possible, even though, for you, the day is bittersweet because she's leaving – I mean, she's been living with Greyson, but somehow this is different, more official. I don't know how those overbearing beauty pageant mothers do it, you know, keeping track of someone else's whole physical being: hair, clothes, makeup, all that.'

'Yeah, right?' Dominique concurred. 'I think – well, I don't know, but it seems to me the real backbreaker is being in charge of manifesting someone else's idea of perfection. Not necessarily Daphne's, just this *idea* floating around out there about what a wedding should be.'

Biddy squared a place card with the edge of the table. 'Manifesting someone else's idea of perfection. Hmm. That's well put.' She wondered if the younger woman was talking about more than just the wedding. Certainly Biddy was no stranger to laboring under another person's vision for life. Abruptly, her enjoyment of her own honesty peaked and fell away. She had wilted quickly under the spotlight. 'I don't know,' she said. 'All I mean is that I don't want anyone to be disappointed.'

'Well, sure,' Dominique said, switching to an offhand tone, 'but there's only so much you can control. Perfection is overrated, anyway. I'm all about meeting basic needs and seeing what's left over from there.'

Laughing in embarrassment, Biddy balled up the tissue and hurried to throw it away under the sink. 'But you! I want to hear about *you*,' she said. 'You have the most interesting life. Tell me everything about Belgium.'

'Oh, it's all right. I don't think it's my forever home. I just kind of live there. In a way, it could be anywhere. You should see my apartment – it's completely barren. Every time I think about buying something, like nice sheets or something to hang on the wall or even fancy hand soap, I think, well, no, because I won't be here for long, and it'll be one more thing to get rid of.' She gave Biddy another searching look. 'Are you sure you don't want to take a break? You could run away for an hour somewhere. Have some time to yourself. I'd cover for you.'

'No, no,' Biddy said, shaking off the last of her tears. 'I'm really fine. It's not the *amount* of stuff I have to do, really, it's – you're so sweet to ask. I just – where *is* your forever home, do you think?'

Dominique's eyebrows climbed a notch higher, but she said, 'I'm not sure it exists. Not Egypt, not Belgium. Not France – that's where my parents live now. They moved a couple of years ago. I don't know if Daphne told you. I like New York but it exhausts me. Not Deerfield. Not Michigan.'

'That still leaves a lot of places,' Biddy said. 'Maybe you're supposed to live in the Bahamas.'

'I hope so. In a hammock.' They giggled.

'How will you find it?' Biddy asked. 'Your home?' She was curious; she had never chosen where to live.

'I think probably I'll look for a job first. But – I don't know. In theory I could work most places. You'd think it would be fun, being able to pick more or less anywhere in the world, but when I think about the freedom I usually just end up feeling lonely. There's nothing pulling me to any particular spot except vague preferences. And sometimes I wonder what it says about me that I can drift like this.' She gave a quick, wry roll of her eyes. 'Total first-world problem.'

'What do you mean?'

'You know, like, oh, woe is me, I'm so exhausted and alienated by my globe-trotting life of preparing expensive food.'

'Don't you have a boyfriend in Belgium? What about him?'

'I don't think he's permanent.' Dominique made a slow, sheepish shrug, her shoulders lingering around her ears for several seconds until she abruptly let them fall. 'It'll all sort itself out. Where do you think I should live? Where would you go?'

Biddy was caught off guard not so much by the question as by her inability to process it. She couldn't think of a single place she might live where she had not already lived. She thought: Connecticut. Waskeke. Maine. Connecticut. Those weren't answers for Dominique. They were shameful in their timidity, their lack of adventure. But she could not imagine living on a tropical island or in the Alps or in Rome or Sydney or Rio. She could not imagine living in Delaware. 'I think you'll know it when you find it,' she said. 'I think you'll find the perfect place. Or at least one that meets your basic needs.'

The side door slammed, and Livia appeared in the hallway, balancing a paper grocery bag brimming with corn on each of her hips. 'Teddy joined the army,' she announced.

'Teddy *Fenn*?' Biddy asked.

Livia set the bags on the counter. 'Teddy Fenn.'

The boy's name, so familiar, sounded foreign to Biddy when Livia pronounced it all by itself, like the Latin name for a rare species, some kind of wetlands bear. 'How do you know?'

'We ran into Jack at the market. He said Teddy just went down to some recruitment center or wherever and signed up. He's not coming back to school. He's not graduating. I don't know why Jack couldn't stop him. What kind of father would let this happen?' Biddy thought Livia sounded like her own father, though Livia would be offended to be told so. The two of them had the same wrongheaded belief in the power of parents over children. A bag of corn tipped over, and the heavy ears thumped onto the floor. Livia gazed heavenward and flapped her arms in defeat.

Biddy was relieved not to be the object of any more scrutiny. 'Easy does it,' she said, approaching her daughter even though she knew her consolation would not be welcome. Since Livia could not admit defeat and accept that Teddy really was lost, she would tolerate no pity. Biddy kept waiting for her to simply get over the boy. As a toddler Livia had been inseparable from her pacifier until the day she was put down for an unwelcome nap and ripped the rubber nipple from her mouth and hurled it to the floor, never to suck on it again.

'Dad was in rare form,' Livia said after allowing Biddy a brief hug and then stepping away. 'He got all, you know, forceful and cheerful, and tried to bring up the Pequod and was weird with Meg, and then, *then*, he goes, "How is Teddy?" Like he was talking about some random acquaintance.

And Jack says, "Oh, funny you should ask. He's made a big decision. He's joined the army." And Daddy says, "Well. Well, well, well, well, well." Like that. "Well, well, well, well, well."'

'Did Jack say why?'

Livia bent to gather up the corn. 'No. I'm not sure he knows.'

'Where does he go? Does he go to . . . boot camp?' Biddy spoke tentatively, uncertain of the expression.

'I don't know. I have no idea where or when or how. I don't know. Why would I know? Did he just wake up one morning and decide, Oh, none of this is really working for me? I'd like a one-way ticket to Iraq, please.'

'They'll give him a round-trip ticket,' Dominique said. She, too, came to hug Livia, and this time Livia seemed grateful, wrapping her arms around Dominique's strong back and hiding her face in the young woman's shoulder. Biddy noticed a strand of corn silk on the tiles and bent to pick it up.

'He might have to come back as cargo,' Livia said, muffled. 'Why can't he just finish college?'

'Livia,' said Biddy, 'I don't want you to think this has anything to do with you.' She reached in from the outskirts of the embrace to squeeze her daughter's shoulder.

'That's what Daddy said.' Livia released Dominique. 'But how could it *not* have anything to do with me?'

Because, Biddy wanted to say, Teddy didn't fall apart after this breakup the way you did. Because Teddy's life no longer includes you. But she could see that Livia was taking Teddy's decision as some kind of sign, an indication that he was becoming unpredictable and erratic, possibly on the brink of a collapse that could only drive him back to her, regretful and awakened. His flight to the army was the last dying flutter of independence, his last binge of freedom before he saw the light. The army would never love him the way Livia did. 'I don't want you to *hope* it has something to do with you,' Biddy said.

Livia began breathing in through her nose and out through her mouth and staring off into space. The therapist she saw at school, Dr Z, had taught her that trick: if you feel like you're about to lose your temper, breathe in through your nose and out through your mouth and count to five or ten, depending on the direness of the situation. Winn hated that Livia saw a shrink. He said she should learn to grin and bear it.

'Anyway,' Livia said after five seconds, 'after we saw Jack, Daddy decided we should go check on their new house.'

'The Fenns' house?' said Biddy. 'Why?'

'I think he wanted to sit there and glower at it and think about the Pequod. Not about how Teddy knocked me up and dumped me, no, no. About how unfair it is – what a great injustice it is – that there's a club out there he can't join.'

75

'Maybe it's easier for him to think about the Pequod,' Dominique said.

Biddy looked at her, annoyed. The casual analysis seemed to violate Winn's privacy. And Dominique couldn't possibly understand what his clubs meant to him, what it was like to live inside their particular social world. Hadn't she just been saying she didn't belong anywhere?

Dominique was standing at the counter with a bottle of white wine she had helped herself to from the fridge, presumably to pour a nerve-settling glass for Livia. The natural melancholy of her face lent an air of pensive deliberation to even her simplest actions, and she contemplated the bottle as though it were a bouquet of condolence flowers in need of arranging. Thoughtfully, slowly, frowning, she twisted in a corkscrew and then glanced up, catching Biddy's eye and, surely, some trace of her enmity.

'You know what I mean,' Dominique said levelly. 'We all have our safe thing to run back to when we get overwhelmed.'

Biddy remembered that only minutes before she had been grateful enough for Dominique's presence to have cried. Apologetically, she said, 'He likes to keep track of new houses on the island.'

'Honestly, I think the house is great,' said Livia. 'They have an amazing location. The house is big, but so what? It's Fenn Castle.'

'The Fennitentiary,' Dominique said, handing a glass of wine to Livia. 'Biddy, may I pour you a glass?'

'No, thanks.'

'Fennsylvania,' said Livia.

Biddy tried to think of a pun but couldn't come up with anything. Had Dominique ever even met any of the Fenns? Most likely not, though certainly she had heard plenty about them – both Daphne and Livia kept up e-mail correspondences with her, and over the past few days the house had effloresced with girl talk. 'Is Teddy on-island?' she asked Livia.

'I don't know. I didn't ask. Probably.'

'Well, you won't run into him.'

'What if he calls me?'

'Do you think he will?'

'I don't know. Maybe. You'd think he'd want to tell me about the whole army thing.'

Biddy sat back down at the table.

Livia stepped closer and studied the mess of cards and charts. 'Shouldn't Daphne be doing this?'

'Seating isn't really Daphne's strong suit,' Biddy said. 'She gives everyone the benefit of the doubt. She doesn't see where conflict might arise.'

'On the other hand,' Dominique said, 'I assume the worst.'

'You're very good,' Biddy said. She reached across Livia to pat Dominique's hand.

'Do you know all these people?' Livia asked Dominique.

'Not all of them,' Dominique said. 'Biddy's been explaining the web.'

'The web?'

'All the connections between everyone. It is impressively tangled, I will say.'

'Do you think Daphne's strong suit might be shucking corn?' Livia asked.

'I'll help you,' Dominique said. 'Wine and corn shucking is an underrated combination.' She turned to Biddy. 'We've pretty much got the seating stuff figured out, right?'

'Sure,' Biddy said, so practiced at concealing her disappointments that she had no doubt she sounded serene, even cheerful, as they abandoned her. 'I'm fine here. You girls go on. Have fun.'

Through the French doors, she watched them settle into Adirondack chairs, glasses of wine on a table between them, and take up ears of corn. They ripped the green husks and pale clumps of silk free of the cobs, and dropped the naked yellow ears in one paper bag and the husks in another. Livia was talking, talking, talking, and Dominique was listening as she expertly shucked the corn, her eyebrows curved in tildes of concentration.

Biddy could no longer bear to watch Livia talk about Teddy, her eyes shining with wounded zealotry. Looking away from the girls, she made a few final desultory attempts at seating gambits that would ensure everyone's happiness at the reception, and then she sat staring into the kitchen, wondering what to do. She could think of no more confirmation calls to make, no more gift bags to fill, no flowers to wrangle, no people to greet until the Duffs showed up for dinner. Usually e-mail was banned from the Waskeke house, necessitating a family trip to the library in town every couple of days, but this time Livia had insisted on having a cable hookup put into Winn's office. Biddy wandered in that direction although she didn't really want to know what new obligations were waiting in her in-box, and she only had to open Livia's laptop and see the photo on the desktop – Teddy was not in the picture, but it was one Livia had taken on a trip with him to Scotland – to decide that, no, she would not check her mail after all. Perhaps she would follow Dominique's advice and take a quiet moment for herself.

She sat in Winn's chair, a winged, brooding, swiveling leather thing, and pivoted slowly around. Out the window she saw Daphne, Piper, and Agatha lounging on the lawn, but she had no desire to watch them and continued turning until she was again facing the green expanse of Winn's blotter, bound at the sides with gold-embossed leather and clean except for a small stack of unopened mail and, all alone out in the middle, a single bobby pin. Biddy picked up the pin and held it in the light, looking for any telltale hairs, but it was clean. She supposed Livia must have left it there, though why she would be fixing her hair at Winn's desk was a mystery.

She swiveled again to look out the window. At the rate Livia was going, she would end up being as scrawny as Piper, whose shoulder blades cast

79

angular, inhuman shadows as she stretched her knobby arms up and out to the side. Of course she might have been as big as Daphne by now, or bigger, or already a mother. Biddy was afraid Livia was the doomed, clever moth who does not just bump against the outside of the lantern but manages to find a way inside and breaks itself against the glass – maybe trying to escape, maybe trying to merge with the flame. Biddy fiddled with the bobby pin, turning it over and over, pinching her fingertip in its tines. Teddy was a handsome kid, comfortable being noticed, impish and urbane under his red hair, not too pale but freckled, almost golden. He was friendly and charming, too, but Livia seemed unaware of how far she outstripped him in curiosity and sharpness and passion. Yes, Teddy had told Livia he loved her, but Biddy, for all her sorrow at her daughter's pain, was disappointed and troubled that Livia had allowed herself to become so vulnerable, mulishly ignoring all the warning signs. How had she, Biddy, managed to raise someone so exposed and defenseless, a charred moth, a turtle without a shell, exactly the kind of woman she most feared to be?

Celeste laughed a hooting, triumphant laugh, pleased to have startled him so completely. Winn, turned pure animal, had bolted off to one side, his body twisting in its unimaginative sheath of polo shirt and salmon-colored pants. His feet, trying to flee, had run afoul of the tree roots, and he had stumbled badly, catching a trunk with both hands. She knew from long experience that taking jokes was not Winn's strong suit, but still she was unprepared for the intensity of the response that crossed his face: first a very brief flash of something odd, like fear but also like despair, and then, once he had steadied himself, pure rage.

'What the hell are you doing?' he demanded.

'Come on, Winnifred, just a little prank. You didn't die.'

He examined the palm of his left hand and held it out for her to see. It was pink and scratched. Tiny white curls of skin stood up like grated cheese. 'This is the last thing I need.'

'Good thing you're not a lefty.' Earlier, Celeste had sensed she was getting too far ahead of the game and had come out for a walk to sober up. She was glad, too, because now she could be confident she wasn't slurring her words.

His face resolved into a grim smile. 'How much have you had to drink?'

'Just the right amount,' she said. She hoped the medically smoothed forehead she wore like a helmet would keep her from betraying the sting of his question. 'What are you doing out here, skulking around?'

'I wasn't *skulking*. You're not the only one who can take a walk. It is my property, after all.'

His discomfort intrigued her. Instinct, honed by years of field experience, had rendered her unable to resist sniffing along a trail of male bad behavior once she caught the scent, and she studied him, increasingly certain that, underneath his bluster, something was off. Winn scowled, backed up against his tree. What had he been looking at in the first place? He moved to block her view, but she leaned around him and caught sight of the girls out in their bathing suits, soaking up the last of the sun like three mismatched lizards. 'Enjoying the view, Winnifred?' she said lightly. There were worse things than being a Peeping Tom.

He gritted his teeth. 'I was taking a walk. I heard a noise, and I went to see what it was. I was about to go up and say hello to the girls when you decided to give me a heart attack. I didn't realize you were taking a break between cocktail hours to sneak around.'

'No need to get huffy with *me*, 007,' she said. He would never dare pick on her drinking with Biddy around, but as they faced each other out in the trees, his dignity ruptured and his adrenaline still running high, they were caught up in a primal energy. She thought he was equally likely to strike her or kiss her. He had kissed her once before, supposedly by accident, and he was attractive in his way, in good shape for his age and with a symmetrical, serious, news anchor sort of face and nice gray temples. But then again she had a thing for repressed men (hello, husbands one, two, and four), and she had a thing for men just starting to go gray (three and four), and she had a thing for forbidden men (three, oh lord, three), and, truth be told, she flirted with Winn sometimes for no more substantial reason than that she liked to keep things lively. She had stolen husband number three in the first place – he had been a charismatic trial lawyer, married, and the authoritarian, despised, partnership-withholding boss of husband number two – and then that little tramp, that child with the long, long legs and the horse face, her best friend's daughter, had gone and stolen him, and off they'd flown to Bolivia.

But Winn was such a square. That was why he and Biddy worked. Ogling through the pine trees was probably the great sin of his life. 'I wasn't sneaking,' she said. 'I was walking, just like you.' She attempted a saucy smirk, feeling a curious deadness in the parts of her face that had been injected into submission. 'So, which is it?' she asked.

'What are you talking about?'

'Is it Agatha or Piper? Oh, don't tell me. I've already guessed.' As she spoke, she realized that she had, in fact, guessed, and scorn rose up in her.

'You are being disgusting,' Winn said with exaggerated deliberateness. 'I hope you get all this out of your system before our guests arrive.'

She poked him in the belly, just above the brass buckle of his needlepoint belt, finding more softness there than she expected. 'Dirty old man.'

'Screw *off*,' he growled and stomped away into the trees.

Celeste watched him go and then pushed through the branches and sauntered out onto the lawn. 'Hello, ladies!' she called. Piper waved; Agatha propped herself up on her elbows; Daphne lolled on her side like a walrus, her chin lost in the soft folds of her neck. Poor dear. Fortunately, she would be the type to shed the baby weight right away.

'What's up, Celeste?' Agatha said.

Piper sat up straight as a yogi and lifted her arms over her head. Her swimsuit stretched over the hollow between her ribs and hips. 'Isn't it so beautiful out?' she chirped.

Celeste flopped onto the grass. 'Absolutely gorgeous.'

'Make sure you check yourself for ticks later, Celeste,' Daphne said. 'Lyme is a problem here.'

'Why would limes be a problem?' Piper asked.

'Not limes,' Agatha said. 'Lyme disease. With a *y*.'

Celeste crossed her arms over her face and wished that a hand would descend from heaven and offer her a cocktail. She was wearing shorts and a striped sailor's shirt, and the grass pricked her calves. She kicked off her sandals and rolled onto her belly, looking uphill at the girls. 'So who's next, ladies? Who's after Daphne?'

'Don't look at me,' said Agatha. 'Piper's the one with a boyfriend.'

'Oh my God,' Piper said. 'Don't jinx it.' She ran a hand through the huge mane of hair that, in

Celeste's opinion, made her look like a member of Whitesnake.

'So marriage is still cool?' Celeste asked. 'It's still something girls your age want? I would have thought you all would be going over to some groovy, Swedish hipster model of commitment.'

'Obviously, marriage is cool,' Agatha drawled. 'Otherwise Daphne wouldn't be doing it.'

Daphne snorted. 'If I had a baby out of wedlock, Daddy would die. Literally die.'

'You mean,' Celeste said, 'you wouldn't be getting married if it weren't for your father?'

'Well, Mom, too. And the Duffs. But, no, if I really had my way, we'd wait a while so I wouldn't have to be pregnant in the pictures.'

'I really want to get married,' Piper volunteered. 'It's so romantic.'

'Yes, it is,' Celeste agreed. She plucked a blade of grass from the soil and tickled her lips with its waxy edge. 'But romantic and prudent are not the same thing.'

'That's good, though,' Agatha said. 'Imagine if there was only prudence.'

'Hmm,' said Celeste. 'Then I never would have married, and the world would be a very different place.'

'My parents would have, though,' Daphne said. She had settled on her back again, and her voice drifted over her belly.

'That's true,' Celeste said.

Agatha crossed one golden leg over the other

and bounced her slender, dirty foot. 'What was Winn like when he was young?' she asked. 'It's just that I can't imagine it. Biddy I can picture, but not Winn.'

Celeste felt a prickle. The nymphet was interested. Never one to torture herself, she preferred not to dwell on the charms of young women and had only allowed her eyes to skim the girl before, assessing her as pretty (really, more than pretty but with the kind of looks that would turn vulgar before too long). But now she gave her full attention to the remarkable body on display in that ratty old bikini, worn to near transparency. Agatha was thin but not hard. Long limbed but still small. Totally devoid of pores or cellulite or stretch marks or stray hairs. Even something as mundane as her kneecap was finely wrought, worthy of study, top of the line.

But this girl must have her choice of men. Why would she want old Winnifred? What about him could possibly light her fire except his forbiddenness, his unlikeliness, the very triteness of his middle-aged crush? Not that any of those should be underestimated. Husband number three, Wyeth, had been the least handsome but most loved of her husbands, and now he lived off his fortune in St Barts, the novelty of Bolivia having long ago worn off, though not, apparently, the allure of long-legged, horse-faced youth. But Wyeth had been stolen property to begin with, an unlucky penny, and Celeste, in the end, had come to accept the bulk of the blame for the sorrows caused by their marriage. Nothing like that should happen to Biddy. Biddy had always been such a docile creature, highly competent but docile, happy to be a kind of ladies' maid to her sisters through her childhood and then an earnest bluestocking and then a selfless wife. To betray her would be the height of cruelty. But this was crazy. Agatha couldn't possibly want *Winn*.

'Oh,' Celeste said, drawing an expansive sigh of phony reminiscence, 'let me cast my mind back. I think – I think – yes. I remember now. Winn was exactly the same.'

Piper made a high squawk that Celeste supposed was laughter. 'There has to be more. Tell! What was he like?'

'Really. I couldn't possibly come up with one thing that's changed.'

Daphne stirred. 'Mom once said he had a bad reputation before they met. Apparently he liked the ladies.'

Agatha's bouncing foot stilled.

'I think he started those rumors himself,' Celeste said. 'Your father is a born monogamist. Boring as hell.'

'Mom seemed kind of proud of it,' Daphne said. 'She's funny.'

Agatha uncrossed her legs and sat up. The shade had fully caught her, and she rubbed her arms as though to brush it off. She said, 'Some people like a little competition. You want to feel like you have someone desirable.'

'You *would* say that,' Daphne said. 'Whatever helps you sleep at night.'

But Piper was nodding. 'No,' she said, 'I think that's true sometimes. You want to feel like the guy had lots of options but chose you. Like you tamed him a little bit.'

'That is so retro,' said Daphne.

'Don't you feel that way?' Agatha asked. 'It's not like Greyson was a virgin when you met. It's not like Greyson was ever a virgin.'

'Well,' Daphne said. 'I don't know. Maybe a little.'

Sadly, but with a certain pleasure of anticipation, Celeste accepted that she needed a drink. 'All right,' she said, hoisting herself to her feet and sliding back into her sandals. 'I'll leave you girls to it. Someone has to tell Daphne what's going to happen on her wedding night, and I don't have the stomach for it.'

'We'll be in soon,' Daphne said. 'We've lost our sun. Check for ticks.'

Celeste walked around the house and greeted Livia and Dominique, who were deep in conversation on the deck beside two bags of shucked corn. Inside, place cards and seating charts were spread over the table, but Biddy was nowhere to be seen. The bottle of gin was out on the counter, and after she poured a little into a tumbler and added ice and a dollop of tonic, she put it away in a cupboard, where people were less likely to monitor its level. The first sip, bitter and fizzy, was unspeakably delicious, and she felt her nerves begin to settle at once. The bottom line was that she was being paranoid about Winn. And even if she wasn't, what could she do?

After retrieving the bottle and splashing out a tiny bit more gin, she climbed up through the house to the widow's walk, where she could have some privacy and fresh air and take in the view. Reclining in a chair, she closed her eyes and pressed the sweating glass against her forehead. She wanted to tell herself she had once been as sexy as Agatha, but her delusions were not so strong as that. Still, she had been seductive. Otherwise she wouldn't have been able to poach Wyeth from his mousy wife and three children. The best she could say for herself now was that she was the kind of woman people called well preserved. But despite all her restorative efforts, she looked tired. Which she was, in the existential sense. There would be no more seductions for her, no more ecstasy, no more destruction. She and Cooper had a pleasant life together, a sanctuary built by two reformed sinners around a policy of maximal calm and minimal communication. Quiet dinners out, long weeks apart when he was off sailing, compatible taste in TV and movies, mutual tolerance of each other's friends, agreement that they would never marry. Maybe she had stumbled on the ideal relationship for a woman her age.

Maybe, after all these years, she had solved the riddle. Even if things fell apart, she would draft another companion from the bush leagues of washed-up lovers, and they would wait out the violet hour together.

CHAPTER 4

TWENTY LOBSTERS

'I've spent the past six months wishing he were dead,' Livia said to Dominique. Immediately, she regretted the melodrama of the statement. Melodrama did not fly with Dominique.

The last of the corn had been shucked, and Dominique was leaning back in her chair and looking out over the lawn. Celeste had walked up the grass a minute before, and they could hear the murmur of bride and bridesmaids from around the corner of the house. 'I doubt that's what you were really wishing for,' she said tolerantly.

Livia considered. 'Everyone thinks I should just get over it,' she said. 'But I don't know what's on the other side of 'it.' I'm not even exactly sure what 'it' is.'

'No need to be all metaphysical about it. You know what you're supposed to do. You just don't want to do it.'

'I don't want to give up prematurely.'

'No one could accuse you of that. I could read you back the fifty e-mails you sent me this winter detailing the ten million arguments you'd pitched to Teddy for why you should be together. But look, you've given it the old college try, he hasn't come around, so cross your fingers and let go.'

A cry came from above and a crow swooped from the roof, trying to gobble something down as it flew, pursued by an enraged seagull. The birds disappeared over the trees. Livia said nothing.

'It's been a while since you've talked to him, right?' Dominique pressed. 'Just keep going with that. Invest some time. I mean, think of it this way. How do you think it looks if you go around mooning over him for months after he dumped you?'

'Why does it matter how it looks?' Livia said hotly, surprised at Dominique. 'Why does everyone care so much about how everything looks?'

Dominique held up her hands in surrender. 'Hey, I'm not a member of this *Great Gatsby* reenactment society you all have going on. I just think it's possible to trick yourself into feeling better by pretending you feel better.'

'Yeah,' Livia said. 'Yeah, I know, but I keep thinking about how far along I'd be. I'd be just as preggers as Daphne.' Two weeks after her abortion, she had been summoned home for a weekend. Daphne and Greyson were coming up from the city for dinner. They had news. Winn roasted a duck. They were still on the salad course when Daphne bubbled over and announced she was pregnant and she and Greyson were getting married. Livia, to her enduring shame, had burst into tears and run from the table.

'Women,' Dominique said knowingly. 'We measure our lives in months.'

'People kept telling me that at least now I know I can get pregnant. Like, phew, what a relief. I'd really be spending a lot of time worrying about infertility otherwise.'

'Yeah, but what do you say to someone about their abortion? The impulse is to grasp for silver linings.'

'I'm not beating myself up over it. I just want to meet someone else. Barring that, I just want to sleep with someone else. To at least create the sensation of moving on.'

'Fine,' said Dominique, 'but beware the rebound guy.'

'I just want a distraction.'

'That's what they all say.'

Biddy was collecting the last of Winn's groceries from the Land Rover when he came walking up out of the trees, frowning and moving his hands to emphasize some speech he was giving in his head.

'Where did you go?' she asked.

'To check on the garden,' he said. 'Depressing.'

'You saw Jack?'

'Livia told you about Teddy?'

'I'm shocked.'

'I'm not. Chip off the old block. At least he'll be far away. Livia won't have to worry about him anymore.'

'She thinks he's leaving because of her. I'm afraid she'll romanticize this.'

'Tell her she's overestimating her own importance. He's a Fenn. He's joining up because he thinks it makes him look good. I tried to get a word in about the Pequod with Jack but didn't get too far. If he's blackballing me because of this whole business with the kids, I think that's poor form.'

'Mmmm.' Biddy was unwilling to enter into another round of the Great Pequod Debate. Was Jack shutting Winn out because Winn had excluded Jack from the Ophidian? Was Fee carrying a grudge over their breakup all those years ago? Were the Fenns so collectively shamed by Livia's ordeal that they simply had no wish to see the Van Meters around the clubhouse? This last hypothesis, she had pointed out to Winn over and over again, was especially silly since he had been on the waiting list well before Teddy's hapless sperm found its way to Livia's egg. To Biddy's thinking, Winn had done everything he could to make his case with the Pequod, and the rest was up to fate. So there was no cause for angst, no need to spin conspiracy theories. In all likelihood, the holdup had nothing to do with the Fenns and everything to do with the club's internal workings and quotas. And even if the Fenns were the problem, most likely Winn, not Livia, was to blame, as Biddy was fairly certain the Fenns had been genuinely fond of her daughter and would not be so unjust as to think she had tried to entrap their son. At the end of the day, why would you want to join a club where you are not welcome? But Winn saw the consequences of Livia's mistake everywhere, as though her womb were the source of all disorder in the universe.

'I'll tell you,' Winn said, 'I have an itch to call up Jack and have it out, get the straight story once and for all.'

'No,' Biddy said, 'not this weekend, Winn, please.'

Celeste's voice clarioned down from the roof. 'Winnifred!' Winn grimaced. 'Oh, Winnifred! The lobsters are here!'

A red-faced man in white shirt and pants appeared around the corner of the house, struggling to push a dolly loaded with two cardboard boxes through the gravel. Each box had a large red lobster stamped on it.

'Van Meter?' he said, consulting something scrawled in black marker on the top box. 'Twenty lobsters?'

'You've come to the right place,' said Winn. He stepped forward and lifted the first box off the dolly, setting it on the ground and pulling off the lid.

The deliveryman watched dubiously. 'Everything okay?' he asked.

'I don't know yet,' Winn said. 'That's why I'm checking them.' He pulled lobster after lobster out of his box, holding each in the air to make sure it was moving its antennae and rubber-banded claws before adding it to a pile on the gravel.

'I'm sure they're all alive, Winn,' Biddy said, blocking one lobster's escape with her Top-Sider. People said lobsters were just giant bugs, and they looked it, creeping along, probing with their long feelers.

'Better safe than sorry, dear,' Winn said. To the deliveryman, who had begun to remove lobsters uncertainly from the second box, he said, 'Here, I'll get those if you'll do me a favor and put these ones back.'

'No,' Biddy said. She bent and grabbed a lobster by its midsection and dropped it back in the box. There was a bed of seaweed at the bottom. 'I'll do it.'

'He doesn't mind.' Winn turned to the delivery-man. 'Do you?'

'No?' the man said, confused.

Biddy set two more lobsters on top of the first, and Winn scooped two out of the second box. 'Slow down,' she said, 'they're getting mixed up.'

'It doesn't matter which box they go in, dear, as long as they're alive.'

'You can go,' Biddy told the deliveryman. 'We're all paid up, aren't we?'

'Just hang on one minute,' Winn said. 'Let me finish here.' Biddy gave up replacing lobsters, and she and the deliveryman watched in silence until Winn pulled out the last one and waved it at them. 'Now,' he said, 'aren't we glad I checked? This one's dead.' The lobster's claws drooped limply, swinging from side to side like a pair of oversized boxing gloves. Setting it on the ground among its living brethren, Winn straightened up and put his hands on his hips, victorious. They all looked down at the lobster.

'That's so weird,' the deliveryman said. 'I've never heard of someone getting a dead one. These things could live on the moon.'

'He just moved,' Biddy said. 'He moved his antennae.'

'No, he didn't,' said Winn.

But Biddy was sure. The lobster had swept his antennae to the side. As they watched, the long, whisker-like appendages flicked again. 'See?' she said.

Winn nudged the lobster with his toe. It didn't move. 'It's sick in any case,' he said. 'We don't want to eat a sick lobster.' He picked up the lobster and held it out to the deliveryman. 'How about running back and getting us a replacement?'

'Well,' the guy said, 'that might take a while. I have a few other deliveries to make first.'

'Not necessary,' Biddy said, reaching out and seizing the invalid from Winn. 'We have more than enough. Winn, Dicky doesn't even eat lobster.'

'But we paid for twenty,' Winn said.

'I can write you a credit,' the deliveryman said, eying the lobsters, which were slowly migrating off the path and into the grass.

'Fine,' Biddy said. 'That will be fine.'

'I don't know,' said Winn.

'It's fine,' Biddy assured the deliveryman.

Agatha and Piper emerged from the side door, Piper catching it before it slammed. Both were in their bathing suits, and the men were, for a moment, too startled to remember to hide their interest in the girls' breasts and legs.

'We heard the lobsters were here,' Agatha said. 'Can we help?'

'Good girls,' Winn said. 'You can catch the runaways.'

'You don't have to,' Biddy said.

'No,' said Agatha, 'we'll do it.'

Winn touched Agatha's elbow. 'Sorry about earlier,' he said quietly.

'What happened earlier?' Biddy asked.

Winn and Agatha looked at each other. Agatha laughed.

'I'm afraid I barged in on poor Agatha in the bathroom,' said Winn.

'Oh, Winn,' Biddy said, 'you know the lock's broken. You have to knock.'

'It was my fault,' Agatha offered. 'I should have—'

'No,' Winn interrupted, 'no, I was careless. I accept full responsibility. Absolutely my fault. I'm not used to so many people being around, that's all. Won't happen again.'

'All right,' Biddy said. 'That's enough, Winn.'

'No big deal,' said Agatha with an ingratiating wink at Biddy. She bent to catch a lobster, her bikini nestled fetchingly in her butt crack.

As the deliveryman wrote up a receipt for the

price of one lobster, Biddy held the dead or dying crustacean in one hand and, slipping the other into her pocket, found the bobby pin there. She rolled it between her fingertips as the laughing young women collected the other lobsters, scooping them up and daring each other to kiss the rust-colored noses while the creatures flipped their petaled tails.

This idea of her father's to cook a lobster dinner for seventeen struck Livia as ill conceived but also immutable. She accepted, too, that he would want her to be his sous-chef and that she would not be able to get out of it. He received the shucked corn without thanks and sent her around to the outdoor shower with a salad spinner, four heads of lettuce to wash and tear up, and an empty laundry basket in lieu of a colander. Agatha and Piper had been in the kitchen in their bathing suits for some reason, padding around like nudists, and Daphne and Dominique came in from outside as Livia was heading out. Daphne had a red sarong tied below her belly. 'Daphne,' Livia said, hefting the basket of lettuce, 'you must be really stressed out, what with the wedding being so close and all. So much to do.'

'Leave me alone, I'm pregnant,' Daphne said sweetly, reaching to accept a glass of iced tea from Piper.

The shower, a stall of cedar planks around a showerhead that stuck out from the side of the house, was near the back door. Livia turned on the water and picked up a head of lettuce, holding it under the spray while she tore apart the leaves and dropped them in the spinner. She felt the way she always did after she talked about her pregnancy: a little embarrassed and slightly unclean, like she had told a crude joke at a party. The sight of Agatha in her bikini had done nothing for her mood. She found herself imagining Agatha and Teddy together, and, arbitrary though the pairing was, the thought sickened her. She had heard about two or three girls he had been with since the breakup, and she thought of those girls with Teddy, too, fragments and pieces of bodies, the whole too gruesome to contemplate. Teddy was still the lone notch on her pathetic bedpost. She dug her fingers into the lettuce, making ragged rips she knew her father would not like, and then she clapped the lid on the spinner and pulled its cord, yanking as though starting an outboard motor.

'Teddy got me pregnant' – that was what she said even though the bulk of the blame was hers. Pills either nauseated her or caused insupportable mood swings; diaphragms caused constant infections; she was afraid to get an IUD; the shot had made her roommate gain fifteen pounds. That left condoms. She fell into a habit of chancing a few days around her period when they could skip the part where Teddy picked at the foil wrapper with his thumbnail, tore it open, held the small jellyfish close to his face to see which way it unrolled, and finally applied it, like some ludicrous hazmat suit, to his penis, which all the condom-related exertions of his brain had robbed of some tumescence. Her gamble succeeded for eight months or so and, with discipline, might have lasted longer if she and Teddy had not hit a rough patch, caused, like all of their rough patches, by his attention to another girl. In the relief of their reconciliation, Livia allowed herself to imagine that they were in the green-lit pastures of the safe zone.

A week after the breakup, she had decided one night to get roaringly drunk alone in her room and dress up in pearls and a party dress. Snow was predicted, but she chose a summer dress patterned with large, old-fashioned roses. From her roommate's closet she fished out high, spindly heels that would have frightened her had she been sober, especially given the iciness of the brick sidewalks. She could not get the zipper in back all the way up, and, for one moment, as she stretched and strained with one elbow poking toward the ceiling and the other bent behind her, she was overtaken by wretchedness and sat down on the futon to shed a few tears. Then the gin kicked back in, and she was out the door without a coat, teetering around patches of snow toward the Ophidian, a few inches of her spine framed by the V of her undone zipper. Around her, girls skimmed by in their going-out clothes, underdressed for the cold and, like her, catching their heels in the divoted ice and the grooves between the bricks. Each group of girls was a single, shimmering consciousness, like a flock of birds or a school of fish, moving together in an elaborate, private choreography, their sequins and silks tossing back the streetlights. The boy at the club's door hesitated when he saw her, but she pushed past him.

She thought she heard him say that Teddy wasn't there, and she said, 'Fuck Teddy,' to no one in particular. She made a tour of the rooms, tripping on the nap of the Persian carpets and the knotty floorboards. Pounding hip-hop filled the clubhouse, at odds with the ponderous, old-fashioned interior, which was all tufted leather, dark paint, carved wood, and grim brass light fixtures. The décor suggested a nostalgic, appropriated Englishness, as though the Ophidian had once possessed faraway colonial holdings. Framed photographs of members, letters they'd written or received, doodles they'd made on cocktail napkins, and other inscrutable ephemera crowded on the walls. 'You're all dead now,' Livia muttered to the class of 1918, 'even though you were in the Ophidian.' The club, she thought, was an institution that existed for little purpose other than to select its members. Once you were in, then what? Then you sat around drinking and gossiping until it was time to choose new members, with whom you sat around drinking and gossiping until the time came to choose the next batch. There was no point to it, not really. The Ophidian was a decoy, a façade, a factory that produced nothing. Her father loved that stupid snake swallowing its own tail. He said it was about self-sufficiency, renewal, and rebirth, shedding skins but persisting, having no beginning and no end. She thought it was about going nowhere, about finding no better option than to devour yourself.

People were looking at her, she knew, and she leered back at them, at the looming faces she knew or seemed to know. She found herself sitting on the arm of a leather couch and laughing at something the boy beside her was saying. She laughed so hard she couldn't catch her breath. She took a sip from the plastic cup in her hand and realized it was full of water.

'This is water,' she announced. 'I didn't ask for water. If I wanted water, I would have asked for it.'

The boy on the couch looked embarrassed. She wondered how she had ever thought he was funny. 'Stephen thought maybe you'd had enough.'

'Oh, is that what Stephen thought?' She was standing now. The room went quiet around her, and she swung left and then right to get a good look at it. 'What?' she said. 'You think I'm drunk? *Stephen* thinks I'm drunk? Well, you can tell *Stephen* that I'm drinking for two! Know what I mean? But don't wait for Teddy to tell you and don't send any cigars!' Water slopped out of her glass and onto her toes. 'Shit.' When she bent down to wipe it away, she lost what was left of her balance and tipped forward, arcing toward the oriental carpet. As soon as she hit (or was it before? did she even fall?), she felt a pair of hands on her sides, righting her. One of them zipped up her dress. 'Teddy?' she whimpered.

The hands did not belong to Teddy, though she spotted him then in the doorway, still wearing his coat, flushed pink under his orange hair, staring at her in a way she knew neither of them could recover from. His contempt radiated from across the hushed room, and she could only send back contrition and animal desperation.

Her rescuer was the despised, vodka-withholding Stephen. 'Okay,' he said. 'That's enough party.'

He took her to a back room, and together they went through her phone until they found a soberish friend who agreed to come get her and walk her home. 'Bring a coat she can wear,' Stephen said into the phone. 'And a pair of boots.'

As they sat and waited, Livia studying the floor-boards and Stephen the ceiling, he said, 'I would take you myself, but it wouldn't look good. Teddy's my friend. I'm the one who called him. He came here to get you.'

All the way home, through the falling snow and the purple-orange glow of the streetlights, while the world rattled around her, jarred by each clumsy step she took in her too-big borrowed boots, Livia convinced herself that Stephen would e-mail the next day to check on her, and something would begin, growing out of the snow like a crocus.

There were e-mails the next day, but none from him.

Livia left her basket of washed lettuce on the deck and went into the kitchen. 'Dad?' she called. 'What do you want me to do with the lettuce?'

Her father approached from his study carrying a thick book bound in blue canvas. 'BIRDS' was stamped in silver on the spine. 'I've solved our little mystery,' he said. 'Listen.' He flipped to a page he had been marking with his finger and read, 'Herons are a large family of wading birds including egrets and bitterns. Egrets are any of several herons, tending to have white or buff plumage.' He closed the book. 'That settles it. We were both right.'

'That book's out of date, and that definition is vague, anyway,' she said.

'But egrets are always herons, and white herons are egrets.'

'But there are white herons that aren't egrets, too. I don't know – I don't remember exactly. I'd have to look it up.'

'I already looked it up.'

'That book is old, Dad.'

'Don't get upset.'

'I'm not upset! I just want to be accurate.'

He looked at her steadily over his glasses as though trying to determine whether she were a heron or an egret. 'Me, too,' he said.

CHAPTER 5

THE WHITE STONE HOUSE

Dominique found she was suffering from the classic dual anxieties of the well-meaning guest: she wished to avoid being asked to help with the cooking (Winn by himself was already too many cooks in the kitchen), but she did not want to appear lazy or parasitical. Escape was the only solution, and so she took a bike and struck off. She rode quickly, standing on the pedals, overtaking some local kids in basketball jerseys on low-riding BMXs who hooted at her as she passed, then a solitary guy in paint-spattered pants, riding slowly and slugging from a brown paper bag, and then a large family of day-trippers in a single-file line of descending size, Papa Bear to Baby Bear on basketed rental Schwinns. Ahead, she glimpsed a cyclist with churning, spiderlike legs in black spandex. His torso was a blaze of yellow. '*Ah, oui?*' Dominique said. '*Le maillot jaune?*' She lowered her head and bore down, imagining spectators lining the bike path, snow-capped Alps above, a peloton of BMX kids behind her riding serpentines and pushing one another. The rickety ten-speed she had chosen from the

Van Meter bicycle jumble jerked side to side as she pumped. She caught him more easily than she had expected, the silver teardrop of his helmet growing rapidly larger until she drew alongside, disappointed. She dallied a little before passing, hoping he would turn to look at her, but he kept his sunglasses fixed on the path's vanishing point.

The lighthouse appeared atop a distant bluff, poking up like a solitary birthday candle. In the day, its light seemed feeble and superfluous, a recurring white spark dwarfed and muted by the sun, but Dominique liked the tower's stalwart shape and jaunty striped paint job. She would ride to it, she decided. She rode a bicycle almost every day at home in Brussels, to and from the restaurant, but she was always having to dodge and dart through fierce swarms of tiny European cars, racing for survival and not pleasure. But this – the air full of salt and bayberry, the sky as iridescent and capacious as the inner membrane of an infinite airship, the slow loosening of her muscles – this was something gorgeous. She needed speed, space, the abrasion of rushing air. Poor Livia was laboring under the illusion of being owed something, some karmic charity, for her pain, but the universe felt no compunction for its cruelties, no sympathy for its victims, especially those who helped misery along with some idiotic bareback sex. Everyone knew, of course; the Ophidian party had become known as 'the Baby Shower.' Daphne didn't seem to have done much to help Livia cope with the situation, but she claimed Livia had been giving her a wide berth, confiding little, taking no interest in her pregnancy or the preparations for the wedding. And Daphne respected other people's privacy, even her sister's, a quality sometimes mistaken for a general lack of curiosity. Daphne had told Dominique that during her worst fight with Greyson, the only fight where each had enumerated the shortcomings of the other, he had accused her of not being *interested* in anything.

These days the chatter about Livia's pregnancy seemed to have died down, and for the most part, little Fenn–Van Meter had been swept under the communal Aubusson rug. Dominique had almost forgotten how these families worked, how they were set up to accommodate feigned ignorance, unspoken resentment, and repressed passion the way their houses had back stairways and rooms tucked away behind the kitchen for the feudal ghosts of their ancestors' servants. She was surprised Winn had not leapt from a bridge or gutted himself with a samurai sword after his daughters got knocked up back to back. Daphne's condition – she imagined Winn, the old Victorian, calling it that – would be grandfathered into the boundaries of propriety by the wedding, but Livia's phantom pregnancy, the missing bulge under her green dress at the front of the church, was a void that could not be satisfactorily filled in and smoothed over. Good thing he had the Pequod to take his mind off things, setting out on his quest for membership like Don Quixote without a Sancho.

Bearing down on the pedals, she shook her head. These people, this pervasive clique, this Establishment to which Winn had attached himself and his family, seemed intent on dividing their community into smaller and smaller fractions, halves of halves, always approaching but never reaching some axis of perfect exclusivity. As long as Dominique had known her, Daphne had rolled her eyes at her father's quirks and blind spots, but until the pregnancy, she had done nothing to differentiate her life from his vision for it. At Deerfield Dominique had assumed that college would be Daphne's time to forge her own way, but then she found herself sitting in her Michigan dorm room, curled up in her chlorine-smelling sweats and watching the snow come down and listening to Daphne natter over the phone about eating clubs and bubbleheaded adventures she had with her new fun friend Piper whom Dominique would *absolutely love* and fancy charity balls in New York and Greyson, always Greyson. Generally willing to be goaded into competition, Dominique had first tried to turn Daphne against these new people, to reclaim her. 'They sound like zombies,' she had said, moving from her bunk to the floor and pulling one arm across her chest, stretching her shoulder. She was always either in the pool or studying or sleeping. The amount of time Daphne seemed to have to get dressed up and drink baffled her. 'They sound like exactly the friends your dad would pick for you. Don't you want to mix it up a little bit? Get out of your rut?'

'My rut?' Daphne had repeated. 'I don't have a rut. This is me. Whether or not you approve. I *like* to fit in. I like people I fit in *with*.' Which of course was what had drawn Dominique to her in the first place, back when she was new and lost at Deerfield. Daphne, so certain of her place in the world, had been the perfect antidote to homesickness. She had been a kind of skeleton key to prep school, and Dominique had taken possession of her gladly.

'I just worry,' Dominique said, 'that you're selling yourself short.'

A few weeks of frostiness followed and then reconciliation and then Dominique visited Princeton and did not love all the activities and people that Daphne loved, and then there was a fight caused by Dominique wondering out loud how on earth Piper had been accepted at a supposedly selective school, a fight that included more references to zombies ('entitled zombie brats') and some harsh words from Daphne about how Dominique was always *judging*, always thought she was *better*, thought she was so *special*, like some kind of fucking *pharaoh* even though she *wasn't*, and sometimes people just liked to go out and have *fun* with people who were *nice* and *fun*.

Distance and time had been good for their friendship. Dominique had come to realize Daphne's life was not her responsibility, and now, in return, almost a decade later, Daphne seemed to value her precisely *because* she was less fun than Piper or Agatha, because she was not tiny and blond, because she preferred quiet bars to lounges crowded with bankers, because she tried to be honest. And Dominique liked Greyson – she did, genuinely. She did not love him, but that was fine. She would see him only rarely. Of her friends who were married, none had chosen mates who matched her aspirations for them. Usually the spouses were steady, kind people who wanted to get married, not the thrilling, elevating, inspiring matches Dominique had dreamed up. She had been accused by her own mother, who was always trying to set her up with eligible expat Coptic doctors, of having unrealistic expectations, both for herself and others, but Dominique thought the disjunction was not between herself and reality but between her desires for her own life and her friends' desires for theirs.

Yet Daphne had accused her of aiming too low. Dominique's boyfriend, Sebastiaan, was a Belgian chef who would brook no shortening of his name. All four syllables must be pronounced, creating a conversational speed bump, a navigational hazard. His name dragged at her tongue and always made her anxious she was talking about him too much even though she rarely mentioned him at all. He was a devotee of traditional, master-sauce French cooking and was moved to actual rage when her

North African spices or Thai herbs invaded his *boeuf bourguignon* or *homard à la Normande*. 'What is this?' he would say, shaking a duck leg at her that bore traces of *baharat*. 'If you want to experiment, then use someone else's goddamn duck!'

'He has a sort of culinary xenophobia,' she had told Daphne their first night on the island, before Agatha and Piper had arrived, when the two of them were sitting alone on the widow's walk. 'But I think he's fascinated by the exoticism, too. Once he came home smelling like Ethiopian food, absolutely reeking of turmeric, and I asked him where he'd been, and he said, "Oh, just to have a beer."'

'Better he cheats with food than with another woman,' Daphne said.

'I'm not sure the difference is so big. I think he likes me because I'm dark and spicy and forbidden. I'm *the other*. He gets to feel like he's breaking a taboo. I can tell from the way he is in bed.'

'How can you be serious about someone like that?'

'I'm not. Not really.'

'Then why date him at all?'

'I like him. He suits me for now.'

'Greyson and I were just talking about how you aim too low.'

'Really?' Dominique was equal parts insulted and intrigued. 'I don't know if that's true. I like to think of myself as making do with what's interested and available.'

'No.' Daphne shook her head and pursed her

lips in a way that reminded Dominique of Sebastiaan sampling one of her soups: the distaste, the sureness of opinion. 'You're not choosy enough.'

How, Dominique wondered, had she come to be embroiled in the Van Meters' lives again? To care about their opinions? Before she had come over for her first year at Deerfield, she had packed her suitcases full of European club-rat clothes and scarves and jewelry from the souks so she could show everyone she was Egyptian and exotic and different. But when she got to her dorm and opened her bags, they were full of clothes she'd never seen before. In her jet-lagged delirium, she had experienced a terrified nausea at finding her things inexplicably swapped out for corduroys, kilts, oxford shirts, and puffy down vests as though her life had been swallowed by someone else's. The old Dominique was gone, left like a vapor trail over the Atlantic.

Eventually she figured out that her mother had spent months plotting and stockpiling and ordering new things from catalogs. Biddy Van Meter had been her accomplice; the school had given Dominique's mother the Van Meters' telephone number when she asked for someone she might call for advice. After she became friends with Daphne and Daphne invited her home for Thanksgiving, Dominique had felt, upon meeting Biddy, that she was meeting her creator, the one who had custom designed her for a prolonged but tangential role in their family life.

The Van Meters were so charming at first. Daphne was sweet and serene. Livia was just a kid then and worshipped Dominique. Biddy was practical, brisk, kind. Winn wore bow ties and pocket squares and attacked all parts of his life with a certainty and precision that Dominique found reassuring. There were no weeds in the Van Meter garden, no unmatched socks in their laundry room. A tennis ball hung from a string in the garage to mark the exact location where the car must be parked. The milk was thrown out the day before it expired. Yet everything they did – playing tennis, cooking dinner, making friends, getting dressed – seemed effortless. Years had to pass before Dominique could see the strain they placed on themselves or, rather, what their grand goal was. They wanted to be aristocrats in a country that was not supposed to have an aristocracy, that was, in fact, founded partly as a protest against hereditary power. That was what Dominique could not understand: why devote so much energy to imitating a system that was supposed to be defunct? Any hereditary aristocracy was stupid, and Americans didn't even have rules for theirs, not really. Lots of the kids Dominique knew at Deerfield came from families dedicated to perpetuating some moldy, half-understood code of conduct passed along by generations of impostors. But, she supposed, people who believe themselves to be well bred wouldn't want to give up their invented castes because then they might be left with nothing, no one to appreciate their special clubs, their family trees, their tricky manners, their threadbare wealth.

She couldn't explain her lingering interest in these people, her patience with them. As a member of an unpopular minority in her home country, secular though she and her parents were, she thought she should be outraged by WASPy illusions of grandeur and birthright, their smugness, the nepotistic power they wielded. But the worst she could summon was a bleak, mild pity, and more often, she felt a bleak, mild amusement. Her sense was that the Van Meters had to throw more elbows than some to keep their status, and at times she caught herself feeling sorry for them. They lived a bit on the fringe – she wasn't sure why and would have been hard pressed to explain the sense of inferiority that she caught wafting through their house every once in a while like a foul wind. Thank God for Belgium, Dominique thought. For Sebastiaan. Thank God she had given up the corduroy and kilts in college and gone back to her tunics and scarves.

A Jeep blew past on the road, then braked with a squeal, veering onto the shoulder. She slowed, wondering if she should speed on by. An unfamiliar head popped out of the passenger window. 'Dominique?' he said as she came alongside. 'Hey. Dominique?'

'Yes?' She stopped and stood straddling the bike,

peering in. Greyson was behind the wheel. 'Oh, hey!' she said.

'I thought that was you,' he said, leaning across his passenger. 'How's it going?'

'You could pick out my butt at five hundred meters?'

'Not your butt, your determination. From a mile away. This is my brother, Francis.'

'Hey,' said the passenger.

'Why do you guys have the top up on such a beautiful day?' Dominique said. 'Are you worried about your hair?'

'I don't like convertibles,' said Francis. He wore old man spectacles and had a vague, placid air about him. 'They give me a headache. I think it's the wind.'

Greyson smiled in his gracious way, acknowledging the oddness of his brother's statement while also indulging it.

'Well,' said Dominique, *carpe diem.*'

'We're going to squeeze in a few sets before we have to get ready for dinner,' Greyson said. 'Do you want to throw the bike in the back and come along?'

She noticed they were both dressed all in white. She was wearing orange soccer shorts and a gray T-shirt from a quiche cook-off she had entered on a dare in culinary school and won. 'No thanks,' she said, even though she had no doubt Greyson would be able to scrounge some whites for her. He probably carried them around with him the same way Sebastiaan, a sometime mountaineer, carried a silver emergency blanket. 'You'd have to put the top down to make room for the bike, and I don't think I know poor Francis well enough to risk causing him a headache.'

Francis fixed her with a yogic stare. 'I don't mind. Really.'

'No, it's cool. I'm going to ride out to the lighthouse.'

They drove away, Greyson tapping the horn twice in salute, and she rode on, again catching the yellow-shirted cyclist, who had passed her while she stood talking. Sweat rolled down her back as she pushed up the final hill to the lighthouse, and she relished it. Dropping her bike on the grass, she walked a slow circle, kicking out her legs and craning up at the light. Up close, the tower was less than perfect. The broad red stripe around its middle had faded to a dull, pinky red. The sun had worn all the shine from the black paint on the dome and balcony, and the glass panes of the lantern room were clouded with salt and streaked with bird shit. Paint flaked from the bricks lay scattered in the grass like red and white confetti. Beyond, behind a discolored chain-link fence and perilously close to the disintegrating bluffs, the rusted skeleton of an ancient swing set stood on a patch of scrubby grass, a relic of the days when there had been a lighthouse keeper and a house for him and playthings for his children. A split-rail fence ran back toward the parking area to keep people away from the edge of the bluffs. '3,048 MILES TO SPAIN' read one of the cautionary signs. She looked out over the water and wondered how many miles to Egypt. How many to her parents' house in Lyon? How many to Belgium? What was Sebastiaan doing? Was he rolling around in an orgy of garam masala and *ras al hanout?* Everything that mattered, that was real, was somewhere across that sheet of ocean, not here in this half-imagined place, this nesting colony for bustling, puff-chested Americans where she, the dark seabird, happened to be breaking a long and uncertain journey.

The yellow-shirted cyclist reached the end of the road, paused, and then reversed course, heading back the way he had come. A propeller plane buzzed overhead, and she shaded her eyes and followed its descent across the island toward the little airport, calculating how much of a head start she would need to give the yellow shirt before catching him would be a challenge.

Winn was stripping the kernels from the ears of corn. He would give them a quick boil and then toss them with the tomatoes and a simple vinaigrette. Two batches, of which this was the first. Ten ears per batch. His favorite striped apron was cinched firmly around his waist, and he was humming to himself. He stood a cob on end and ran his very sharp German knife down its side, watching the satisfying curtain of yellow crumble after the blade. Turning the cob, he repeated the exercise until he was left with a reticulated peg. The mindless repetition was soothing, even delicious. He descended into the rhythm of falling knife and sweeping hand, pushing the sweet-smelling kernels into a red metal bowl while a pot of water steamed on the stove.

Piper appeared in a bathrobe. 'Oh!' she said. 'Hi.' Her wet hair hung down her back in uncombed clumps, and her face, robbed of its shaggy headdress and devoid of makeup, looked gaunt and beaky. She hesitated, drawing her hands up against her chest and twisting her bony fingers together.

'Looking for something?'

'Daphne wanted a cucumber.'

'A cucumber?'

'We're putting slices on our eyes. To make them less puffy.'

'Does that work?'

'We don't know.' She emitted the high, tickled *hee hee hee* laugh of a cartoon mouse. The bathrobe – an old one of Daphne's, pink terry cloth – dwarfed her. Something about her thin neck and angular face made her look strangely old, like an aged monk, pale from living in a cave. 'That's part of why we're doing it. Daphne says it's an old wives' tale, and Agatha swears by it. We're taking before and after pictures.' Again the squeaking giggle.

'There's one in the crisper, but I was going to use it in the salad.'

'Oh. Okay.' She pulled her damp hair around her head and picked at the tangles. He turned back to the corn, and when he next glanced over his shoulder, she was gone. Resuming his humming, he tipped the cutting board over the red bowl, adding more kernels to his tall heap of corn, a perfect cone like sand from an hourglass.

Agatha said, 'I hear you're withholding our cucumber.'

Winn whipped around. She was standing where Piper had been, her hair also damp but combed away from her face, and she was back in the gauzy white dress from earlier. 'I'm what?' he said.

'We just need to borrow a little bit.'

She dug in the refrigerator and emerged with a green, warty phallus, neatly edging him aside so that she could take over his cutting board and his knife and lop three inches off the unfortunate vegetable. Then she pared the stub into eight thin slices. 'Voila! Instant beauty.' She waved the maimed cucumber at him. 'Should I leave this out for you?'

'I'll take it.' When he went to take it from her hand, she held on to it, making him pull. He snorted.

'Your ears must have been burning earlier,' she said.

He set the cucumber aside and ran his knife down the last corncob. 'Why is that?'

'I can't remember how it came up – we were out on the grass with Celeste, and somehow we got speculating about what you were like in college. And Celeste said you were exactly the same.'

'Hmm,' he said, unnerved.

'So were you?'

'Celeste would know better than I would.'

'Do you want to know what Daphne said?'

'I don't know. Do I?'

'She said Biddy told her you had a bad rep.' She waited. He was silent, and she went on, 'Supposedly, you were a bit of a player.'

Winn picked up the bowl of corn and dumped it into the boiling water. He set a massive colander in the sink, then wiped his hands on his apron and turned to face her, folding his arms over his chest. 'A player?'

She aligned the cucumber slices into a neat stack, holding them loosely in her fingers like poker chips. 'We were just curious because you're one of those people who seems to have been born an adult, with a house and a marriage and everything. I can imagine Biddy when she was young but not you.'

'Hmm,' he said again.

'Well?'

'I don't remember. I don't think I was dramatically different. I had girlfriends, but nothing out of the ordinary. I wasn't some kind of Casanova.' He turned, pulled the pot from the stove, and poured its contents into the colander. His glasses steamed up.

'That's what Celeste said. She said you were a born monogamist.'

121

He pushed his glasses to the end of his nose and looked at her over them. 'I'm sorry you girls don't have anything more interesting to talk about.'

She reached up and grasped his glasses by the earpieces, tugging them from his face. He closed his eyes, and when he opened them, she was wiping the steam away on the hem of her dress.

On the day in 1966 when Winn left for Harvard, his father presented him with a gold wristwatch and an absolution. 'Youth is the best excuse you'll ever have,' Tipton Van Meter said, giving his son's hand a valedictory shake on the sidewalk of a leafy Boston avenue, not far from the Public Garden, in the shadow of their white stone house. He spoke slowly, with deliberate weight. That he had been planning this moment for some time was clear. Winn opted for manful silence. No response would measure up to whatever line had already been scripted for him in his father's imagination, and so he returned the handshake with a fervor he hoped would express strength, vigor, and gratitude. Tony the driver sat waiting behind the wheel to convey him the not quite four miles to the gates of the Yard.

'Well, good-bye, Dad. See you for dinner Sunday.'

Tipton only nodded.

Until Tony turned a corner, Winn looked out the back window, at his father standing in the street in his gray suit, hands behind his back.

Winn had crossed the Charles countless times before, but he could not help feeling that the splendor of this particular September afternoon was a benediction meant just for him and that the familiar green water, gilded by the same sun that skipped dazzling prisms off his new wristwatch, was an important threshold. He was crossing into a new era, and his father's parting words were carved above the gates. Tipton Van Meter was a great believer in youth, and Winn believed in Tipton. Most fathers would have asked their sons to do the family proud or to stay out of trouble or to find their place in the world. That his own father had given him permission to do none of those things was a tremendous relief to Winn. He resolved to allow himself a great deal of freedom on the condition that someday he would take up the right kind of adulthood. For now he would be carefree, unencumbered, full of mischief and frivolity, and then, later, he would be an honorable man, a true citizen, a man whose portrait might hang on a wall: someone like his grandfather Frederick, whose countenance supervised the billiards room of the Vespasian Club, or like his father, whose painted image regarded its living twin from across the dining room in the white stone house.

As a child, Winn's favorite spot was the carpet beside Tipton's chair, where he sat and watched his sire drink gin from a cut crystal glass and listen to the radio. Now that Winn had entered into what Tipton predicted would be the most glorious years of his life, he perceived the dawning of a perfect symbiosis of father-son esteem. Tipton was a Harvard man himself, and in the years since his graduation, he had fashioned in his own mind and that of his son a tanned and tousled vision of the ideal collegian. This young man was a dedicated sportsman, an unostentatious student, a giver of witty toasts, and a debonair wanderer through the candyland of female companionship. While some boys dreamt of being the president or an astronaut, Winn passed through boyhood aspiring only to grow into the broad shoulders and brass buttons of his father's half-remembered, half-imagined Harvard man. In the stories Tipton chose for the afterdinner hour, he himself was that man, the cocksure ringleader of a band of high-spirited rascals. Always he recounted every detail, projecting the glimmering past onto the soiled tablecloth, the faces of his listeners, and his own portrait in its elaborate, gilded frame high on the wall. A few weeks before Winn left for Harvard, his fifth-form English master and his wife had come to dinner, and Tipton told a classic.

'We had the cook at the club pack us a cold lunch,' Tipton said, 'and we climbed out a window of Sever to have a picnic on the roof. Cort Wilder, Moody, Kreegs, Tom Patten, and myself – they were the fellows I was running with at the time. You know Cort Wilder, don't you?' This was directed at the English master. 'Oh, I thought you might have crossed paths. He was a classics man, too. Anyhow, it was the first nice day of spring, which is always a marvelous day, isn't it? Everyone comes out of hibernation. We wanted to get the bird's-eye view, so we had a picnic basket that belonged to Kreegs's girlfriend and sandwiches from the club, and we were drinking champagne straight from the bottle, which is always such fun, isn't it? I doubt anyone would have noticed us, except the wind picked up Kreegs's sandwich wrapper and whooshed it around for a minute before dropping it right down on the head of Professor Fieldston, who was on his way to lecture. You know Fieldston, don't you?'

'The name rings a bell,' the English master said, dropping a cube of sugar into his coffee with silver tongs.

'Anyhow, it turned out that Kreegs, the goose, had been using that wrapper to wipe the mayonnaise off his sandwich, and so it stuck rather wetly to the side of Fieldston's face. He looks up, and there we all are, lined up on the roof like pigeons. So, of course, he goes charging into Sever, and I'll tell you, we panicked. We thought we were done for; Kreegs started whining about how he was on probation and would get kicked out, and Moody said his dad was already talking about cutting off his allowance and this would be last straw and so on and so forth. But fortunately I knew Sever inside and out, and so I led the bunch of us over to the other side of the roof where I scrambled around and found an open window. I'll tell you, there's never been a more surprised French class, you can bet on that, seeing the five of us drop in one after the other. Cort was a wit and managed to turn around and say something about *la fenêtre* before I brought us out and down a back stairway. Fieldston was probably still craning his head around out the window and wondering where in hell we'd gone when we were already back at the club. We had to leave the picnic basket behind, and someone told me Fieldston kept it on a shelf in his office for a whole year. If anyone happened to glance at it, he'd get a suspicious look on his face and say, 'Look familiar?' He held out hope, the old coot. Kreegs did get kicked out, though, a few weeks later. I can't remember for what. Something silly. He went back to Baltimore.'

Leaving it at that, he began forking up his *tarte tatin* while the others sat marooned in a silence broken only by the clinking of silver on china. It was typical of Winn's father to append his story with a sad and vague fact, oblivious that his listeners were still waiting for a punch line. The English master raised an eyebrow at Winn from across the table. 'Coffee spoons,' he said, tapping the air with one such implement. 'Van Meter, I have measured my life in what?'

'Sorry, sir?'

'Finish the line, Van Meter. 'I have measured my life in . . .' what?'

'Coffee spoons?'

'Yes, who's it by?'

'Sir?'

'What is the poem and who is it by?'

As the silence stretched out, student and teacher recognized in each other's eyes the same growing alarm, the student because his father would think he had not learned and the teacher because the father would think he had not taught. The coffee spoon wavered between them. Just before Winn was going to take a guess and say Eliot, the master's wife stepped in and said, 'James, you are *merciless*. Quizzing the boy at dinner. He's going off to Harvard in a week; he's too excited to remember all the this-and-that you taught him.'

The master, pipe clenched in his teeth, began patting his pockets. 'Fortunately for you, Van Meter, I learned long ago to listen to my wife.' Tipton flicked a book of matches from the head of the table, which the master missed and swatted to the floor. 'Looks like you're off the hook,' he said to Winn, straining to reach under the table.

'Thank you, sir.'

'I never had much of a mind for poetry myself,' Tipton said.

When dinner was cleared away and guests gone home, Tipton told the stories that Winn would have preferred he keep to himself.

'Probably one of the fellows in the Ophidian had a grudge against me. I overheard one of them maligning my father once, passing on trash he'd heard from his own father, no doubt. I would have liked to have joined, though. I made it to the final dinner. Willy Abernathy was president at the time, although they have some odd word for it in the Ophidian. Oro-something. Can't remember. But what a stand-up fellow Willy was. Always dated the most beautiful girls, and they loved him even after he broke their hearts because he did it with such perfect manners and so much kindness. He had a straw hat that I admired, kind of a boater. I got one just like it. But it never looked right on me, and I tossed it in the river as a joke.'

In his undergraduate years, Winn was everything he had been raised to believe a Harvard man should be. He belonged to many clubs, appeared in farcical plays, sang tenor in an all-male ensemble. The top of his bureau was obscured by a masculine still life of half-forgotten objects: a cigar cutter, a flask in a leather sleeve, a pile of coins, a large plaster duck stolen as a joke from someone's garden. In his mirror was a young man who wore a tennis sweater with confidence and about whom blew the salt breeze of youth and promise.

The gold wristwatch turned out to be not quite right. The boys who seemed most aristocratic wore watches with straps of plain leather. The more Winn observed those boys, the more evidence he found to support certain suspicions that had sprouted at Deerfield: his father, not always but from time to time, behaved like a member of the nouveau riche, a glitzy echelon much less desirable than the dusty shelf that held the old money and where he, Winn, had eked out a rickety perch. By junior year he had perfected a certain calculated shabbiness and showed it off with the scuffed toes of his cracked and flattened loafers and the tiny rip that he made and then mended on the lapel of his favorite sport coat. Though he enjoyed squash and the occasional game of touch football, his brief association with freshman crew ended when an older boy, a boy in the Ophidian, remarked that a sunrise should only be seen from the sidewalk outside a girl's room or on the opening day of deer season. He bought a new watch with a plain brown strap at a store in Boston. The gold one was brought out only when he went home for Sunday dinner. Certain boys in the Ophidian got away with wearing dandyish clothes or pursuing sport or school with unabashed striving, but Winn was given neither to idiosyncrasy nor ambition and was never tempted to risk deviating from the Ophidian way of doing things, an unspoken code that prioritized irony, insouciance, and drunken mischief above all else.

Eventually he forgave his father's rare gaffes because he knew that Tipton's father had been the one to pull the family up and establish them in the white stone house. Tipton, then, really *was* new money, and his missteps, while unfortunate, were understandable. Winn's mother came from genuine society stock, but she had been away for much of his childhood making her slow migration through various places of recuperation. She returned home

129

for good only when he was fourteen and off at Deerfield.

The Ophidian Club was a brick building on a brick street, tall and narrow with black shutters and, over its door, the graven image of a snake swallowing its own tail. Though it would not have Tipton – Tipton had been a member of the slightly inferior Sobek Club for Gentlemen – the Ophidian welcomed Winn, and after his initiation (a night of equal parts revelry and good-humored humiliation), he went home for a day to rest and to gloat. He had thought his father would ask about the secrets he was now privy to, and he looked forward to demonstrating the dignified silence all Ophidian members were sworn to adopt in the face of inquiry, even though, really, he longed to tell about the roasted rattlesnake, the Greek mottoes, the medal with the club seal he was given to wear around his neck, the bawdy recitations, the feeling of being anointed. But Tipton only sat in his chair and listened to the radio, and for dinner he went out to the Vespasian Club and did not invite Winn along. Winn ate alone beneath Tipton's portrait and then went up to see his mother.

'Is this club any good?' she said. She was lying on a sofa beside a window, a tray of untouched dinner on a low table beside her. She seemed much older than she was. Her hair had been allowed to go gray; her hands and neck were withered, her face slack, and the rest of her was hidden in the folds of her robe and blankets.

'It's the best one,' Winn said. 'They hardly take anyone. Everyone wants to be in it.'

'That's fine, then,' she said, gazing down at the street below.

He waited, and then he said, 'Daddy wanted to join, but he wasn't invited.'

She turned back to him, her colorless lips pursed. 'Really?' she said. 'How marvelous for you, Winnie, how really wonderful. What did your father say when you told him?'

'He congratulated me.'

'But was he happy? Did he seem truly happy for you? Tell your mother the truth.'

'He was happy.'

She picked at her bedclothes. She waggled her head and shrugged her shoulders as though engaged in silent conversation. A car passed outside, drawing her eyes to the window.

'Actually,' Winn said, 'he wasn't as happy as I thought he'd be. I thought he'd want to know things. I thought he'd be pleased a Van Meter got himself on the Ophidian books.'

'Do you think he's jealous?' Her fingers clutched her blanket. 'Oh, my Tipton. Jealous as can be. It was the same way with him and his father – you couldn't tell where the envy stopped and the disappointment began. They'd rather have you think they're disappointed, you know. Keeps them up on their throne.'

Winn thought of the Ophidian snake with its tail in its mouth, called, like the club's president, the

Ouroboros. 'I did what he wanted me to do. He wanted me to be in a club, and since he always talks about the Ophidian, I thought he'd want me to be in the Ophidian. If he wanted me to be in the Sobek, he should have said so.'

'Cold fish,' his mother said to her hands as they worried the blanket. 'Cold fish.'

Beneath the Ophidian's beamed ceiling, long days were lavished on the triangular bliss of club chair, snifter, and cigarette. His nights, whenever possible, were spent pursuing girls. Radcliffe girls were fine when he could get them, but since they tended to be serious and scholarly and lived in chaperoned fortresses, he mixed in some local girls who worked in the shops in the Square, a few Wellesley girls, and the occasional high school girl. *Youth is the best excuse you'll ever have*, he told himself. He dated girls as varied as the dogs in a dog show – tall and studious Miranda Morse; busty Deborah Latici; Michelle Fleming, the violinist and rank bitch; Bobbie Hodgson, who worked in a bakery. All had something to contribute to either his social standing or his sexual experience, and any girl who was an asset to both he was happy to call his girlfriend for a while. These were the liaisons of youth, made lightheartedly and extinguished with a delicate touch. And when, in one memorable afternoon, Winn kissed Lily Spaulding and touched her breasts and then walked up a flight of stairs to kiss her friend Isabelle Hornor and make forays beyond the woolen frontier of her hemline, he did so in the spirit of good fun.

As graduation approached and then passed, sending him into the city to join the white-collared, steel-livered ranks of young working bachelors, he began to experience a nagging inkling that his father's benediction was nearing its expiration date. Tipton never said so, never expressed any disapproval, but neither did he make any further mention of youth and excuses. When Winn went home, which he did with diminishing frequency, Tipton took him to the Vespasian for long, somber meals during which father and son commented only on the news of the day and the deaths and marriages of family acquaintances.

While Winn believed that worthwhile young men must be carefree, he also believed that worthwhile grown men must bear up under the burden of respectability. He puzzled over when exactly the music should be stopped and the drunks sent home and the crepe paper swept from the floors to make room for cribs and Labradors. *Is it now?* he wondered as he set down his drink and turned from a conversation with a beautiful girl to vomit into the swimming pool of his friend Tyson Baker. When he heard some months later that Tyson Baker had died during a game of pond hockey, dropping through the ice like a lead weight, he thought, *Is it now?* Waking up to find a clammy section of his date's stocking draped in a gauze mask across his face, breaking a champagne flute with a butter knife at a wedding when he meant only to chime for a toast, chipping a tooth on the sidewalk outside an all-night pancake house. At Christmas. Every New Year's. Every birthday. At funerals, weddings. When he listened at the door while a girlfriend lay crying in her bathwater. *Is it now? Is it now? Is it now?*

He had thought in college that the age of twenty-eight sounded like an appropriate endpoint to youth, and he resolved, as the day drew nearer, that he would indeed turn over a new leaf. He spent his twenty-eighth birthday at the house of a friend, playing croquet on a lawn that, beyond the last wicket, dropped dramatically to the sea. His partner was a silly girl who said, 'I thought I had that one!' after every botched shot. She tried to turn her incompetence into a joke by saying that he didn't like her for her croquet skills anyway, but he had, in fact, brought her along because she claimed to be good at croquet. Between her ineptitude and the rum cocktails they had invented at lunch, he managed to lose a hundred dollars on the game. He decided he could not begin his adulthood so ignominiously and postponed it yet again.

In the end, it was his father's death that made Winn, then thirty-one, a man. At the funeral, while some school friend of Tipton's droned a reading from scripture, Winn felt the last grains of his youth run out. His father had kept the hourglass tilted up on one edge for him, cheating time a little, but now, with the evaporation of those paternal hands, the glass had thumped level, the sand an ash heap in the bottom. Tipton had been seventy-one, taken out by an aggressive prostate cancer that he refused to fight. His golf partner stepped up to the podium and cleared his throat. 'A reading from the book of Revelation,' he said into the microphone. He looked strange in his dark suit, without his argyle vest and pom-pommed club covers. 'And I saw a new heaven and a new earth: for the first heaven and the first earth were passed away; and there was no more sea.' With his father gone, Winn was the man of the family, and since his mother was certain to be soon pulled under by the collective suction of her imagined ailments, there would not be much time before he would, in fact, *be* the family, one man with all the departed Van Meters riding on his shoulders. He had pockets of cousins and aunts and uncles around the Northeast: none on his father's side but all drooping from the same listless Brahmin branches as his mother, all short and with overlarge Hapsburg chins, members of a dynasty that had lingered a few generations too long. He scarcely counted them as family.

While giving his eulogy, Winn noticed a girl in the fourth or fifth row, Elizabeth Hazzard, called Biddy, whom he knew but not well, only as the daughter of a distant associate of his father's. She handed her handkerchief to the woman beside her, perhaps her mother, but she did not dab her own eyes. The sight caused him to pause, and he cleared his throat as though fighting back tears. When he continued, he found himself speaking mostly to Biddy, telling her about his father, how Tipton had been a dignified, honorable man, well respected by all who knew him, a fine role model. He liked that she was not someone who cried at funerals as though tears were a requirement like applause at a tennis match. He liked her navy blue dress, the no-nonsense cut of her hair, the lingering traces of her summer tan, the upright way she held herself. Possibly he was being untoward to cruise for a girlfriend at his own father's funeral, but he could summon no guilt, only gratitude, for Biddy's presence. In her tidy face he saw hope and freshness, while all around him hung tapestries of decay.

They married less than a year later on the lawn of her parents' house in Maine. The guest list was kept short because he was still mourning his father. Biddy put a cherry blossom in his lapel that later fell out unnoticed. His mother stayed inside and watched from a window, claiming she was too fragile for the sea air. Biddy's dress was restrained, almost plain. Harry Pitton-White, Winn's best man, had a stomach flu and swayed beside him during the vows like a nearly felled tree. In his toast, Biddy's father said he was glad Biddy had married a man who would never do anything foolish, which Winn took as both compliment and threat. After he and Biddy departed for their oppressively floral room in a creaky bed and break-fast, the tanked-up groomsmen and bridesmaids went skinny-dipping in the frigid springtime Atlantic, a stunt that made Winn wistful and jealous when he heard about it at brunch the next day. Underneath her wedding dress Biddy wore a white garter belt and stockings that he found unbearably sexy but did not tell her so, not wanting to embarrass her by making a fuss and also incorrectly assuming she had a whole trousseau of lingerie that she would, without prompting, trot out over their first year. Silence over stockings – the first regret of his marriage.

He thought he remembered most of his wedding day, but he had no memory of the preparations for it, certainly not of anything like the hullabaloo surrounding Daphne's. His wedding had been a wedding, not a family reunion and missile launch and state dinner all rolled into one. Possibly Biddy and her mother had gone through agonies of decision and obsession, comparisons of all the shades of white and all the flowers in the world, but he had been off doing other things, working and golfing and fulfilling the drunken rites of his last hurrahs. These days, though he could still plead work or golf, his absences did nothing to slow the flooding of his house and in-box and the entire consciousness of his wife with invitations and hairstyles and flatware and string quartets and the question of whether chocolate ganache on caramel cake would be too rich. He found himself forming strong opinions on things he had never before contemplated – guest books and party favors, napkins and centerpieces. 'Daylilies,' Biddy incanted in her sleep. 'Tulips.' Painful quantities of checks, bushels of them, enough for a ticker-tape parade, flew from his desk, alit briefly on the fingertips of Biddy or Daphne, and then winged off into the ledgers of the florist or the dressmaker or any other of the gang of tradeswomen who were merrily chipping away at his bank accounts.

'Well, it's a rush job,' Biddy said, 'and that's an additional cost, and there's nothing we can do about it.'

She was right. There was nothing to be done. Greyson was perfectly appropriate. He wore neckties and belts printed with ducks or whales and was affable at all times. He enjoyed sailing and rowing and dancing and parties. Five years out of college, he had already made headway on a fortune for himself but shied away from anything flashy or crass, choosing to wear frayed khakis and drive a Nissan remarkable for its antiquity and smallness, which Winn took as a mark of good breeding. Indeed, Winn would have felt nothing but proud pleasure about the match if not for the bump in Daphne's wedding dress. Already her finger had swollen beyond the capacity of her carefully chosen wedding band, and a stunt ring had to be bought at the last minute for use in the ceremony.

'They both went to Princeton,' Winn had said to Biddy after the simultaneous announcements of impending birth and nuptials. 'They have responsible jobs. You would think they could figure out how to use birth control.'

Biddy said, 'I think they might not have cared very much. Daphne wanted a baby. They knew they were getting married eventually.'

'They should have thought of us,' Winn said.

CHAPTER 6

YOUR SHADOW AT EVENING

The Duff family arrived ten minutes before they were expected. Winn was in the kitchen snipping chives when Celeste's voice rang down from the widow's walk. 'Duffs, ho!' she called. By the time he gained the outdoors and was standing, still in his apron, by the red front door with a hand raised in greeting, a caravan of rental cars had emerged from the trees: first a plain white sedan – good old Duffs not going in for any frills – and behind it two Jeeps, tops down, roaring up the drive as though bringing General Patton to the front lines. They parked in a neat row along one edge of the clearing, and Greyson sprang out of the first Jeep, calling out a greeting to Winn and in the same breath tossing back some nonsense to the two boys with him. Winn gave a hearty, 'Hi there, men!'

Greyson's brother Francis had been riding in the cargo space behind the seats, and he unfolded himself and stepped over the tailgate and onto the bumper with an air of wounded dignity. Descending to the gravel, he paused to inspect his pants (red, embroidered with white whales) for dirt, and as he

140

did so, the other boy, Greyson's best friend, Charlie, grabbed him and pulled him into a hammerlock. Francis, limp as kelp, accepted the assault without protest. 'Did you get a headache?' Charlie asked him. 'Are you in agony? Is the night ruined?'

'I won't know for a while,' Francis replied. 'It doesn't happen right away.'

'Winn,' Greyson said, bounding up, 'you remember my little brother, Francis. And my friend Charlie.' Greyson always had a robustness about him, but he seemed even more energetic than usual. Had a football been at hand, he would have been firing passes to Charlie and Francis and to his other brothers, the older ones, who were sitting in the second Jeep having a murmured argument.

Greyson had three brothers and no sisters. Four boys born at regular two-year intervals, four Duffs in a row. To Winn, four sons in one family was an embarrassment of riches despite the uneven quality of the boys. Greyson was the pick of the litter, certainly. The eldest, Sterling, spent all his time in Asia and had a slimy reputation. The next one, Dicky Jr, was congenitally stiff – and why Dicky and Maude had decided to pin the Jr on their second son, Winn could not guess. Then came Greyson and then this youngest, Francis, the family queer fish, who gave off an appearance of ordinary preppiness, standing on the doorstep in his horn-rimmed glasses and whale pants, but who was always on some spiritual quest or other,

141

embracing a series of Eastern religions, professional ambitions, and artistic passions.

Winn ushered them toward the door. 'You boys do me a favor and go inside and see if you can find my wife and send her out, would you?'

When Greyson and Charlie had gone jostling into the house with Francis shuffling in their wake, Winn turned to the other arrivals. The white sedan was flanked on one side by Greyson's father, Dicky Sr, and on the other by Greyson's mother, Maude. Dicky raised both his arms and waved them over his head. 'Hello, the house!' he shouted.

'Hello, the car,' Winn returned at a lower volume.

'Thank you so much for having us, Winn,' Maude called. 'Look at your lovely house. It's just *lovely*.' She shaded her eyes with one hand in a kind of salute.

Maude and Dicky opened the car's rear doors, stretched out their hands and, like two magicians performing identical tricks, each pulled out an old woman. Dicky's old woman brushed him away, saying loudly, 'I'm fine, I'm fine.'

'I was trying to be helpful,' he said.

'Well, you're in the way.'

Tall and solid, her white hair cut short and left uncurled, she wore a blue pantsuit with pearls and, on a cord, eyeglasses as large and round as portholes. This was Oatsie, Dicky's mother. On Maude's side, the rubber tip of a cane emerged first, probing for the ground, followed by a pair of tiny feet in white Keds, then rickety calves in suntan nylons, and finally a frail bundle of a woman in a pink Chanel suit, topped with a cloud of Barbara Bush hair. She was Mopsy. Her trembling hands grasped indecisively at the cane and then at Maude and then at the car door. Maude passed her mother off to Dicky and went around to the trunk. 'Bloodies!' she announced, lifting out a canvas bag and straining to hold it aloft so Winn could see. 'I had an absolute craving. I made them at home and brought them on the plane, can you believe it? Daphne can have the recipe when I die but not a moment sooner. You can't beat them.'

'I wouldn't dream of trying,' Winn called back.

The two older boys had finally wrapped up their discussion, and Dicky Jr hurried forward to take the bag from his mother, while the other, the elusive firstborn, Sterling, portly in seersucker, stood by the Jeep taking a few last drags from a cigarette. The second he dropped it to the gravel, Oatsie barked, 'Sterling, pick up that butt!'

Sterling obliged, tossing it in the back of the Jeep before he ambled toward the house. Winn allowed his hand to be wrung by Dicky Sr and pivoted through the grandmothers and Maude, kissing cheeks. He took the canvas bag of thermoses from Dicky Jr, who frowned suspiciously up at the house, and was introduced to Sterling, the only member of the Duff contingent whom he had never met.

'The best man,' Winn said. 'You've been in Hong Kong?'

'That's right,' said Sterling.

'We appreciate your making the trip. I know it means a lot to Daphne and Greyson that you came.'

'You bet.'

Sterling was only in his early thirties, but his face had a libertine puffiness, and his belt was overhung by the settled, bankerly paunch of an older man. His eyes, though long lashed and of an unusual caramel color, betrayed no sense of fun. His gaze was oddly steady, even cold.

'Proper Dews,' Oatsie said, reading the house's quarterboard. 'Clever.'

'Oh, isn't that funny,' said Maude. 'Did you think that up, Winn? You're so creative. You must be where Daphne got her imagination. Thank you so much for having us, really. This is a treat. And Greyson says you're *cooking*? Really, you're too generous.'

'Don't overdo it, Maude,' said Oatsie.

'What a day this is. What a day,' Dicky Sr chimed in.

'Isn't it, though?' Maude said. 'Can you believe the wedding is so soon? These two wonderful young people starting their lives together. We *are* fortunate, aren't we? Aren't we?'

'We are indeed,' said Dicky Sr.

'Hup,' said Dicky Jr.

Maude went on gabbling to Winn as though she'd mistaken him for a talk show host. 'I have to tell you, I really do think of Daphne as a daughter. I really do. And to finally have another woman around, I can't tell you how wonderful that is. After all these boys, I just, I can't tell you – well, *hello!*'

Biddy had at last appeared. The kisses began again, as did Maude's trills about her recipe for Bloodies and the generosity of the Van Meters.

'Quite a day,' said Dicky Sr.

'Come inside,' said Biddy.

Mopsy took hold of Winn's arm from behind, surprising him with the strength of her grip. 'I'm afraid I do need to—,' she said.

He bent his ear toward her. 'What?'

'She needs to sit down,' said Dicky Jr loudly. 'She gets tired. Come, Gran. This way.' He detached her from Winn.

'Oh, this house,' exclaimed Maude as soon as she was through the door. 'How *lovely*. And how beautifully you've decorated it. Look at this painting.'

'A friend painted it,' said Winn. 'It's only up because Biddy insists.'

'I should hope so,' Oatsie said, examining the canvas, an Alpine landscape, through her enormous spectacles.

Maude pressed her palms together. 'Well, it's *lovely*. And so sweet of you to hang it. Greyson is so lucky to be joining a family with a house like this.'

'Daphne says wonderful things about your Maine place,' Biddy said over her shoulder, leading the way

145

toward the kitchen. 'The pictures she's shown us are stunning. I asked Daphne how many acres you were on, but she's terrible with that sort of thing.'

'Bless her heart. She's *wonderful*,' said Maude.

Dicky Sr cleared his throat. 'About fifty-five acres.'

'Must be a chunk of the island,' Winn said.

'Well, it is the island.'

'My word,' said Biddy, dropping back at the doorway. 'Leave it to Daphne not to mention that.'

'You know,' Maude said, 'the house is very modest, very rustic. We bought it ages ago when land was so undervalued there. But it's our little place. We like it.'

Dicky said, 'Lots of family memories.'

'Just a little family place. Very rustic.'

Dicky nodded. 'It was good for the boys when they were young.'

'We can't wait for the new baby to be there. It's a *wonderful* place for children.'

In Winn's imagination, a lifetime of dueling island homes took shape, campaigns waged on both sides to lure the children and sway the favor of the grand-children. Daphne had probably been to the Duffs' place ten times and had never thought to drop the crucial detail that the Duffs' summer home was not *on* an island but *was* an island. In all likelihood, she had never asked, never thought anything of it.

'We got you a tuna steak,' he said to Dicky. 'Daphne said lobster doesn't agree with you.'

'It certainly doesn't,' Dicky said. 'Nor does death

by asphyxiation. Such a shame because I'm always watching other people eat them. Francis got the gene, too, poor kid. He's worse than I am. Can't even touch the things.'

'Daphne didn't tell me that. Damn it, I'm afraid I only got one—'

'Oh, don't worry about it. Francis can scavenge. If he's lucky I'll give him a bite of my tuna. Ah, there's Daphne!'

He swept off. Winn stood at the edge of the kitchen. Biddy was pouring Bloody Marys from Maude's thermos into a glass pitcher and chatting with Oatsie while Celeste hovered vampirically over her shoulder, eyeing the tomato juice. Dicky and Maude were out on the deck embracing Greyson and Daphne; the bridesmaids and groomsmen were weaving a maypole dance of cheek kisses; in the living room, Mopsy sat in a wing chair gazing out the window in the direction of Sterling, who stood on the lawn with his back to the house smoking another cigarette. Winn was glad to see Livia out there in the mix, kissing cheeks with the rest. She was wearing a blue dress that suited her, and the day's sun had pinked her up a little, though she still looked too thin. Before Livia had dwindled into a wisp and Daphne had taken on the dirigible shape of late pregnancy, they had both been so lovely and young and ripe. The promise of fertility (preferable to its proof) had hung around them, in their large eyes and full mouths, their narrow waists and violin hips.

147

Where the girls' hips had come from was a mystery. Biddy was built like a blade of grass, and Winn, too, was straight and narrow. But the girls complained that they could never find jeans that fit, that everything in their closets had felt the tailor's needle. Biddy swore her family was populated exclusively by walking, talking yardsticks, bamboo poles, and rails, so Winn's lineage must be the source, their hips the bequest of some long-dead woman, an anonymous Eve of the Dutch lowlands, trailed by a gaggle of children as she plodded from stove to field to barn and back again. Now that Livia had shed her hips and Daphne's were dwarfed by breasts and belly, Winn found himself looking out through the open doors at two young women who wore his daughters' faces and inhabited versions of their bodies but were strangers, too.

Livia knew, as soon as the family Duff burst on to the scene, that the party would be one of those small, successful gatherings that effervesces from the start and continues on, buoyed by a tide of alcohol, until an unnoticed apex of high spirits passes, followed by a long, queasy slide into sloppiness, sleep, and regret. She had not dared go to any parties since the incident at the Ophidian. She had willfully humiliated herself in front of the pupating elite, whose judgment would, in all likelihood, hang over her for the rest of her life, and since then she had kept to herself. But this party, this little family shindig, seemed like a safe way to get back in the saddle.

The evening was mild. To the west, the sky was shades of sherbet, while overhead the dome was still blue and streaked with white contrails darting off like the paths of minnows. Everyone was outside except her father. After deputizing her to put out a cheese plate and trays of smoked salmon and shrimp cocktail, he had knocked back a perfunctory half glass of wine and returned to the kitchen to bustle around in his theatrical way, chopping with rat-a-tat speed and tossing and stirring and grating with the verve of someone conducting a philharmonic orchestra. Even Mopsy had been squired from the house by Dicky Jr and sat rubbing her arms and complaining of the chill. Livia stood with a Bloody Mary and listened to Dicky Sr rhapsodize about the Duffs' latest batch of Labrador puppies.

'They're wonderful, wonderful puppies,' he said. 'Just wonderful.'

As best she understood, Dicky Sr had retired while at the top of his game in an amorphous and lucrative career of doing things with money in order to write plodding historical tomes that he self-published, books with one-word titles like *Napoleon, Berlin,* or *Verdun*. He had a Rooseveltian smile, his jaws perpetually clamped around an imaginary cigarette holder. Would anyone ever write a book called *Duff*? Or *Dicky*? 'Dicky' wasn't even short for anything – Daphne said so. The name was on his birth certificate. His late father, Richard Duff IV, had not wanted to burden him with a V, but then Dicky had gone ahead and started the cycle all over again with Dicky Jr.

'Are you working on a new book?' she asked him.

'I am indeed,' he said. 'I've got my assistant started on the research for a biography of Oliver Wendell Holmes.'

'Do you have a title?'

'Funny story. I thought I would call it *Holmes*, but someone pointed out that people might think I meant Sherlock Holmes, so now the working title is *Justice*.'

He embarked on a detailed description of his interest in Holmes and had reached the college years in a synopsis of his life when Oatsie, who had been hovering nearby, said, 'Dicky, that's enough book talk.'

'All right, Mummer, what would you like me to talk about?'

'Why don't you ask this young lady something about herself.'

'All right, Livia. You're at Harvard, yes? Going to be a sophomore?'

'A senior.'

'That's right. And do you have any plans for afterward?'

'I'm going to get a Ph.D. in marine biology,' she said.

'Oh.' He hit her with his biggest smile and swirled his wine.

'I thought your father said you were going to law school,' said Oatsie.

'He says that sometimes,' Livia said. 'Only because for a while Daphne thought she was going to law school, and he got comfortable with the idea.'

'You want to be like Jacques Cousteau?' asked Dicky. 'Down with the fish?'

'You ought to go to law school,' Oatsie said decisively. 'You'd make a wonderful lawyer. You have beautiful hair.'

'Thank you,' Livia said. When she was old, she wanted to be like Oatsie: imperious, brusque, and given to non sequitur.

'That woman Janet Reno,' Oatsie continued. 'Her hair was an abomination.'

'Sterling did a year of law school,' Dicky said, swinging around. 'Sterling!' Greyson's brother had wandered almost to the edge of the lawn, down by the trees. He turned at his father's voice. 'Come up here!' Dicky called.

Obediently, holding a tumbler brimming with amber liquid, Sterling walked up the grass. 'Have you met Livia?' Dicky asked, opening his arms around them like they had just signed a peace accord.

'Hello,' Sterling said, shifting the glass to shake her hand.

Livia was taken aback by the blatancy with which he looked her up and down. Dicky didn't bat an eye. 'Livia is considering law school,' he said. 'I thought you might have some advice for her.'

'Where did you go?' Livia asked.

'UCLA.'

'Really?'

'Not Ivy enough for you?'

'I was just expecting somewhere in the East.'

'Francis,' Oatsie called, 'don't leave that glass there. Someone will break it.' She marched off, and Dicky Sr drifted away, drawn inexorably toward the lawn, where Greyson and Charlie and Dicky Jr and Dominique had begun a game of badminton. Livia and Sterling were left alone. In Duff family lore, of which Daphne had become an evangelist, Sterling was always portrayed as a lady killer, and Livia had not expected someone so terse and dissipated looking.

'I needed a break from the village,' he said.

Livia was confused. 'Greenwich Village?'

'No, this village. All these people who know my parents. This little world where everyone reports on everyone. Not that Hong Kong is much better. The expats are all tied up together.'

'Kinky.'

He stared at her, then half smiled.

She waited for him to say something, but he didn't. 'Do you like it?' she prodded.

'Being tied up with expats?'

'Hong Kong.'

'I like how the Chinese do business.'

'How is that?'

'Drunk.'

She laughed. Again, she waited for him to say

something; again he only stared at her in silence. His blankness made her feel itchy, jumpy. 'Where did you go for undergrad?' she asked.

He took the nearly empty Bloody Mary pitcher from a low table and poured the thick dregs into her glass. 'Bowdoin. I'm the lone holdout from Princeton, although I don't think Francis counts because we had to buy his way in.'

She couldn't resist the bait. 'What do you mean?'

'Little Franny couldn't keep his eyes on his own paper. The teachers looked the other way. The kids noticed. Eventually, someone got tired of it and busted him. Rather than let him swing, Mom and Dad made the whole thing go away. He got caught again at Princeton. He almost got kicked out. Princeton got a remodeled library of dramatic arts.'

'I didn't know any of that.' Livia studied Francis, who was out on the lawn with the others. He swiped lazily at the birdie and missed.

'It wasn't in the Christmas letter.'

Livia had always liked the Duffs. They were painless companions. Dicky and Maude lived within familiar confines: the Ivy League, the Junior League, *The Social Register*, Emily Post, Lilly Pulitzer, the Daughters of the American Revolution, Windsor knots, cummerbunds, needlepointed tissue box covers, L.L. Bean, Memorial Day, Labor Day, waterfowl-based décor. They were old-fashioned, myopic, beyond reproach. Greyson was a modernized version of his parents, still an upright citizen but loosened up, enlightened, gone wireless. Dicky Jr, though only thirty, seemed to belong to an earlier generation. He had the joylessness of someone who had seen too many cycles of war, social upheaval, and financial ruin to bother with the caprices of modern youth. According to Greyson, Dicky Jr had been a dour Young Republican in his teens and in his twenties applied himself to his finance job and to a methodical investigation of eligible women that ultimately yielded a female mirror image who fused with him in a marriage as cold and perfect as the bond between two adjacent blocks in an igloo. She was known as Mrs Dicky and would not be arriving until just before the rehearsal dinner – work, Dicky Jr explained. Since entering his thirties, he seemed to be settling in beside an eternal fireplace for a lifetime of newspaper rattling and irritable rumination. Francis was the classic baby of the family, indulged and flattered, but Livia had always assumed that Sterling, not Francis, was the black sheep.

She had been interested to meet the protagonist of the lurid stories Daphne told with mock horror, and now a whiff of Sterling's allure came spiraling down as though on a breeze. His willingness to abandon the family press release was titillating, and he had a lazy, reptilian confidence that appealed to her. Recognition dawned on her – here he was, the rebound guy, gift wrapped and delivered to her door. If she and Teddy got back together, she wouldn't be so angry at him for having strayed once or twice if she'd had a fling of her own.

'But you decided not to finish,' Livia said to him. 'Law school.'

'I needed to get farther away.'

'You're wearing seersucker pants. How far can you have gone?'

For the first time, he smiled fully, showing teeth that were unexpectedly white and even, a movie star smile. He looked down at his lower half. 'Don't tell anyone, but this seersucker is ironic.'

'There's no such thing.'

'Don't go to law school.' He was serious again.

She rolled her eyes. 'I never said I was. I never even said I was thinking about it. I'm studying marine biology.'

'Like Jacques Cousteau?'

She smirked. 'That's exactly what your father said.'

He shrugged. 'It's the obvious thing to say. I've never met anyone over the age of six who wanted to be a marine biologist.'

'I'm going to get a Ph.D.'

'That's what you want?'

'Yes. Definitely.'

'Well, as long as you're so definite.' He sipped his drink. 'Sounds great. Chasing grant money, chasing fish, chasing tenure. Sounds fun.'

Livia said, 'You told me not to go to law school,

155

and now you're making fun of me for having something else I want to do?'

He stepped closer and clasped her forearm. His gaze was unwavering, not intrusive but strangely inactive, like his eyes had landed on her and he could not be bothered to move them. 'I'm only teasing. I'm not used to talking to people who know what they want.'

He released her. She couldn't tell if anyone had noticed the touch; no one seemed to be looking. 'What makes you so immune to it all?' she asked.

'To what?'

'The village.'

'Nothing. I'm not. I'm undone by the evils of my upbringing and the turpitude of my kind.' He smiled.

'Sterling,' Oatsie called from across the deck, 'what are you saying over there?'

'Just talking, Grammer,' Sterling said. He drank his whiskey, his eyes suddenly dark, like Oatsie had kicked his plug out of the wall.

Lightly, Livia said, 'Your grandmother told me I have beautiful hair and would make a wonderful lawyer.'

He snorted. 'I'd rather see you on the prow of a boat, looking for dolphins.'

'And you'll be somewhere in Asia, wearing ironic pants.'

'In Asia my pants are very, very sincere.'

She stepped closer to him. 'You said you don't talk to many people who know what they want. Do you know what you want?'

He did not blink. 'Always.'

In the air around them, the evening tuned its orchestra. 'What?' she asked, feeling bold and fearful at the same time.

'Right now,' he said, 'I want to sit down.' He pivoted around, turning her with him, and sat in an Adirondack chair, pulling her onto its arm. The two of them surveyed the lawn: the bright, running figures and the white flash of the birdie.

The lobsters needed cooking. Winn whisked the first unlucky six two at a time from their box on the kitchen floor and dropped them on their backs in the pot of boiling water. The remaining lobsters crawled slowly over one another, purplish, alien, their bound claws sad and impotent. They had been packed with layers of green and brown seaweed, and some of them wore glossy wigs where it had caught on their plates. Winn did not know why the seaweed was included – when Livia was a child, he had, out of laziness, told her the lobsters ate it, but she'd consulted a book and corrected him. Most likely the box was supposed to seem homey for the lobsters, not for their benefit but so people could feel better about the way their dinner spent its final hours. He had already covered the kitchen table with a red and white checked tablecloth and put out green salad, the corn and tomato salad, sliced French bread, and plastic plates and utensils. They would eat on the deck or the lawn, not ideal for a strenuous, two-hand food like lobster but better than having all the mess inside. Biddy came in with an empty wine bottle and looked in the pot. 'They're flipping their tails,' she said. 'I hate how they flip their tails.'

'They're none too pleased about things,' Winn said. 'Leave the lid on and it'll be over faster.'

'I feel sorry for them.'

'They're overgrown insects.'

'I feel sorry for them anyway.'

'They have very basic nervous systems, Biddy. They don't feel things the way we do. They're just *reacting*. They're not *emotional*.'

Biddy stood for a moment, looking down into the pot, billows of steam rising around her. Carefully, she replaced the lid. She turned around and smiled brightly. She held out the wine bottle. 'Do we have any more of this? Our nearly in-laws say it's exceptional.'

He pulled another bottle from the refrigerator and opened it for her. Watching her go, stiff shouldered, back outside, he noticed Agatha and Piper jumping around, cheerleading the men and Dominique as they ran complicated patterns across the grass, a shuttlecock bouncing above them, the net disregarded in favor of a kind of free-roaming scrimmage. Agatha leapt in the air with her knees bent so her white dress floated up and the dirty bottoms of her bare feet flashed him, and for a single filthy second he fell through a trapdoor and into a delirium of Agatha on her hands and knees in the grass, his fingers gripping a golden handful of her hair. The vision lasted no time at all, striking him like the blast of air from a speeding train. Then he saw the deck, his guests, his wife, the lawn, and the braided paths of the badminton players. He willed the thought away, and it went.

He loved Biddy – indeed she was deeply lovable, and loving one's wife was a requirement of marriage. She was so entirely the kind of person he should be married to that he loved her, in part, out of gratitude for her very appropriateness. There had been times, only a few times, when her prim, calm, polite, essential Biddyness had seemed to waver (for instance, when he had seen her straining in that tub of French water, calving Livia into a cloud of blood), and so, too, had his love tipped and teetered. But even he, with his accountant's view of emotion, grimly consigning its bits and pieces to the correct columns in a secret ledger, recognized there was more to his feeling for Biddy than simple appreciation. He could not be sure he had ever been *in* love with Biddy, or with anyone for that matter, but Biddy was the woman he had felt the most for, which was enough for him to consider himself fortunate in matrimony. He would not give himself over to fantasy, especially not when he had lobsters on the stove. If he let his thoughts run wild, then thirty years of marital fidelity, professional integrity, and social rectitude might be trampled into the same muck that stained the bottoms of Agatha's feet.

Livia was sitting on the arm of Sterling's chair,

talking, her face tilted down to him while he gazed at her crossed knees. Beyond, Agatha and Piper had stopped jumping and were talking with their heads close together in the intent way women had, pawing each other's hands and arms with little darting touches to mark salient points. Once, when she and Daphne were seventeen, Agatha's parents had gone to Mauritius for the month of December and declined to invite their daughter along, arguing that her short, two-week break would disrupt their stay, and Agatha had spent the holidays with the Van Meters, giving Winn two weeks of nervous stomach. At his own Christmas party, he had watched Agatha perch on the arm of a chair occupied by their next-door neighbor, Mr Buckley, a man so ancient he resembled a reanimated mummy and who had once reported Biddy to the police for driving with one headlight out. Agatha laughed at whatever drivel was wheezing from his desiccated lips, and eventually the geezer grew bright eyed and bold and rested one Methuselan hand on Agatha's bare knee, which she rewarded by tapping that claw with her fingertips as she spoke, causing Winn to turn away in disgust and spill eggnog down his pant leg.

Sterling was the only young man not engaged in sport, though he looked like he could use the exercise. Around him, women lounged like seals on a rock. Dominique made a spectacular save, smacking the birdie at Greyson from just inches above the grass. She, too, had been at the Christmas party when Agatha captured Mr Buckley's aged heart, but she had been in the kitchen, putting the finishing touches on Winn's signature Black Forest Yule log. Daphne shouted encouragement through cupped hands. Biddy pulled up a chair beside Maude and the grandmothers. Sterling, imperial, enthroned, looked up at Livia and spoke. He touched her knee with one finger. In three strides Winn was at the door. 'Livia,' he called. 'Would you come in here?'

The sound of her name barked as though through a bullhorn made Livia jump. 'What?' she said. Her father stood in the doorway, beckoning her with an eggbeater motion of one hand. She crossed the deck, chin high, ignoring Oatsie's raised eyebrows and Celeste's wink. 'What is it?' she asked.

'Don't be difficult, Livia. I want you to set out that bluefish pâté with some crackers,' Winn said.

She wondered if she had done something wrong by sitting on the arm of Sterling's chair. If her father had decided to run such obvious interference, then maybe she had wandered beyond flirtation into the red lace slums of apparent desperation. But no, she thought. Sterling had been the one to draw her down beside him.

'That's what you shouted at me for?'

'I did not shout.'

'You did, too. You completely interrupted my conversation.' She glanced back at where Sterling

161

was sitting motionless, lizardlike, one hand wrapped around his glass. 'Haven't you done enough today?'

'What are you talking about?'

'"How *is* Teddy?"' she said, mimicking her father's chummy tone to Jack Fenn.

He gave her a long, steady look over his glasses. 'I've known the Fenns for a long time,' he said. 'I was only being polite.'

'I've had enough politeness,' Livia said. 'Why can't you be loyal to me and just the tiniest bit impolite?'

'There's no *reason* to be impolite,' said her father.

She began Dr Z's trick, breathing in through her nose and out through her mouth and counting to five.

'Stop it,' he said, pointing at her. 'Don't do that.'

'Do what?'

'You know what. That breathing thing. That shrink thing.'

She pushed his finger away. 'If it's so important to you that I forget about Teddy, you should leave me alone out there.'

'What does one thing have to do with the other?'

From the stove came the hissing and clicking sounds of the lobster pot boiling over. 'You should check on that,' she said. She did not know if he watched her go, but she strode across the deck as though it were a stage and settled, preening, back on the arm of Sterling's chair.

★   ★   ★

Oatsie was drinking her vodka neat because she did not care for the way Maude made Bloody Marys, and the Van Meters did not have any clam juice with which she might have been able to doctor one to her satisfaction. Lately her drink of choice was a bullshot. Her friend Doris had put her on to the concoction – vodka mixed with cold beef bouillon – and she took it as a sort of curative tonic, even though her grandsons laughed. Cold beef vodka soup, they called it. She watched Sterling sitting with that Van Meter girl on the arm of his chair. He looked like he could use some nutrition mixed with his booze. He had gotten fat but also sallow. The girl didn't appear to mind. A wedding was always an aphrodisiac, full of temporary pairings driven by vicarious hope. Love was in the air, weak and snappy as static electricity. Let them do as they liked. She had met Harold at a wedding, and their marriage had been tolerable enough. She sipped and watched the boys and the Egyptian girl running on the grass. Francis swatted listlessly at the birdie, missing it.

Waskeke made Oatsie uncomfortable. She disliked the expectation that she should always be looking at the water, the sky, and so on. The sun had fallen into the trees, leaving behind air that was sweet and full of entomological strummings, but Oatsie could find no delight in a sunset. Beauty strained her nerves. The loveliness of the evening twisted itself into the sensation of

163

longing – but for what? For more. For more, or for some end to it, some climax, but the sweetness only stretched on, like a violin string that is tuned to unendurable tautness but will not snap. No release, only fading, light leeching away.

Out on the grass, Francis shouted something rude at Greyson, and Oatsie thought of scolding him but could not be bothered. The Van Meter girl looked pleased with herself, there beside Sterling, even though he seemed to have gone off into one of his silences. Propellers droned overhead. One of those buzzy little twin-engine planes. Beyond, the almost-full moon was ascending in time with the purpling of the sky. A string of birds sped by. Oatsie could feel the world pivoting away from her, the unstoppable entropy. Was longing a pleasure in itself? She had been at a party once, not unlike this one, back when she was married and newly pregnant with her first child, and Freddy Maughn, whom she had known since childhood, had grabbed her hand and kissed its palm as she passed him in the hall on her way to the bathroom. She remembered Freddy's dry lips and the tip of his tongue on her hand. He was three sheets to the wind and probably only meant to be playful, but for months afterward, until her pregnancy became too much of a distraction for Harold, she had pressed her hand to his mouth while they made love and told him to kiss it. His lips never produced the same effect as Freddy's, but she had persisted, irritably casting around for satisfaction. Her disappointment made her wish so fervently to be kissed again by Freddy Maughn that her desire spilled over and made her cling tightly to Harold, who strutted around afterward like a rooster.

And now she was an old woman, about to become a great-grandmother, sitting at a party on a summer evening and thinking about death. Greyson swatted the birdie over Dicky Jr's head into the grass and turned to make sure Daphne had seen. Love was just one more thing that would make it difficult to die. When had she become so morbid, so resigned? She didn't know. The sun's daily arc might have tricked her into believing she was following an infinite circle, but she knew she was marching a straight line. What a party guest she was. What terrible vodka the Van Meters had. She closed her eyes and pressed her palm against her lips.

CHAPTER 7

THE SERPENT IN THE LAUNDRY

The lobsters had turned the clownish red of death. Winn pulled them out of the pot with tongs, cursing under his breath at the heat and at Livia. Oil smoked in a skillet, and he tossed in Dicky's tuna and thought again of Agatha sitting on the arm of Mr Buckley's chair. Why did these girls think they could go around sitting on the arms of men's chairs? Livia acted as though *he* were the one provoking *her*, yet his behavior had been unimpeachable. All he asked of her was basic civility and an ounce of propriety, but she was like one of her sea creatures, goaded by the slightest disturbance into puffing up and flashing warning colors.

The two terrible phone calls had come not long before Christmas, the first on a night when Winn and Biddy had been to a party and were sitting at the kitchen table, half drunk and flipping through catalogs. Winn's red bow tie was undone around his open collar, and Biddy, who usually did not drink much at all, was flushed and pretty from mulled wine, a sprig of mistletoe tucked behind her ear. When the phone rang, she answered. She smiled, and then her face changed.

He looked up from a page of dog cushions in different colors and plaids, monogrammed with dog names. 'What?'

'She's pregnant,' Biddy said.

'Who's pregnant?'

'Livia.'

'Livia?'

He had wanted to seize the phone, had in fact attempted to seize the phone; he felt an insane and overwhelming conviction that he had the means to nip the whole situation in the bud. All he needed to do was talk some sense into his daughter, to tell her that this was unacceptable, would not be stood for, was not the way this family worked. She absolutely could not, and would not, be pregnant if he had anything to say about it. But she was not standing on a ledge somewhere debating whether or not to get knocked up. The thing was done, the die was cast. Biddy fended him off, first with shooing motions, then by catching him by the belt when he made a break to pick up a phone in another room. She pressed the receiver against her shoulder. 'No, Winn,' she said. 'Not yet. You're on the bench.'

He supposed she had been right to send him, scowling, back to the kitchen table, where he could only watch the conversation, spy on it really, gleaning from Biddy's side that Livia had simply, whimsically decided to do without any kind of protection and had no illusions of keeping it. He felt a need to be busy, and he opened all the doors in an advent calendar that Biddy's sister Tabitha had sent, popping the chocolates and their crumbs onto the table and then fetching the trash can from under the sink and sweeping the whole pile into it. There were long periods when Biddy said nothing, only made soothing noises that told him Livia was crying on the other end. What had she expected, he wondered. What on earth had she been thinking? He smacked the kitchen table with his palm and gritted his teeth.

In a few days, he calmed down. He had, at first, taken for granted that Livia's situation would be obvious to the world. He had imagined her waddling home for Christmas break in maternity clothes, needing to be hidden away, the season's celebrations ruined by public shame, but gradually the realization came to him that Livia was only barely pregnant, the keeper of a tiny, rudimentary embryo and nothing more. He felt generous enough to send her an e-mail expressing his support. 'Dear Livia,' he wrote. 'I was sorry to hear about this unfortunate turn. Everyone makes mistakes, and we will handle this discreetly. I hope you are not too distracted from your studies. Hang in there, kiddo. Dad.'

And Teddy Fenn of all people. Winn liked the boy well enough (they were, after all, fellow Ophidians), and Livia was enraptured by him, but the relationship had obviously never been anything permanent. They were young; Livia was too emotional, Teddy less than committed. In truth,

Winn had counted on the relationship ending, and the sooner the better because the thought of being tied to Jack and Fee Fenn with anything stronger than the gossamer threads of puppy love was repugnant. He hoped against all odds that Teddy had not told his parents about Livia's condition, that Jack Fenn was not sitting in his own kitchen, in his own Christmas dishabille, pondering the possibility of their shared grandchild. Preferring not to dwell on the idea, Winn shut it away and prepared to wait the whole thing out. Then Livia phoned to tell them Teddy had broken up with her.

He had been at work in his study, worrying over some financial documents, and while Livia talked, his eyes strayed to the pages.

'I'm sorry to hear that, pal,' he said. 'But everything will work out in the end. You'll see.'

'No, it won't.' A snot-filled snuffle traveled down the line and into his ear, nearly making him gag. 'I lost my virginity to him, and this is what he does?'

Winn covered the receiver with one hand. 'Biddy!' he called. 'Phone!'

Biddy picked up in another room, and Winn listened to Livia tell the story again. Teddy had come to her and said he had been considering leaving the relationship for some time, and the pregnancy, for him, was too much to bear.

'He said it had gotten too hard,' Livia said. 'Cry me a river, you know? Like this isn't hard for me?

169

And then he said he couldn't be part of *this*, of what I was going *to do*. Oh, and the best part is that suddenly he's Catholic. And I was like, well, you never go to Mass. And he was like, well, you don't have to go to Mass to be Catholic. And I said maybe not, but it would be good corroborating evidence that you're abandoning me because of religion and not because you're a chickenshit dickhead.'

'I seem to remember that Jack was Catholic,' Winn said.

'Well, this is the first I've heard of it.'

'Hmm,' Winn said, digesting. 'Has he told his parents?'

'I don't know. I doubt it. None of his friends know, of course.' Livia was gaining steam. 'Because heaven forbid he should look like an asshole.'

'Or maybe he thinks the situation is private,' Biddy put in, 'and doesn't want to make you vulnerable to gossip.'

'His friends actually threw him a party,' Livia went on. 'They called it the Emancipation Celebration. And they invited all these girls, slutty girls, like stocking a fishpond, who knew their fucking job was to fucking fuck my boyfriend. Congratulations, you're easy! You're really special! I know lots of people who went. People I thought I was friends with. Isn't that so fucking obnoxious?'

'No need to swear,' Winn said. He twiddled his pen. He knew about these parties. You made sure there was enough booze, and you invited a few girls who would be sure bets for the newly single brother. Harmless, really. Just a show of support.

'It is obnoxious,' Biddy said. She was in the room above Winn's study, and he heard her chair shift. 'But, Livia, the bottom line is that you don't want to be with someone who doesn't love you.'

'He loves me,' Livia said. 'I know he does.'

'If they're throwing him a party then he must be in pretty rough shape,' Winn offered. 'They probably wanted to cheer him up.'

'Daddy, they were supposed to be my friends, too.' Her voice broke. 'But it turns out I'm just something to be free of.'

'Try not to take everything so personally.'

'Winn, how is she supposed to not take that party personally?'

'How would you feel,' Livia said, 'if Mom left you, and then all her friends threw a party at the house and tried to get her laid?'

'Mr Buckley could be the deejay,' Biddy said.

Livia hiccupped, almost a laugh.

'You have to understand,' Winn said, 'that the fellows in his club have to be loyal to him first, and they're doing what they can to help him through a hard time.'

'Winn,' said Biddy.

'This is just what they do, Livia. The party doesn't have anything to do with you. It's a tradition. If your friends had thrown you a party like that would you have turned it down?'

'Yes.'

'Really?'

'The point is,' Livia said, 'couldn't they have done something nice for Teddy without rubbing it in my face that they think all I've done for the past two years is prevent Teddy from enjoying his God-given quota of pussy?'

'Livia,' said Biddy. 'Find a different word.'

Winn struggled to control his voice. 'I'm sure,' he said, 'they just meant to give him a good time, take his mind off things for a night, show him there are other fish in the sea.'

'Winn,' Biddy cautioned.

'*Daddy*. Other fish in the sea? Could you please be on my side? I'm your daughter. Your jilted, *pregnant* daughter.'

The stairs creaked, and Biddy appeared in the doorway, holding the phone between her ear and shoulder. Eyes wide, she sliced horizontally at the air with one hand and mouthed, *No*. He waved her away. 'Livia, all I'm saying is that the less importance you place on this party and the less attention you pay to what Teddy's doing, the better you look. Pretend you're not bothered. Go on with your life. People will respect that.'

The phone was quiet. 'Livia?' said Biddy.

'There's something else.'

Winn straightened the papers on his desk. 'What?'

'The Emancipation Celebration was on Thursday, and then on Saturday there was a normal sort of party at the club. I went to it. I was pretty drunk.'

172

'Yes?' said Winn.

'I'm only telling you this because people were there whose parents you know. You'd find out eventually.' She sniffed. Winn wanted to tell her to blow her nose. 'But I kind of lost it and told everyone I was pregnant.'

'What do you mean you told them?' Biddy said.

'I might have sort of shouted it.'

'Oh, Livia,' said Biddy, 'you didn't.'

'Obviously I did, Mom. It's not just a fun lie I made up.'

'Don't snap at Mommy,' Winn said. 'How many people could have heard you? Not too many?'

Livia's voice was small. 'A lot. Pretty much everyone who was there. And they all told other people.'

'What other people?' Winn said.

'Like the whole Ophidian, their girlfriends, their friends. The entire world.'

'Have you lost your mind?' Winn exploded. 'What in God's name were you thinking?'

'I don't know. I went crazy.'

'No, Livia, tell me what you were thinking.'

'I don't know. I wasn't. I'm sorry.' The last word was swallowed by a sob.

'This kind of behavior is unacceptable. I have been very understanding about this whole situation because I thought we agreed this would remain private. We need to get these outbursts under control. You were way out of line. Out of line. It's bad enough that you go around acting like a floozy, but then you throw your dignity right out the window and the whole family's with it. It's not becoming. It's not adult. People won't respect you.' He stopped, his well of censure unexpectedly run dry.

'Please, Daddy. It's done. I'm sorry. Please don't torture me. However embarrassed you might be, I promise I feel a million times worse.'

'Everything's always worse for you, isn't it? As though that's an excuse. You can't keep your knees together, and now we see you can't keep your mouth shut either. You need to think about other people for once. The Ophidian is something I respect, and you chose that place, of all places, to drag this family through the mud. I can forgive many things, Livia, but I'm not sure this is one of them.' He could hear her ragged breathing. 'Hello?' he said. 'Livia?'

'The Ophidian?' she said. There was a high tremor to her voice. 'You think the worst part of this is that it happened at the Ophidian?'

'The Ophidian is very important to me.' He wanted to shout at her that he had wanted a son who would be a member of the Ophidian, not a daughter who got knocked up by one.

'You can take your stupid club and shove it up your *ass*, Daddy. You know another thing people respect? An ounce of fucking loyalty from their own fathers.' The line clicked.

'Hello? Livia? Don't you hang up!'

'She hung up,' said Biddy.

Winn took off his glasses and rubbed his face. Then he put his glasses back on, picked up his pen, and turned crisply back to his papers. Biddy stepped closer. 'Winn?' she said.

Winn held a sheet up to the light and frowned at it. 'What?'

'I think you could have handled that differently.'

'She told me to shove the Ophidian up my ass. Is that the way civilized people speak to their fathers? No. I will not indulge her with a response. She's too worked up. She's hormonal. I can't get through to her when she's like that.'

'You graduated almost forty years ago. Do you really have to put the Ophidian above your child?'

'I did no such thing.'

She came around the corner of his desk to face him, tapping at the wood to get his attention. He wanted to slap her hand. 'Really?' she asked.

'No!' he said, nearly shouting. He took a deep breath. 'Well look, dear. Look.' He set down his pen and folded his hands. 'I was one of those boys once. I was only trying to provide her with some insight into what they were doing because I thought another perspective might be useful. You know, maybe they don't all need to be summarily shot. One thing I don't know, I am willing to admit, is what it's like to be a pregnant twenty-year-old, you're right. Especially one who goes into a crowded party full of our friends' children and announces that she's gotten herself' – he pushed his papers around – 'in a bad way. So, if

175

I wasn't as diplomatic as I might have been, I apologize.'

'Livia's suffering,' Biddy said. 'What she did was wrong, but she's obviously miserable about it.'

'She should be!' he erupted. 'She deserves a little misery. I'm trying my damnedest to be reasonable here, Biddy, but she's making it awfully difficult. What more do you want?'

'It would be nice if we didn't always just have to assume you love us.' Biddy's voice rasped, but Winn was in no mood to console any women.

'Have I or have I not been a good husband to you?' he said. 'Have I provided for you? Given you freedom and support? I don't treat you badly. I don't complain about your family. I've given you free rein over this wedding. What more do you want from me, Biddy? Have I or have I not been a good husband?'

Biddy stood up straight. 'I think,' she said, 'you've been the best husband you probably could be.'

As quickly as Winn could dish them up, the lobsters were carried off and devoured, hollowed out into empty red armor piled high in ceramic bowls. He wondered what Biddy had done with the sick lobster – he couldn't imagine her killing it, nor did he think she would have left it somewhere to die.

All the Adirondacks were full, so he carried a straight-backed chair out from the dining room and sat in it with a gin and tonic – the fourth and strongest of a quick succession – sweating a dark circle onto his knee. He had poured the first after Livia had flounced out of the kitchen and the second and third not long after that, as he ate his own lobster alone in the dining room, preferring to sit at a proper table and not to sprawl on the deck or lawn. In his left ear, Dicky was telling a long story about, he thought, Oliver Wendell Holmes. In his right ear, Maude laughed arpeggios at something Biddy was saying. He was tipsy. Quite tipsy. Around him, the party was gaining a pointless momentum, becoming a parade to nowhere. Night had fallen, and Biddy had gone around setting out hurricane lanterns and lighting them with a kitchen lighter. Their orange glow, extending from the murky edge of the dark lawn into the thick of the crowd, was warmer and more enticing than the wan grids of pale incandescence that fell from the doors and windowpanes, turning people to shadows as they passed near the house. Agatha was standing and leaning over Sterling, giggling and pouring him a drink in a pose that cried out for go-go boots and a stewardess outfit in loud, groovy colors. Sterling's eyes meandered from her face to her neck to her waist and back again.

'And we got hold of a bunch of lobster shells,' Dicky Sr was saying, having moved on from Justice Holmes. 'Bags of them, already starting to smell – I mean they were *decidedly* ripe – and we put them in the heating ducts of their building. This guy Jeffrey Whitehorse broke in; he could pick locks. He said he had an uncle who was a jewel thief. Strange guy, Jeffrey. While he was at it, he stole this club coat of arms they'd cooked up and had gotten carved somewhere, and we mailed it as a gift to the prime minister of Iceland. The next day you could smell their building from three blocks away. Terrible, terrible smell. Nothing quite like rotting shellfish for a stink.'

Winn was watching Daphne, flushed and bleary eyed from laughing, leaning against Greyson with a bottle of nonalcoholic beer balanced on her belly, but Dicky's story, issuing with clipped precision from his thin, Rooseveltian lips, disoriented him, keelhauled him through a chaotic wash of memory, and when he came up on the other side, he had to check to see that it was indeed Dicky speaking, Dicky's aquiline profile in the shadows and not the dark silhouette of his own father.

'No,' said Maude, pulling Winn back into the present, 'you don't mean Iceland. You mean Ireland. And his name was Whitehouse, not Whitehorse. Whitehorse makes him sound like an Indian.'

'You tell the story then, dear.'

But Maude had already lost interest. 'Sterling is certainly popular with the ladies tonight,' she said sotto voce.

Agatha and Sterling had begun playing a hand-slapping game. Sterling's reflexes were surprisingly

178

quick. He flipped his hands out from under Agatha's and slapped the backs of hers before she could pull them away. 'Rematch!' she said, and he did it again. 'How are you so fast?' she cried. Livia was watching them from across the knot of chairs, her face without expression but her eyes dark and active, and Celeste, who sat beside her, was watching them all. Winn didn't know if he was more distressed by the idea of Sterling sleeping with Agatha or Livia. Probably he should be most bothered by finding himself swimming in the same pool of potential partners as his daughters, but all he could summon was a fatalistic apathy.

'Girls have always liked Sterling,' Dicky said.

'Go figure,' said Winn. Maude laughed one uncertain trill.

Just then Greyson stood up, clinking two beer bottles together. 'Everyone,' he said. 'Everyone.'

'He's a prince. He's a catch,' said Maude, leaning close to Winn's ear as though telling a secret. He did not know who she meant. She winked and nodded.

Greyson sang a song, not a short one, that Livia had not heard before. It was old-fashioned and brassy and provided an abundance of opportunities for the singer to drop to one knee and mime with pumping hands the tromboning palpitations of a heart in love. He sang well enough, in a reedy tenor Livia remembered from Christmas caroling. Charlie and Francis, former Tigertones both, sang backup and provided goofy slide-whistle sound effects. Daphne beamed. Agatha, drawn to the spotlight, danced her way to a post just behind Daphne, where she shadowed her friend's delight – clapping her hands in time with the song and shimmying from side to side. She winked at Sterling, who tipped his glass at her, and Livia felt squashed and defeated. Never before would she have argued that Daphne was more beautiful than Agatha, but the sight of joyful, radiant Daphne beside vaudevillian, showboating Agatha convinced her.

Dominique sat off to one side, a little apart, a drink in one hand, watching the action with a pained expression badly hidden under an indulgent smile. She wore white canvas sailor pants and a blouse in stiff black cotton with an asymmetrical neckline, and her legs and arms were both crossed, one foot in a silver ballet flat bouncing just off the beat of Greyson's song. A thick silver bangle was pushed high up on her forearm, but otherwise she wore no jewelry. For most of her life, Livia had wanted to be Dominique, and the desire returned with new strength: to be aloof, impassive, queenly with close-cropped hair, classic in a way that had nothing to do with pastels or goofy little whales but was about elegance and coolness. Did they all seem ridiculous to her? Livia longed to be more mysterious, more self-possessed, more neutral in her color palette, the kind of woman whose thoughts were the object of speculation. Dominique rubbed her biceps and then turned to retrieve a folded square of fabric that she shook out, revealing a bright yellow and orange batik, embroidered with flowers, loops, and abstract squiggles and studded with tiny mirrors that flashed in the lantern light. Wrapping it around her shoulders, she was transformed from chic, minimalist European into something more vibrant and arresting, a dark head emerging from folds of saffron and canary, a sun priestess.

Growing up, Livia had always assumed that Dominique would one day be fully integrated into their circle, married to a boy like the ones Daphne had been friends with at Deerfield, settled somewhere around New York, still cool, still exotic but also neutralized, fully adapted, a happy convert. Her differentness had seemed all the more precious because Livia had not believed it would last. But instead Dominique had gone to Michigan when she could have gone to Brown, to culinary school when she had been accepted at Wharton, to Belgium when an equally good job was on offer in Boston. She abandoned the clothes, the music, the mannerisms, and most of the friendships of her prep school self, and yet through all that shedding she seemed to become more calm and assured than ever.

Transformation captivated Livia, but she was squeamish at the thought of changing her own life. To change would be to admit that she had been going about things all wrong. Her people noticed change, discussed it, speculated about its superficiality, its vanity. The only kind of change they understood was the flickering skin of the octopus, blending in with its surroundings, or the real estate flipping of the hermit crab, always shopping for a slightly roomier prison. Dominique would probably advise her to leave, to go somewhere else and start fresh and then come back when she had become who she wanted to be. But Livia couldn't see the way. It was too late for her, already too late.

After the applause died down and Greyson finished kissing Daphne, there could be heard, from somewhere on the island, the sound of a bagpipe.

'What is that tune?' Oatsie said.

Winn said, 'Is it "Amazing Grace"?'

'Dad thinks every song is "Amazing Grace,"' Livia said. 'It's like he's color-blind but for music.'

'Tone-deaf?' posited Francis.

'No,' Livia said, 'it's that he only knows the name of one song.'

'Maybe it is "Amazing Grace,"' said Piper.

'No,' said Dicky Jr. 'It's from that movie about the *Titanic*.'

'*Titanic*?' said Dominique from her corner, tickled. 'Dicky Duff Jr, I would not have expected you to come up with that.'

Dicky Jr shrugged. 'It's what it is.'

'Everybody,' said Greyson, 'my brother is a twelve-year-old girl.'

'In 1997,' put in Francis.

Daphne sighed and stretched. 'I have to go lie

down,' she said, rubbing her belly. 'I might be back but probably not.'

Escorted by Greyson, she went inside. 'Don't neglect your cocoa butter!' Oatsie bellowed after her.

Winn stood. 'Drink orders?'

There was a chorus of requests, and when they died down, Oatsie said, 'What about you, Livia? Do you have any beaux?'

Livia was aware that only the wobbly partition of Celeste separated her from Sterling. She struggled for a few seconds with how to answer, not wanting to seem either unavailable or too available and also wondering what information had already reached him through the pneumatic tubes of gossip, but before she could formulate anything, Celeste piped up with, 'Livia's pining over the one who got away.'

Livia rounded on her and gave an incredulous flick of her head. Celeste seemed to think that because she'd been through so much romantic tumult herself, seen so much, she had the right to impose a policy of total openness on everyone around her, certain they understood their troubles didn't amount to much in the grand scheme of things.

'Oh?' said Oatsie. 'How did he get away?'

Celeste tapped the side of her nose with one finger. 'In the worst way. Without permission.'

'We don't need to talk about it,' Livia said.

Oatsie's glasses caught the lantern light. 'Don't worry, dear. There are other fish in the sea.'

'Are there?' Livia said, heating up. 'I thought there was just the one.'

'It ain't over till the fat lady sings,' Celeste said. 'Maybe it'll be a second marriage for both of you.'

'Second marriage for who?' Piper said, appearing with a glass for herself and one for Dominique.

'No one,' Livia said.

Sterling spoke. 'Daphne and Greyson,' he said, exhaling a cloud of smoke. 'Celeste has uncovered the dirt. They were both married before. Go on, Celeste. You were about to tell us about Daphne being a showgirl.'

'At the Golden Nugget,' Celeste said without hesitation. 'She married a craps dealer. It only lasted a month.'

'My parents were both married before,' Piper said brightly, pleased to be sharing good news. 'My mom's first husband died, and my dad's first wife ran off with her ophthalmologist. Things always turn out well in the end.'

'That's true,' Livia said. 'They always do. One hundred percent of the time. How many times have you been married, Celeste?'

'Oh, about a million,' Celeste said around the cigarette Sterling was lighting for her.

'My husband and I were philanthropists,' Oatsie said. 'But since he's passed, I've lost the knack.'

She regarded her grandson with such fixed interest that Sterling said, 'What?'

'I don't know whether you should ever marry,

Sterling, dear. I think maybe not. You are not the type.'

'Why is that?'

They stared at each other with their indolent, unblinking gazes, each perfectly comfortable under the scrutiny of the other. 'You're a clever boy,' Oatsie said. 'But you're not very nice.'

Sterling absorbed his grandmother's pronouncement with equanimity, and in the quiet, an odd sound could be heard from somewhere nearby. 'What is that?' asked Francis.

'What?' said Piper.

'Shh,' said Dominique. 'I hear it, too.'

The sound, a regular sort of huffing like the respiration of a train, grew louder until suddenly a dog, an immense black Labrador, burst like a cannonball from the darkness of the lawn, bounded onto the deck, and began rushing from chair to chair, panting and wagging solicitously as though in apology for his late arrival. His nails tapped a flamenco beat on the wood. Livia pushed his snout from her crotch, and he went directly to Sterling, who watched the intimate explorations of the inquiring nose without interest. The lanterns burnished the dog's coat and caught the whites of his eyes. He was the size and shape of an oil drum. 'Hey, get away from there,' Francis said when the dog went for the plate beside his feet.

'Come here,' called Agatha. 'Here, boy! Here!'

'What is he looking for?' said Dominique as the dog bustled past, his black nose searching the air and then following an invisible trail along the deck and then revisiting the air.

'He's looking for the treasure of the Sierra Madre,' Oatsie announced in her loud, round, plummy voice.

'He's probably from the IRS,' said Sterling.

Agatha patted her thighs. 'Here! Here, doggie. Why doesn't he like me? Come here!'

Winn, who had been sitting back by the house with the other parents, lurched to his feet. 'Whose dog is this?' he demanded. 'Who brought this dog?'

'No one did,' Livia yelled at him over the hubbub. 'He just appeared.'

'I thought we were getting a stripper,' Charlie said.

'Here!' cried Agatha.

'Keep him away from those lobster shells,' said Dicky Sr, not stirring from his chair.

Greyson reemerged from the house, took in the scene, and with one lunge caught the dog by his collar. The animal sat down, jovial and inky black, pink tongue hanging from the corner of his mouth and tail tick-tocking from side to side. 'Everyone,' he said, 'I'd like you to meet' – he looked at the collar – 'Morty.'

'Morty?' shrieked Piper. 'That is *not* his name.'

'Where did he come from?' Winn kept asking. 'Why is he here?'

Grinning, the dog looked rapidly from side to side, craning around at all the faces. A thick string of drool unfurled from the edge of his lip and draped itself over Greyson's hand.

'Shit!' said Greyson, releasing the collar. 'He slimed me!'

The dog, free again, was in more of a hurry than ever and ran slip-sliding around in a circle, dodging everyone who reached for him. The party was on its feet, darting around calling the dog, wanting to pet the dog, trying to grab the dog. Finally Morty saw his chance and leapt from the deck, vanishing down the dark slope of lawn, and Agatha, focused entirely on her pursuit and not on her feet, went headlong after him, belly flopping into the night. A stunned silence hung over the party for as long as it took to draw breath, and then they were all in hysterics, rocking and tipping in their chairs, wheezing and gasping. Livia, doubled over in spasmodic laughter, looked out through her tears and noticed the peak of the party as it passed.

Her father was kneeling on the edge of the deck. 'Agatha?' he said. 'Are you all right?' Her face with its tousled yellow mane appeared and then a hand as she dragged herself up, keening with laughter. He reached out for her and hoisted, struggling to get her on her feet. She teetered from side to side, disheveled, a barefoot urchin, trying to wipe her eyes and brush the grass and dirt from the front of her dress. For a moment she clutched the front of his shirt.

'Ooh,' she said, catching sight of a ribbon of raw skin running down her forearm. 'Oopsidoodle.'

'Are you all right?' he asked. He took hold of her wrist and held her arm up to the light.

'Why wouldn't he come to me?' she asked. 'He went to everyone else.'

Livia did not like the way her father was patting Agatha on the shoulder – clumsily, sort of like she was a horse, but with a fixed, embarrassing attention. She looked at her mother, who was sitting with the Duffs and studying her own hands in her lap with raised eyebrows. Maude said something to her, and she turned, smiling, her brightness switched on again.

Celeste was still undone by giggles. 'Because,' she said to Agatha, barely getting the words out, 'he's neutered. He's not interested.'

'He's a dog,' Agatha said testily.

Celeste waved a hand in apology but couldn't stop laughing.

From her chair, Dominique said, 'Morty didn't like you. That's all.'

'It's true,' Agatha said, looking hurt and slurring faintly. 'He didn't like me. Oh, God, why didn't Morty like me?'

'He liked you,' Winn said, leading her to a chair. 'Of course he did.'

'Dogs don't have to like *everyone*,' Oatsie said.

Livia stepped off the deck and lay flat on her back in the grass. An airplane crossed the sky, and she imagined its interior – people packed in rows like eggs in a carton, the chemical smell of the toilets, pretzels in foil pouches, cans hiss-popping open, black ovals of night sky embedded in the rattling walls. How strange that something so drab, so confined, so stifling with sour exhalations and the fumes of indifferent machinery might be mistaken for a star.

'Do you think your mother is happy in there?' Winn said, returning to the corner of the deck where Biddy and the Duffs were sitting. He had gone inside to get a beer and the first aid kit, but somehow the kit had passed from his hands into Sterling's, who was now sitting beside Agatha, daubing her scrape with a cotton ball while she bared her teeth at the sting.

'Oh, did she go inside?' Maude said.

'She's there.' Winn tilted his head at the window through which Mopsy could be seen sitting in the dark living room, a narrow shadow dwarfed by a wing chair. She reminded him of how, at his wedding, he had searched the windows of the Hazzards' house for his mother's face. 'I asked her if she wanted some light, but she said no.'

'Thank you so much for checking on her, Winn, but I'm sure she's fine. She might be a little tired. She gets tired. She's probably resting. This is a *wonderful* party. You are so sweet to go to the trouble.'

'It's nothing,' said Biddy. 'Really.'

'Well now, Dicky,' Winn said. 'Have you gotten out on the golf course much lately?'

'Not much, I'm afraid,' Dicky Sr said,

189

mournfully shaking his head. 'Things have been awfully busy.'

'Don't listen to him,' said Maude. 'He was out on Wednesday with Marshall Hattishaw.'

'Thank you, dear. Next time I'll let you answer the question.'

'Marshall Hattishaw?' Winn said, fumbling with a bottle opener. 'Do I know him? Where did he prep?'

'Andover. Do you know him?'

Winn nodded, summoning an indistinct image of a blond man holding a squash racquet. Finally he managed to pry the cap off the bottle, but the toothy disc slipped through his fingers and rolled away somewhere under the chairs.

'He's a *doll*,' said Maude.

'I don't know him,' Biddy said. 'Where do you know him from, Winn?'

'Here and there. We move in the same circles.'

'What about you?' Dicky asked. 'How's the working life?'

'Ah,' Winn said. 'Fine. I'm not golfing as much as I'd like, though. I played a few rounds last month. Actually, I'm hoping that soon I'll be able to take you out on the Pequod course. We've been on the waitlist for a while. I can't imagine it'll be much longer.'

'No,' Dicky said. 'I'm sure not.' But a glance had passed between him and Maude.

Winn peered at them. 'Jack Fenn's on the membership committee. Do you know him?'

'I do, very well,' said Dicky. 'We go way back. He's a solid guy, Jack. A class act.'

'Yes.' Winn nodded. 'Yes. We were at college together. Unfortunately, there's some bad blood between Livia and his son.'

Another communication passed between Dicky and Maude, but this one was not so much seen as felt, just a subtle shift in their postures. 'I'm sorry to hear that,' Dicky said.

'The mistakes of youth,' Winn said, raising his bottle. 'May they not be visited on the old.'

Biddy patted Winn's thigh. She turned to Maude. 'Tell me – Daphne was saying something about Francis spending time in a monastery?'

'Yes, my goodness, can you believe it? My little Buddha. Francis is very spiritual. I keep telling him he'll have to give a little family lecture on, you know, serenity and, what is it he says, acceptance, and, let me see, the *middle* way. Francis says—'

'I only hope,' Winn said, 'that Fenn can look beyond our differences when it comes to the Pequod.' His hand had escaped Biddy's, and his index finger was pointing at Dicky. He let it drop into his lap.

'Winn,' said Biddy. 'Leave it for now.'

'I can't imagine Jack would hold something like that against you,' Dicky said. 'That's not Jack's way. He's a stand-up guy, Jack.'

'If there's a problem, it couldn't be Jack. No. No, no,' Maude said.

'What do you mean?' asked Winn, the finger creeping back up and swinging toward Maude like a dowser's stick. Biddy grabbed his hand and held it, squeezing.

'Young love, it's so dramatic, isn't it?' Maude said. 'That's all I mean. Greyson and Daphne are so lucky to be settled.' She glanced between Winn and Dicky. 'I'm sure you'll be teeing off at the Pequod before you know it.' This last was spoken so kindly, like a nurse telling a doomed G.I. he'd be going home soon, that Winn was sure she knew something. Suddenly, he felt very drunk.

Biddy was talking about Teddy. 'I was so shocked when Livia told me. She was shocked. His mother must have been shocked. Or maybe not. What do I know? The decision just seemed so sudden.'

'Chip off the old block,' said Winn.

'With four sons,' Maude said, 'the draft is my biggest fear. If they ever came for *my* boys, I don't know what I would do. I would be a *lioness*. I would bundle my babies off to Canada.'

'Dicky would be all right,' Dicky Sr said. 'And Greyson. Francis couldn't hack it, though.'

'Maybe Sterling could be a medic,' Winn said bitterly. They all looked over at Sterling pressing a row of Band-Aids onto Agatha's arm.

Maude shook her head. 'I hate even to think about any of them going. It's a terrible, terrible thought.'

Winn stopped listening. The light from the lanterns was ghoulish, and the scene swung slowly from side to side as though they were on a ship. There were Agatha's bare knees, and there was Celeste's glass catching the light and Mopsy's dark shape in the window. The young men wore shirts the colors of saltwater taffy and drank from bottles of beer. Their ankles were bare beneath the cuffs of their pants. He couldn't tell them apart. There was Maude gesturing, drawing a jagged heartbeat in the air.

'Must be hard for Livia, though,' Maude said. 'After everything.'

'Livia,' Winn said, doggedly trying to restore order, 'is laboring under the illusion that Teddy's joining the army had something to do with her.'

There was a pause. 'We don't need to get into it,' said Biddy.

She was right, of course, but her rightness only prodded Winn into elaborating. He said, 'It's time she faced the fact that men break up with women because they *don't* want to plan their lives around them. Teddy isn't thinking about her.'

Livia appeared from nowhere, standing over them. 'Thanks, Dad,' she said. 'Glad you're on my side.'

'Livia!' said Biddy. 'Where were you hiding?'

'I was right there,' Livia said. 'I was lying in the grass. I heard everything you said.'

'Make sure you check for ticks,' said Maude.

Winn reached for Livia's arm, but she brushed him off. 'Pal,' he said, 'we might as well be realistic. He isn't planning a future with you.'

'I didn't say he *was*. Is this your idea of party chitchat?'

'If that's what he wanted,' Winn floundered on, 'he wouldn't have broken up with you. End of story. This isn't about you. You and Teddy are no longer connected. He has his life and you have yours. You'll be better off as soon as you accept it. End of story.'

She lifted her chin very high. 'Well,' she said, loudly enough for everyone to hear, 'then you should get it through your head. You are never going to be in the Pequod. They don't want you to join. They don't *like* you. They have a golf course, and you can't play on it. End of story.'

The deck seemed very quiet. Winn felt sour, shriveled, and old. 'I think you ought to apologize,' he said.

'Absolutely not!'

'Biddy,' Winn said, 'don't you agree that Livia owes me an apology?'

Biddy looked miserable. 'Let's just enjoy the party,' she said. 'Let's talk about all this later.'

He glared at her and then around the deck. Agatha was watching, but Sterling, who was mummifying her head in gauze as a joke, went on with his task, covering her nose, her lips, her chin. Her eyes blinked out of the whiteness. 'I need some air,' Winn said, standing. 'I need to take a walk.'

Bringing his drink, he passed through the waste-land of the kitchen, piled with dirty plates and

194

crumpled paper napkins like little dead birds, and climbed the stairs, all the way up to the widow's walk, leaving the hatch open behind him. The air felt fresher on top of the house; the day had been flaccid and still, but now a breeze stirred along the roof. He should have been angry, but drink had always dulled his temper, leaving him thwarted and bitter when, sober, he would have been furious. The island was always being buffed clean by salty air and rolling fog, its colors softened, its surfaces rubbed smooth, and he gave himself over to the same process, closing his eyes and breathing in and out like Livia's shrink had taught her. Beyond the wash of light seeping from the house, the island was dark, but he knew the view so well he could picture the patchwork perfectly: windswept interior, green amoeba of golf course, shrubs and low trees punctuated by chimneys and gables. On the edge of it all stood the lighthouse. The beam flashed across, heading out to sea. When he was young, he would bring his girlfriends out to the tower just after sunset, and, standing at its base with the island at his feet, he had felt he was at the center of the compass, the horizon a perfect circle drawn by the revolving beam.

'The silent flight of the lighthouse light,' he whispered to himself, liking the sound. 'The silent flight of the lighthouse light.' From below, he heard the clinking of ice cubes drawing nearer. Celeste climbed the stairs one-handed, plunking her glass down on the planks and hauling herself out after it.

'Winnifred,' she said, emerging from the floor. 'There you are, naughty boy, up here like the bell ringer.'

'Whose dog was that?' Winn said. 'Who lets their dog run loose like that?' He knew that Celeste, through long experience, could gauge drunkenness the way the older salesmen at Brooks Brothers could fit him for a suit with a single glance, and he didn't bother disguising the gliss that hitched his words into one long chain. He trusted her not to comment, not even in retaliation for his cheap shots at her drinking that afternoon out in the trees.

'Everyone loved the dog. He just added a little spice to the party, something to talk about, just like your little tiff with Livia. Don't worry about it, old friend. Come on back down. The Duffs are getting ready to leave.'

'I need some fresh air,' he said. 'Did Biddy send you up to get me?'

Her tight, painted face floated out of the gloom, seeming to precede the rest of her. 'No,' she said. 'I needed some air, too. So much talking down there, you can't breathe. I love these widow's walks. They're very romantic.'

'I'm told the correct term is "roof deck." "Widow's walk" is a salesman's idea. Romantic, like you said. So people can think of themselves as seafarers.'

'I like it,' Celeste said. 'It's all about loss and female fortitude. If I were out at sea, I'd want to know someone was waiting for me, wouldn't you?' She pulled a pack of cigarettes from her pocket. 'Do you want one?'

He hadn't smoked in years. 'Yes,' he said.

'I don't know if I'll be able to light it in this breeze,' she said, putting the stalk between her lips. She produced a lighter and turned away from him, her cupped hand an orange band shell behind the flame. 'There,' she said, handing him the lit cigarette. 'All yours.'

He took a drag. The sensation was marvelous. She lit another for herself.

'Do you think,' he said, sorry for having been harsh with her earlier, 'that Livia thinks she and Teddy will wind up together?'

'Probably,' she said.

'I hate the irrationality of it.'

'Where's the fun in being rational all the time?'

'I'm not talking about fun.'

'Fun's not your thing. Let Livia think what she wants. It won't change anything.' Celeste gave his arm a gentle punch. 'The wedding is going to be beautiful,' she said. 'Just beautiful. I can tell. I wish my wedding had been so beautiful.'

'Which one? To Wyeth?' She had married Wyeth furtively, in a municipal courthouse.

'No, no. The first one. Mother and Daddy hated David so much I had to beg every last rose out of them. We had chicken at the reception. *Chicken.*

Not that an entrée should matter when you're starting your life and so on, but it seemed like a big deal at the time. Maybe David and I were doomed from the first.'

Winn thought the problem with Celeste and David had been rooted more in her drinking and his prolonged and petulant unemployment, but he said, 'Your wedding to Herbert was a great bash, though.'

'And the marriage was still doomed? Is that what you mean? It's a fair point. Four thousand dollars on oysters alone, and we were done in two years.'

Winn drank from his bottle and Celeste from her glass. She leaned over the railing. 'Look at that,' she said, pointing down. He could just make out the shapes of Sterling and Agatha sitting close together on the edge of the deck. 'A perfect match. Trouble and trouble.'

'Oh, I don't know,' he said, trying to seem unconcerned.

Celeste was quiet. Then, in a low voice and without looking at him, she said, 'Do the right thing here. Make sure Biddy has a nice weekend.'

He stiffened. 'Of course Biddy will have a nice weekend.'

'Just please think of her. I know I have no right to lecture anyone on self-control, but I have a lot of experience with mistakes.' She exhaled through her nose, suggesting mirth.

'I don't know what you're talking about,' he said.

She slapped his cheek lightly with the backs of her fingers. 'The girl, Winn. Stay away from the girl.'

Decades earlier, during a drunken game of sardines at the Hazzard ancestral home, Winn had mistaken Celeste for Biddy in the darkness of a closet and kissed her. Not until she pulled away and whispered, 'Well, I do declare!' did he realize his mistake. Though he had apologized profusely, he had never been sure if she believed the kiss was an accident, and he had not confessed it to Biddy. He wondered if there was any grand pattern to who blunders into whom in the dark. After kissing Celeste, he had been troubled that someone who was not his wife, who resembled her in neither vice nor virtue, could be so identical to her in the dark, redolent with Biddy's smell and presence, the sound of her breath.

'Winn!' called Biddy from below. 'Come down! The Duffs are leaving!'

By midnight the party had burned down to its embers. The elder Duffs had departed amid a flurry of kisses and garbled promises about the next day, and Biddy had gone up to bed without a word. Wading through the mess in the kitchen, Winn filled a garbage bag with a pungent hash of lobster carcasses, corncobs, lurid bits of tomato, scraps of lettuce, blobs of cheese. He took another bag and filled it with beer cans, beer bottles, wine bottles, gin bottles. He dismantled skyscrapers of dirty pots and pans and dishes, loading what he could into the dishwasher and piling the rest in the sink. Murmurings and burbles of laughter drifted in from outside, where the young people were still sitting in their circle. He admired their stamina, but he wondered what the point was. There wasn't much to be gained from dragging the party out. A worse hangover, maybe. The chance to say something ill considered. Of course, there was the tantalizing mirage of sex, always shimmering just out of reach until, sometimes, if you waited long enough, it unexpectedly engulfed you, turned tangible.

He had once relished all those prospects; indeed he recognized that a similar drunken need to *do* something, to channel his blurry impulses into activity, was spurring him through the sponge-smelling calisthenics of the compulsive cleaner. When he married he had turned his back on boozy, nocturnal abandon, learned to resist the tinkle of a beaded curtain, the alluring, subterranean racket of female laughter and popping corks. He rinsed tomato residue from Maude's thermos. A spoon, examined for signs of use, showed him the upside-down balloon of his face. He wiped the counters and the backsplash and gathered up the tablecloth and dish towels for the wash.

Celeste lay asleep on a couch in the living room, her silver sandals and a bag of pretzels on the floor beside her. At the top of the book-shelf, the ship's clock still insisted it was half past four. A lamp blazed down on her face, but she had always been someone who could sleep anywhere, under any circumstances, without registering discomfort. She was curled on her side with her head resting on her folded hands, and she would have been a vision of peace if not for the deep, arrhythmic splutters issuing from her open mouth. Hugging his laundry with one arm, Winn tiptoed nearer. The harsh beam of the lamp exposed the fissured and spotted topography of her face, the leavings of her makeup, the brittleness of her bleached hair, the faint tracery of blue veins at her temple. Her toenails were painted shocking pink. He reached and switched off the light.

All day the house had seemed to have a honey-combed permeability. Every bathroom contained a woman; everything he did was observed; every hallway was a gauntlet of girls to smile at and scooch around. The joists hummed and resonated with chatter. And Celeste's warning on the widow's walk had unsettled him. He had no desire to be the aging dog, limping and panting after the mocking young thing.

On the floor of the laundry room he found a tangled heap of beach towels and bedsheets that, after dumping his kitchen cargo into the washer, he bent over and began trying to sort, stepping from side to side in a slow, drunken elephant dance. The room had one window, a tall rectangle of black panes that threw back a flimsy violet portrait of himself, hollow eyed and anxious looking. When Agatha spoke from the doorway, he had already seen her purple ghost slide across the glass, but still he jumped in surprise.

'Hi,' she said.

'You scared me.' He stepped back, bumping up against a narrow counter cluttered with half-empty bottles of bleach, clamshells holding safety pins and buttons, and a box of detergent that gave off the bright scent of phony springtime. He put his hands in his pockets.

'I was looking for a room that wasn't spinning. But this doesn't seem to be it.' She leaned against the washing machine. She was barefoot, as she had been all night, and there was a maroon stain down the front of her white dress.

'No,' he said. 'This is as bad as anywhere else.'

'I want to go on a walk. Do you want to take a walk?' She smiled. Red wine had dyed the insides of her lips burgundy and her teeth a chalky lavender.

'Sterling wouldn't take a walk with you?'

'I haven't asked him. I wanted to ask you first.'

He was unprepared for the surge of lust that caught him, and he grasped the edge of the counter and held on as though it were his only handhold over a chasm. 'I shouldn't.'

'Oh, okay,' she said. He was so accustomed to seeing her look confident and unconcerned that he was shocked when her face puckered into a knot of distress. She put one tan hand over her eyes.

'Agatha,' he said. 'Come on, now.' He stepped across the laundry pile and patted her shoulder. When she uncovered her face, the unsightliness of her first tears was gone, and she wore an expression of beguiling desolation. Her lips were swollen and flushed, and a few plump tears dropped from her eyelashes.

'I'm sorry,' she said. 'I'm just drunk. And the dog didn't like me. And now I'm embarrassed.'

'There's no need to be embarrassed.'

'You're always so nice,' she said.

'It's easy to be nice to you,' Winn said. He found himself squeezing and petting her upper arm.

'I've always had a crush on you.' She hung her head.

'Really?' he said.

'You're so nice to your family. They're lucky. They don't even know how lucky they are.'

'Well,' he said. She understood, this girl. She *saw* him. Her allure for him, perhaps, wasn't just December lusting after May but one familiar recognizing another. He wanted to tell her that, but instead he said, 'Maybe.'

'You cooked that dinner,' she went on. 'You made everyone feel welcome, and everything you do seems so effortless, like you don't even have to try. Livia shouldn't have said those things. They're not true.'

'I thought you liked Sterling,' he said.

'I was just flirting with him to make you jealous.'

Winn reached out and took hold of her wrist as

he had after her kamikaze leap after the dog. He bent her elbow back and examined the row of Band-Aids Sterling had used to cover her scrape. With his thumbnail, he separated one from her skin and tore it off. He did the same to the next one and the next until they were all gone. He pressed his thumb hard against her raw skin, and she twisted her wrist free. Her arms wrapped around him. He burrowed his face into her neck, inhaling her smokiness. She turned her head, searching for his mouth, and as soon as he kissed her, he knew all his fortifications, his safeguards, his laws and bylaws were for nothing. He pinned her against the washer and bit her mouth while his hands pulled at her thighs, ran up them to clutch at her ass. His fingers raced along the elastic frontier of her underwear and breached it. When he touched her, lost as he was in his rapacious frenzy, he registered the uncanny absence of pubic hair. The sensation shocked him. He had known, through hearsay and his rare ventures into the cybermetropolis of pornography, that this was common now, but his sexual heyday had been during an era of bush. Agatha could have been a different species from the other women he had touched. Thunderstruck, he bent down to look at her, pulling up her dress. Her naked sex, plaintive and exposed, reminded him of children and animal paws and the noses of horses and the word 'pudenda.'

'You like it?' she said.

'I don't know,' he said. 'Yes.' He straightened up and, closing his eyes, kissed her. Tentatively, after a moment, he touched her again, prepared this time for her hairlessness but not for her dryness. He opened his eyes.

She was gazing over his shoulder at an equestrian print that hung on the wall, an arbitrary decoration in an unimportant room: a mottled river of hounds flowing after a fox. Leggy horses with red-coated riders stuck like boulders out of the white and tan waters. Her face bore no trace of arousal, no particle of interest in what was being done to her. She might have been in the waiting room of a dentist's office, idly wondering what unpleasantness awaited both her and the beleaguered fox. She must have sensed the change in him, his moment of recoil, because she threw back her head and released a whimper. Her throat pulled tight. When she looked at him again, her face was a wanton mask of pleasure: eyelids at half mast, wine-stained incisors gripping her lower lip. He jerked his fingers from the soft mousetrap that had caught them and stumbled backward, the laundry dragging at his feet, until he was again clinging to the tenuous safety of the sink.

'What?' she said. 'What's wrong?'

At first he could not reply but could only gape at her, conscious of the obviousness of his excitement but also feeling the first inkling of the enormity of his mistake. 'We shouldn't have done that.'

'But we want each other.'

'This was a moment of weakness.'

'Don't say *was*.' Her face was tense and determined. She stepped forward and started to reach for him, for his groin or belt buckle – he couldn't tell – but changed her mind and let her hand drop. 'I know what the problem is,' she said, 'but I just get that way sometimes. It doesn't mean anything. It's because I've had a lot to drink. It doesn't mean I'm not into doing this, really. I really am attracted to you.' She attempted a pout. 'What do you see when you look at me?'

He looked at her, at her face, her miraculous limbs, the humid tangle of her hair. 'I see the fountain of youth,' he said.

Unfazed, she barely blinked, as if she were often taken for such fountains. 'This is your chance,' she said.

'I'm sorry,' he said. He felt foolish, gullible. 'This shouldn't have happened. I need to know you won't tell anyone.' Something hardened in her eyes, and, alarmed, he put his hands on her shoulders, trying to seem kind, fatherly. 'Look. Listen. You're a beautiful girl. There's no shortage of men who want you. I'll admit I want you. But this isn't something I should be doing. I'm married. I'm your friend's father. All right? Now, let's agree to pretend this never happened.'

'I knew you had a thing for me. That's all.' The hardness turned to quartz. She wore an expression he had often put on his own face, meant to convey warning, disdain, and censure. Again, sadly, he thought that they were familiars, she and him. She angled her head at the fingers resting on her shoulder, the same fingers he had so hastily removed from her mysterious and disappointing interior. 'Do you mind not touching me? I don't want to smell like pussy.'

He dropped his hands to his sides, and she slid past him, face averted, leaving him alone with the laundry and his reflection in the window.

CHAPTER 8

A PARTY ENDS

To Livia's horror, Francis was coming on to her. When he got drunk, he assumed a devil-may-care, man-about-town posture – rakish and self-consciously anachronistic, a dissolute Edwardian cad – and he had started laying it on thick, leaning toward her with wiggling eyebrows and ardent eyes behind his horn-rims.

'May I tell you a secret?' he had said, winking and pulling his chair up so his whale-spotted knees were touching her bare ones.

'Knock yourself out.'

He leaned forward and took her hand, pulling it so close to his mouth that she felt his breath on her knuckles. 'You have to swear – swear on Daphne's baby – that you won't tell anyone.'

'I'm not swearing on her baby.'

Without hesitating, he said, 'I'll tell you anyway.'

'If you insist.'

'You're the most beautiful girl here.' He kissed her fingers.

She laughed, high pitched, incredulous at her own bad luck. She had thought before dinner that Sterling was a sure bet, but then Agatha had moved in. Things had become even more dire because now Sterling was off somewhere – Livia did not know where – and Agatha was missing, too. The coincidence had not escaped the notice of the holdouts on the deck, the party's rear guard: Greyson, Dicky Jr, Francis, Charlie, Dominique, and Piper. Piper, bright eyed from liquor, was curled into a tiny, delighted, sideways ball in her chair, giggling at nothing, a lime green cable-knit sweater pulled over her knees and her bare toes poking out from under the hem. Dominique peeled the label from her beer while Dicky Jr talked, her head angled toward him to suggest she was listening.

After she'd lost track of Sterling, Livia had felt compelled to move on to plan B, which she supposed was Charlie. She'd gotten attached to the idea of having a romp and at this point was willing to take what she could get, within reason. (She did not consider Francis within reason.) But Charlie was one of those confusing boys who was nice all night long and then gave you a kiss on the cheek and went home alone. They had chatted, and she had snuck in some flirtatious touches, but after a while he had excused himself and gone to talk to Piper, who wasn't even single. Livia was deflated. A willing partner shouldn't be so hard to find. Shouldn't she, a twenty-one-year-old girl – a twenty-one-year-old girl who had recently caused a scandal and dropped two dress sizes – be fighting them off with a stick?

'I'm really not,' she said to Francis, 'and we both know it.'

In one quick movement, he dipped his head down and pressed his cheek to her open palm. She looked around the deck, mortified. Charlie smiled at her. 'You are,' Francis said, raising his head. 'I'm smitten.'

'Since when?'

'Since I saw you in the moonlight.'

She snorted and freed her hand.

'It's true!'

'I thought you had a girlfriend, anyway.'

'That's over.'

'What happened?'

'Her tits were too big.'

'What?' Livia said, loud with disbelief. 'Did they grow?'

'No, they were always too big. One day I couldn't take them anymore.'

'Francis, a gentleman would never say that about a woman,' Dicky Jr interjected from across the circle, sounding like Oatsie.

Francis winked at Livia again. 'Only kidding.'

Trying to sound light and teasing, she said, 'How can you say the word "tits" to me when you're doing this whole moonlight and roses thing? Just be normal, Francis.'

'Sorry. You asked.'

Livia caught Dominique's eye, beseeching. 'Hey, Francis,' Dominique called. 'What's this I hear about you being in a monastery?'

Piper, whose gradual withdrawal into her sweater had advanced until not only her legs and feet but hands, chin, mouth, and nose disappeared, popped like a gopher from the crewneck. 'You were in a monastery?' she asked.

'I was.'

'Only for four days,' said Dicky.

Francis fiddled with the beads of his bracelet. 'The monastic environment wasn't for me. But Buddhism is still a very important part of who I am.'

Livia rolled her eyes, and the others saw, and Francis saw them see and looked at her. She met his quizzical gaze with an expression of attentive innocence.

'And,' he went on, 'to be honest, leaving the monastery was a rough transition. I found myself looking around at everyone – you know, people going about their business, going to the post office, going to Whole Foods – and it depressed me that no one stopped and examined the moment in which they were living. Life is all just like, that's my parking space, you're taking too long, I want the last bagel. I don't know. I was feeling very lost. I still think the moment is what matters. You have to *be* in the moment. The moment is the unit of being.'

'So,' Piper said, subsiding back into her sweater, 'are you a vegetarian?'

'I am tonight. I'm allergic to lobster.'

'You ate your weight in smoked salmon,' Dicky said, attempting to smother a burp. 'Salmon isn't a vegetable.'

'Do you meditate?' Piper asked. 'Do you believe in reincarnation?'

Livia could tell Francis was annoyed. She had had a similar conversation with him when they first met and since then had witnessed others trying to get to the bottom of his Buddhism. People tended to be intrigued by the idea of an Upper East Side WASP turning away from materialism and cleaving to lotus blossoms and banyan trees, but since Francis hadn't gone so far as to back up his faith with actual practices, his inquisitors were left with a muddled feeling of having been duped, and he, in turn, felt thwarted and misunderstood. 'Not exactly,' he said.

'Francis is going to be reincarnated as a dung beetle,' said Dicky.

'You're going to be reincarnated as a pig's asshole,' Francis shot back.

'You can't be reincarnated as just part of something. Even a fake Buddhist should know that.'

'Hey,' said Greyson. 'Hey now.'

'Aren't you supposed to believe in that stuff, though?' asked Piper.

'Unfortunately,' Francis said, 'I was born with a logical mind. I'm always struggling to reconcile my spiritual side with my intellect.'

'Don't worry, Piper,' said Greyson. 'We've all tried. We think he's in it for the bracelet.'

Francis held out his wrist. 'This was a gift from a lama in Nepal.'

'You bought it on Canal Street,' Dicky said.

'No, I didn't.'

'Your glasses aren't even prescription.' Dicky almost spat the words.

'So?' Francis said. 'I like them!'

An uncomfortable silence. Dominique shrugged at Livia.

'Maybe we should think about packing it in,' Greyson said, and then Sterling came walking up the lawn.

'Where have *you* been?' Livia demanded, striving for mock haughty but coming off, she feared, as shrill.

He sat down beside her, filling the only gap in their circle. At once Francis backed off, pulling his chair away. There were eight of them, and Livia felt like they were on a camping trip, sheltering in the lee of the house, getting ready to tell ghost stories. 'I went for a walk,' he said.

'Where's Agatha?' said Francis.

Sterling shrugged. 'How should I know?' He seemed perfectly sober. Daphne had said he was like a black hole for alcohol, swallowing it up without a trace.

Francis lifted his eyebrows above his decorative glasses. 'We thought maybe she was with you.'

'Well, she wasn't.' He glanced at Livia, and something slid through his eyes that she did not like. In the short time she had known him, she had seen him wear either a blank, shuttered expression or a knife-and-fork-sharpening look of sexual appraisal. This was neither. Breaking her stare, he pulled a beer from a six-pack under his chair and cracked it. Foam welled up. On an impulse, she leaned forward and sipped the yeasty froth off the top of the can. When she straightened, his odd expression had returned. Through the whirl of her own intoxication she could not be sure, but it looked like compassion.

'Livia.' Her mother was peeking around one of the French doors. She was wearing a cornflower blue cotton bathrobe and sheepskin slippers. The bathrobe was one of Livia's father's, with navy piping and a monogram on the breast pocket.

'What is it?' Livia said rudely. Was it so impossible that she be allowed to sit on the deck and enjoy the party?

Her mother beckoned, almost furtive. 'I need to ask you a favor.'

Livia stood. She was reluctant to leave Sterling alone now that he had come back, but she extricated herself from the circle of chairs and went to her mother. Biddy pulled the door shut behind them. 'Did Daddy tell you about the lobster?' she asked.

'What lobster?' Livia glanced out at the deck. Sterling hadn't moved, but she was afraid he would make a break for it as soon as her back was turned. It was the maneuvering part of the night, time to stalk, feint, wait each other out.

'The sick lobster.'

'What sick lobster? I don't know what you're talking about.'

'When they delivered the lobsters, Daddy unpacked them all on the driveway, and one seemed sick.'

'He unpacked them on the driveway? Why?'

Her mother turned one of her slender hands palm up, like *Who can explain Daddy?* Only the light above the stove was still on, but even in the dimness she looked worn out. She said, 'I didn't know what to do with the sick one, so I put it in the refrigerator in the garage.'

Livia wasn't sure she was keeping up. 'What?'

'I put it in the refrigerator in the garage.'

'Is it dead?'

'I don't know. Will you just please go over there before you go to bed and take care of it for me?'

'You mean like feed it?'

'No.'

Comprehension worked its way through her intoxication. 'You want me to kill it?'

'It's probably already dead.'

Livia looked outside again. 'Can't it wait until the morning, then?'

Her mother followed her gaze. Her hand moved up her robe and held the neck closed. 'Never mind,' she said. 'I'll do it. Otherwise I'll worry all night. I felt bad for it. I put it in the fridge because I heard that the cold makes them sort of hibernate.'

'Why can't Daddy do it?'

'I don't know where he is.'

Her mother seemed vulnerable, almost frail,

standing in that bathrobe, its sash tied neatly at her waist. Livia remembered how she had not forced her to apologize to her father and was grateful. She said, 'You go to bed. I'll take care of the lobster.'

Biddy seemed more relieved than Livia could understand. 'Thank you,' she said, backing toward the doorway. 'See you in the morning.'

Livia watched her go, momentarily distracted from her own sexual prospects. Her mother was as unknowable as Dominique, possibly more so, but she excited neither envy nor curiosity in Livia, only tenderness and anxiety – anxiety for her happiness, her approval, anxiety that Livia might end up being just like her. This last fear was improbable given how different their temperaments were, but her mother had always seemed to live in default mode, gliding along in a well-oiled rut that, theoretically, Livia might be unknowingly shunted into at any moment. She heard a door close upstairs and went back outside and sat down.

'Is everything all right?' Dominique asked.

'Yeah,' said Livia. 'My father has disappeared, and Mom just put a hit out on a lobster.'

Dominique was unfazed. 'He sleeps with the fishes.'

'My dad?'

'The lobster.'

'I think he's sleeping with the beer in the garage,' said Livia.

Francis frowned. 'Your dad?'

'The lobster,' said Livia and Sterling together.

Livia led the way around the back of the house with Sterling following behind her, Indian file they had called it when she was little, as though by walking one after the other any group of school-children was transformed into a band of hunters creeping silently through a forest. Sterling's silence bore down on her, heavy with what was to come, and she was aware of the muscles in her legs working and the damp springiness of the grass under her feet. Patches of fog obscured the stars. She turned onto the path that led to the garage and heard Sterling stumble and land hard in the gravel. 'Fuck,' he said. 'These little rocks sting.'

A flashlight would have been a good idea. She was not fully prepared, either logistically or psychologically, to embark on a drunken mission to kill a lobster, but Sterling had offered to come with her and, as he said, do the dirty work, and she had been so eager to be off the deck and away from the late-night grumpiness brewing there that she had immediately accepted. She wanted to make good on the promise of the early evening and their easy, carnal rapport, which had felt so adult, so mutually recognized and accepted but then had been tainted by the bitter anticipa-tion of a letdown. Was it possible that Sterling had, in fact, already hooked up with Agatha and now was going for her as a nightcap? No, he wouldn't. But she did wish he were more obviously the aggressor.

As soon as they were out of sight of the deck he should have seized her and kissed her to break the ice instead of just trudging along in her wake.

Only a faint light filtered through the trees from the porch, and as she reached to help him up, her fingers accidentally found the softness of his face. 'Sorry. Didn't mean to poke your eye out,' she said.

'Don't worry about it.' He squeezed her hip as he stood, whether to steady himself or as an overture, she couldn't tell. 'We've got a lobster to kill.'

In the garage, she did not turn on the lights but told him to wait and ventured alone into the musty darkness. She set her course by the refrigerator's hum, moving slowly with her arms stretched out, worrying about spiders and rodents but more about how she would look in the harsh fluorescent overheads: tired, and with smudged mascara and an oily nose. She caught her shin on one of the sawhorses that held the canoe and cried out in surprise. 'Did the lobster get you?' Sterling asked.

'Just a canoe.' She made the final blind crossing to the refrigerator and pulled it open, wincing at the sudden light. There was no lobster she could see, only beer and wine and cartons of orange juice and liter bottles of tonic, but then she found the unfortunate crustacean on a bed of seaweed in the salad crisper, its mottled purple claws limp as the gloves of a passed-out boxer. A troop of beer bottles stood in even ranks on the floor, and Livia supposed her mother had taken them out of the drawer to make room.

'Is it dead?' Sterling asked from close behind her.

'I think so.' Grasping the lobster by its thorax, she held it up and studied it. Its claws and antennae dangled. None of its legs so much as twitched. 'Yeah,' she said. 'Looks like it.'

'Kind of sweet that your mom put that seaweed in there.'

Livia set the lobster on the cement floor and reached in to scoop out the seaweed. 'I guess. I don't know what she wants us to do with him.'

'Bury him?'

'Seems like she might as well have left him in the fridge until morning. I don't think she wants us to dump him in the trash.'

'How do you know it's a him?'

'Here.' She held out her handfuls of seaweed to him.

He accepted them. 'Hey, thanks.'

Brushing off her hands, she picked up the lobster and turned it over, pointing to the swimmerets on the underside of its tail. 'I didn't. But it is a he. These ones closest to the body would be soft and feathery if it were a girl. Female lobsters are called hens.'

'What are the males called?'

She put the lobster on the floor. 'Cocks,' she said. She wondered if he had already known that and was teasing her. She began stacking the displaced beer bottles back in the salad crisper. 'This is weird for Mom,' she said. 'Usually she's not so tenderhearted. She's more practical.'

'People get weird at weddings.'

When the beer was put away, she looked around. 'Do you have the lobster?'

'No, I have the seaweed.' He shook the bunches of dark strands like sinister pom-poms.

'Didn't I put him right here?'

'Maybe he ran away.'

'He was dead. Wasn't he?'

'Can we turn on some more lights?'

Livia opened the freezer, widening the wedge of light on the floor. One long, whiskery antenna swept across the cement, almost brushing her foot. 'There he is,' she said. Grateful the lobster's claws were still banded, she reached into the darkness and found its cold carapace. When she picked him up, his claws did not droop as they had; there was life in his body. 'He's alive. Wow.'

'It's the Christ lobster,' said Sterling.

'Now what do we do? After all this, it seems like a shame to kill him, and I don't just want to leave him.'

Sterling tossed the seaweed into the air like confetti. Bits of it landed on Livia, cold and slick. 'Obviously,' he said, 'we have to set him free.'

They walked down the driveway and along the bike path beside the road, bound for the nearest salt water, a marshy inlet off the long harbor. Livia had gone inside for a flashlight and had also retrieved a canvas bag monogrammed with her mother's initials for the lobster to ride in.

'I don't know if he'll survive in the marsh,' she said to Sterling, who was carrying the lobster bag. 'Crabs do. I don't actually know very much about lobsters. I know they like rocky places, and they move around quite a bit, in different depths, but I don't know about this kind of brackish environment. We'd have to drive to the marina for anything better, though, and neither of us is in any shape for that.'

'I could drive,' Sterling said. 'You should have said so.'

'Really?' she said, skeptical but not wanting to sound prissy. 'Next time.'

'What's the matter, Jacques? Don't you trust me?'

'Jacques?'

'Cousteau.'

'Oh.'

'The majesty of *la mer*,' he said in a French accent. 'The genius of zee lobster oo pretends to be dead zo as not to be for zee eating. 'E waits in his silent refrigerator tomb, 'oping zat rescue will arrive.'

'Lobsters have really simple brains,' she said.

They walked on, the flashlight bobbing over the asphalt path and the sand and sharp grass at its edges. She should have been playing along, she knew, keeping the flirtation going the way Agatha would have, but she was beginning to sober up and to worry that Sterling was slipping off the hook. If she were with Teddy, she would know what jokes to make, what to say and do. She was always missing Teddy at the wrong times. 'I weesh,' she said, putting a lame, semi-Gallic elongation on her vowels, 'zat I could be sure ee could survive in zee marsh. I simply do not know.'

Sterling was silent. She wanted to shine the flashlight full in his face to see what he was thinking. 'Well,' he said finally, 'starving in a marsh beats getting boiled.'

'Does it?'

The few inches of darkness between their shoulders seemed to widen as they walked, spreading into a gulf, and by the time they reached the marsh, he might have been miles away, out to sea even, in a boat she had not been invited aboard. The flashlight, as though powered by the energy between them, began to dim and flicker. 'Come on,' Livia said, shaking it. The beam steadied, and she led the way down a side path, through a clump of maples and down to where reeds and cordgrass took over and the soil turned oozy and pulled at her sandals. She stopped where the water began: inert and ominous, punctured by reeds and steamed over with fog. It was no more than a thin black membrane on the silt, but it stretched to become the surface of the harbor and then the skin of the open ocean, touching all the continents.

'This is no good,' she said to Sterling. 'It's too shallow and mucky. He'll just die.' She turned and shone the dying beam down another path. 'I think, though, if we go this way, there's a little beach at the end of the marsh. It's not too far.'

She expected he would say no, even mock her for wasting so much effort to save a lobster identical to the one making its way through her digestive tract, but he said, 'Okay,' and they walked ahead, following the wan, bobbling light. By the time they reached a strip of clear sand, the flashlight was in its death throes, but Livia knew they were in the right place because she could hear the water moving in the harbor and, farther out, rolling waves.

'So,' Sterling said, 'we just put him on the beach, and he goes galloping in?'

'I think he'll have the best chance if we toss him out a ways.'

'Assuming he's not already dead.' Sterling opened the bag, and as Livia shone the light on what looked to be a dead lobster, the last of the batteries ran out, leaving them in the dark. 'I think we knew that was going to happen,' Sterling said.

'Yes.'

'Well, let's do what we came to do.'

For the second time, Livia's blind fingers found the lobster's shell, which was still cold but now dry. She lifted him out of the bag, willing him to give some sign of life. 'We have to take the bands off his claws,' she said to Sterling.

'Sure.'

'Can you do it?'

His fingers found her arms and traveled up them to the lobster. She felt him tugging. 'If I had never seen a lobster,' he said, 'I don't know what I would make of the thing I'm touching right now.'

'Careful not to pull his arms off.'

'I'm trying.' He grunted. 'Okay. Done. He seems dead to me, but he's tricked us before.'

'Agreed.' She stepped out of her sandals and walked toward the sound of the water until its coldness lapped over her feet and then up to her ankles and knees. The hem of her dress dragged in the water. Under her feet the harbor sand was pebbly and a little slimy. Holding the lobster with both hands, she drew him back to her hip and then flung him out over the water, trying for a long, low toss. A splash in the dark. She felt a tremendous relief, as though she had done a great and necessary good. They were having an adventure, she and Sterling. They were going to great lengths, silly lengths, to treat an animal with dignity, but he hadn't complained once. And if he had come along this far, he must want her. Striking off into the dark, back toward shore, she felt almost giddy, overflowing with anticipation. But quickly she realized she wasn't sure she was heading in the right direction. How simple it seemed to get back to dry land – not far – but the darkness under the fog was absolute. She walked a few steps this way, a few steps that way, trying to follow the rise of the sand, but she stepped into a sudden hole and her dress was soaked up to the thighs. She climbed out in the direction she thought was shore, but the water only got deeper. She stopped. 'Sterling?' she called. A sensation of precariousness came over her, a feeling that he was gone, that land itself was gone, and she was wandering along the edge of a great depth.

'I'm here.'

His voice was farther away than she had expected and muffled by the fog, which was settling in droplets on her hair and eyelashes. She hugged herself, chilled. The water around Waskeke was always cold, even in summer. 'Keep talking so I can follow your voice,' she said.

A silence, and then he began to sing her name. 'Livia,' he sang. 'Livia, Livia, Livia.' His voice was pleasant, baritone, not reedy like Greyson's but gruff and sly.

She moved toward him, and the water receded to her knees and then her ankles. He stopped singing. She stopped moving. 'Don't stop,' she said.

A tiny light appeared, like a distant lighthouse, diffusing through the fog in a soft, pale sphere and then fading to something smaller, like a firefly. He had lit a cigarette. She was close enough that she could smell the tobacco and hear him take a drag. The firefly floated in a little curlicue, enticing her. Or maybe it was not a firefly but the bioluminous lure of an anglerfish, lighting the way to a set of nasty jaws. Maybe she had stumbled out of an ordinary night and into a benthic underworld. 'Livia,' he sang again. 'Livia, Livia.'

Winn sat in the driveway behind the wheel of the Land Rover. He had needed a place to hide, somewhere smaller and safer than the outdoors but not in the house, which had been such a welcome sight when he arrived but now loomed like an enemy fortress. The window of his bedroom was still lit. Biddy must be reading. That warm yellow room seemed so far away, the bed with its white sheets, the wooden whale spouting on the wall, his wife propped up on her elbow, her face shiny with nighttime lotions. A while before, he had seen Livia and Sterling go walking down the driveway, her with a flashlight and him with a canvas bag. Ordinarily, he would have accosted them, asking what was in the canvas bag and where they were going and why (although the why was obvious enough), but tonight he lacked the heart and, after the laundry room, the authority. So he sat, alone in the car, trying to think of nothing. He wished for his father. If he could have been anywhere in space and time, he would have been sitting across from his father in the lounge of the Vespasian Club, reading the newspaper and not speaking.

After Winn's wedding, his mother refused to venture outside the white stone house ever again, preferring to live out her days sequestered on the top floor. When he came to Boston for Ophidian dinners or business meetings, he had sometimes detoured past the house at night and stood on the sidewalk or peered out from the back of a taxi, looking up at the lit window of his mother's room atop the dark mass of the sleeping house, an eerie beacon of unseen life. His mother did not once leave in the two years she lingered, and he saw her only three times: twice when she summoned him to what she imagined was her deathbed and then the last time when, after a sickly lifetime of false alarms, she died. Her room, even at the end, was perfectly tidy, kept in order by her Ukrainian nurse. When he thought of his mother, he always imagined her surrounded by hypochondriac squalor: jars of foul-smelling tinctures, balled tissues, rows of potion bottles, trays of mold-covered food. But those three times he went to bid her farewell, she was sitting upright in a bed of worn but fresh-smelling blankets in a clean room, her withered hands folded neatly on a crisp strip of turned-down sheet.

'What does she do all day?' he had asked Eva once as he left.

'She is waitink for God to find her,' Eva said, crossing herself. 'Every day she wait. She is a saint, your mama.'

The house, when Winn sold it after his mother's death, was a wintery landscape of sheeted furniture. He hired an appraiser to go through the whole place, taking away whatever could be sold, and then he went in to sort out the personal debris left behind in rooms where missing lamps and chairs were memorialized by clean, dark voids on the faded carpets and dusty floors. The Vespasian had politely declined his offer of Tipton's portrait, and so it had still been in the dining room, wrapped in brown paper and propped against a wall, waiting for some boys from the Sobek Club to come pick it up. They had promised to give the painting a place of honor in their clubhouse and to fix a plaque on the frame with Tipton's name, dates, and graduation year.

'Why don't we take it home with us?' Biddy had said.

'No,' said Winn, having already considered and rejected the idea of installing his father's judgmental gaze in their newly purchased Connecticut house. 'He would want it to go to one of his clubs.'

In his father's study Winn found a decades-long paper trail of soured investments and minutely recorded household expenses, antiseptic letters from longtime friends, playing cards, unidentifiable currency, stationery from clubs and hotels, clipped newspaper articles about people Tipton knew. Opening an Exeter yearbook from 1926, Winn found, written in his father's spidery hand across the youthful faces of the boys, 'deceased, 1943,' 'deceased, 1965,' 'deceased, 1941.' There were bits of ephemera from Winn's school days: a program from his turn as Colonel Pickering in *My Fair Lady*, a stained necktie patterned with the Ophidian crest that Tipton must have rescued from the trash, a poorly typed essay on the financing of World War I.

The appraiser had taken away Tipton's desk – a vast, oaken extravagance with as many nooks and cubbies as a dovecote – and left behind stacks of papers and boxes of miscellaneous junk on the floor. One box was topped with a note that said its contents had come from a locked drawer and to excuse the intrusion but the key had been found in another drawer. Inside was a thin stack of hopelessly quaint girly magazines, a chrome tube of old lipstick that had acquired a translucent yellow rind, a palm-sized photo album mostly containing black-and-white snapshots of women Winn did not recognize, a cryptic letter signed only 'L,' and an old photo case, its velvet dappled and squashed with age. This held a portrait of a smirking teenage boy and a stern old man. The image was faded, the background erased except for a floating piece of drapery, bound with a fat cord and tassel, part of a photographer's set. The figures had turned so ghostly and transparent that the grain of the paper showed through their clothes. Winn knew that his grandfather, Tipton's father, Frederick, was the boy, although his longish hair and old-fashioned suit were unfamiliar and his features, heavy and morose by the time he became the old man Winn remembered, the man beneath whose painted visage the Vespasian billiard balls spun and clacked, were tender and wicked as a faun's in the photograph. Pretty and slight, he stood leaning against the old man's chair, and his sardonic eyes were trained on some spot above the camera, his narrow mouth pursed. The old man stared into the lens with what might have been defiance, scowling beneath a voluminous thicket of white eyebrows and the twin tusks of his long moustache. He had one leg stretched out into the obliterated white space of the photo's perimeter. His hands were balled in fists on his lap. This was Winn Cunningham, source of Winn's name and of the white stone house and whatever fortune still rolled around the increasingly empty Van Meter vaults. Winn took the photo from its case and turned it over. The reverse was blank.

He had delegated Biddy, six months pregnant with Daphne, to go through his mother's clothes – what she would find he could not imagine, perhaps a wedding dress and then fifty years of nightgowns – and floorboards creaked above him. He put the picture in the trash and, after he leafed through them, also the magazines with their plump, bare-breasted pinups. Taking up the other photos and the letter from L, he wondered, as he often had, if his father had strayed. Surely he must have. Winn found himself hoping that he had, that Tipton had known some flicker of human warmth in those long years between marriage and death. The little photo album might have been a trophy case for conquests. He paused over one woman whose portrait had been tinted by an inexpert hand, her cheeks painted a feverish red and her irises a light green that bled out to her lashes, giving her a blind, alien appearance. He set the album on top of the magazines.

Many times Winn had regretted discarding the contents of that drawer, especially the photo of his grandfather, and as he sat in the musty darkness of the old Rover, he wished again that he hadn't. The act of dropping those bits of paper in the garbage seemed, in retrospect, unutterably cruel. He had discarded the image and the letter and the photos to prove his own lack of sentimentality, not pausing to consider that they were reliquaries of his forefathers' secret hearts. He would, he knew, leave behind no trace of his encounter with Agatha, his one physical infidelity in a lifetime of mental adulteries, bodies he had touched only with the curious fingers of supposition. As he looked up at the lit window of his bedroom, the full weight of shame settled on him: guilt for having betrayed someone as fine as Biddy, fear that he would be exposed, sadness that the dignity and restraint he prided himself on were illusions, embarrassment at the tawdriness of the washing machine, the girl half his age, the lustful murmurings and groans she had heard escape his lips. He needed some air. He cranked down the window, letting in damp air and the sound of crickets. Biddy's light upstairs went out.

A movement at the side of the house, and a male voice said, 'Don't slam it. The sign says.' Three figures emerged to the sound of crunching gravel. He couldn't quite make out which boys they were, what iteration of Duffs. Ordinarily, he would have hounded them for proof of sobriety, or at least a convincing imitation, and threatened to call a taxi until one of them swore he had stopped drinking hours before and was by now as unpolluted as a Shirley Temple. But he sat as still as he could, hoping they would not see him. It was Francis, Dicky Jr, and Charlie. They had almost passed safely by when Charlie did a double take and peered at him from across the driveway.

'Mr Van Meter?' he said.

'Heading out, boys?' Winn said. 'Is one of you fit to drive?'

Listing sideways, Francis raised an imaginary drink in a toast. 'I am.'

'Good,' said Winn. 'All right then.'

Charlie stepped closer. 'Everything okay?'

'Fine. Just came out to listen to the radio, check the news.' Winn gestured at the dashboard. The radio was not on.

'Cool,' said Charlie. Behind him, Francis turned abruptly and rushed into the darkness.

'I think he had to puke,' said Dicky Jr.

'Are you sure you're okay out here?' Charlie asked.

'Yes, perfectly fine. Good night, boys.' He rolled the window back up. He and Charlie watched each other through the rising pane of glass, then the younger man shrugged, waved, and turned away.

When their taillights had disappeared down the driveway, Winn went into the house. Someone had turned out the lamp, but Celeste was still on the couch, emitting a low splutter. He passed her by without a second glance. Out on the deck, the lanterns burned unattended, but he left them. He wanted nothing but to be in his bed, next to Biddy, safe in the absolving darkness. He had started up the stairs when he heard, from above, the unmistakable swampy sounds of two people kissing. A woman whimpered softly. He stopped, exasperated. Was there no end to it? When he started to ease back down, the stairs creaked a parody of the feminine cry he had just heard, and he stopped again. The kissing sounds continued unabated. Those brazen, suctioning smacks, the sheer audacity of the stairwell kissers seemed outrageous, and he decided he would not be cowed by whatever lascivious display was being put on in his home. He stomped purposefully up and, rounding the bend, was greeted by the sight of Greyson and Daphne clinging to each other. Daphne, in her nightgown, was leaning against the wall, framed family photos hanging askew around her, and Greyson craned over her belly, his hands braced on either side of her head, kissing her with singular purpose. Winn cleared his throat and edged around them.

'Oh,' Daphne said. 'Daddy. I got up to see if people were still here.'

'All right,' Winn said. 'Good night.' He pushed by with the harried, businesslike air of a man leaving his office and waving farewell with a folded newspaper.

The bedroom was dark and quiet. Biddy lay still.

In the distance, a foghorn sounded, not the deep warning bellow he remembered from childhood but an automated tone, dulcet and polite. He lay watching the lighthouse beam swing across the walls. Livia had been to parties at the Sobek, but she said she'd never seen the portrait of Tipton. Perhaps over the years it had migrated to some inner sanctum. Perhaps it had been thrown out. He counted off five seconds between flashes, his lips moving in the dark. One, two, three, four, five, and then light shot through the window and raced across his robe hanging from the bathroom door, touched the chest of drawers, the oil painting of a crab, the basket of shells the girls had collected long ago, the soft rise in the blankets where Biddy's legs were. Winn felt honored by the beam's presence in his bedroom, included. The brief wash of light, flying over the shingled houses and dark salt grass before sweeping out to sea and back around again, was so quick that it might have been a ghost or headlights from a passing car except that it came back every five seconds, like clockwork, exactly as he expected.

FRIDAY

CHAPTER 9

SNAKES AND LADDERS

After Winn settled into a measured snore, Biddy slipped out of bed. Fog sieved through the window screens and hovered in a cool gauze through which the lighthouse beam swept like an oar. For a moment she stood looking down at her husband, his shadowy mouth agape, and then she went into the dark bathroom and sat on the edge of the tub. She was so very tired. She had been lying awake for too long, her thoughts skipping between daughters, rattling down lists of to-dos, ricocheting irresistably into the future, where an infinite number of potential calamities lay in wait for the baby or the girls or herself. Usually, she could control her thoughts; usually, she fell right to sleep, but tonight she couldn't fight the current. Nor could she stay beside Winn, listening to him sleep.

She reached out and turned the bath tap, releasing a gush of water. Winn would not wake, not once he had begun snoring. She fit the rubber plug into place, pulled her nightgown over her head, dropped her cotton underwear onto the bathmat. Her shadowy reflection loomed in the half-steamed mirror, setting off a childish thrill of fear along a wavelength that extended back through the decades to when Celeste and Tabitha had held her by the wrists as they chanted in dark bathrooms, summoning spirits. She eased herself into the water, feeling a stinging in her chilled toes and another, blunter shock as her shoulders met cold porcelain. She arched away, bracing the bony crook of her skull on the tub's edge, and then lowered herself more carefully, settling in, scooping hot water up over her chest and shoulders.

When the bath was comfortably deep, she reached with a toe to turn off the tap, and silence fell, broken only by the drip of the faucet and the distant tone of the foghorn. She sighed, loudly but only once, purely for her own benefit. Winn, helping Agatha after she'd fallen off the deck, had been so chivalrous, so attentive, so *obvious*. The obviousness was what she could not tolerate. She had known what he was when she married him, had expected to be the kind of wife who looked the other way from time to time, but she had also expected him to be discreet. And he had been. She assumed there had been other women, but she had never come across any evidence of them, which was all she asked. A simple request, she had thought: cheap repayment for her forbearance, her realism, her tolerance. At times his discretion had been so complete she had allowed herself to think maybe there *hadn't* been others, but she didn't like to risk being foolish enough to believe in something as unlikely as her husband's fidelity. He must know how comical his lust for Agatha was, how vulgar. Over the years Agatha had never shown any reciprocation beyond the laziest, most reflexive flirting. But tonight she had grasped his shirt after he pulled her back up onto the deck.

Biddy cupped water in her hands and brought them to her face. There was no way around it – she would be exhausted in the morning. She inhaled, tasting the steam. The bath began to perform the magic she had experienced in water all her life, draining away stress like infection from a wound, restoring balance. After the wedding, her life would go on as it always had. The baby would be healthy. Livia would find a new boyfriend. Winn would go to work and come home. What had Dominique asked? Where she would live if she could live anywhere? Maybe they could move to Waskeke full-time in a few years. Maybe they could go abroad for an extended trip, rent a house in France, visit Dominique's restaurant, take a river cruise.

She was walking through a field of lavender, alone except for buzzing bees when something choked her. The air turned thick and terrible, and she awoke, coughing up lukewarm bathwater.

Again, Winn woke before dawn. He was too hot, and his heart was beating too quickly, racing along in the futile hurry he remembered from hangovers past. Everything came back. Agatha leaning against the washing machine. The smell of her hair. The feel of her arms and thighs, the shocking lifelessness of her face, the sticky friction of her arid pussy. Bringing his fingers to his nose, he found only a mild sourness that might have been the odor of his own clammy, boozy sleep. Beside him, Biddy breathed evenly, and though the sound shamed him, he couldn't keep from imagining what would have happened if he had not seen Agatha's face in that one unguarded moment or if he had ignored its troubling vacancy. If their encounter had reached its natural conclusion, his sin would be more severe, but in the disenchanting postcoital lull, her face with its wine-stained teeth might have summoned the antidotal regret he remembered from the more ill-advised couplings of his youth, a little curative disappointment.

And Livia. Had she returned? He told himself Sterling would take care of her, and then he told himself not to be ridiculous. Fumbling for his glasses, he picked up the clock, angling it toward the window and waiting for the lighthouse to illuminate its face. Five fifteen. Less than three hours' sleep, but he saw no possibility of dozing off again. He had a tennis match arranged for nine o'clock, an hour that seemed exasperatingly distant. Rising, he went into the bathroom and flipped on the light. The face in the mirror was haggard, gray skinned, and filmed with a sickly sheen. He gulped some water from the faucet, and the pain in his head expanded like a sponge. There was no oil in his joints, no spring in his step, no bend in his spine, no forgiveness in his stomach. When he was young, he hadn't appreciated what a marvelous gift it was to be able to shrug off any depravity, upchuck all toxins, and drop back into a contented sleep. The towel he reached for was damp, as was, he realized, the bathmat under his bare feet, and indeed the bathtub itself had a shallow puddle around the drain. Biddy must have taken a bath before turning in. Probably she had a lot to soak away. He was sorry for his spat with Livia; there had been no need. Blame the drink.

He returned to bed, but sleep did not come. Instead, he was bombarded by fantasies, grim ones of Livia floating on the tide, inexplicably drowned, and also lewd visions of Agatha. He was pinned against the mattress, pilloried by dread and longing. He pressed his face into his pillow and groaned with contrition. As though she sensed something amiss, Biddy rolled from her side to her back and made a small, disapproving sound. He turned to face her, studying the dim contours of her brow, nose, lips, and chin, and then he tunneled an investigatory hand under the sheets to her hip. She wore a short tunic of white cotton, plain as a pillowcase, without sleeves or embellishment of any kind, the latest in a long succession of such nightgowns, each indistinguishable from the last, that she had been wearing for all the summers he had known her. The garments had a tendency to ride up and expose the equally white and plain underwear she favored, but now, puzzlingly, he found a naked flank. Never had he known Biddy to go to bed without underwear. Her skin was warm, a little tacky, as though she had just put on lotion. He caressed the bare knoll of her hipbone and slid his hand across her lower belly, her pubic hair tickling the side of his pinky. Agatha's fantastical, indecent softness flared in his memory, but he scooted closer, pressing his face into the crook of Biddy's neck. She turned her head away but did not wake.

'Biddy,' he whispered to the underside of her earlobe. 'Bid.' He ran his hand up to her small breast, feeling the lazy beat of her heart under his palm. He touched his lips to her shoulder. The skin there was cool. Suddenly he was desperate. He could not remember when he had last wanted her so badly. Possibly never. The breast under his hand was soft and warm, the skin loose over the convoluted plumbing of its interior, the nipple permanently enlarged by breastfeeding twenty years in the past. If he had only wanted to exorcise his frustrated passions, he would have gone instead to jerk off in the bathroom like a guilty teenager, but this was something else, something surprising. Her body was no longer pristine; her skin had lost its youthful pliancy; she had none of Agatha's thrilling newness, the black magic he had sucked from her tannic mouth. Every inch of Biddy was known to him. But still her sleeping presence acted on him more powerfully than anything under Agatha's skirt.

'Biddy,' he said. 'Biddy, wake up.'

'Hmmm?' she said, stirring under his proddings. 'What is it?'

He kissed her. The gentle fug of her breath only inflamed him more, and he shifted his weight onto her body, nudging her knees apart.

'I'm sleeping,' she said into his mouth. 'I'm so tired.'

'Please, sweetheart,' he whispered.

The word 'sweetheart' was a signal, used only under cover of deepest privacy and need. Biddy said, 'Mmm,' and then nothing more, and Winn wasn't sure if she was considering her options or if she had fallen back asleep. After a moment he nudged her and said, 'Biddy.'

'Oh,' she said. 'You're serious. All right, fine.'

With profound relief, he eased his creaky, lusty, penitent, weary, gin-soaked sinner's body onto and into the sanctuary that was Biddy. He thought he might embarrass himself by weeping. He would not have much in the way of stamina, but given the pain in his head and the miasmic fumes rising from his stomach, that was just as well. Biddy seemed to have intuited that his requirements were basic and animal, with no room for frills, and she lay without moving, her hands resting lightly on his back, while, breath hissing and shorts tangled around his ankles, he took his succor. He was close to finishing, could hear the harpsongs and see the cloudy peaks, when a reservoir of saliva that had been collecting behind his bottom teeth overflowed and fell in a long, thin string onto Biddy's chest. He paused. She did not seem to notice that he had drooled on her. In fact, she seemed to be asleep. His first impulse was to wake her, but then again she had not given the impression of being so concerned with the details of this specific sexual episode that she would insist on witnessing its climax. The gentlemanly thing might be to write off the whole attempt as ill-fated and accept his frustration as karmic punishment for being a sorry old goat. But. He could not ignore the fact that he was, at the moment, within hailing distance of the shores of paradise. As his wife, would Biddy begrudge him the use of her body in attaining this one moment of desperately needed release? Well, said the heckler who lived under his bleachers, she would if she knew what you got up to last night. And with that, he went soft.

He stood in the shower for a long time, but it washed away nothing, neither his shame nor his hangover, and he cranked the water off in desolation. He peed and worried fleetingly about prostate cancer, and then he put on his tennis whites and his bathrobe over them, shuffling his feet into an ancient pair of calfskin slippers. Dense, milky fog filled the house, its infinite particles riding air currents in swirls and swarms that appeared in the yellow pulses of lighthouse light and then vanished again into the dormant gray air. The light was like something breathing. On his way downstairs, he paused outside Livia's door, listening to Celeste's snores. Carefully, he turned the doorknob and peeked inside – no Livia.

In the semidarkness of the kitchen he put on a pot of coffee and poured a glass of orange juice. The regular sound of the foghorn felt suspenseful and jarring, and in between tones his ears rang with silence; the sandpapering of his slipper soles on the kitchen tile was shockingly loud. In the living room, Greyson was asleep on the couch, flat on his face, still fully dressed. Winn crept past him and paused in the doorway to the laundry room, taking in the hospital-white enamel of the washing machine, the nest of twisted linens on the floor. The Band-Aids he had peeled off Agatha's arm were scattered around, their undersides spotted with blood, and he went in to pick them up, scraping with his fingernails at one that had stuck to the tiles.

He was still in there when the screen door creaked. Poking his head into the hall, he saw Livia's back as she set down her sandals and canvas bag and eased the door shut. The immensity of his relief surprised him. She was alive, whole and herself, trying not to be caught, up on tiptoe, slender fingers splayed against the door as she pushed it gently into place. Winn ducked back into the laundry room and hid behind the door, holding his breath as she padded down the hall. He listened to her whispering to Greyson, trying to wake him. Greyson grunted, and the couch

245

springs squeaked. He wondered if they smelled the coffee, if they would discover him, but in a minute, Greyson tiptoed down the hall and let himself out. The Jeep started in the driveway. Gravel crunched; the engine faded; Livia's footsteps trailed up the stairs.

Winn settled in his study, in the tall, winged chair behind his desk, and eyed the pull chain of his brass lamp without reaching for it. There was enough light now. A thin stack of envelopes sat on the corner of his blotter, stray mailings periodically collected by the caretakers: advertisements for a cable company, requests for donations, an ancient thank-you note regarding a dinner the previous summer that he could not recall. These he tossed into the wastebasket. He wrote the caretakers their quarterly check and a note requesting possible explanations and remedies for the vegetable garden's dismal yield, and he sealed these in an envelope that was rippled with damp, its flap already gummy. He wanted the distraction of work, but there was no work to be done. His blotter was pristine and uncluttered. He had left everything at home, bundled and stacked on his desk. If only he could be paying bills, signing his name, squaring stamps, licking bitter flaps. He considered calling in to the office, but no one would be there.

His eyes passed over the spine of an old photo album on a bottom shelf, and he thought again about the lost photographs from his father's desk.

Over the years he had banished most of his familial artifacts out to this house, where they might peacefully decompose in the salt atmosphere. Old possessions led to reminiscence, and reminiscence meant reckoning his accounts, scanning his ever-lengthening columns of deeds, being reminded that one day there would be a final total, carved in stone. Such dreary thoughts had no place in his workaday life of commuter trains and industrial averages, and so he sequestered them on the island, where morbidity, like all other things, was tempered by the breezes and contained by the comforting moat of the Atlantic. But now he took the album to his desk and sat with it.

The first pages were occupied by portraits of his grandfather Frederick as an old man and one of his mother on her wedding day, followed by a series of black-and-white prints of his father and his father's friends: pale, well-tonsured men standing side by side or sitting, knees crossed, in rooms Winn recognized from the Boston house or from his father's clubs. He paused over the one he always paused over. It was a small snapshot, three inches square, of his father standing beside the billiards table at the Vespasian Club, cue in hand, smiling broadly at something off to his right, while above him Frederick looked sternly down from the wall. Of all the photos, this was the only one in which Tipton looked happy.

The Vespasian, on a hill near the State House, had been Tipton's home, really, much more so than the pallid house where he and his wife dwelt like strangers. He ate most of his dinners there, read his newspapers, and convened his friendships. It was a large, dapper building touched with classical details – acanthus leaves, white pediments over the windows, columns flanking the front door. A bronze plaque on one of the columns read 'Est. 1901,' marking the year a Mr Arthur Andrew Depuis died and bequeathed his home to a collection of industrialists and politicians who had previously been known as the Seahorse Society and who, after moving into their new headquarters, renamed themselves the Vespasian Club.

The building was grand, gloomy, and over-heated. From the front door, a long entranceway led into a round sort of foyer, floored with black-and-white tiles from which a nautiliform staircase twisted upward. The foyer was referred to as the Keep and was the hub of all the other rooms, tall, square chambers lit by chandeliers with burned-out bulbs and dusty crystals. From the street, the club looked like four stories, but it also had an attic that accommodated a small but functional theater and a sublevel made possible by the angle of the hillside that held a swimming pool with a mosaic bottom depicting a chariot race. Glass doors wrapped in wrought-iron ivy gave access to a walled, sloping garden.

The major alterations to the Vespasian since Winn's boyhood were the acceptance of female members in the early 1980s and, in 1991, the replacement of the pool's treacherous and eroded marble deck with cement. But otherwise, little had changed. The same huge copy of Canaletto's mossy *Colosseum* still hung in the dining room. Vichyssoise was still offered for lunch every day in summer. At meals, diners still scooped their own side dishes from silver trays held low by uniformed staff. For Christmas there were still Yule logs, pine boughs, carols, and buttered rum, and every year on the attic stage members put on an impromptu (though not really) pageant with a red-nosed old man draped in tablecloths as the Virgin Mary and, as the baby Jesus, a ham. A certain Mr Grimshaw, more spots appearing each year on the hands that proffered the pen for the registry, still presided in gartered shirtsleeves over the front desk, which was not really a desk but a room off the entrance hall – Grimshaw's little fiefdom, crowded with trays of loose papers, battered mahogany mailboxes, and a hanging row of keys with heavy brass fobs that opened the handful of rooms on the fourth floor where members could spend the night. In one of these rooms, the key stolen when Grimshaw wasn't looking, Winn had been relieved of his virginity by sixteen-year-old Lucette Winters (not a virgin) while downstairs his father and her parents finished dinner.

In his bachelor years, he found the club was a good place to bring dates. Girls who were not part of his world were impressed by it, and those who already belonged felt reassured. They thought that by bringing them to the club he was making a promise to abide by the rules of their common caste. If you fit in here, they reasoned, and I fit in here, then we are two puzzle pieces molded by nature and nurture to fit nicely together, me with you and you with me. If you take me up to the billiards room and show me the portrait of your grandfather, you are showing me that you are mindful of family, that you are someone who has a line to carry on, as I do. If you stand when I leave the table and stand again and pull out my chair for me when I return, then you are telling me you take me seriously and that this is a serious courtship, and later, when we are standing on my doorstep, I will understand that what you are asking for is not a freebie but a deposit on our future.

Before Biddy, the only girl who got at all under his skin was Ophelia Haviland (the future Fee Fenn, wife to Jack and mother to Teddy), whose father had been in the Ophidian and had chosen her cruel name because its first syllable reminded him of his club. Haviland Sr had many clubs in common with Tipton, and though Haviland's passion for the Ophidian and Tipton's failure to gain admission was a source of tension, the two men were friendly. Winn had been dimly aware of Ophelia for years but thought of her as a kid until he was twenty-eight and she twenty-three and they kissed at the Vespasian's New Year's Eve dance. She was not as beautiful as he would have liked (her eyes bulged slightly), but she was intelligent and athletic and always light and pleasant in social situations and could be counted on never to embarrass him by being overly serious or overly flighty. Plus, he was still holding out hope that his twenty-eighth year would be the witching hour when he gave up his boyish ways, and he took his regard for Ophelia as a sign of his own growing maturity, even though he remained troubled by the possibility that he might find an equally compelling woman whose eyes did not bulge.

After six months, on a hot summer night when the Vespasian's windows were open in hopes of catching any torpid breeze that might happen by, Winn found himself playing pool with Ophelia's father while the girl and her mother were in the attic attending a slide show put on by a member about his travels through the Soviet Union. Haviland had unbuttoned his collar and rolled up his sleeves in concession to the heat, but he was a tall, immaculate man who never seemed to suffer physical discomfort or indignity of any kind, and his face and shirt were perfectly dry. Winn, lining up a shot, was tormented by the dark circles under his arms and the sweat on his face that, as he focused on the cue ball, dripped off the end of his nose, leaving a dark spot on the green baize. He shot poorly and then turned to collect his drink from the windowsill and to mop his face with a cocktail napkin. Haviland marched around the table, chalking his cue with deadly focus, and knocked first the seven ball and then the three tidily into a corner pocket.

'I think you've got me, sir,' Winn said, standing against the window with his arms slightly raised in the vain hope that the muggy air would dry him.

'Hmm,' Haviland said. 'Yes.' He moved to the end of the table and, after again attempting to drill his cue through the chalk cube, bent and reached out one long arm to line up the eight ball. Winn gazed up at the portrait of his grandfather. Frederick looked glum in the painting, jowly and frowning above his white tie.

'He was a queer, you know,' Haviland said casually. 'Side pocket.' He shot the stick between his knuckles and sent the cue ball sailing into the eight ball with a clunk. The eight ball bumped off the cushions, narrowly missed the side pocket, and spun to a stop.

'Pardon?' Winn said.

'Your grandfather.' Haviland angled the cue back over his shoulder at the painting. 'He was a queer.'

Winn half smiled, unsure what the joke was. 'I don't know what you mean.'

'How much more plainly can I say it? He was a queer, a fairy, a homosexual. Didn't you know? It's your shot.'

Winn stood rooted. 'I think you're confused. He was married. He had my father.'

A long, shaded lamp hung over the pool table,

illuminating it like a stage. Haviland rested his hands on the edge and leaned forward into the light. He looked perfectly serious. 'Don't worry,' he said, 'it's not common knowledge, but it is the truth. Probably you've run across a few people who know, but your father has been very effective at making sure the whole story gets forgotten for your sake. I only know because I've become the unofficial club historian. A few stray clues in old letters caught my attention. I followed up. Even in Tipton's day most people didn't know. He was very discreet. My father knew him. I knew him well enough, too, and I would never have guessed. Do you know who Winn Cunningham was?'

'He was my grandfather's uncle. He helped him get into business.'

Haviland grinned. 'That's the line? Well. Tipton's wise to keep the story simple. No, Winn Cunningham was *not* related to Frederick. Cunningham owned a paper mill. Frederick and his father worked there. You see where I'm going. Your great-grandfather essentially sold Frederick to Cunningham when he was fifteen or sixteen. Naturally, they were extremely poor. Desperate. Frederick was supposedly very handsome as a young man. Cunningham took him in and paid for his education and kept him in fashionable clothes, and then he was considerate enough to die while Frederick was still young. Cunningham had no family, or at least none who wanted to contest the will, and so Frederick inherited several mills, several ships, your house,

253

whatever else there was.' Haviland regarded the table and then thoughtfully leaned over and sank the eight ball. After it disappeared with a soft *plunk* into the pocket, he recollected himself. 'Oh, it was your shot, wasn't it? I apologize. I didn't even call the pocket. I don't know what I was thinking. I concede the game. Rack them again, will you?'

'Wait,' Winn said. He wiped his forehead with his sleeve. 'Hold on.'

'That's fine. Take a minute.' Haviland retrieved the triangle and began pulling the balls from the pockets. The sight of him moving so calmly around the table, sending the shining spheres gliding and clacking into one another with a flick of his wrist, infuriated Winn.

'Now, wait,' Winn said. Haviland stepped away from the table and stood with his hands in his pockets. 'I'm sorry, sir,' Winn said, 'but you're mistaken. Very mistaken. I don't know what you – I don't see what reason you could have to say these things. Vicious, disgusting things.'

'I don't like being the bearer of bad news any more than the next fellow. But I can see you do believe me. That's why you're angry. You must have sensed something was off. Haven't there been stray comments? Odd silences? Your grandfather was smart enough to go away for some years after Cunningham died, I think to Europe. Then he came back and started over. He lived respectably. It was easier for everyone to pretend to forget.

Your father tries to erase the past, he tries admirably, but there are still people around who remember. Frederick should have gone to another city. You've come much farther than could have been expected. You can almost pass for what you think you are. I haven't told Ophelia – she would probably say I'm being old-fashioned. Nonetheless. Here, I'll break.' Haviland lifted the triangle. Gleaming and inert, the balls held their orderly formation until, with a clatter, they flew apart like flushed birds. None went in. 'Heck!' said Haviland.

Winn bent over the table. The crook between his fingers was sweaty, and the cue slipped, bumping the ball and sending it dribbling sideways. 'You don't think—,' he began. 'You can't mean – Ophelia isn't – In 1976, you still—' He stopped and tried to collect his thoughts. He had always been told that his family had been established in Boston society by Frederick's working his way up from a clerk to mill owner. The idea of Frederick as the child consort to a lecherous old queen could not be made to fit with anything Winn knew. This was a perversion, a sordid prank. He wanted to run Haviland through with his cue. Why would the man say such things? He must want to sabotage Winn's relationship with Ophelia. But why? Haviland should be grateful he was interested. Winn had assumed it would be abundantly obvious to everyone that he was capable of doing better and that his courtship of the girl was a sign of maturity, that he was letting go of some youthful romantic ideal.

'Do you disapprove of my taking out Ophelia?' he asked.

Haviland looked at him curiously. 'No. But I thought we should talk before it got too serious. It would be best if it didn't get too serious.'

With as much dignity as he could muster, Winn crossed the room and set his cue in the wall rack. Turning back, he said, 'I think, *Brother* Haviland' – this was the way Ophidian members addressed one another – 'that you have made several mistakes tonight, and eventually you will regret them all.'

Haviland tilted his head to one side. 'You know,' he said, 'it's interesting to me that your father named you after Cunningham. I think it must have been his way of trying to legitimize the situation. The best defense is a good offense, as they say.'

'I was named for my grandfather's uncle,' Winn said stiffly.

'If you say so.' Haviland began bending and shooting, bending and shooting, indiscriminately sinking balls with expert thrusts of his cue. 'If it's any consolation, the Vespasian has a long history with men like that. Do you know what they found when they came into the building for the first time after Arthur Andrew Depuis died? Caligula's vacation house. Nude statues, suggestive paintings, very unusual tribal objects. The floor of the Keep was a mosaic of a naked shepherd boy caressing the horn of a goat. I wish I could have been a fly on the wall when the Seahorse Society stepped through the door. No one knew, of course. He left it to them as a kind of joke because they hadn't let him join their club. People will go to great lengths for revenge on those who have excluded them – isn't that interesting? I could have black-balled you from the Ophidian, you know, but I didn't. I admire you, Winn. You're a striver. Fortunately for the Seahorse, Depuis was an appreciator of antiquities in general as well as the male form, and they could salvage some things, like the pool, for instance. And I think most of these paintings came from Depuis. It was easier just to keep what they could and change the name. That way they didn't have to gut the place entirely. Probably for the best. If they had decorated it with seahorses, I'm not sure it would have looked any less queer than when Depuis had it.' Again the table was an empty green field. Haviland set down his cue and took up his glass.

'You seem to have a lot of knowledge about this sort of thing,' Winn said. 'Kind of a hobby for you?'

Haviland smiled without humor. 'I hope you understand it's nothing personal. If you ever have a daughter, you'll know.'

Winn had broken up with Ophelia as cruelly as he could stand to. He stopped calling her, broke what dates they already had, and brought the most beautiful girl he could find to a party where he knew she would be. He felt a twinge of conscience when he saw Ophelia standing in Harry Pitton-White's doorway, her stricken face, her protuberant eyes filling with tears, and then her valiant effort to pull herself together. She wore a short summer dress patterned with pink and green elephants – the fact was she had terrific legs. He turned away, feigning absorption in the story his date was telling about her years smoking forbidden cigarettes out the dorm windows at Foxcroft. 'It was wild!' she kept saying.

The night, for his purposes, began as a success. Ophelia looked miserable. His date looked stunning. Harry Pitton-White took him aside and flicked a thumb in the direction of the date, who could be heard exclaiming 'Wild!' from across the room, and said, 'Where'd you find Helen of Troy?'

'At a dinner,' Winn said.

'Great face. Great ass.'

Winn studied the twin protrusions in the paisley jersey of the girl's dress. 'I'd say her face could launch seven or eight hundred ships, tops. But that *is* a thousand ship ass.'

'Bon voyage,' Pitton-White said, taking a handful of almonds from a nearby bowl and dropping some into his mouth and some onto the carpet.

'You can have her after tonight.'

'Really? Anyway, what happened with you and Haviland?'

'I was never very excited about that one.'

'And you don't want to hang on to this one?'

'Not for long.'

'Must be all right being you,' Pitton-White said. He went and turned down the lights and put on a record, and everyone pushed back the furniture and began to dance. Winn's date hopped up and down in the middle of the mob, looking around in all directions and tossing her hair. Soon Pitton-White was pogoing beside her and reaching for her hips. Ophelia swayed on the periphery, smiling slightly. A guy Winn didn't know tried to dance with her, but she refused. Winn leaned against the wall and watched. Had he been sober, he would have been more careful, but he was drunk and let himself stare. She glanced up and caught him looking. He turned his attention to the almonds, but out of the corner of his eye he saw her coming toward him.

'Did I do something wrong?' she asked.

'No,' he said.

'Well, then, why—'

'It's just not for me. Sorry.'

'You could have told me that. You didn't need to let me twist in the wind. It seems like you not only want to break up with me, you want to be as mean about it as possible.'

'Sorry.'

'I would like to know why.'

He watched the dancers jump and turn exuberantly, elbows flying. He had not expected Ophelia to be so persistent. Unwittingly, she was presenting him with an irresistible opportunity to really lower the boom on the Havilands. 'It's nothing you can help,' he said. 'It's the way you look.'

She recoiled. 'What?'

'It's your eyes. They bulge. I see myself with someone more attractive. I've never been very attracted to you. I don't like looking at you.'

She flushed. Her bug eyes expanded with anger. He had expected her to run away, to cry. He found himself nervously munching almonds one after the other. 'You couldn't keep your hands off me,' she said in a hard voice. 'I think you found me plenty attractive. You left that girl, that Wellesley girl, for me. You lasted five seconds in bed. I felt like I was with a fifteen-year-old. You don't like to look at me – then why have you been staring at me all night? Your date's noticed.'

On the dance floor, his date was watching them over Pitton-White's shoulder and frowning. Winn shrugged and ate another almond. What Ophelia said was true, but happiness in the bedroom was something separate from his expectations for physical beauty. 'I'm sorry. There's nothing I can do. Why don't you try to have some dignity about it?'

'And,' she said, 'I don't know if you've noticed, but I'm at least as attractive as you are. You're good looking enough, but your skin is bad and . . .' – her eyes alit on what he already knew to be his most regrettable feature – 'you have a weak chin.' She shook her head, still staring at that disappointing spot below his lips. He wished she were not so willing to seize the advantage – something he had loved about her. His fingers crept up to his chin, squeezed it tenderly, like a piece of fruit. A clear delineation existed between his neck and face, but still his chin was not the strong, crisp, masculine escarpment it should be. The problem was that there was a smidge too much softness *underneath* his chin, a yielding swag of flesh he had possessed since childhood that tended to swallow the lower edge of his jawline, especially if he wasn't careful and pulled his head back into his neck. Weak chins were for weak men, symptomatic of cowardice, corruption, deviant appetites, and poor breeding, and he was forced to conclude that, both on a cosmetic level and as a sign of his essence, his mandibular failings made him less attractive than he might have been with a perfect, Gregory Peck kind of chin. But there was nothing to be done.

'I can't help it if I'm not attracted to you. There's no cause to get mean,' he said breezily.

Her eyes bulged farther from their sockets. 'I knew you didn't know what love is, but I thought you knew what attraction is. You're an idiot.'

'Well,' he said, 'you're the one who said you loved me.'

'You're right,' she said. 'I'm a bigger idiot.' She turned and vanished into the party, reemerging in a swirl of summer coat and angry eyes and slamming door. No one else seemed to notice that she had left.

He went home with his date, who was dewy and excited from dancing and jealousy, but he was so rough that he frightened her. Fear was something he had never roused in a woman, and a part of him was pleased to be seen as threatening even though he knew he was being selfish, even wicked. When she asked him to stop, he acquiesced without argument, leaving her on her bed with her face turned toward the wall. For weeks afterward, his fingers kept straying to his chin, worrying at it, trying to sculpt it into a finer shape. Eventually, he lost track of Ophelia, who seemed to have moved away, and though he saw her father sometimes at the Vespasian or at Ophidian dinners, he avoided speaking to him. When exactly she became Fee, he didn't know, nor did he know how she met Fenn, but he heard through the grapevine that they were dating and later that they were engaged. He was not invited to the wedding but heard it was a great party, and he heard about the birth of their children and then about Meg's problems. The merging of two people he had rejected unnerved Winn, but whenever he bumped into them over the years, they were perfectly cordial. After she took up with Teddy, Livia said they were nothing but nice to her, and until his problems with the Pequod, Winn had begun to think the bad blood between them existed only in his imagination.

Somewhere in the house, a toilet flushed. Floorboards creaked. Winn sat up. He had been leaning forward at an unforgiving angle, resting his cheek on his desk, and now his neck was cricked. Already most of the fog had burned off, and his study was filled with a warm, lemony light. He returned the album to the shelf and shed his bathrobe and slippers. Barefoot, he crept to the side door and took his tennis racquet and shoes from the closet. While he was tying his laces, he heard female voices overhead. More floorboards creaked, and there was another rush of water through the pipes. Easing the screen door shut behind him, he went out, swung astride his bicycle, and peddled frantically down the driveway, slipping on the gravel and feeling that he had made a narrow escape.

CHAPTER 10

MORE THAN ONE FISH, MORE THAN ONE SEA

Dominique sat in a beach chair reading a cookbook borrowed from Winn's collection. A furled umbrella lay beside her in the sand; the morning was still cool, and the sun was pleasant. Livia was lying nearby on a towel. She wore a sweatshirt over her bikini and had her arms folded across her face. To dramatize her hangover, she was emitting a steady groan.

'Go jump in the water,' Dominique told her. 'Clear the fuzz.'

Livia parted her arms and craned her neck to look at the waves. 'I don't know,' she said. 'I'm still chilled.'

'I can't believe you guys slept on the beach.'

Livia let her head drop back onto the towel. 'I know. Not much sleep, though.'

Dominique watched a gull carry a scallop up in the air and hover, flapping, before dropping it on the hard sand and swooping after it to pick out the meat. Piper was dawdling along the wrack line collecting shells while Daphne wallowed in the surf, floating on her back and admiring the diminishing island chain of her belly, knees, and toes. Greyson dipped under and resurfaced, heaving her up in his arms and roaring over her shrieks before he slipped her gently back into the water like an egg to be poached. Her belly bobbed up and disappeared and bobbed up again. Francis was lying on a towel in the sun. Charlie was playing paddleball with Dicky Jr, who wore a polo shirt and had zinc smeared on his nose. Celeste and Biddy lounged in the shade of an umbrella. Agatha, complaining of a headache, had stayed at the house.

A breeze had kicked up and blown away the last of the fog, and fat cumulus clouds slid purposefully out to sea. The sun ducked in and out of their towers and peepholes; diagonal columns of light made jade islands in the water.

'How did you guys leave things?' Dominique asked.

'I don't know,' Livia said. 'Ambiguously. Once it was light enough, we walked back to the house, which took forever because I got us lost in the fog – we didn't really talk – and then he kissed me on the cheek and got in the Jeep to wait for Greyson. And that was it. Thank God he didn't come to the beach. I don't think I could handle interacting with him right now in front of all these people.' She groaned again and pressed the heels of her hands to her eyes, but Dominique had the impression that, really, she was peacocking a little bit, proud of her boldness, her seduction of a man who was older and not Teddy. She kept touching her concave belly where her sweatshirt was riding up and crossing and uncrossing her knees like someone who had just rediscovered her own skin. Members of wedding parties, Dominique thought, were almost contractually obligated to sneak off to kiss and grope one another. The union of groomsman and bridesmaid was a symbolic consummation, a rain dance, a pagan rite fueled by proximity to love and optimism and free booze.

A wave washed thin on the sand, catching the yellow paddleball. Charlie charged after it. He made a show of doing a shallow dive into the surf, flashing the pale bottoms of his feet. Livia added, 'A party always seems like a letdown if you don't go home with someone.'

'Maybe,' said Dominique, 'but I don't think you should go down that road again. Not with Sterling.'

'Well,' Livia said, rolling onto her stomach and cupping her chin in her hand, 'that might be hard.'

'I'm not trying to be a party pooper. Sex with your brother-in-law is a bad idea.'

Livia swung her feet, pert and childish. 'Isn't there something to be said for ill-advised lust? What's the point of being single if you don't stock-pile some good stories to live off of when you're old and boring? Doesn't caution pale in comparison to raw passion?'

Dominique closed the cookbook around her index finger. 'Raw passion?'

'You know what I mean.'

'I know what you mean, Madame Karenina, but people are assholes. They'll cheer you on while you make all your little mistakes, and then they'll be there to rubberneck when your adventure comes to a bad end.'

'But he doesn't really matter. If he hurts me, it'll be a distraction. Like pinching yourself after you've stubbed a toe so you can focus on the little hurt.'

'Don't say I didn't warn you.'

'I won't.'

Dominique settled back, resigned that she had done as much as she could. Female friendship was one-tenth prevention and nine-tenths cleanup. Livia would do what she would. Her sad-girl hormones would bind her to another man who didn't want her, and when Sterling sloughed her off, Dominique would be called upon to indulge her defense mechanisms, tell her that *of course* there was some complicated reason he would not allow himself to open up to her, *of course* he knew she was too good for him (no man ever thought that – it went against natural selection), *of course* he was afraid of getting hurt. When Dominique had come upstairs from the party, Agatha had been tucked into her little brass bed and was sniffling and sighing to signal she needed consoling over something. Dominique ignored her, and Piper had already pitched face-first onto her own little bed and fallen asleep in her underwear and green sweater. Whatever Agatha was up to, Dominique wanted no part of it.

A lifeguard Jeep rolled by, and the driver lifted one tan hand in lazy greeting. Two men in rubber boots rode in the back with buckets and a half-dozen tools that looked like narrow shovels on long handles. They dwindled into the distance, following the curve of the shore out of sight.

'I wonder what's going on,' Livia said.

Daphne lumbered out of the water and up the beach. She wrapped a towel around her shoulders and pulled open a canvas chair, setting it in the sand.

'Good swim?' Dominique said.

'You can't appreciate weightlessness until you're pregnant,' Daphne said, squeezing out her hair. 'It's fantastic. I understand why hippopotamuses spend so much time in the water.'

'Hippopotami,' corrected Livia.

'You can say hippopotamuses, can't you?' said Daphne.

'You're the bride,' Livia said. 'You can say whatever you want.'

Daphne eased down into her chair. 'Dominique, don't they have hippos in the Nile?'

'They do. I believe the plural is "scary fuckers."'

Livia tsked at her sister. 'Are you going to ask her about the secrets of King Tut's tomb?'

'I don't know why you're getting snippy with me.'

'I'm not snippy.'

'You are.'

'Isn't there wedding stuff you should be taking care of?'

'Like what?'

'It just seems odd that you can sit around at the beach the day before you get married.'

'Mom said that's what the coordinator is for.'

'Who's greeting the relatives?'

'I don't know. They're greeting themselves. We'll see them tonight. What time is it, anyway?'

Dominique consulted her phone. 'Eleven.'

'I guess the day is your oyster,' Livia said.

Daphne ran her hands over her belly like a seer consulting a crystal ball. 'You're acting like *I'm* the one who embarrassed *you* last night.'

'It's none of your business.'

The two of them had always been perfectly comfortable fighting in front of Dominique. She thought they might even prefer it to fighting without an audience. Each believed she was right, and each was equally sure Dominique would take her side. They never seemed to notice whose side she really did take, and, in fact, she was usually never asked. But both Daphne and Livia would remember her as an ally, and in that way, without expending any effort, Dominique managed to come out on top of most Van Meter family disagreements.

'Obviously, it's my business,' Daphne said. 'Greyson is exhausted. He got almost no sleep.'

'Why didn't you just let him sleep in your bed?'

'We're trying to be romantic. And, Livia, Sterling is bad news.'

'Just because you're getting married doesn't mean you know everything about men.'

'Why set yourself up?'

'God!' said Livia, outraged. 'Just let me make a bad decision, just this once. I've had enough endings. I'd like a beginning for a change.'

Dominique and Daphne exchanged a skeptical glance.

Coloring furiously, Livia said, 'Agatha does whatever she wants all the time, and you guys don't act all concerned, hovering around and telling her to be careful.'

'What does Agatha have to do with it?' Daphne asked.

'If Agatha had slept with Sterling, would you be giving *her* this speech?'

'It's not a speech. You *slept* with him? I thought you just fooled around. God.'

Dominique said, 'You don't want to be like Agatha.'

'Maybe I do.'

'You don't,' Daphne said firmly, emboldened by Dominique's endorsement.

'Don't tell me what I want!'

Daphne threw up her hands. 'You know what, Livia? I don't care what you do.' She took a book about parenting from her beach bag and flipped through the pages. Livia put her cheek on the towel and closed her eyes.

Dominique looked at the water, at the people swimming. The previous spring, she and Sebastiaan

270

had taken a trip to the Red Sea and had gone out on a snorkeling boat. At one point, they anchored a short distance offshore, maybe a quarter mile. The captain said they could swim to the beach, and so Dominique did while Sebastiaan stayed on deck smoking black cigarettes and reading Dutch poetry. The water was warm; the swim felt good. Even though she hadn't swum regularly since college, her shoulders were still strong, and she cut through the water with authority. Halfway to shore, she paused to go under and have a look around. The water was very clear. She saw the sloping sea floor, the pale hull of the boat, and, beyond it, huge black shadows moving through the water. They were whales: distant and indistinct and astonishingly enormous. She had never told the story to Livia because she knew Livia would ruin it by asking what *kind* of whales they had been and what they were doing (feeding? traveling? playing?), and Dominique did not know, nor did she want to think about them that way, as animals acting out normal behaviors. She preferred them as lurking mysteries.

Piper approached. 'Hey,' she said, holding out a small object. 'What is this? They're all over the place.' The object was a hollow pod shaped like a large scarab beetle, dry and black with the texture of papyrus and two curving prongs on each end.

'It's a mermaid's purse,' Daphne said.

Livia gave a superior sigh. 'It's a skate's egg case.'

Piper looked confused. 'So, which is it?'

'Both,' said Daphne, reaching up to take the pod. 'Mermaid's purse is just something people call them. I can't remember who taught me that. Maybe Dryden.'

'Who's Dryden?' asked Piper.

'Our gay cousin,' said Livia.

Dominique imagined young Daphne had probably been disappointed by the object that went with the name. A mermaid's purse should be green and sparkling, but this thing, with its smooth black surface and curving horns, was strange and sinister.

Piper thought a minute. 'What's a skate?' she asked.

'A flat, cartilaginous fish,' said Livia. 'Kind of like a ray. They bury themselves in the sand.'

Daphne tossed the pod aside. 'God, I have this urge to do cartwheels. If I weren't pregnant, I'd do some. Greyson! Do a cartwheel!'

Down the beach, Greyson waved and turned a perfect cartwheel and then another and another. His limbs turned like spokes in the sun. 'I want to do a cartwheel, too!' Piper said. She hurtled down the sand like a gymnast about to vault and turned an energetic cartwheel in front of Francis, who applauded as she stood, arms over her head, in a ta-da! stance. 'Wait,' she shouted. 'Watch!' She jogged some distance away and then came racing back, did one preparatory skip, and flung herself forward into a handspring. She didn't get enough leverage on takeoff and underrotated, descending at the angle of a lawn dart and whumping forcefully onto her butt. Charlie and Dicky Jr went running to her.

'Are you okay?' Daphne called from her chair.

Piper, sitting in her crater, flapped one hand in response. 'Is she laughing or crying?' Livia said.

Dominique shaded her eyes with her hand and watched the boys haul Piper to her feet, spindly as a child. 'Beats me.'

'Where are all these people *going*?' Daphne asked, watching another Jeep cruise by. 'Hey!' she called. 'Hey! Where are you going?'

One of the men in the back of the Jeep cupped his hands around his mouth and yelled over the wind. 'There's a hail!'

'What?'

'There's a *wha-le*! Around the point! Beached!'

'Is it alive?' Livia shouted. He was getting farther and farther away. He pointed at his ear. She cupped her hands around her mouth. 'Is it alive? Is the whale alive?'

Winn, resplendent in his tennis whites and triumphant after beating his old friend Goodman Perry in straight sets, was pedaling home with a bicycle-basket cargo of blueberry muffins when he rounded a bend and saw a golf cart parked on the side of the bike path. He was in high spirits. His hangover had lifted sometime during their warm-up rallies, and the magnificent relief of no longer feeling awful was enough to get him off to a good start, winning the first three points and then the first set. Perry was the better player, and Winn's tidy dominance had puzzled them both at first and then, by the middle of the second set, elated Winn and lowered Perry into a sulk. Between points, Perry prowled the net, running his racquet along the tape and scuffling the red clay, keeping up a steady mumble to himself. 'It's this wedding,' Winn had called. 'I have more pent-up aggression than usual.'

Perry nodded and swung through a courtly backhand. 'Your serve,' he replied.

Winn won the next point with a dainty tap that brought Perry swooping up from the baseline with racquet outstretched as though trying to net a butterfly. 'Good hustle,' Winn said. Perry only glowered. Pressing his hand against the strings of his racquet, Winn watched his flesh bulge through the gaps. His sudden genius for tennis suggested he might be full of physical talents not yet discovered or fully realized. As he bounced the ball and watched Perry take up a determined crouch at the opposite end, the perverse thought surfaced that his conquest of Agatha – and he considered it to be a conquest because, really, a woman's permission was the central obstacle – was responsible for his improved game. He wondered if their tryst was acting on his masculinity like some Chinese herb or voodoo powder, making him stronger and more agile, able to – and here he reared back and sent an ace past Perry and ringing into the links of the fence – assert himself.

He celebrated by stopping at the market and buying five of the good muffins, not enough for everyone but all the store had left. Then, on the stretch of path that skirted the twelfth hole of the Pequod, before he was even halfway home, he saw the golf cart. It had no business being where it was. There were separate paths for bikes and for carts, and this cart was most certainly on the wrong path. Winn's habit was to ride quickly but casually, leaning back on the seat and taking occasional practice swings with his racquet. As he went zipping along, knees pumping a lively rhythm, swatting at the air to fight off the sight of the rogue cart, he saw there was a man behind the wheel and above him, at the top of a slope, two more in visors and pleated shorts, leaning on clubs. The man in the cart was bending sideways to extract a tiny white ball from a mess of grass and poison ivy. Winn steered out to the edge of the path and glared at the golfers.

Perhaps he ought to have called out or thumbed a peal from the silver bell on his handlebars, but as it happened, just as he passed behind the cart the driver popped upright with golf ball in hand and went whizzing into reverse without a glance behind him. Escape was impossible. There was the flip of a lever, the high whine of the machine's warning buzzer, and then the square plastic bumper flipped Winn and his bicycle sideways off the path. Later he remembered a series of crooked, trapezoidal images, like the feed from a damaged antenna: the sky, the asphalt, the back of the driver's head, the grass where he landed. In the aerial instant of the crash, one pedal spun viciously around and sliced into the flesh of his calf, leaving a sickle-shaped wound, and, to add insult to injury, his tennis racquet flew out of his hand and up onto the road, where it was promptly run over by a passing van. Two muffins escaped from the bag, one coming to rest in the gutter and the other standing upright in the grass like a stout toadstool.

Lying on his back, leg aflame, Winn stared up at the sky and grimaced. A tall, cauliform cloud blew in front of the sun and then was blotted out by a face. 'Hey!' the man from the golf cart said, lifting the bike off Winn. 'Are you all right? Did you hit your head?'

Beneath the brim of the man's cap and behind thick glasses blinked two small, watery eyes. The ruddy flesh of his snub nose was aerated by deep and abundant pores, and the skin of his face sagged slightly as he leaned over, close enough for Winn to smell his breath. It was musty, horsey, the breath of something that ate only grass. Perhaps he was turned loose at night to graze on the fairway.

'Ah, Jesus,' Winn said. 'Christ, that hurts.'

The man leaned close and stared into Winn's eyes like a hypnotist. 'Did you hit your head?' he asked again.

Winn rolled his neck. 'I don't think so. No, my

leg's the problem.' They looked at his leg. It was bleeding.

'You should put pressure on that,' the man said. He pulled a red paisley handkerchief from his back pocket and handed it over.

'I agree,' Winn said. He pulled off his signet ring and tucked it in the pocket of his shorts before pressing the handkerchief over his wound. The golfers who had been on the top of the hill were gone.

The man thoughtfully pinched his lower lip between thumb and forefinger. 'Would you like to use my phone?'

Biddy was summoned from the beach, and Winn sat in the grass to wait for her, gazing up at his new antagonist. He expected the man to speak, but he just stood in silence, gazing into the distance as though waiting for a bus.

'Do you belong to the Pequod?' Winn asked.

'No, I work there.'

Winn chalked up a point for himself. He could spot a caddy a mile away. 'With all due respect,' he said, 'you didn't have the right of way. You were in a motorized vehicle on a bike path.'

The man looked back at the golf cart in surprise, as though it had tapped him on the shoulder. 'Motorized vehicle?' he said.

'That's right,' said Winn.

The man shrugged. 'It's a golf cart.'

'It has a motor.'

'But it's not a car.'

'It doesn't have to be.'

'I think it does.'

'Well,' Winn said, 'regardless, it's dangerous to bring it on the bike path. This is exactly why there's a separate path for carts in the first place and why you're supposed to stay on it. If you need to come on the bike path, you are to do so on foot.'

'Doesn't say that anywhere,' the man said. He put his hands in his pockets.

Winn blinked, flabbergasted. This man, he realized, this man who had knocked him off his bike, causing him a wound that would obviously need to be stitched and would give him a limp as he walked Daphne down the aisle in little more than twenty-four hours, this man had no intention of apologizing. An apology was simple courtesy, not necessarily an admission of fault, certainly not of legal liability. He should say he was sorry for causing Winn pain even if he was the kind of person whose understanding of a motorized versus nonmotorized vehicle was, at best, murky.

'What is your name?' Winn said.

'Otis Derringer,' the man said.

'Mr Derringer,' Winn said, 'all this time I've been waiting for you to apologize, as would be the natural thing to do given the circumstances and the events of the past few minutes, and you haven't.'

Again, Otis looked back at the golf cart, this time like he was appealing for backup, saying to the cart, *Get a load of this guy*. He took off his hat and wiped at the indentation left in his forehead. A whitewash of old sweat ghosted the brim. 'Well, sir,' Otis said, replacing the hat, 'I don't think I need to apologize. I did the right thing. I stopped and asked about your head. I offered you my phone. You asked me to wait with you, and I'm waiting with you. Other than that, I think we can say accidents happen and leave it at that.'

Winn's right index finger came up and trained itself on Otis's face. 'But some accidents are *caused*,' he said, his finger jerking toward Otis like a leashed attack dog, 'by people who get off scot-free while other people pay the price.' Winn wondered how much blood he had lost. His fingers were sticky where the handkerchief had soaked through. Lifting the cloth, he watched a bright crescent well up from his flesh.

'I think you should have braked,' Otis said. 'I didn't see you coming.'

'You didn't look.'

'I believe I did.'

'All right, how's this,' Winn said. 'Even if you apologize, it doesn't mean the accident was entirely your fault. I'll just take it as a gesture of friendship.'

Otis stuck his jaw forward, making his face even more bulldoggish. 'I'm a friendly guy,' he said. 'I don't really think I owe you an apology, but if you'd like me to apologize, I will.'

'Okay,' Winn said, 'I would like you to apologize.'

'I just did.'

Winn stared at him in wonderment. 'Hey,' Otis said, sitting in the grass beside him. 'Hey, you look really pale.' He took one of Winn's hands and rubbed it briskly between his own. 'Here, put your head between your knees.' He pressed Winn's neck downward. 'Deep breath, buddy.'

'Have I lost that much blood?' Winn asked. 'Where is Biddy?' He lifted his head, and Otis gently pushed it back down.

'You haven't lost enough to fill a thimble. You're feeling the shock.'

'I've lost more than that.'

Otis gave a little puff of laughter, and Winn smelled the warm stable smell of his breath again. 'You're probably from New York.'

'Connecticut,' said Winn. 'I work in the city. But I've been coming here for fifty years. Since I was a kid. Back when it was a rough old fishing village. It wasn't fancy at all.'

'Yeah.' Otis took his hand off Winn's neck. 'I was born here.'

Winn said nothing. They sat. In the distance, the ocean was mottled with cloud shadows. One of the things he loved about the island was the sensation of being inside an envelope of sea and sky, how the horizon was a clearly ruled line between one thing and another, entirely different thing. 'Do you know Jack Fenn?' he asked.

'Sure,' Otis said. 'Great guy.'

The familiar shape of the Land Rover shot past.

There was a squeak of brakes, and Biddy reversed onto the shoulder. She came toward him over the grass, tall and lean, crisp as a white sail on a blue sea. 'You,' she said, touching his head with one finger, 'are a real Hazzard!' Biddy had never lost the habit of her old family joke, nor had her sisters, even though it had been decades since any of them had been Hazzards. 'Hello,' she said to Otis.

'This is Otis Derringer,' Winn said. 'My assailant.'

Otis wiped his fingers on his pants before shaking Biddy's hand. 'Sorry. I've got a little bit of blood on my hands.'

'Coming from you that means a lot, Otis,' Winn said.

Otis hesitated, pinching his lip again and giving it a little twist. Then he said, 'If anyone asks, I apologized.'

After a pause, Winn said, 'Like hell.'

Biddy looked back and forth between the men, alert and friendly. 'Come on, ducky,' she said to Winn finally, offering him her hand.

Because Winn was woozy and the ground soft and uneven, he was of little help to Biddy. The pain, too, was considerable, and each time he put pressure on his injured leg, more blood trickled out of the wound and down into his sock.

'The muffins,' he said, pointing at the bag where it lay.

'Let's get you first.' Biddy turned to Otis. 'Would you mind helping him?'

Winn thought Otis would only take his other

arm, but, to his shock, the caddy knelt in the grass and lifted him up. Winn had not been carried since he was a child, and he would never have expected to find himself cradled in the massive arms of a man with breath like a hayloft. He heard himself whimper. Craning his head around Otis's shoulder, he said Biddy's name. She was standing motionless, an astonished hand over her mouth.

CHAPTER 11

FLESH WOUNDS

The whale was dead, long dead. It had died at sea and drifted in, relatively unmolested by sharks, nudged up onto the beach during the night. A fisherman discovered it at dawn. From passersby Livia had learned it was a sperm whale, but no one could tell her how big it was or if it was male or female or how it had died. Francis was the only one who wanted to come with her to see it, and they walked up the beach together toward an outcropping that made a narrow point. A man coming the opposite direction on an ATV told them they would find the whale on the other side. Couldn't miss it. Smelled worse than they could possibly imagine. While lying on her towel, Livia had gotten the impression of a steady flow of human traffic heading to the point, but as they walked and left behind the popular section of the swimming beach, they found themselves alone, trudging along beside a crumbling bluff. Occasional wooden staircases built into its sandy face led up to the houses Jack Fenn was trying to save from the ocean.

Livia found herself in a bleak mood. She wondered

what Sterling was doing, why he hadn't come to the beach – was he avoiding her? She was curious to know how he would have acted. Maybe he would have come with her to see the whale instead of Francis. Maybe they would have paused to sit and kiss on one of these wooden staircases – the thought made her stomach roil with pleasure and anxiety, churning up acidic dregs of liquor.

Francis wore large, square, cheap black plastic sunglasses and had a Sanskrit tattoo on his shoulder. She had never seen him without his shirt before, and he was stockier than she would have imagined, and hairier.

'I can't believe no one else wanted to come,' she said.

'You probably wish Sterling were here.'

'No,' she said. 'It's not every day you get to see a whale. I would have thought everyone would want to come. But heaven forbid anything should interrupt their pleasant day at the beach. Why go see something dead when you can stay where you are and play paddleball?'

'Absolutely,' said Francis. 'I'm with you on that. Whales aren't totally my thing, but I see this as a chance for a real experience. I'm trying to be spiritually open to the world.'

'Right,' Livia said, not sure what he meant. 'I mean, this island wouldn't exist without sperm whales. We all hang wooden whales on our walls and wear whale pants and have whale-tail door knockers and put stainless-steel kitchens in old whaling captains' houses, but given the chance to stand in the presence of a real flesh-and-blubber whale, we lose interest.'

'I was wearing whale pants last night,' Francis said, 'but ironically.'

'Sterling said his seersucker was ironic, too.'

'So he stole my joke, and then he stole you.'

She had been hoping he would choose to forget his halfhearted attempt on her. 'I think your approach to irony might be a little off,' she said. 'If everyone expects you to wear seersucker or little whales, and then you do, how is that ironic?'

He looked at her over his sunglasses. 'Why did you choose Sterling? I'm not really mad. I'm just curious.'

'Francis, you weren't serious. You don't have feelings for me.'

'How do you know? Don't laugh. Whether I do or not is beside the point. My question is, what's wrong with me? What makes him more attractive? Because he is. I know that. Even though I'm arguably better looking and probably a better person.'

'Nothing's wrong with you. I just don't feel that kind of connection with you.'

'But you do with Sterling.'

'I don't know. I did last night.'

'Hmm.' Francis walked along in silence. The farther they walked, the less protected the shore became, and blowing sand stung Livia's shins. 'It's funny how families work,' he said. 'Sterling and I are a lot alike, actually. We both have contemplative natures. We're both drawn to the Far East. But Sterling doesn't have any kind of belief system, and he's depressed all the time. I channel my dark thoughts into bettering myself, which explains why I'm a serial monogamist while Sterling – no offense – will sleep with anything. If you want my two cents, you should steer clear of him.'

'Those aren't the first two cents I've been given today.' Truth be told, she didn't mind the family gossiping about her and Sterling. If she couldn't be cool and aloof like Dominique, then she might as well be thought of as a little impetuous, a little wanton, a bit of a maneater. In her experience, people in a group envied the ones among them who managed to pair off. Even if they criticized a choice of partner or pretended to disapprove of flings in general, most people would rather be the ones fumbling in the dark and then reemerging, sheepish and smug, than the ones who got tired and washed their faces and went to bed just like on any other night. Plus, now she had proven she could move on from Teddy.

Livia stooped to pick up a pumpkin-colored scallop shell. She turned it over in her fingers and then tossed it away. That morning she had woken in darkness, chilled and shivering. The tide had come up, and her feet were wet. Reaching for Sterling, she found only cold sand. A wavelet washed over her feet, and she felt afraid and profoundly alone, about to be swept away. But then she had scrambled to her feet and tripped over Sterling, who groaned and said he was fucking freezing.

Francis kept talking. 'Sterling acts like this jaded renegade, but he's not. If anyone is, it's me. I don't know how he gets away with all the shit he pulls and yet I'm the family whipping boy.' The first putrid whiff arrived on a gust of wind, and he threw his bicep over his nose. 'Oh, Jesus, did you smell that?'

'If you weighed forty tons and died, you'd smell bad, too.'

'Why do you love them?'

'Who?'

'Whales.'

'I don't know.' He wasn't the first to ask, but she didn't understand why she was supposed to know the answer. Why did anyone love anything?

'You must have some idea.'

She shook her head. 'It's something about their being so big. It makes me sad, how big they are. They're rare enough that every time I see one I get a thrill. I think they're beautiful. How can you not love them? They're fascinating. Did you know they hunt as a team? Humpbacks *herd* fish by making clicking sounds and blowing bubble nets.'

'Yeah? Wild.'

'It is wild.' She thought of the dense, silvery ball of confused fish packed tight together, the lucky eaters rocketing up from underneath with their mouths open wide, yawning portals to the underworld. The whales' throats, ribbed like elastic, bulged with fish and seawater, billowing from the sloshing and swimming going on inside. When, she wondered, did the herring know that they were not in a new, darker sea but inside another animal? Or were herring too stupid to know that they were being eaten? She thought probably all things knew when they were being eaten.

'I heard about Teddy joining up,' Francis said, his voice high and thin because he was pinching his nose. 'That must be hard.'

'He can do what he wants.'

'Sure. You know, in a way I envy you. You really seem to feel things. I'm never sure I'm experiencing genuine emotion because I'm always wondering if I'm only feeling what I think I *should* be feeling. If that makes any sense.'

'I guess so.' The smell of the whale was beginning to make her sick.

'Do you still love him?' Francis persisted. It was another familiar question with an answer that eluded her.

'No,' she said.

'What made you stop loving him?'

'I don't know. Maybe exhaustion.'

She wondered when she would stop loving Teddy. Before him, she had loved only her mother, her father, and her sister, and love was something to be tamped down beneath decorum. Her father, returning home from work when she was already in her nightgown, hair damp from her bath, would catch her by the shoulders as she ran to embrace him and, holding her safely at arm's length, stoop to kiss her cheek with his dry lips. On the occasions she managed to sneak up on him and hug his legs or waist, her arms were gently detached and the kiss administered from a polite distance. Eventually, she learned what Daphne seemed to have been born knowing: he was happiest if she did not grapple with him but presented herself like a soldier with a stalwart cheek and waited for him to bend to her. As a child, despite her profound girliness, Daphne had not been one for physical affection or declarations of love – those were things she learned, like algebra, at prep school. Livia's mother was the warmest of the bunch, responding to her 'I love you's' in kind (not with her father's 'All right, dear's') and waking her for school with a brisk but gentle rub of her back as if brushing her clean of snow.

After Daphne had left for her first year at Deerfield, there had been a period of two or three weeks when Livia would come home from school and her mother would take her onto her lap in a deep, plaid armchair and hold her for a whole, silent hour, stroking her hair while they looked out the window at birds and squirrels in the summer-green trees. The first invitation surprised Livia, who was used to being left to her own devices in the afternoons. She had perched gingerly on her mother's narrow lap, only gradually settling back against her shoulder, letting the tan arms encircle her, breathing the neutral, soapy smell of Biddy's skin, the sharp hint of bleach from her shirt. Not since the womb had she had her mother so much to herself, nor had she been given such access to the rhythms of her body – the resolute beating of her heart, the swelling of her lungs – and she absorbed them hungrily, her voluptuous pleasure colored with anxiety because the prolonged quiet closeness, never discussed between them or mentioned to her father or Daphne, seemed somehow illicit. Then one day, when the first leaves were turning yellow, Biddy did not go to the armchair but gave Livia her snack in the kitchen and went upstairs by herself, signaling that their time of indulgence had run its course.

'Sometimes love just ends,' Francis said author-itatively. 'Also, I wanted to say, about what I said last night about Hannah's breasts being too big – I didn't mean to sound shallow. I would hate for you to think of me that way. Like Hannah was only breasts to me.'

'I think you said tits.'

'Spiritually, Hannah and I were all wrong for each other. If she had been the one, I think I would have known. But I also know I'm afraid of opening up and letting myself be vulnerable to another person, so I made everything about her tits.' He was addressing the side of Livia's head as she walked. 'I like talking to you,' he said. 'Other girls can be so judgmental, but I feel like I can tell you anything and you'll understand. You're very compassionate. Maybe because you've been through hard things, too – you don't have to talk about it, but I know all about what happened.'

Livia walked faster, trying to hurry him along, but he hung back, forcing her to slow. 'Can't we talk about something else?' she said. 'Something a little lighter?'

'Sure. I just wanted you to know that I'm here for you. Another reason I like you is that I think we have similar roles in our families. We're the critical ones. We represent a threat to their way of life, a new order.'

A loose gang of seagulls hung in the air on the other side of the point, circling and diving, croaking at one another. They were picking at the whale, Livia knew. Far above, a trio of turkey vultures carved slow spirals. Watching the birds, she said, 'Yeah, Sterling told me about the trouble you got in at school.'

He stopped. 'What trouble?'

She felt tense ripple of pleasure at getting a rise out of him. 'I shouldn't have brought it up.'

'What trouble?'

'Sterling said you almost didn't get to go to Princeton.'

'I never cheated.' He aimed his big, square sunglasses at her. 'Those other kids were lying. They were jealous.'

'Okay,' she said. 'Never mind. It's none of my business.'

'I *deserved* to go to Princeton. I *earned* it.' He was wheedling, almost begging.

'Okay,' Livia said again. 'I'm sorry. I had no right to say what I did.'

'That's true.' He punched her lightly, cheerfully on the arm. 'Hey,' he said with hard brightness, 'you know, I've heard Teddy's slept with half of New York since word got out about the army. Apparently, the old wisdom is true about girls and uniforms.'

She gaped at him and then turned and hurried down the beach, struggling in the deep sand. The smell of the whale was getting worse, and as she started panting from her efforts, gasping in the foul air, her stomach turned. Francis was coming after her. 'I'm sorry,' he called. 'I'm an asshole. Livia. Please. It's just that I'm not good with rejection.'

Breaking into a jog, she reached the tip of the point, where the currents came together and made a seam in the ocean. An alcoholic vapor came into her nose, and her mouth filled with saliva, and she knew she was about to puke, which she did, splashing into the water and retching a thin green liquid into the foam. She had skipped breakfast.

Francis waited on the beach while she rinsed her mouth with salt water. She walked heavily back toward him and when she was close enough said, 'Please just shut up.'

To her surprise, he obeyed and followed a docile two steps behind as she started walking again. In the quiet, her guts still cramping, she wondered if what he really wanted was for some girl, maybe her, to get all suited up in black leather and slap his ass with a whip and make him lick her feet. She wasn't good with rejection either. She thought of herself at the Ophidian party, shouting and spilling her counterfeit vodka, and she cringed.

In a minute they rounded the point, and the whale appeared, not far down the beach. A crowd of people and Jeeps surrounded it, and seagulls bombarded from above, but Livia saw only the whale, an onyx teardrop, a great black river rock.

'Oh,' she said, awestruck, putting her hands over her heart.

'Fucking Christ,' said Francis, 'that's a smell.'

The stink of the whale was powerful, gummy, almost tangible. The wind was depositing particles of decay on her clothes and skin, but Livia did not mind. Her nausea had stabilized into something endurable. The whale's fluke, flat on the sand like a giant discarded spade, filled her with pity.

The last time Biddy remembered waiting in an emergency room was when Livia was fifteen and home for Christmas and had passed through the swinging galley door into the kitchen, where Daphne was attempting to bake a red velvet cake. Livia had become incensed at something Daphne said or did, and a mysterious tussle occurred, at the end of which Livia came running back out through the door with a deep gash in her left thumb. She told them the wound was self-inflicted and accidental, but still she had seemed to cast a glowering blame at her sister and at the meaty hearts of all red velvet cakes. That waiting room and the waiting room where Biddy now sat beside Winn, his injured leg propped up on a chair, were nearly identical – the same linoleum, the same vinyl chairs, the same isopropyl tang in the air. All waiting rooms were essentially the same, not really places in themselves as much as rehearsals for purgatory. On the opposite wall hung a large framed photo of an orange crab held by its claws, its pale belly facing the camera, jointed legs flexed in outrage. A television showing the weather hung high in a corner; a grim-looking ficus tree sheltered beneath it. At the juncture of two hallways, a seen-it-all receptionist with a pencil in her hair reigned over a high, curved desk cluttered with papers.

The chairs were sparsely occupied. Biddy turned Winn's wrist so she could look at his watch. Only twelve fifteen, still early in the day for summer injuries. Midafternoon and early evening were probably the prime hours for heads to be koshed by yardarms and softballs, fishhooks to go astray, shucking knives to slip. A young couple waited in seats near the receptionist's desk. The woman looked green around the gills and was gazing dolefully into an empty plastic grocery bag she held on her lap while the man, who wore a sun visor, rubbed her back and stared at the television. Presently the woman stood and bolted for the bathroom, one hand clapped over her mouth, and the man watched her go with wistful resignation, as though she were a wayward balloon. An old woman and a small boy sat beside the ficus tree, not talking, neither with any obvious injury or malady. The boy's hair was parted in a severe white line down the middle of his skull, and he was dressed in an oddly old-fashioned way: shorts, kneesocks and brown lace-up bucks. Biddy thought he looked like he should be rolling a hoop down a Berlin street beneath zeppelin-crossed skies. The only other patient was a lanky, gray-haired man in pants the color of Pepto-Bismol. He had a bloody bandage over one eye and was standing in the mouth of one of the hallways practicing his golf swing. Over and over he squared up at an imaginary tee and, focusing with cycloptic malevolence on an invisible ball, torqued back at the waist and then whipped through his stroke, ending with his hands up behind his head and one toe pointed balletically on the linoleum while he gazed down the hall at an illuminated sign that said 'NO SMOKING.'

Flipping through a magazine about home décor, Biddy paused at a spread on a beach house in the Hamptons. Sand and salt grass, a blue swimming pool, rooms with no one in them. 'Don't read that,' Winn said, peering over her shoulder. 'You'll want a new kitchen.'

'I'll risk it,' Biddy said, not looking up.

'Those magazines only exist to foment discontent.'

She turned a page. 'Let them eat cake.'

'I wonder what those Pequod folks will think when they hear about this,' he said, hoisting up his leg and turning it so she could get a good look. The caddy's handkerchief, stiff and stained brown in spots, still bound the wound. 'Talk about adding injury to insult. They're probably already worrying about whether or not I'm going to sue. This might turn out to be a nice bit of leverage, when you think about it.'

He frowned out at the waiting room. The vomiting girl returned from the bathroom. The golfer, wary of interference, waited for her to sit before settling into his stance.

Biddy studied her husband's profile, his graying eyebrows and thin lips, the chin that concerned him so. Had she only dreamt that they made love in the early morning? After she nearly drowned herself? Her exhaustion had made her brief sleep heavy and thick with dreams. She thought it really *had* happened, unlikely as that was, but she was too embarrassed to ask him. From the beginning of her romantic life, back when she was a quiet, good-looking, well-liked girl going out with the most staid, earnest sons of her father's friends, she had accepted that men would not be changed. The boys she danced with at the boat club would never, she knew, turn into men who excited her, nor would their polite hands ever stir her passion. Really, until she went to bed with Winn, she had not experienced anything like passion, but she had known it existed and known she wanted it. Funny that he was the one who lit her up – he was nothing like the exotic lovers she read about in her mother's stash of risqué novels. Although, admittedly, he was known as a bit of a tail chaser, and since the tail-chasing men never came after her (she supposed she didn't strike them as a good bet), his reputation gave her a thrill.

He had sought her out through the crowd of mourners after his father's funeral; at first she had thought he'd mistaken her for someone else. She remembered his eyes, lit with purpose, finding her among all those black hats and black shoulders, coming closer and closer until he was there shaking her hand and asking her to dinner while she was simultaneously offering her condolences. The very strangeness of his interest had flattered her. How alluring she must be to distract a man from grieving for his own father. How irresistible her sex appeal must be to drive away the pall of death. Her thrill lasted through their first dinner and the ones after that, through their first amorous skirmishes, persisted even after she realized that he was yet another man pursuing her not for fun but with a mind to long-term investment. Occasionally, they ran into some girl or other whom Winn had taken out before her, and those girls thrilled Biddy, too, the way they tried to flirt past her, to get him to betray her by showing some interest, which sometimes he did and sometimes he didn't.

She knew her tolerance was unusual, but she

couldn't help the way she was. Just like Winn couldn't help the way *he* was. 'Does it hurt?' she asked, pointing at his leg.

'Of course it hurts.'

'Poor dear.' She looked down at her magazine, at a long, empty picnic table between two rows of olive trees somewhere in Spain, set for twelve people. 'I couldn't believe,' she said, 'how that man lifted you. Like you were nothing.' His silence in the car had told her he thought a great indignity had been done to him, but she had felt only wonder at the sight of her husband cradled in another man's arms. She wished he could have seen himself, witnessed the abject confusion on his own face. When he had said her name, it had been the tremulous query of a child seeking reassurance in the night.

Winn folded his arms over his chest and said, 'That was very inappropriate, very intrusive. I'm very troubled that he did that. I'll be mentioning it to the Pequod as well. You can't go around picking people up like that.'

'I think he was trying to help. I asked him to. He wasn't' – she lowered her voice – 'molesting you. I don't think he's the brightest bulb in the box.'

Winn fiddled with the knot in Otis's handkerchief. 'Let's change the subject,' he said.

A nurse in lavender scrubs appeared with a clipboard. The vomiting woman looked up hopefully. 'Chamberlain,' said the nurse. The boy in the

298

kneesocks and his companion stood and followed her back into the innards of the hospital. The vomiter rested her head on her knees. The golfer whistled softly as he drove another ball toward a green that only he could see.

'What would you like to talk about?' Biddy asked.

'I'm thinking,' said Winn, 'that maybe I should call Jack Fenn and let him know what the situation is. That seems like the fair thing to do, given that he's one of the people responsible for the reputation of this club. I think he might like to know that his caddies are going around maiming people without apologizing and picking them up without invitation.'

Biddy paused before she answered to make sure her tone stayed light and friendly. She didn't want to give Winn something to push against. 'To be honest,' she said, 'I don't think Jack will feel personally responsible.'

'My leg is just something else to put on his tab.' He fixed his eyes on the photo of the orange crab as though feeling a kinship with it.

'What do you mean?'

'Well, after that whole business' – Winn rolled his hand in an etc., etc. motion – 'in the winter, with Livia, the Fenns owe us.'

'Oh, Winn, that's insane.'

'No, it certainly is not. Livia's procedure cost five hundred dollars. Not to mention the damage done to her reputation.'

'You can't exploit your daughter's private life to worm your way into a golf club.'

'She didn't keep it private, did she, and I shouldn't have to *worm* my way into anything. This whole situation is ridiculous. Untenable. You know, Dicky and Maude seemed to know something.'

Unable to hide her exasperation, Biddy said, 'I don't think there's a conspiracy against you, Winn. And Dicky and Maude said Jack Fenn isn't the problem. To be honest, I have trouble believing that with Teddy about to leave for boot camp Jack is giving either you or the Pequod much thought.'

'Another poor decision from that boy. I could have kept Teddy out of the Ophidian, you know. Maybe I should have. He's sure turning out to be a chip off the old block. Jack was so self-righteous about the whole army thing. Jack Fenn the hero, Jack Fenn the brave. I guess Teddy needs something to lord over everyone, too. You would have thought he would have been happy enough to get in the Ophidian after Jack didn't. Good for the Fenns. They're just very, very impressive, the whole bunch of them.'

Biddy could see Winn's emotions beginning to spin off their reel, something that happened so rarely she had never learned how to stop him from unraveling entirely. He glared around, his lips pressed together as though in defiance of some insidious antagonism buried in the pale hospital walls, the pronged silhouette of the ficus tree, the slow whirligig golfer, the wraiths of weather-report storm clouds swirling over the television. She disliked men when they pouted, and her sympathy silently and invisibly abandoned him, her early morning dream of lovemaking forgotten and replaced by a vision of him as a golf club pariah, a tantrum thrower, a man of so little heft that another man could lift him up and pack him away in a car without the slightest strain.

'Klausman,' the purple nurse said. The golfer, who had moved on to perfecting his putt, raised a hand in acknowledgment and followed her. The vomiting girl watched them disappear with a castaway's desolation. She buried her face in her hands. Her boyfriend continued polishing her hunched back with light, circular, reassuring strokes. A new nurse appeared. 'Van Meter,' she said.

'Finally,' Winn murmured, pushing himself up. Biddy rose, too, but he shook his head at her. 'Wait here.'

'Are you sure?' she asked, still standing.

'Very sure.' He hobbled after the nurse, past the weeping girl and her plastic bag, and disappeared down a long, pale hallway of many doors.

Livia walked a slow circuit around the whale. From a distance it looked black, but up close she could see its skin had deteriorated to a mottled reddish gray and was marked all over with white scratches and scars, mementoes of a life spent tangling with sharp-beaked squid. It lay on its left side with its belly facing inland. Its right pectoral

301

fin was swollen into a useless flap, a pathetic tab stuck to the bloated side of an immense dark balloon. Half a dozen men in foul-weather gear had begun to peel away the skin and blubber. The whale could not be left to rot on the sand. Thirty or forty tons of fat, meat, and briny offal could not be left to erode according to nature's sluggish timetable when there were summer beachgoers to be kept happy. Probably the museum in Waskeke Town would want the skeleton – they had one already but why not another – and the bones could not be had without digging them out of the oily flesh. The men were sweating and cursing, spattered with particles of the leviathan. It looked like hard work, flensing, but they had made progress. Wide tracts of blubber were exposed along the whale's side. A cutter in yellow overalls stood on top of the animal, bracing his rubber boots against the slippery skin and leaning on the long handle of his knife (an antique borrowed from the museum) to push the blade through dense strata of fat. A bulldozer, Livia overheard people saying, was coming to help bury the pieces.

Below the massive, blocky head, the whale's jaw hung open – long and narrow and studded with conical teeth – and Livia peered into the odiferous cave of its mouth. In its upper jaw there were no teeth, only sockets. The opening to its throat was surprisingly small, no grand, fishy portal leading to a ribbed and lightless cathedral with room for Geppetto and Jonah. It was a female, and she wondered how many calves it had produced, how far it had ranged. Sperm whales dove thousands of feet to feed in total darkness. They could hold their breath for an hour, dive at five hundred feet per minute, slow their metabolisms, collapse their lungs, tolerate huge amounts of lactic acid as their muscles burned through stored oxygen. They allowed cold water into their nasal passages so the oily spermaceti in their heads turned from liquid to solid, helping them descend. They were, in all ways, miraculous diving machines.

And yet they could drown, did drown, tangled in transoceanic phone lines or held under ice or wrapped in fishing nets. The bones of older whales showed lesions from nitrogen emboli caused by ascending too quickly – the bends. Livia wondered if an upside-down cosmology existed for whales, if heaven was something deep and dark and cold, and this bright, sandy beach was hell. She thought again about how she had woken up that morning, the darkness of the beach and the water washing over her feet. The whale was already dead by then, close to shore if not yet beached, rolling in the surf only a few miles from where she and Sterling had been. Fortunate whales sank to the sea floor when they died and were picked to bare bones by fish, crabs, and worms. This whale had fallen through some loop in the universe and descended from the sky, sinking through the night to be picked at by humans.

Francis was talking to some men clustered

around a truck. He was speaking with great animation – probably, she thought, about genuine experience and his desire to have it. Eventually the men shrugged and nodded, and Francis lifted an axe from a pile of tools on the sand. Livia knew at once what he intended. He carried the axe to a spot below the pectoral fin, set the blade in the sand, and grasped the handle with both hands. The man in yellow atop the whale paused in his cutting and looked down. Francis looked like a blinkered horse in his big sunglasses, turning his head from side to side, getting his bearings. 'Francis,' she called, walking in his direction. 'Wait!'

'Why?' Francis shouted against the wind.

She had no answer. A cut-up whale was a cut-up whale. No one else seemed inclined to stop him. But Livia did not want Francis, someone who didn't even like whales, to drop an axe into this one's belly. 'Just wait!' she called.

'Here we go!' he said, raising the axe behind his head. The blade sailed down and stuck into the blubber. Francis grinned. He worked the axe free and raised it again. Uneasy, Livia watched. She had almost adjusted to the reek of the whale, but it seemed to have become more pungent. She thought she might vomit again.

'One,' he said, lifting the axe, 'two, three!' The blade descended, glinting against the sky. She was never sure if the whale exploded before or after the axe hit home. She would have sworn the weapon was still in flight when she was knocked back by a wall of crimson and pinned to the sand under a heavy rope of intestine. She could never recall the sound of the massive corpse ripping apart. She remembered the axe, and then she remembered being on her back, looking up at the startled seagulls.

CHAPTER 12

FORTUNATE SON

Winn met Jack Fenn in October 1969. Winn was a senior, and for the members of the Ophidian, October was a flurried month of social sport. In the third week, invitations to an Ophidian cocktail party were bestowed upon likely sophomores, who, as the lingo went, could consider themselves 'punched.' Most punches were chosen because they were acquaintances of Ophidian members. Some were chosen out of the freshman register for their last names. The punches who did not irritate any of the members by behaving in a way that was too boyish, boorish, earnest, serious, slick, falsely modest, hammy, eager, or bookish were invited to another event and then another until the pond of potentials was drained down to the last drops of purest blue. The punches whose brothers or fathers had been in the club were considered the nearest thing to shoo-ins that the Ophidian, for all the rigor of its selection, could have. For a legacy to be denied admission was unusual but decidedly possible if the apple fell far from the tree or the tree had been problematic in the first place.

Jack Fenn was a legacy of the best kind. Not only his father and brother but his father's father and his mother's father and a slew of uncles had belonged to the club; three Fenns had been elected Ouroboros, and all Fenns had been popular and remained active as alumni, donating money or gifts every year and maintaining an open-door policy in their homes for members. In the club's upstairs great room, mounted in a central position on the longest wall, was an enormous, curved sword like something out of *The Arabian Nights*, its handle finialed with a fanged python's head, the empty eye sockets of which supposedly once contained rubies. For obscure reasons, the sword was known as Fenn's Fiddle, and during the most raucous of club gatherings, it was taken down to be brandished during songs or used for comic effect to slice cheese. On occasion, the blade opened Ophidian fingertips in impromptu ceremonies of blood brotherhood.

When young Jack Fenn arrived at his first punch event, coppery as a new penny and with an abundance of summer freckles, he was greeted enthusiastically and passed from member to member with the same glee and lighthearted reverence as the sword itself. So boisterous were the members that none of them (save Winn) noticed the fatal trace of seriousness hanging over Fenn. He was always holding a glass but seldom drinking from it, and he chatted with the members and took their jokes amiably enough without ever shedding his air of reserve and judgment. Punches were not meant to judge but to be judged. When Winn tried to express his doubts, the other members brushed him off, calling him 'Old Sour Grapes.' The Ouroboros himself, an impeccable boy named Frost Jameson, came up with 'Van Whiner.' Not until punch season was almost over, in the gray days of winter when the remaining punches were being scrutinized as carefully as yearlings about to go up on the block, did Winn get his hard evidence.

Along with another senior named Bill Midland and a strapping, rigorous, red-faced alum called Denton, Winn was assigned to take Fenn and two other sophomores, twin brothers with the last name Boothe-Snype, out to lunch. Denton chose an oak-and-brass restaurant that was a club favorite, and a dour maître d' in a tailcoat led them to a curtained alcove where they sat in a horseshoe-shaped leather banquette beneath an oil copy of *The Raft of the Medusa*. Winn, Bill Midland, and Denton each ordered steak, onion soup, corn pudding, baked potatoes, and Caesar salad, and Denton selected two bottles of good burgundy.

'Chilly out,' Denton announced, spooning chives onto his potato. 'A nice, hearty lunch is just the ticket.'

The punches nodded, eying the members' feasts while slicing – elbows well off the white tablecloth – into the more modest entrées they had tactfully chosen: a game hen for Fenn and sole meunière for the Boothe-Snypes. Winn felt a flash of sympathy. He had been in their shoes not so long ago. He remembered the anxiety of trying to choose food that would appear sophisticated and Ophidian but not presumptuous or greedy, the struggle not to say the wrong thing but also not to think so long about what to say that he missed his chance to speak at all, the gnawing self-consciousness of being evaluated as a social entity – that was the point of these lunches, of course: to see if the punches were, first, the kind of men worthy of the Ophidian and, second, the kind of guys the existing members would want to pal around with. They were meant to be brothers, after all, but brothers who chose one another. This process of selection, of rational choice, was, in Winn's opinion, more profound than any accidental genetic bond. Ophidian members made a mindful commitment, swearing a solemn vow after the mutual recognition of something in one another's . . . Winn did not like the word 'soul,' but the Ophidian ideal, when you came right down to it, was of a brotherhood bound not by parentage but by souls.

When he was a punch, he had been taken to this same restaurant, and the conversation had revolved mostly around sports – tennis, football, and lacrosse – until one of the other punches revealed that he was an accomplished figure skater, a national champion. Winn had thought

Thank God as soon as the words 'figure skating' left the other boy's mouth because even then, as a lowly punch, he knew it was not Ophidian to figure skate, and if he joined in the subtle, oh-so-subtle mockery of this boy (who, it turned out, would go to the Olympics the following year in Grenoble and place a very un-Ophidian twelfth), then he would have succeeded in forging a bond with the members. This lunch, however, Jack Fenn's turn in the hot seat, was held on December 3, 1969, only two days after they had all endured the crucible of the draft lottery, and inevitably the talk turned to numbers. Bill Midland's number, he volunteered, was 248.

'July eleventh,' he said. 'Lucky seven-eleven. Didn't let me down.'

'Good,' Denton said. 'That's a good draw, Midland. Not that you wouldn't make a fine soldier, but I imagine you have other priorities.'

'A girl drew my number,' Midland said. 'Did you see her? From Washington State. Seems odd to have girls draw. What do they have to do with anything?'

'Did you hear about David Eisenhower?' said one of the twins.

'Got called tenth or something like that,' said the other.

'Something like that,' agreed Denton.

Fenn, who had so far said little, spoke up. 'Thirtieth.'

'He'll be all right,' Denton went on. 'Fine military

tradition in that family. I expect he'll go over, but he'll be used appropriately. I'm sure of it.'

'I knew him at Exeter,' said Bill Midland. 'Not well, but he was in my class.'

'And?' asked Denton, looking up sharply from his corn pudding. Denton was a fixture at these punch lunches because he had a relentless instinct for digging to the bottom of a man's character like a pig snuffling for truffles.

Midland shrugged. 'Good enough guy.'

Denton nodded. 'There you have it,' he said.

Fenn said, 'I heard he's going into the navy reserves.'

'Frost Jameson pulled something low, too,' Winn said. 'In the fifties, I think. I told him he should pretend to be queer.' The memory smarted. Jameson had only replied with a look of annoyance.

'What about you, Van Meter?' asked Midland. 'What did you pull?'

Winn had gone home to watch the drawing. As soon as he passed beneath the porch lantern of the white stone house and into the tall and chilly entryway, he wished he'd gone to the Ophidian instead. Most of the members had convened at the club. Television watching was usually considered too prosaic for the clubhouse, but they kept an old set on the uppermost floor in a room reserved for unwanted odds and ends: a retired pool table with faded felt and one short leg propped up with a ball of candle wax, a trunk full of moth-eaten costumes occasionally hauled out for charades and pranks, an ancient Victrola, a library of handed-down textbooks, a few decommissioned lamps. The room was also used to store gifts from alumni that did not make the grade for more prominent display. There was a large African drum that no one knew what to do with. There was a porcelain doll dressed as a yeoman of the guard and a globe with the names of countries written in German. Mostly, though, there were snakes. Haphazardly strewn about the room and stacked among the books and lamps were dozens of snakes collected on exotic travels and mounted by inexpert taxidermists, given walleyes or lumpy bodies or buck fangs or other deformities that disqualified them from exhibition downstairs, where the Ophidian had enough snakes to open a museum of herpetology. A rattler emerged from the bronze lily of the Victrola's mouthpiece, and an asp coiled beneath the mammoth burgundy Hercules of an armchair that stood opposite the television and spat wooly stuffing from two slits in its back and one in its seat.

To that room, that aerie of the unwanted, Winn's true family had repaired to await their collective reckoning in the company of their heraldic animal while Winn sat on the rug beside his father's chair and listened to the radio as he had as a child. Eventually he went into the basement and turned on the black-and-white television there, just for five minutes, because he wanted to see exactly who was conducting this morbid raffle. A young man in his Sunday best stepped up to a plain glass jar and pulled out a capsule, which he handed to a woman at a desk. She opened it and unrolled a slip of paper, handing it to a balding man in a blue suit, who read the date aloud and handed the slip to yet another man, who stuck it to its place on a long, dreary board, halfway down a column of identical slips, next to several identical columns, and announced the numbers again. After a few draws, a new young man appeared in suit and tie and reached into the jar. Each bit of paper was passed rapidly along, held by each person for as short a time as possible. May 19 was slotted into its place on the board (75) and then November 6 (76). Winn wondered what would happen if a boy drew his own birthday. Would he ruin the whole charade with his grim face, his trembling fingers? After September 5 (82) was pulled, his father called from upstairs. 'Winnie,' he bellowed, 'come have a talk.'

Bitterly, Winn switched off the TV and climbed the stairs. He should have known he would not be allowed simply to sit and listen. No, he had to hear for the hundredth time Tipton's story of how he had, at the age of thirty-three, tried to join up. He claimed he would have been among those who landed at Normandy if not for a grace note in his heartbeat. Instead he had been forced to stay home with the women, women who wanted to date soldiers and not men with complicated heartbeats who worked for their fathers. Faced with few options, he had married Winn's mother, not a fresh young girl but a woman his own age – well bred, humorless, and dyspeptic. They had both been thunderstruck when, as she neared forty, she became pregnant, an ordeal for which she never forgave either husband or son. 'Once,' Tipton intoned while Winn edged closer to the radio, straining to hear the numbers, 'Cort Wilder's brothers were home on leave at the same time, and Cort and I dressed up in their spare uniforms and we all went out to a dance hall. What a night that was. Lord.' The word expanded slowly from his lips, filling up like a bubble with the romance and shame of that one night as a glamorous impostor – *Lord* – before it popped into silence.

The voice on the radio announced that June 6 was number 110. Winn looked over his shoulder at his father. 'Close one,' he said.

Tipton was studying the bottom of his glass, turning it so the crystal facets caught the lamplight. 'If they call your number,' he said, 'you will go.' At once Winn was tearful and full of rancor. Given the chance, he might have declared his manfulness unprompted. *If they call my number*, he might have said, *I'm going*. And then, in a perfect world, Tipton would have said, *No, you're my only son. Run to Canada. I don't care what anyone says.* But Tipton had the moony look he got when he was lost in his dreams of the past. This wasn't World War II, Winn wanted to tell him. No one thought so. He didn't need to dress up as a soldier to get girls. He had thought that his father, who had never gone to war, would not mind if his only son, his only child, followed suit and stayed home to live a long and peaceful life. If Communism could be distilled into a single combatant, a juggernaut in a red singlet, then Winn would offer his own body, throw himself into the arena as a martyr, but to leave the comfortable brick womb of Harvard and the promise of a good career to be shot at by Vietnamese villagers . . . it didn't sit right. Everyone Winn knew felt the same way. He suspected Tipton would feel the same way if it were Tipton's head to be shorn, Tipton's life to be interrupted, Tipton who would crawl through the jungle. Not that the situation would come to that, of course. At least Winn didn't think so. If push came to shove, Tipton could at least be convinced to pull strings to get him into the National Guard or the reserves. He would only carry this warrior-father charade so far. And so Winn, without looking at his father, said okay, he would go, and then they had waited, and the numbers had followed one after the other, until finally, after Tipton nodded off, his glass spilling its clear dregs into his lap, Winn's number had come up.

'June eighth,' he said to Bill Midland. 'Three hundred sixty-six. Dead last. And my name starts with V. Last in the alphabet lottery.'

Midland's face filled with awe. 'Holy moly. The

Cong could take the White House, and you wouldn't get called up.'

'Well done, Van Meter,' said Denton. 'Good day to be born.'

'Do you oppose the war, Mr Denton?' asked Fenn, cutting into his hen.

Denton head bobbed backward in perplexity like a struck speed bag. 'Christ, no. You can't have the Russians rolling down the Mekong. No, not at all. It's got to be fought, but we need a certain kind of young man here to keep things running smoothly. I think you all are more use to capitalism than you are to the army.'

'Here, here,' said Winn, trying to close the subject.

'Then who do you think should do the fighting?' Fenn persisted. He seemed relaxed, curious, unaware of his treacherous footing.

The question was an obvious one, but Winn would never have asked it. A cardinal rule of Ophidian punch events was that butting heads with a member was discouraged but possibly forgivable while offending an alum was suicidal. Denton colored and sawed at his steak. 'Well, son, starting off with the delinquents is a good idea. If you're causing problems for us over here, you might as well go cause them over there. And then, to be frank, I think we should call on the lower classes. If you're not in school and you don't have much of a future in any event, then get out there and do your part. Greater good, and so on. Boys'll amount

316

to more in the army than by working in, I don't know' – he waved his knife in a thoughtful circle – 'an auto body shop or someplace. They do their part, then they come home and get a free education. Lift themselves up.'

'So,' Fenn said, 'the poor should fight.' He spoke in a mild, secretarial tone as though he were reading back shorthand notes of Denton's speech.

Denton looked at him narrowly, his eyes traveling over the bright hair that covered the tops of his ears and brushed his collar. 'You're Auggie Fenn's boy?'

'That's right.'

'And what does your father think?'

Fenn smiled. 'Rich man's war, poor man's fight.'

'*Auggie Fenn* thinks that? He *said* that?'

Bill Midland, who had nearly dropped his fork at Fenn's words, turned to the twins. 'What was your number?' he asked.

'Actually,' said a Boothe-Snype, 'we were born on different days, technically. I made it out just before midnight on June eighteenth, and he was born an hour later, on the nineteenth.'

'Well then, where does that leave you?' Denton asked. His cheeks and forehead were redder than usual, and he spoke with impatience, through a purple and white mouthful of meat and potato.

'I'm one hundred four. He's three hundred forty-one,' said the other twin, his face full of dismay at the consequences of his slow trip through the birth canal.

317

'Bad luck for you,' Bill Midland said. 'Can't you say something like you can't be separated from your twin and you should have the same number?'

'They'd probably give us both one hundred four,' said Boothe-Snype 341.

'Maybe they'd give you the average of the two.' Midland looked pleased with his solution.

'Could be worse, could be worse,' said Denton, laying a large and reassuring hand on Boothe-Snype 104's shoulder. 'You've got three more years of two-S, don't you? This will all be over by then. Or at least you'll have time to figure out something else. Too bad they did away with the graduate deferments; otherwise I'd say you're completely in the clear. As it is, I think you'll be just fine, not as fortunate as your brother there, but just fine.'

'That makes me think of that song,' Bill Midland said. 'You know the one I mean? "Fortunate Son"? I heard it's about David Eisenhower.'

'I don't know it,' Denton said. 'How does it go?'

Conducting himself with little twitches of his knife and fork, Midland sang in his glee club baritone, 'It ain't me. It ain't me. I ain't no senator's son.' He cut off and reached for his wineglass, blushing because, as it happened, the Boothe-Snypes' father was a senator.

'Poor taste, that,' said Denton. 'Eisenhower will do his duty. That's more than I can say for these so-called musicians sitting around and whining.'

'I was watching the draw in Eliot,' Boothe-Snype 341 said, 'and a guy got pulled fifth and put his

318

foot through the television. Cut his ankle up. We all had to go find somewhere else to watch.'

Denton nodded. 'Long-haired type?'

'Not really. Just a guy.' The Boothe-Snype shrugged.

'No good going around making scenes,' Denton said with finality. 'You have to accept your duty and do it with honor.'

'That's easy to say when you're out of the running, though, isn't it?' Fenn suggested.

'Pardon?' said Denton, disbelieving, a forkful of beef arrested on its way to his mouth.

'All I mean is that since you've never had to sit in front of a television and wait to see if you're going to be sent off to defend some jungle from a particular system of government, I don't think you're in any position to judge.' As he spoke, Fenn lifted and turned the remains of his game hen with delicate maneuvers of his silver, probing for any last morsels.

Denton's big, robust face turned a sweaty shade of tomato. 'And you? Are you packing your bags for Canada? Or did you get a nice high number?'

Fenn set his knife and fork on the edge of his plate and dabbed his mouth with his napkin. 'My birthday is September fourteenth,' he said.

Activity at the table ceased. Winn stared across at Fenn. Fenn met his eyes and then looked away. The others had remembered Winn now, too, and were glancing back and forth between him and Fenn and then at one another.

'Well, well,' said Denton, leaning back in his chair and surveying the boys and the ruins of lunch with the air of a satisfied khan. 'The alpha and the omega. Together at one table.'

'But you're taking your two-S,' Winn said. 'You still have two years after this one.'

'No. I'll go when I get called up.'

'God, why?' blurted Bill Midland, agog.

'Don't be stupid, Fenn,' Winn said. 'Why would you do that?'

'I don't like all this squirming that goes on. Begging the doctors, begging the draft boards, pulling strings, running to Canada. I don't blame guys for wanting to get out, but I don't have it in me. My number came up. I intend to do as I'm intended to do.'

'That's insane,' Winn exclaimed before anyone else could speak. He was surprised at his own vehemence. He pointed at Fenn. 'It's one thing to dodge, but it's another to turn up your nose at your deferment. Two-S is meant for people like you. You can't just *go*. At least get into ROTC or something, Fenn, really. You don't know what it'll be like. You want to be in the mud with a bunch of guys who would have killed for three years of two-S? You don't have to be a hero. Be reasonable. For your own sake.'

'I have to say,' Denton put in, 'I agree with Van Meter. Deferments exist for a reason – a good reason – and you should take advantage. Think of your mother. No sense in throwing everything away for . . . for some kind of gesture you'll regret as soon as you get over there. Probably sooner. But then it'll be too late. Christ, carrot-top, you'll be a sitting duck.'

'What is the reason?' asked Fenn.

'What?'

'The reason deferments exist.'

'We've been through this, Fenn,' Denton said, taking an indulgent, paternal tone. 'It's to keep men like you from getting cut down before their time. There's no sense in it. It's a waste. Take my advice. Take the two-S. At least for a year. If you feel the same way after a year, then go. I wash my hands.' He lifted his voluminous white napkin from his lap and scrubbed his lips.

Fenn spoke in a wry echo of Denton's false patience. 'Thank you, Mr Denton. I'll take that into consideration. But I believe I drew number one for a reason.'

'What?' said Denton. 'Why? Because of God and that?'

'Whatever you want to call it.'

'Fenn,' said Winn, 'don't take this the wrong way, but you're sounding stupider and stupider.'

Fenn seemed calm, almost sad. 'Oh, I don't know, Winn. I think you'd like the military. There are lots of rules, and you always know where you stand.'

Winn said, 'Why do you want to be in the Ophidian anyway, if you might not even last this year? What's the point in punching?'

'Well, you invited me to lunch, and I was available, and I've been taught that it's rude to turn down an invitation when you're not otherwise engaged.'

Bill Midland snorted. The velvet curtain was flung aside and the waiter appeared, shouldering a silver tray of cakes and tarts. 'Something sweet?' he said.

The doctor, a man of about forty, swung through the door. He was tall and lean and moved in smooth, rapid glides, like a water bug. His sparse blond hair was combed without vanity straight back from a hairline in deep recession. Only a narrow, downy peninsula survived between two long incursions of forehead. 'Ah, Mr Vanmeter,' he said, glancing at the chart in his hand and pronouncing the name as one word with a Germanic emphasis on the first syllable. 'You fell off your bike.' He offered a brief smile, a quick flex of the mouth. Above the crenellation of pens in the breast pocket of his lab coat, 'DR FINLAY' was embroidered in blue script.

'Van *Meter*,' Winn said. 'I didn't fall. I was hit by a golf cart.'

'I'm sorry to hear that,' the doctor said, taking two long glides toward Winn and wiggling the knobs of his stethoscope into his large ears.

'There's no need for a checkup,' Winn said, twisting around to fend him off. The paper on the exam table stuck to his thighs and crinkled loudly. 'You can go ahead and stitch me up.'

'Mmmhmm, just routine. Breathe in.'

Winn filled and emptied his lungs, followed a bright light with his eyes, admitted a thermometer into his mouth, allowed the dank, bristly caves of his ears and nostrils to be illuminated and observed, and watched with detachment as his tennis shoes kicked feebly in response to the tapping of a rubber mallet.

At last the doctor peeled Otis's handkerchief back from Winn's shin and lightly touched the edges of the crescent-shaped wound. 'Mmmhmm. Yes, yes,' he said to himself. Without another word he turned and vanished out the door, reappearing twenty seconds later with a rolling metal tray laden with sharp silver instruments that gleamed maliciously in the light. The doctor busied himself at the sink: washing his hands, opening and closing drawers, pulling out packets of gauze, wiggling his long fingers into surgical gloves he plucked from a box. So deft and rapid was his routine that he appeared to have three or four arms; Winn wondered if he might juggle tangerines or spin a plate atop a wand at the same time he stitched up the wound.

'Been a busy summer?' Winn asked, trying to fight off the first ripples of queasiness as the doctor slid the needle of a syringe through the rubber seal in the lid of a small glass vial and pulled back the plunger.

'Hmm? Oh, yes. Yes, yes.' Dr Finlay propelled himself across the floor on a wheeled stool and coasted to a stop beside Winn's leg. 'This may sting.' He swabbed briskly with a square of gauze that left behind a trail of fire. 'All right now, a little prick,' he said, lowering the needle to the edge of the wound. He punctured the skin. Winn watched him depress the plunger ever so slightly. A drop of blood appeared at the site of the injection, and the doctor wiped it away. 'And another one,' he said, his voice sounding far away as he moved the needle to a new spot. 'And another one.'

A sour layer of cold sweat sprang out on Winn's forehead, but he also felt overheated. He wondered if he had gotten sunburned sometime during this godforsaken morning.

'One more,' the doctor said from a great distance. Winn looked down and saw the needle pierce his flesh before it dissolved into white sparks and flares. 'Oops, spoke too soon. One last prick,' came the doctor's voice through a shimmering darkness as Winn fell sideways out of the world.

CHAPTER 13

A CENTAUR

Livia walked a few steps ahead of Francis, across dunes and through sharp grasses, her skin sticky and chafing, her whole self reeking. The smell was a potent cocktail of salt water, kitchen sponge, and death. They were looking for a path from the beach out to a road where Dicky Sr could come and pick them up. Livia's phone had been destroyed when, panicked after the explosion, she had run into the ocean, but Francis's had survived. Even his sunglasses had emerged intact, if smudged. They paused to watch a Jeep jostle over the sand with a stretcher propped like a surfboard against its roll bar, one paramedic riding shotgun and the other crouched in the back. In the distance, the lights of a waiting ambulance blinked silently.

'He'll be fine, won't he?' Francis asked.

'I hope so,' Livia said. 'For your sake.'

'I don't see how this was my fault.'

'I'll walk you through it. You hit the whale with an axe. The whale exploded.'

'How was I supposed to know that would happen? They *gave* me the axe. They *said* I could.'

After the initial chaos, after Livia had come back out of the water, she found a crowd standing in a circle, looking at someone on the ground. Sidling in, she saw that the object of their attention was the man in yellow foul-weather gear, the one who had been standing atop the whale when Francis dropped his axe. He was lying on the sand with a shard of bone sticking out of his shoulder like a pin from a butterfly, and he pointed a finger at Francis and said, *You did this*. But Francis had denied it, saying he hadn't done anything; he was just another innocent bystander.

'When you see a bloated raccoon on the side of the road,' Livia said, stepping over a dune fence, 'do you run over and pop it with a fork?'

'Sorry if I don't know everything about stupid fucking whales,' said Francis. 'Everyone was cutting it up anyway. If not me, someone else would have hit the sweet spot. If you think about it, I kind of *released* it from all that pressure.'

Huge clumps of meat and blubber had been strewn across the sand. The whale's outsize organs and all its piping and wiring and insulation were on display – lungs like hot-air balloons, bones of dinosaurian dimensions, a meaty colossus of a heart. Great pale ropes of intestine lay scattered like joke snakes sprung from a can. The impaled man had a long gray beard trimmed square at its bottom, and his face was contorted in rabbitlike agony, his large front teeth gripping his lower lip and his small, dark eyes darting over the circle of faces looking down on him. A woman Livia took to be his wife knelt beside him, her hands fluttering helplessly around the bone. Once accused, Francis had pulled Livia forward by the wrist.

'I swear it wasn't me,' he said. 'Ask this girl. Just ask her.'

Livia had studied the dour, spattered faces. For the most part they looked like locals, not summer people. One blond woman in a bloodied Lilly Pulitzer dress stood holding the hands of two small, tearful boys, but otherwise the faces were creased and weathered, toughened by long winters on the island. She had intended to cover for Francis, more for her own sake than his, but lying to these people, grim and weary as the crew of some wrecked ship, seemed unconscionable. She hesitated for just a little too long. The man's wife stood up. She was a short, hunched person with a gray cloche of hair and stuck-out chin.

'You're going to jail,' she told Francis.

'There's a misunderstanding,' he said.

'What misunderstanding? Look what you did to Samuel. Look at him!'

'It just blew up! I didn't do anything. He's wrong. It just blew!'

His voice rose above the low grumble of the crowd, which had begun to stir and close ranks. Samuel's wife looked around, almost sly, gauging the allegiance of the others, and then, one eye squinted shut, lips folded in a turtle smile, she faked a quick jab, her fist stopping just short of

Francis's jaw. Francis stepped back from the fist and onto the rubber boot of the man behind him, which the man quickly reclaimed. Francis stumbled sideways, grabbing at Livia for balance.

Now the crowd began to look less like castaways and more like a band of Gothic villagers, armed with flensing knives instead of clubs and torches. Francis sized them up with a shifty, darting glance. Then, as though pulled by a falling weight, his face slid downward into an expression of deep grief.

'Maybe you're right. Maybe it was me,' he said, looking at Samuel's wife through lowered lashes. 'I am so sorry – I didn't realize. I should have been more careful. I acted without thinking, and now this poor man is gravely injured. I feel terrible. I don't know how I'm going to live with this. I just wanted to feel like a part of the island, you know? I just wanted to participate. And now look what I've done. I ruin everything I touch. I'm cursed.'

He brushed at the sand that encrusted his cheeks and sniffed. Then he plopped onto the beach, wrapping his arms around his shins and lowering his head to his knees.

'Francis?' Livia said.

He pressed his hands over the top of his head. His voice was muffled. 'I deserve to go to jail. I deserve whatever's coming to me.'

Livia looked at Samuel's wife, recognizing her to be the arbiter of their fates. The woman narrowed her eyes and looked out to sea like a captain considering a change in course. Finally, gruffly, she said, 'Get up, kid. Only a lunatic would have done that on purpose. You're not a psycho. You're just a little dumb.'

With the wonderment of a condemned man granted a last-minute reprieve, Francis lifted his chin and gazed up at her. Livia nudged him with her toe, urging him to his feet, and he stood and reached to shake the woman's hand. 'Thank you,' he said. 'You've been more generous than I could have possibly expected or deserved.'

'Yeah,' Samuel's wife had said. 'Go on and get out of here.' And they had obeyed, trailing away down the beach like two outcasts.

'Still. You got lucky,' Livia said to him as they walked, turning inland, out of sight of the ambulance. 'They were ready to string you up.'

He shrugged. 'The trick is to be sorrier than anyone could expect you to be. Then they feel bad and want to do something nice for you.'

'Is that what the Buddha would do?'

'I never said I was the Buddha,' Francis said. 'The best anyone can do is to *try* to emulate him. The trying is what matters. I live in a constant state of failure.'

They traversed a narrow, sandy trail and came to a wider track that led through a gathering of beach cottages and eventually joined the road where Dicky Sr had agreed to pick them up.

'What I don't get,' Livia said after a long silence,

as they stood on the graveled shoulder and peered into the distance for Dicky's rental car, 'is why you would choose that particular religion, when it's so easy for people to call foul on you. You have to know everyone's going to wonder why you're not a vegetarian, why you don't meditate. You're supposed to be eliminating desire, but, as a person, you seem pretty willing to indulge all kinds of desires. Why do that to yourself? Why not just say you're a nihilist and be done with it?'

They were both caked with a fine layer of powdery sand, blown onto them by the persistent wind. Francis glittered in the sun as though sugared. 'I like the struggle,' he said, 'even if I never make any progress. At least this way I have an aspiration. I'm set in contrast to *something*. Otherwise, I would just blend into the scenery, and no one would ever have anything to say about me.'

On the drive home, Winn wanted the windows open in hopes that fresh air might dispel the headache and nausea that had settled in shortly after Dr Finlay resuscitated him with an acrid packet of smelling salts and stitched up his numb flesh. Biddy's hair, bobbed in a blunt and practical line at her shoulders, streamed backward and flew around her ears before standing straight up in an electrified coxcomb. The morning breeze had gathered force, and clouds advanced under full sail, more of them than before, merging to block out the sun and then sliding apart in a burst of light.

Some vital part of him had been depleted, if not by his wound alone, then by his fainting spell on the doctor's table, by Otis scooping him up like a damsel in distress, by Agatha and her wine-red mouth, by all the people in his house sucking lobsters out of their shells. Agatha had been driven from his thoughts, but now her decoys started popping up everywhere, like targets in a shooting range. She was the blond jogger they overtook and the visored driver of the car behind them; she was in a tennis skirt holding the leash of a dog lifting its leg on a stop sign. Again the trees waved him up his driveway with evergreen fans. As it had when he first arrived, the house looked strange, like an impostor house. A Jeep was parked to one side of the driveway, and a white car was stopped near the front door, a bedraggled version of Livia standing beside it and speaking to the driver.

'Good lord!' said Biddy. 'What could have happened?'

Before Biddy had time to park, Dicky Sr waved out the window of the white car, gave a cheerful toot of the horn, and sailed off down the driveway, leaving Livia alone. 'Stop,' Winn said to Biddy, opening his door. 'Just stop here.'

She jolted the Land Rover into park. 'I'm stopping, I'm stopping.'

Winn slid from his seat in a hurry and landed awkwardly on his bad leg. 'Damn!' he said at the squirt of pain. He limped toward Livia. 'What in God's name happened?'

'A whale exploded on me. What happened to you?'

'A golf cart hit me. A *whale*?'

She told the whole story while Biddy made exclamations of surprise and Winn looked her over for damage. She seemed fine, if grimy and sandy and odiferous. The ends of her ponytail clumped together like the bristles of a dirty paintbrush. The way Livia looked, the general gruesome mess of her, reminded him of something, but he couldn't place it.

When she had finished, he said, 'Let me make sure I have this straight. You heard there was a dead whale on the beach. You decided you wanted to see it.'

Livia nodded. 'Yes.'

'You left your sister behind and walked around the point. You—' He stopped. Ordinarily, he would have repeated the whole story back to her to make sure he had the facts pinned to their proper places in their proper drawers, but his head ached and his leg ached and his usual routine seemed too arduous to bother with.

'Livia,' Biddy said, holding hesitant fingers above her daughter's hair, 'you look just like you did on the day you were born.'

That was it, the thing Winn had been reminded of: Livia as a newborn. He saw her emerging into that tub, underwater like a drowned thing, and

332

then being lifted into the air, bloodied and shrieking, the crimson cloud drifting from between Biddy's legs, the doctor saying *C'est une fille.* A more recent memory intruded: he was pacing the front hall of the Connecticut house, waiting for Livia and Biddy to come home from *getting it taken care of,* and he watched out the window as the car appeared and Livia slid out of the front seat and retched into the flower beds.

'But,' he said, 'no major harm done? Everyone's fine?'

'Well.' She hesitated. 'A guy got a shard of bone stuck in his shoulder.'

'What guy?'

'An island guy. An ambulance was there when we left.'

He kneaded his forehead with two fingers. His headache was thriving. 'Is there anything I need to do about any of it? Is Francis getting arrested?'

'I don't think so.'

'Fine then.' He turned to Biddy. 'Where are the other girls? The bridesmaids?'

'I don't know. If they're not here they're still out doing makeup practice or getting their nails done – I can't remember.'

'Makeup *practice*? Seems extravagant.'

'Well,' Biddy said, 'it's what people do for weddings, Winn.' And off she went, around the side of the house.

Livia looked after her. 'Is Mom mad?'

He reached to pat her on the back but stopped

short. 'Come with me to the garage. I want to bring over some more wine now that the locusts have come and gone.'

'Dad, I'm dying to shower.'

'First we'll do this, and then of course you'll use the outdoor shower.'

'Dad.'

'First we'll do this.'

An exhausted stupor had begun to overtake him, sweeping like a thunderhead after his retreating adrenaline, but he would outrun it. He set off at as rapid a limp as he could manage, following the driveway through the trees to the garage. 'Take it easy, Ahab,' Livia said behind him. Usually, he would have gone in at the side door, but he wanted to make a large physical gesture to fight off his grogginess, and he seized the handle of the big up-and-over garage door and heaved.

A moment passed before he understood what he was looking at. In the dusky cave he had so theatrically thrown open were two figures. One figure, really. A mangled centaur: Agatha, naked, on all fours, and Sterling Duff rearing up behind her, also naked, kneeling on an unzipped pink sleeping bag that had belonged to one of the girls. They froze, blinking at the light like animals surprised in their den, and then there was a flurry of covering hands and futile scrambling. Winn stood and watched them. He suspected that later he would feel something about all this, but he also knew that, at the moment, he was too tired to jump and exclaim and hide his eyes. He gazed at Agatha's bare breasts, her hairless body. Behind her bobbed Sterling's pale bulk and embarrassing erection. When the two of them finally settled down and were standing side by side like Adam and Eve, shielding themselves with the sleeping bag, Winn said, 'I just came for some wine.' He limped past them back to the corner where cases of wine were stacked beside the old refrigerator. Dry black strands of something were scattered on the cement floor – seaweed, but why? He picked up a box of reds and, turning to tell Livia to come get a few whites out of the fridge, was rewarded instead with the sight of Sterling's and Agatha's asses: Sterling's white and flat, Agatha's round and tan. Livia had vanished. He had not noticed her go. He had only a vague, peripheral memory of her bolting away before the door was even all the way up. What had happened between her and Sterling? He could guess. He didn't want to guess. The wine was too heavy for him. Wobbling on his bad leg, he set the box down with a clank. Sterling turned so he and Agatha stood back to back, rolled by the sleeping bag into a kind of burrito.

'I can get that,' Sterling said.

Winn tore open the box and pulled out two bottles. 'Bring the rest when you come in,' he said. 'No hurry.' Without looking at Agatha, he stumped out of the garage and back to the house.

*　*　*

'Look who's here!' Biddy exclaimed in the kitchen. She was at the sink washing strawberries. Winn, clutching the wine bottles like two clubs, thought at first she was talking about him, not to him, until he realized the eldest Hazzard sister, Tabitha, had arrived and was sitting in the breakfast nook with Celeste. Celeste had a glass of something in front of her; Tabitha was drinking orange juice through a straw so as not to disrupt the precise vermillion lacquer on her lips. 'Hello, Tabitha!' he said, bending to kiss her cheek. 'Celeste.'

Biddy brushed past him and sat down with her sisters, setting a bowl of strawberries in the center of the table. Celeste took one. 'Biddy was just telling us how you were maimed,' she said. 'Poor thing. Shouldn't you be getting off your feet?'

'You're a real Hazzard!' declared Tabitha.

'I'm fine,' Winn said, setting down the wine.

'And a caddy scooped you up?' Celeste's face was unreadable, but he thought they had probably been laughing at him.

He turned on Biddy. 'Why did you tell them?'

'Was it a secret?' she said, not meeting his eyes.

Tabitha, a practiced changer of subjects, said, 'Are you sure you're feeling well?'

'I'm sure.' He did feel okay, if fuzzy around the edges. He leaned against the counter and looked them over. He had always enjoyed comparing Biddy to her sisters because he liked to be reminded that he'd gotten the best one. On the level of basic armature, the three women were almost identical,

336

all tall and spare with long, elegant bones and an innate economy of movement. They had pointed chins, thin, tan, deliberate fingers, and wrists that expressed queries through small, tidy swivels. As young women they had shared a scrubbed, athletic, flat-chested look, but Celeste had gone to Switzerland for her fortieth birthday and returned with buoyant, inviting, unsettling breasts. Without intervention, Tabitha and Celeste would have had the same two vertical lines between their brows as Biddy did and the same friendly deltas of crow's feet, but temperament and divorce and lovers had left the elder sisters wealthy and discontented and their foreheads immobilized. Biddy, though she complained about her skin and was touchy about the secret gray cores of her sensibly dyed brown hairs, had elected, with Winn's encouragement, to face the degradations of age with a minimum of fuss. She wore sunscreen but little makeup, and since her skin was naturally olive and resilient, the effect was not of neglect but of cleanliness and practicality. He would not have had her any other way and told her so, discouraging her from messing around with her disused stash of blushes and lipsticks, but sometimes still she spoke wistfully of her sisters' visits to doctors in Europe and the Caribbean and their pricey treasure troves of unguents and creams.

'Is something bothering Livia?' Tabitha asked. 'She flew through here a minute ago. She didn't even stop to say hello. I wanted to hear about the whale.'

337

'She was supposed to shower outside,' Winn said, 'not come in here.'

'Did you have an argument?' Biddy asked. She would not have asked in front of anyone but her sisters, and yet he deplored discussing anything of significance in front of them.

'No, we didn't have an argument.'

'Well, why was she upset?'

'I don't know. She's Livia. Tabitha, how is Dryden?'

'Oh,' Tabitha said, 'you know. He's fine. Busy. He's here – on the island – but as soon as the ferry docked he had to go meet friends for drinks. Gone, just like that. He knows everyone everywhere. Do you think I should go check on Livia?'

'I'm sure she's fine,' Winn said breezily.

Celeste's face was stretched with curiosity. 'You're hiding something,' she said. 'Out with it, Winn.'

Under normal circumstances, he would have resisted longer, at least long enough to tell Biddy in private first, but he had no stamina for the usual thrust and parry with the Hazzards. 'I suppose you'll find out anyway,' he said. 'We went to the garage to get wine, and we found Agatha and Sterling . . .' He gritted his teeth, unable to finish the sentence.

'*In flagrante*?' Celeste asked.

Winn tilted his head, half a nod.

'No!' Biddy said. 'Really?'

'Who are Agatha and Sterling?' asked Tabitha.

Celeste clapped her hands. 'Now we've got a wedding.'

'No,' Winn said. 'A wedding is not an excuse for bad behavior.'

'Who are Agatha and Sterling?' Tabitha asked again.

'You've met Agatha,' Biddy said. 'She's Daphne's friend from Deerfield. Pretty girl.'

'Ah,' Tabitha said archly. 'That one.'

'This sort of thing isn't supposed to happen,' said Winn.

'Lighten up, Winnifred,' said Celeste. 'Don't be such a prig.'

Biddy said, 'And Sterling is Greyson's oldest brother.'

'Oh.' Tabitha looked unimpressed, as if Winn had said they'd been discovered playing table tennis. 'What did you do?' she asked him.

'I told them to bring in some wine when they were done.'

'That was nice of you,' Biddy said lightly, 'to let them finish.'

Uncertain if she was alluding to the *interruptus* of their morning, he scrutinized her for signs of irony, but she was selecting a strawberry from the bowl and did not look up. Celeste gave him a look that was knowing but not unkind. He frowned at her. So far he felt only an analytical interest in what he had seen. There had been something Olympian about the sight of them, something archetypal: man and woman mating

339

amongst the spiderwebs, amid swirls of dust. There were three Agathas: the one in his fantasies, the one whose body he had kissed and probed, and the one he had just seen naked head to toe, giving herself to a greedy, bumbling, grasping, haplessly engorged male intruder.

'What did Livia do?' Celeste asked.

'She took off,' said Winn. 'Tabitha, how was your trip over?'

'Poor thing,' said Celeste.

Biddy looked perplexed. 'You mean Livia? Why poor thing?'

Celeste leaned in a conspiratorial way across the table, one coral-nailed hand gripping the edge. 'As the kids say, last night Livia and Sterling hooked up.'

Sam Snead, the wedding planner, pulled open the screen door ('DO NOT SLAM,' it instructed her) and peered down the hallway. She heard voices from the direction of the kitchen. 'Yoo-hoo!' she called. The talking stopped. 'Yoo-hoo!'

Biddy called, 'In the kitchen! Come on in!'

Sam Snead was not a resurrection of the great dead golfer but a woman named Samantha who had married a man named Snead. She was never known as Samantha or as Mrs Snead but was someone whose first and last names had become permanently fused and so was only ever referred to as Sam Snead. The absurd label hung over her like a pseudonym although she preferred to think her name had not robbed her of self but given her the gift of inherent branding. She was not Sam Snead the woman; she was Sam Snead®, Elite Wedding Planner. She had considered keeping her maiden name (Rabinowitz) but in the end had decided to shrug her shoulders, find the silver lining (many of her clients had a deep fondness for Sam Snead the golfer and less for people named Rabinowitz), and make do, which, as she told her clients, was how she handled all crises and embarrassments and why she was an excellent and very expensive wedding planner.

The first thing she noticed was the bandage on Mr Van Meter's leg and the grubby state of his tennis whites. 'Dearheart, your leg! What *happened* to you?'

Something was afoot in the kitchen. While Mr Van Meter explained – some business with a bicycle and a golf cart – she kept her face bright and friendly and nodded to show she was listening but studied the group with her expert eye. His leg aside, Mr Van Meter looked distinctly the worse for wear. He had shadows under his bloodshot eyes and was smeared with blood and dirt. The others, the women, looked evasive, like they'd been caught gossiping. Sam Snead hadn't gotten to be where she was in the wedding-planning world by being insensitive to human discord. How many disasters had she prevented over the years, how many abandonments? How many cold feet had she warmed with rosy talk about future and family and nonrefundable deposits? Too many to count. Perhaps, too, she had aided and abetted a few mistakes, but she didn't know the statistics because she didn't like to follow up with her couples. She liked to wave them off on their honeymoon and then never see them again except as a pair of names atop her final invoice.

When Mr Van Meter finished, she said, 'Well then, Father-of-the-Bride, the question is, can you walk the length of an aisle? And if you can't, can we drug you up so you can?'

'I'm fine,' he said. His eyes were glassy and unfocused, and his manner was less prim and prickly than usual. He would bear watching.

'Wonderful!' she said. 'Now, listen, Mother-of-the-Bride, I know you told me you didn't want to do anything once you were on-island, but do you have the seating charts? Tomorrow's, and then also the one from Maude for tonight? Because I'm about to whisk tonight's over to the restaurant if you have it. You do? Wonderful. Homework is done, then, nothing left to do but enjoy, enjoy. Oh, look what you've done, clever girl. Perfect. Perfect. Thank you.' She took the seating charts from Biddy, tucked them away in her woven-leather tote bag, and pulled out a cloth-bound planner. 'All right, time for a briefing. Currently, it is three thirty. Guests have been arriving all day. No new cancellations that I'm aware of. The wedding party needs to be at the church by five thirty for the rehearsal – two cars will be here at five ten on the dot. Cocktails start at six thirty, and in theory dinner will be at seven thirty, probably closer to eight. All right? Now, I've heard from—' She broke off as the French doors opened and one of the bridesmaids, the one who seemed like trouble, stepped inside carrying a case of wine. According to Daphne, this one had missed makeup practice and getting her nails done because of a stomach bug. Why they didn't call a hangover a hangover, Sam Snead did not know. 'Hello, dear!' she said. 'Are you feeling better?'

The girl set down the wine. She took in the lanky collection of older women at the table and avoided looking at Mr Van Meter, who was avoiding looking at her. 'Much,' she said. 'Thank you.'

'I'm sorry,' Biddy said. 'I didn't know you were ill.' Her sisters simpered.

'Anyway,' Sam Snead went on, 'I was saying I've heard from our on-island tailor who's going to swing by and sneak a last check on the dress with Daphne before we leave for the rehearsal and will stay here and steam it. I just spoke to Daphne – they're done with manicures, except for Livia, who vanished at the beach, and poor Agatha here, who was under the weather.'

Winn saw Celeste's mouth twist and knew she was dying, *dying* to say it hadn't been the weather Agatha was under. Agatha leaned on the counter near Winn, the sole of one bare foot pressed against the other ankle like a Masai, her yellow cotton dress falling off one golden shoulder. What insouciance, he thought, what insolence to stand in the middle of all these interlocking rings of knowledge and ignorance and act like she had nothing to be ashamed of. He caught, or thought he caught, the bitter, animal smell of sex. Why hadn't she slunk off somewhere to wash herself? Was it so simple for her, once rebuffed, to settle for the next available male? Had the memory of their encounter even crossed her mind before she went with Sterling into the garage? He frowned and then turned the frown into a yawn when he caught Celeste watching him.

Biddy was explaining to Sam Snead about Livia and the whale, and Sam Snead was nodding rapidly.

'Okay,' Sam Snead said, absorbing the story with aplomb, 'but Livia will be ready for the rehearsal? If she's having a hard time getting the smell out, tell her to try tomato juice. If it works for skunk, it might work for whale. Great. Anything else? I'm running out the door.'

'Good-bye,' said Winn, extending his arm and herding her toward the hallway.

'Are you going to the restaurant?' Tabitha said. 'Our rental house is over there. Could I ask you for a ride?'

Biddy cocked her head. 'I thought that was your Jeep out front.'

'No,' Tabitha said, 'not mine. Skip dropped me off.'

'Well, whose was it?' asked Sam Snead.

'Sterling's,' said Agatha. 'But he's gone now.'

A silence fell. Biddy wiped crumbs from the tabletop with a napkin. Agatha picked at her chipped nail polish. Sam Snead smiled at everyone. 'Shall we be off?' she said to Tabitha.

'Good-bye,' Winn said again. But the front door slammed, and Daphne and her retinue blew into the kitchen. Daphne wore a white cotton beach dress, strapless and smocked at the chest, bellied out by the dome of Winn's grandchild.

'Tabitha!' Daphne exclaimed. There were greetings and introductions, and through it all Daphne looked blissfully happy, pink with a bride's radiance or pregnancy's glow or perhaps just sunburn, even as she declared she was exhausted and would die without a nap. Winn could not imagine being so happy, not in this kitchen full of women who had all fused together into one entity, one chattering hydra that he had married and fathered and fingered in the laundry room and kissed accidentally while playing sardines and paid to plan a wedding. He wasn't sure he had *ever* been as happy as Daphne looked. If he had, he could not remember, nor did he have any hope of being so again in the future. There weren't any great surprises in store for him, no twists of fate that would uncover new deposits of happiness. Grandchildren would be pleasant, but with his luck they would all be girls and, in any event, named Duff. He had chosen the walls of his prison,

345

and they suited him: this house and the house in Connecticut, his clubs, his station car, the grimy windows of Metro-North, the crystalline windows of his office, the confines of Biddy's embrace, the words 'husband' and 'father' on a tombstone. What else was there? He had no unsated wanderlust. He did not want a young wife, a new family, nor did he crave solitude, a cabin in the north woods, a lake to fish. He had almost everything he could think to want, and yet still ambivalence bleached his world to an anemic pallor. Maybe if he had been given a son, life would be different.

Livia, really, did most of the things he had imagined his son doing. Women couldn't join the Ophidian, but at least she went to Harvard. She was a decent squash player and an avid socializer. She was pretty and sporty and friendly, if also susceptible to cyclical black moods brought on by the lunar rhythm of womanhood. She should have been enough, but when Winn was carrying her bags and boxes up to her room on the first day of her freshman year, he had passed an open door to a suite filled with boys and their fathers, all shaking hands. A maroon banner with a white *H* already hung above the fireplace. He stopped on the landing, a laundry basket full of Livia's sheets in his arms, and stared at these strangers who seemed so familiar. He stood long enough that one of the boys turned and asked, 'Are you looking for someone, sir?'

'Oh,' Winn said. 'I'm sorry. I was just looking.'

When they nodded and glanced at one another, he said, 'I used to live in this room.'

'No kidding,' said the boy. 'That's cool. They gave us a list of everyone who's lived here.' He picked a piece of paper up off his desk and held it out to Winn. 'Which one are you?'

'Alexander Tipplethorn,' Winn said, pointing. 'Nineteen seventy.'

'I think I might have known your brother,' said one of the fathers, a tan, squinty sort of man. 'James Tipplethorn, class of seventy-five?'

Winn hefted the laundry basket. 'That's right.'

'What's James up to now?'

'I don't hear much from him, actually,' Winn said.

'Oh.' The father hesitated, then asked, 'Moving in your kid?'

'That's right,' Winn said. 'Pete Tipplethorn. Keep an eye out for him.'

Winn confessed his lie to no one, but his pleasure in visiting Livia was ruined. He avoided the other freshman parents, and even during Livia's sophomore and junior years, he was always nervous he might, at any moment, be unmasked as the sad imposter who had once tried to pass himself off as Alexander Tipplethorn, brother of James and father of Pete.

'Here she is!' announced Sam Snead.

Livia was standing just inside the doorway. Her hair, still damp, was braided and pinned in a garland around her head. She wore a black sheath that did nothing to distract from her paleness or her thinness. She looked like a consumptive. Her eyes were lined in black, and they glittered in her strained face.

'I understand you had a little emergency,' said Sam Snead to Livia, 'but everything will be fine. The makeup artist is very good. She'll know what to do tomorrow even without a dry run. Tell her lots of bronzer.'

Livia smiled unhappily. Winn could see the tension running through her. Were she to be plucked, she would sound a very high note. Daphne, Piper, Dominique, and Sam Snead were still jabbering about makeup and nails. Biddy cracked ice cubes from a tray. Celeste and Tabitha spectated from the table, affecting casualness.

Livia moved slowly in Agatha's direction. Agatha held out her hands palms up in a helpless gesture. The expression on her face was trying to be many things – conspiratorial, amused, apologetic, innocent, defiant – but fear showed through. Livia took hold of one of Agatha's hands with both of hers. There was a crack. Agatha cried out.

CHAPTER 14

THE SUN GOES OVER
THE YARDARM

The church stood on the eastern bluffs, white and sharp edged with a white steeple, like a paper cutout set against the sky. Only a short, eroding expanse of green lawn separated the tidy structure from the bluffs' edge. Grass lapped at its foundations, pushing up blue and white bursts of lupines and snapdragons like the bow wave of a ship, and ran on for another hundred feet until there was nothing more to root in and the last blades peeped out over the precipice. Each of the church's long sides had five tall, narrow windows of wavy, bubbled glass in a pale, almost colorless blue. A rose window over the altar admitted a disc of sunshine, and its twin at the back of the nave let in the periodic flash of the lighthouse. The walls were white, the pews cherry, and the air was seasoned with old books, flowers, and furniture wax.

Livia stood miserably at the front beside Dominique and across from Sterling. Daphne and Winn appeared in the bright square of the open doors, their forms solidifying out of the dazzle.

Daphne was smiling; Winn, who limped, was frowning. In what struck her as a grotesque parody, Livia had been made to walk down the aisle arm in arm with Sterling. He had said nothing except to ask if she'd really broken Agatha's finger. She had glowered and tried to hustle him along even after Sam Snead stage-whispered from the front, 'Slow down! Look serene!' Piper was on Dominique's other side and then, at a safe distance, Agatha. There hadn't been time for another trip to the hospital, but Sam Snead had told Agatha she could go after dinner if she wanted an X-ray. Uncle Skip, a doctor, was summoned by Tabitha from the comfort of the rented couch in their rented cottage to set the bone and splint Agatha's finger to a Popsicle stick. Doctors don't need X-rays to fix broken fingers, he had assured Agatha, wrapping her hand with some of the white tape sent home with Winn for rebandaging his leg. Especially not a finger like hers, which had snapped neatly as a breadstick. Skip had eyed Livia over his shoulder with twinkling reproach, not minding his chance to show off his resourcefulness while women passed in and out of the kitchen with wet hair, dry hair, wearing towels, wearing dresses. So it was that Agatha held, as a rehearsal bouquet, a bag of ice wrapped in a towel, her hand taped into a scout's pledge.

Sterling stood with his hands behind his back and stared up and away, off in the direction of the organ pipes and choir loft. The same seersucker trousers that Livia had pushed off his hips and kicked away in the sand were making an encore appearance, miraculously clean and pressed and accompanied by a matching jacket, its buttonhole stuck through with a white daisy.

At the steps to the altar, Daphne and Winn stopped. 'Now you lift up her veil and kiss her farewell,' said the minister.

'Very well,' Winn said. He did not bother with a practice kiss but nodded at Daphne and stepped sideways into the front pew to sit beside Biddy.

'Okay,' said the minister, 'but tomorrow make sure you remember to actually do it. Now the bride comes up here, gives her flowers to the maid of honor, and joins hands with the groom. Good.'

Winn shifted in his seat, leaning to hear something Biddy was whispering in his ear, and the wood creaked. Livia heard the snap of Agatha's finger again. She had breathed in through her nose and out through her mouth, counted to five, and broken it. She remembered the cool digit between her own fingers, Agatha's eyes expanding with fear. Agatha had begun gasping, almost hyperventilating, cradling her hand against her chest. Her father had gone to Agatha first, his hands hovering uselessly over her shoulders, before he had rounded on Livia, snarling, 'What were you *thinking*? What is *wrong* with you?' She had not realized she was crying, but later when she went off to collect herself, she saw that run mascara had left dark wings on her cheekbones.

'Livia.' Daphne, her hands joined with Greyson's, was looking at her. The minister and Greyson and all the groomsmen were looking at her, too. 'Did you hear that?'

'What?'

'Sam Snead told you to straighten out my train when I get up here.'

'Okay.' Livia crouched behind Daphne and mimed arranging an invisible dress. Sterling snorted, and she sprang up and returned to her place. She was only trying to cooperate with this silliness. She and Sterling would hand them pretend rings; they would all retreat down the aisle past pews filled with pretend people in the invisible wake of Daphne's train and the hummock of her unborn child.

But first Greyson had to pretend to drop his pretend ring and scramble around looking for it beneath the skirts of Daphne's pretend gown, mugging up at her. When the rehearsal was finally over, Livia walked beside Sterling to the church doors and dropped his arm before they reached the last pew. She marched out and across the lawn until she came to the split-rail fence at the edge of the bluff. Below, the ocean was blue-black and roughed up by the wind. There were dangerous shoals underneath. Dozens of wrecked ships, maybe hundreds, rotted away on the sea floor. At night the light from the lighthouse passed through the water above their bones like a ghost. All those wrecks had been the reason for building the lighthouse in the first place, but now the rescuer needed rescuing. The lighthouse, perched precariously on the crumbling bluffs, had become a quaint reminder of a dead island, where there was no radar or GPS, only a revolving light.

Sterling drew up beside her. They stood in silence. 'Starting to look like rain,' he said.

She turned. The others were clustered around the church doors. Her father was nodding at whatever Maude was saying, probably that the rehearsal had been *lovely* and wouldn't the wedding just be *wonderful*. Agatha was holding out her bandaged hand for Dicky Sr's inspection and laughing even though Dicky had never said anything funny in his life. 'It wouldn't dare. Not on Daphne Van Meter's wedding day.'

'Listen.'

Livia picked at some lichen on the fence. 'What?'

'I wanted to say – if I had known how much it was going to upset you, I wouldn't have done it.'

'What is "it"?' she asked. 'Is "it" her? Or me?' He stared at her, his whiskey-colored eyes flat and expressionless as buttons. 'Fine,' she said. 'Don't say anything. Just stare at me.'

'I thought eye contact was a good thing.'

'Eye contact with you is like eye contact with a taxidermied moose head.'

His gaze did not stray from her face as he patted his pockets in search of cigarettes. 'Look, I didn't mean for what happened with us to be this big thing. If I wasn't clear, I'm sorry.' Finding the pack, he tapped it against his palm. 'I don't think I'm anything to break someone's finger over.'

'That's great, but it's not like I'm so distraught. I didn't have some grand plan for revenge. I'd just had enough of Agatha.'

'She's not so bad. Just a little lost.'

'That's what Daphne always says. It's bullshit.' Livia picked more aggressively at the lichen. She was a pathetic dupe. She had known Teddy did not love her enough but had plowed ahead anyway. Worse, after one goose-bumped night on the beach, she had let herself hope that Sterling would be the one to exorcise Teddy. She supposed she must be a masochist, drawn to those who didn't want her. Her mistake had been to fancy herself a prize, a quarry, someone who would stand out from the hoi polloi of Sterling's conquests. Now she saw that his experience had not given him the choosiness of a connoisseur but the indifference of a glutton. His body, dumpy and flat-footed in the garage, could not have been the body that had pressed her into the sand, and yet it was. The body Teddy was sharing with half of New York – that was the same body she had imagined belonging to her. The indignity was too much. Seeing them humping away beside the old upside-down canoe with bike pumps and forgotten beach toys arrayed around them like props on a rustic porno set, she might have laughed, but instead she found herself converted, suddenly and with a zealot's certainty, to the belief that sex was meaningless. People spent their lives searching for something beyond the simple friction of skin on skin, but there was nothing. The void between two people could never be closed, and in trying to close it, they would only learn everything that was to be despised in the other. Even the sanctified sheets of the most devoted union were a platform only for empty animal thrustings. Before, she had been too naive to see, but now the grand farce was obvious.

Whitecaps blew over the hidden sandbars. Sterling smoked. Bits of black and green lichen flaked from the fence. Her nails looked terrible. She would ask Dominique to paint them. 'You really embarrassed me,' she said to Sterling. 'Men never think about what goes on between women.'

He sighed, making sure she knew he was trying his best to be patient. 'What do you mean?'

'You think, well, if this girl doesn't matter to me, then she doesn't matter in anyone's scheme of things. But girls always think they're the one who mattered, and then you meet up with some other girl who thinks she mattered to the same guy, and even if you hate that girl, if you think she's stupid or ugly or too beautiful or a bitch or slut or someone you'd otherwise want to be friends with, you now have this very intimate thing in common.'

'So?'

'My point is that it matters who you sleep with.'

Sterling swiveled away from her as though he

was about to leave and then turned back. 'Of course, you apply these standards to yourself, too. You went to the beach with me after thinking things over long and hard and weighing all the pros and cons.'

'I didn't let you find me doing it in your garage with some slut, now did I? I thought you were going to apologize.'

'I'm sorry.'

'I accept.' She walked off, leaving him smoking his cigarette on the edge of the cliff.

Winn went straight to the bar and ordered a gin martini.

'It'll be just a minute,' the bartender said, drying glasses.

'Winn, what are you doing?' Biddy said, passing by with Maude. 'Come outside. They have a little bar set up just for us.'

'Still want it?' asked the bartender.

'Whenever's convenient for you.'

He tucked his towel in his back pocket. 'What kind of gin?'

'The cheap stuff's fine.'

The bartender took a bottle from the bottom shelf.

Daphne swept through on Greyson's arm. 'Daddy, what are you doing? It's this way.'

'I'll be out in a minute.'

For the rehearsal dinner the Duffs had chosen a restaurant in a hotel on the harbor. Winn had warned them the chef was new and the food reported to be inconsistent, but there was a broad outdoor deck overlooking the water that Maude said would be divine for cocktails. Through the windows, he saw Daphne being engulfed by Biddy's relatives and miscellaneous Duffs. There was a hubbub of kissing and chatting. Agatha's golden arms and wounded hand appeared on the bar beside him.

'Quiet in here,' she said.

Only two other seats at the long mahogany bar were occupied, by two men who had been talking and picking at a tiny silver bowl of mixed nuts but were now studying Agatha.

'You should go out to the party,' Winn told her, giving a one-fingered salute to Dicky Sr as he passed.

'I'll have a drink first.' To the bartender she said, 'Gin martini with three olives, please.'

He did not ask which brand of gin but poured from a bottle that looked like a cut gemstone.

'Cheers,' Agatha said to Winn.

'I don't drink these much,' Winn said, allowing her to graze the edge of his brimming glass with her own. 'They're terrible.'

'You might want to think about upgrading your gin,' the bartender chimed in.

'What did he have?' Agatha asked. The bartender pointed, and she laughed.

'Look what was in my gift bag,' she said, lifting her chin so the skin tightened over the hard tube of her throat. With her fingers she indicated a silver necklace in the notch at its base, a starfish.

'Very nice.'

She lavished him with spaniel eyes. 'It wasn't what I wanted.'

The bartender had been wiping the same patch of bar for much too long. Winn cleared his throat, and the man inched away. 'I'm sorry to hear that. How is your finger?'

'You could kiss it and make it better.'

He stood up, slopping some martini on the green leather seat of his bar stool. 'Shit,' he said, grabbing a handful of napkins to mop it up.

'I was only kidding,' she said. 'Just fooling around.'

He paused, clutching the soggy clump of white napkins, and searched her face for clues to her meaning. What had always drawn him to her – her unknowability beyond the obscuring haze of sex that hung around her – now seemed frustrating and perverse.

'Another one?' the bartender asked, leveling a finger at Winn's glass.

'No. Just the tab for both.' He dropped the napkins on the bar. Perhaps he should simply commit to the idea that their flirtation had been one big joke, with what happened in the laundry room as a punch line. Maybe that's what it had been to her. He could have imagined the whole thing. He could be losing his mind – who was to say?

'Sorry about today in the garage,' she said,

touching his arm. Her expression had softened, her eyes grown large and importunate, but still he felt suspicious and baffled, like the object of a con. 'I didn't know about Livia and Sterling until afterward. I swear. I'm always causing problems.'

He bristled at the memory. 'Did you want to make me jealous?'

She bit her lip. The rosy skin yielded to her teeth, slightly yellow from nicotine. 'It just kind of happened,' she said regretfully. 'I'm sorry about last night, too. Red wine makes me weepy.'

'It's fine.'

She slipped off her stool and offered him her hand. 'Forgiven?'

'Of course,' he said, standing and giving her hand a solemn shake. 'Absolutely.' As she started to move away toward the doors to the deck, he felt a violent disappointment. 'Agatha.' He took a few hobbling steps after her. She paused.

A woman's voice came from behind him. 'Winn?'

He turned, expecting to see some relative or one of the Duffs. It was Ophelia Haviland, Fee Fenn.

'Fee!' he said, startled into speaking too loudly as he moved to kiss her cheek.

She accepted his kiss, but she was looking past him, her expression amused and somehow satisfied, like she had been proven right about something. 'Hello,' she said to Agatha.

'I'm sorry,' Winn said, beckoning Agatha forward. 'Fee, this is Agatha, one of Daphne's bridesmaids. Agatha, this is Fee Fenn, an old friend.'

The women shook hands. 'That's a stunning dress,' Fee said.

'Is it?' Agatha said, looking down at herself. She wore an unembellished gray satin slip. No bra. 'I can't decide if I like it.'

'We're having the rehearsal dinner here,' Winn told Fee.

'Tonight?' she asked. Square diamonds glittered in her ears, and her eyes were made up, but her clothes were simple and unobtrusive: white blouse, narrow slacks, loafers. He had to admit she was a pretty woman. Her eyes *did* bulge a bit, but all in all, she was nothing to be ashamed of.

'That's right.' Winn pointed out the window at the party on the deck.

'What are you two doing hiding in the bar?'

'Taking a hiatus from humanity,' he said. It was a phrase from when they were dating, when they would sneak out of a crowded party for some fresh air or when they decided to spend a weekend in his apartment, just the two of them.

Fee's smile turned brittle. 'Is Livia here?'

'Of course.'

'Jack said he told you and her about Teddy.'

'That's right,' Winn said. 'A chip off the old block.'

'We like to think so. He's here, too. With Jack and Meg in the dining room. I was just on my way to the ladies'.'

'How is the food?' Agatha inquired.

'I don't know,' Fee said. 'There's a new chef.'

'Say,' Winn said. 'Tell Jack I have a bone to pick with the Pequod.'

Fee glanced in the direction of the restrooms but stood her ground. 'I'd be happy to.'

'It was the damnedest thing. I was riding my bicycle home from a tennis match this morning – with Goodman Perry – do you know him? – I was on the bike path, and one of your caddies was down there in a cart – on the bike path – retrieving a ball for a couple of gents. Right as I passed by, this caddy put the cart in reverse without even a glance behind him and' – he clapped his hands for effect – 'slammed right into me. Knocked me off my bike. Look.' He set his foot on the bottom rung of the bar stool and hoisted up the leg of his bright green pants. A rusty flower of blood had worked its way through the gauze. 'I had to go to the hospital and get stitches. Tomorrow I have to walk Daphne down the aisle, and the timing couldn't have been worse.'

'I'm sorry to hear that,' Fee said. She gestured at Agatha's hand. 'Were you injured as well?'

Agatha gave her guttural, abbreviated laugh. 'Under different circumstances.'

'Otis Derringer,' said Winn. 'He was the caddy. And you know, Fee, the most extraordinary thing about it was that he wouldn't apologize.'

'Wouldn't or didn't?'

'Wouldn't. I told him I would appreciate an apology, no legal strings attached, and he said he hadn't done anything worth apologizing for. I don't know how you make that argument when you've sent a man to the hospital, but there you have it.'

Fee had been listening with her chin in the crook between her right thumb and index finger, the other fingers curled against her mouth, obscuring it, but he could tell from her eyes that she was smiling a particular bittersweet, superior smile he remembered. 'Sometimes people don't apologize when they should,' she said. 'That's the way it goes sometimes.'

'Under these circumstances,' he said, faltering, 'it seems clear . . . it seems clear . . .'

Fee dropped her hand, and that old smile swelled and twisted into a suppressed laugh. 'What seems clear, Winn?'

He couldn't think of anything to say.

'I should go outside,' Agatha said. 'I'm not being a very good bridesmaid.'

'I shouldn't keep either of you.' Fee moved toward the ladies' room. 'Please tell Daphne I said congratulations.'

Winn followed Agatha out to the deck, daring to swiftly touch the bare skin between her shoulder blades with one finger as they passed through the doors. She arched her back but kept walking, away to where the young people were. Winn found the little bar set up as Biddy had said, just for them, and ordered a gin and tonic.

'How are you holding up?' Sam Snead said, popping up beside him. 'How's the leg? You were

362

limping a little during the rehearsal, and of course that's fine. No biggie at all. No one minds if the father of the bride is a little off kilter. But it's a wedding and everything's supposed to be perfect, so I got you these from my trusty bag of tricks, my bag of potions, just in case. It's up to you. They might help. Take them, don't take them. I've given Daphne a little something for tomorrow, too. I give something to all my brides. Takes the edge off. Like I said, take them, don't take them. I'm here to make sure you have a good time. All right? Okay. We'll start moving everyone in for dinner in twenty, yes? Good.'

She pressed a small envelope that rattled with pills into his palm. He pocketed it, feeling surreptitious. He had spent more time feeling surreptitious in the past twenty-four hours than he had in his whole life. Dryden, Tabitha's son, floated by in a white suit with a sky-blue pocket square. 'Uncle Winn! Long time no see.' The young man air-kissed him and drifted toward a group listening to Francis recite the story of the whale. Dryden always made Winn think of his grandfather Frederick. Had he been anything like this young man? He thought of Fee's father, old Haviland, chalking his cue under Frederick's portrait like he was sharpening a weapon.

'Boom!' said Francis. 'And then it rained blood.'

Agatha sat on the arm of a chair occupied by the groomsman who was not a Duff, Charlie. She laughed and touched the young man's arm and looked at Winn. Daphne took Greyson's hand and swung it back and forth. Piper fished a maraschino cherry from her drink and casually flung it over the railing and into the harbor. Sterling stood alone, leaning on the wooden railing and gazing moodily out over the water. A waiter approached him with a tray of hors d'oeuvres, and Sterling stared at the toothpicked morsels as if he had never seen such a thing before. He shook his head and the waiter moved on. Dicky Sr and Maude were holding court in a circle of their family members. Taking a bacon-wrapped date from the tray Sterling had rejected, Winn chewed and watched Dicky Sr. Why had this man of all men made so many sons who wanted to fuck his daughters? The sun had dropped into the clouds like a flame into a lantern, and in the orange light the tireless breeze was tossing around the cocktail napkins and the hair and skirts of the women. They were blooming, all of them, the young people. Their cheeks were flushed from sun; their eyes were bright from drink; the shoulders of the girls were as smooth and appetizing as marzipan. They laughed so easily. They laughed at everything. They were laying hands on Daphne's belly, and she was guiding them to where the baby was kicking. 'Do you feel it?' she asked.

'Yes!' they said. 'Yes!'

Watching Agatha, he felt uneasy, dissatisfied. He had expected, long ago, that marriage would be an antidote to his youthful hedonism – with my body,

I thee worship, and so forth – but he had found it was only a partial balm. The number of years he had lasted without a dalliance seemed like a miracle, or, rather, a feat of miraculous self-discipline. He had always suspected that a little sexual diversion was likely to be more trouble than it was worth. What was the point? However many women he screwed, he would never want to leave Biddy. His life would be unchanged. But now he thought maybe he was due a little adventure for adventure's sake. He might have underestimated, all these years, how refreshing a new body might be. In the morning he would have done anything to undo his brief grappling with Agatha, but then, when she had walked away from him in the bar, the possibility that they would go no further had seemed unendurable. If he could give this itch a good, thorough scratching, just this once, he might find the relief he needed. And, even better, he might feel really and truly sorry about it – maybe, more than sex, he needed a good scare, a wake-up call. Downing the last of his drink, he snatched a glass of wine from the tray of a passing waiter. Taking out Sam Snead's little envelope, he shook the pills around – there were three – and then hooked one out with his finger and swallowed it. Yes, he would give in to temptation just this once. Of course, he abhorred weakness in himself, but to look at the thing logically, he had already committed the sin. How much worse could a small escalation make it? Not much. Perhaps not at all.

Agatha had left her perch beside Charlie. Winn could not see where she had gone. He wanted to communicate his decision to her somehow – perhaps a wink would do the trick – and to stop her from filling up her dance card for the evening with Charlie or, heaven forbid, Sterling again. Sterling was still there, on the railing, contemplating the harbor. Winn thought of the garage door flying up, their naked shapes. Despite the nearness of his sixtieth birthday and the dustiness of his bag of lover's tricks, he was certain he would be able to drive all memory of Sterling or anyone else from Agatha. Too bad Sterling would never know and would only complacently pat himself on the back for having both Agatha and Livia. Winn flinched at the thought of Livia and wondered if he should warn her that Teddy Fenn was in the dining room. He had half a mind to go in there and ask the Fenns to leave, Pequod be damned, to take their high and mighty selves home to their rented house and let Livia have a nice night for once. Looking around, Winn spotted her sitting alone at a little table with a cocktail, funereal in her black dress. He thought of the garage again, except he saw his daughter instead of Agatha.

Sterling looked at Waskeke harbor and missed Hong Kong. All the slips at the docks were taken, the outermost ones by a showy fleet of brilliantly white motor yachts and magnificent teak-decked sailboats. Out in the basin, boats on floating moorings bobbed in the chop. The car ferry was on its way out, big and blunt, chugging around the small lighthouse at the harbor's mouth. A pair of seagulls teetered on the wind. The sight was lovely, but he preferred the grand scale of Victoria Harbor with its crystal garden of skyscrapers. He liked the huge, ugly container ships and the red sails of the tourist junks.

He was not in the mood for small talk. He felt no need to ingratiate himself with Daphne's family or to see what his own relatives were up to, to find out which colleges his cousin Annabelle was considering or to hear about Uncle Digbert's boardroom triumphs. He knew he was supposed to store up nuggets of trivia about everyone so he could regurgitate them later and prove to the family that he *cared*, that he was *involved*. Thank God in a few days he would be back in Hong Kong and free again to live without much obligation to anyone. With the other expats, small talk was ritualized; they all knew the script; he could keep up his part without exertion. He only enjoyed chit-chat when he was working on a girl, and only for the gamesmanship involved, the razzle-dazzle, the strategy of fitting together words and phrases and laying them out just so until he had paved an inviting path down which he and the girl would walk, arm and arm, to the bedroom. Or kitchen. Or bathtub or car or movie theater. Or bar bathroom. Or fucking freezing beach. Or garage.

Neither Livia nor Agatha had been small-talk

girls. Livia was a big-talk girl, and Agatha was a no-talk girl. He'd bungled the situation, although he didn't see how he could have avoided that particular bungle except by turning down Agatha, which would have been insane. Still, all evening he'd kept thinking of Livia's face after Winn had flung up the garage door, infantile and ancient at the same time, full of loss. Her hands had contracted like two claws against her bony clavicle (he remembered kissing it, hard as a copper pipe under her skin). Meanwhile Agatha was popping off him and running around like a headless chicken.

Gazing down into his drink, he shook the bergs of ice so they collapsed and sank below the yellow surface. Something bright flew past his ear. He turned. The albino-looking bridesmaid was giggling with Francis.

'I'm sorry,' she said. 'I was trying to toss a cherry into your drink.'

'I put her up to it,' Francis said, lifting a hand. 'Sorry, bro.'

Sterling pursed his lips. Mopsy was sitting down and complaining about the cold; Dicky Jr was at her side, playing nursemaid as usual. Dicky Jr's wife, Mrs Dicky, who had just arrived, stood nearby, frowning passionately at her BlackBerry and punching it with her thumbs. Grammer was berating Greyson about something. Livia was sitting alone, forbidding as a widow. Sterling appraised his drink and was about to return to the bar when he saw Winn Van Meter heading for him and guessed from the determination on the man's face that a time of reckoning had come.

'Listen,' Winn said, taking him by the bicep and drawing him toward the least populated corner of the deck, 'I wanted to have a talk with you.'

'Oh?' Sterling looked piningly at the bar.

'What you do isn't any of my business. What you do in my garage, however, starts to become my business, and what you do with my daughter is my business.'

'Really? Does she think so?'

Livia had perked up and was watching them through the crowd.

'This is between us now,' Winn said. 'I have to say, you've really caused a problem here. Livia is pretty good at going off the deep end. You probably didn't know that, but you didn't get to know her before you . . . you didn't get to know her, now did you?'

Sterling shrugged. 'Livia wanted to hook up, so we did. Then today the other one wanted to, so we did. I don't think I did anything wrong.'

'Livia is very upset. She's had a hard time of it this year and your' – he seemed to search for a word – 'philandering didn't help.'

'Philandering.' Sterling took a pack of cigarettes and a lighter from his pocket. He offered the pack to Winn, who sneered at it. He pulled out a cigarette and lit up, turning away to shield the flame from the breeze. 'Livia and I,' he said, releasing a lungful of smoke, 'in no way had a committed relationship, given that we'd only just met, so I don't think you could call what I did this afternoon "philandering." Getting greedy, maybe. To which I'd plead guilty. On many counts.'

'But you've made all this trouble between the girls. I don't think it's too much to ask for you to limit yourself to one girl per twenty-four-hour period. Just for this weekend. Then you can go back to Hong Kong and your usual schedule of eight or ten girls a day. Because of you, the brides-maids hate each other.'

'Look, Agatha's attractive. I don't need to tell you that. I like Livia, too. She had the bad luck to be first. Nothing personal. If Agatha had happened last night and then Livia was interested today, it would have happened the other way around. Anyway, Livia and I have already talked about this. I've apologized.'

'That's not nearly enough.'

Sterling exhaled, squinting against the smoke. 'It's interesting you think you have the moral high ground.'

A ripple of apprehension crossed Winn's face, but he lowered his chin and glared over his glasses. He pointed at Sterling. 'We are standing outside the restaurant where you are supposed to go in and make a toast to your brother, who is marrying my daughter. You're a grown man. You should take some responsibility. I think in time you'll learn the value of being a gentleman – it puts you above reproach.'

Firmly but not roughly, Sterling pushed Winn's accusing finger away with the side of one hand. 'I'd rather get laid,' he said. 'The way you've got it all worked out, the burden is all on the men to regulate the morality and happiness of the sexual world. But I think there's something condescending about that. Should women's impulses be over-ridden by my patriarchal duty to keep order among them? Shouldn't women be allowed to choose who they sleep with and when, regardless of the conse-quences? Do you really think men should police them? Or do you just want special rules for your daughter?'

'I don't want to debate philosophy with you.'

'What do you want?'

'I want you to apologize to my daughter.'

'I did apologize. I already told you that.'

'One day you'll be married, maybe with daugh-ters of your own, and you'll learn the value of respecting women. You'll also see that what you're doing now, what you did yesterday is . . . it's tacky.'

'Tacky?' Sterling had not planned to play his next card, but he had also not planned to be scolded like a schoolboy by Greyson's new father-in-law. 'How was your night last night?' he said. 'Did you get caught up on your laundry?'

Winn tipped back like a buoy on a wave, eyes wide with shock. Just as quickly, he recovered his expression of flinty resolve. Whatever the cost, he would not be deterred from his original plan for this conversation, and Sterling was almost impressed.

'You're not fit to shine Livia's shoes,' Winn said.

'You're probably right,' Sterling replied, 'but she was a willing participant.'

'You don't know how to be a man or a gentleman.' Winn was beginning to slur his words ever so slightly, and his pupils were large and dark. Sterling wondered if he could possibly be on drugs – wouldn't that be something? Taking careful aim, Winn poked him in the chest.

Sterling knocked the finger away. He had been in enough bar fights to know when words were about to come to blows. They weren't quite there yet. So far, they had kept their voices down, and the party continued around them, though Livia was still staring at them, transfixed. 'I'm sorry – given what I saw through the window last night, I'm not sure I'll be signing up for your correspond-ence course on being a man and a gentleman.'

Winn frowned, put his hands in the pockets of his green pants, and tried for a kind of cowboy bluster. 'I don't know what you're talking about.'

Sterling, entertained, spoke mildly. 'You think I'm bluffing? I just reached into the ether and plucked, at random, the idea that you were up to no good in the laundry room last night?'

'So you're a Peeping Tom now, too.'

'I was taking a walk to try and sober up. Don't worry – I won't tell on you. Agatha's weird, isn't she? She's so aggressive, but then once things get going, there's not much there. You know what I mean? She's wild and frigid at the same time.'

Recognition was all over Winn's face, but he said, 'I don't know what you mean.'

'I wouldn't take it personally. A lot of these kinds of slutty girls are like that. In my experience, anyway.'

'You sleaze,' Winn barked, his index finger jabbing painfully into Sterling's sternum again. 'You think you can just oil your way through your life, but you can't. You have to take some responsibility. Youth is the best excuse you'll ever have, but you aren't a kid anymore. You've got to take some responsibility for yourself.'

Sterling thought it over. He swallowed the last of his drink. 'To each his own,' he said.

'No,' said Winn. 'Everyone has to grow up. You don't get to be an exception. If everyone just did whatever they wanted, where would the world be?'

'Friend,' said Sterling, 'I don't have the answers.'

'Dinner!' cried Sam Snead. 'Dinner is served!'

CHAPTER 15

RAISE YOUR GLASS

Everyone was funneling into the restaurant, but Biddy was moving in the opposite direction, toward the railing and the water. Dominique paused at the doors and then followed, lightly touching her back as she drew up beside her. 'Can I do anything to be helpful?'

'Oh, no,' Biddy said. 'I just need a second.' She rested her hands on her hips and leaned forward with her elbows out like a sprinter recovering from a race. Besides her wedding band and a wristwatch with a leather strap, she wore no jewelry, and her dress was a simple sheath in cream linen that left her thin, brown arms bare.

'Everything okay?'

'Of course.'

Sam Snead stood beckoning at them from inside. Dominique shook her head and held up an index finger. Looking at Biddy's unfussy person and unfathomable profile, she felt a deep puzzlement about how to proceed. She wanted to repay some portion of the comfort this woman had given her when she was a lost, foreign teenager, but if she ventured to say she was sure Livia hadn't *meant* to break Agatha's finger or that Winn hadn't *meant* to get in a fight with Greyson's brother, she would certainly be blundering across Biddy's invisible boundaries of privacy and propriety. This was truly advanced WASP: how to comfort a wronged wife and mother without acknowledging any misdeeds done or embarrassment caused by loved ones. Too advanced for her. Dominique was ready to leave Waskeke. Spending so much time with the Van Meters was like returning to a cherished childhood home and discovering that either her memory had been wrong or time had taken its toll, and the place was not magical or special at all but ordinary, flawed – a revelation doubly offensive because it made a certain swath of past happiness seem cheap, the product of ignorance.

'I checked the weather,' Dominique said, 'and this is all supposed to have passed by the morning.'

Biddy gave a wan smile. 'Good. Thank you for checking.'

'Yoo-hoo!' called Sam Snead. 'Mother-of-the-Bride!'

Dominique said, 'Should we go in and see how our seating chart is working out?'

'I just need one more minute.'

Dominique waved at Sam. 'Go ahead,' she called. 'We'll be right in.'

'We didn't put Sterling near Winn, did we? Do you remember?' Biddy asked. 'I've gotten all mixed up.'

'I don't think so. Do you want me to go look?'

'Who's next to Winn?'

'You are, I think. And maybe Maude? Do you want to sit somewhere else?'

'Why would I want that?' She seemed taken aback by her own sharpness and touched her fingers to her temples. 'Sorry. I'm sorry, Dom. I didn't mean to snap. Do you think everyone's having a good time?'

'Hmmm,' Dominique said, pretending to mull over the question. 'No.'

Biddy gulped a laugh that swerved quickly toward tears. But all she had to do was take a breath, and the usual friendly composure returned to her face. 'I'm glad you're here. It's nice to have someone around who's so honest.'

'I'm definitely from the village of truth tellers. Not everyone loves it.'

'What do you mean, the village of truth tellers?'

'You don't know that old riddle? There's a jungle with a village of truth tellers and a village of liars, and an anthropologist is looking for the truth-telling village. He comes to a fork in the jungle path, and there's a native standing there. What question does he ask?'

Biddy bowed her head for a moment and then looked up, pleased. 'Which way to your village?'

'Exactly. The magic question.'

'Is there a village for people who stick to pleasantries?'

'Maybe. What question would you ask to get there?'

'Where does Biddy Van Meter live?'

They stood for a moment in silence. A waiter moved around the deck collecting left-behind glasses and chasing after stray napkins.

'I'm joking,' Biddy said.

'I know.'

Intertwining her slender fingers, Biddy brought her hands up under her chin and blinked over them at Dominique. She looked earnest, even prayerful. 'You seem so strong. I wish Livia were more like you.'

Dominique didn't know if she was strong or not. All she knew was that her best decisions had been the ones that brought her freedom, but talking about freedom with Biddy would be like explaining Africa to a giraffe that had been born in the Bronx Zoo. She felt like a fraud, a sham healer whose only hope was to keep spinning bullshit and hope no one caught on before she could make her escape. 'I think Livia is strong,' she said. 'She's just going about things the wrong way right now. She'll be fine. Everything's going to be fine. We should go inside.'

'You're right.' But still Biddy did not move.

'Mother-of-the-Bride?' Dominique said. 'O, Mother-of-the-Bride? We can't have a rehearsal dinner without the mother-of-the-bride.' She offered her arm to Biddy, who took it and allowed herself to be led back to the party.

Livia was seated with Dicky Jr on one side, Dicky Sr on the other, and Mopsy across from her.

Dinner was in a private room with two long, white-draped tables topped with vases of irises. Three of the walls were taken up by ranks of twelve-paned windows, shut against the wind and full of the boat-crowded harbor, now dark and ruched with whitecaps. A waitress in a blue necktie and white apron moved along the tables, lighting tall white tapers in silver candelabras.

Livia's position as the filling of a Dicky sandwich was fine with her. If she had been stuck between Francis and Sterling or her father and Sterling or anyone and Sterling, she would have cried into her field greens. But the Dickys were a sturdy, lock-jawed bulwark against whatever had transpired between her father and Sterling out on the deck. She hadn't been able to hear them, but her father had kept poking Sterling in the chest, never a good sign. On the way to dinner, she had lingered in the doorway and caught his arm, whispering, 'What was that? What did you say?' But he had only hustled her through the dining room, hissing at her that he wasn't the one who had broken somebody's finger that day, and now he seemed to have already buried the incident somewhere in his vaults. He took his seat and shook out his white napkin. Glasses pushed to the end of his nose, he raised his wineglass and swirled it, inspecting the burgundy liquid in the candlelight.

'Dicky,' said Mopsy, 'I'm under a vent.' She rubbed her arms and stared accusingly at the ceiling, which was made of white planks and dark beams and had no vents. 'Could you ask them to turn down the air-conditioning?'

'Certainly,' said Dicky Jr, getting up.

'I don't think the air-conditioning is on,' Livia said. A waitress folded Dicky Jr's dropped napkin and set it back on the table.

Dicky Sr eyed the ceiling as though he had been asked to speculate on the weather. 'Mopsy,' he said loudly, leaning across the table, 'are you cold?'

'A little.'

Dicky Sr nodded and forked up a bird's nest of frisée, satisfied that, having been cold for the forty or so years of their acquaintance, his mother-in-law was still cold.

Livia leaned forward. 'Do you ever think about moving somewhere warm?'

The old woman cupped a hand behind her ear. 'You'll have to speak up. I'm hard of hearing.'

'She asked,' Dicky Sr bawled, 'whether you ever think about moving someplace warm.'

Mopsy looked over at the table where the lesser relatives were sitting. 'Do you think it's warmer at that table?'

'I meant,' Livia shouted, 'do you ever think about moving to Florida or someplace like that! A warm place!'

'Oh,' Mopsy said, shaking her head. 'No. What would I do in Florida?'

Dicky Jr returned and sat back down. 'All taken care of,' he said, shaking out his napkin.

Mopsy beamed and stopped rubbing her arms. 'Thank you, dear. It's much better already.'

The meal progressed. Daphne and Greyson smiled at each other as they sipped ice water, as they passed the bread basket, as they chose between sea bass and lamb. Livia ate sea bass and listened to Dicky Jr and Dicky Sr discuss the traffic situation in New York City, their cutlery flashing in tandem, the pair of them rolling along like two wheels hitched by her axle. Mopsy picked at her food and passed the time between bites by staring at Livia with distaste. When Livia offered pleasantries and questions, Mopsy only said, 'I'm afraid I can't hear you.' Neither of the Dickys made a move to serve as a bullhorn, probably because they knew Mopsy could hear her perfectly well. But still Livia was grateful not to be next to Sterling, who sat between Piper and Dominique and stared petulantly into space like someone enduring a ride in a crowded subway car.

Livia wondered what would happen to them, Daphne and Greyson. When they were children, Daphne's favorite game had been to dress Livia up in a pillowcase veil and give her a bunch of flowers picked from the yard and marry her off to some inanimate object dressed in one of their father's bow ties: a stuffed elephant, a tree, a leaky inflatable shark dug out from a heap of disused pool toys. 'You must take this very seriously,' Daphne would tell her. 'You are a princess now. And a wife. You must care for him' – she gestured at the slowly crumpling shark – 'and for your kingdom. It won't always be easy. Do you accept this as your duty?'

'I do,' Livia would say solemnly, worrying about the pilfered bow tie and if her father would find out they had broken the rule against playing with his things.

Where Daphne had picked that stuff up at such a young age and how she had managed to combine sparkling pink fancy with a stoic sense of marital endurance, Livia could not guess. The general consensus was that, as a couple, Daphne and Greyson were perfectly suited, both for each other and for the institution of marriage. It was a match both appropriate and timely; they were two people joined by their desire to join. They were pleasant, predictable, responsible, intelligent, and practical, not full of fiery, insupportable passion or ticking time bombs of impossible expectations. What they had was a comfortable covalence, stable and durable, their differences understood, cataloged, and compensated for. They were perpetuating their species. Livia saw her own parents as having a marriage of habit and mutual tolerance; the Duffs went together like two shades of beige, bound by a common essence of optimism, narrow-mindedness, and self-satisfaction. Daphne and Greyson were the perfect next generation.

Except for the baby. The baby was the snag. Sure, women were getting pregnant all over the place; people got married years after having kids;

people skipped marriage altogether; people got married a hundred times and accumulated a thousand stepchildren; people shook their gametes like a martini in a shaker and poured them into a stranger's womb. (A perennial ad in the *Crimson* had informed Livia that plenty of loving, upstanding, barren couples would pay $30,000 for her eggs, provided she was white, athletic, and met their minimum SAT scores.) People shuffled the order of love, marriage, and baby carriage all the time, but not people who had grown up under the contiguous roofs of Winn Van Meter, Deerfield, and Princeton.

Daphne was passing around a print of her last ultrasound. The latest technology: a close-up of the baby's face, yellow and waxy, its eyes partly open. Livia did not like the picture, which reminded her of a death mask, nor had she anticipated how Daphne's burgeoning belly made her feel a corresponding void in her own. After New Year's, she had stayed home for the first few days of reading period to have, as they said, the procedure. Biddy drove her a few towns over to where there was a clinic in a plain brown office block. A lone protester stood out front in the strip of grass between the sidewalk and the two-lane road zipping with commuter traffic. His dented green hatchback was parked nearby, decorated with an abundance of bumper stickers: 'It's a child, not a choice'; 'LIFE'; 'Abortion is murder.' 'Good morning!' he called out in a jolly voice, holding out a pamphlet.

'That asshole,' Livia muttered to her mother.

Biddy put an arm around her shoulders. 'I know. We can just ignore him. We won't change him, he won't change us.'

'It's seven a.m. on a Friday,' Livia said, and when they reached the glass doors, she spun around and shouted, 'Get a job!' In response, the man held aloft a lighted candle in a jelly jar. Livia gave him the finger.

'Livia!' her mother said, pulling her inside. 'Don't engage!'

'He's an asshole,' Livia said again, but she wondered what it would be like to stand there every day, praying and praying for the vaporous stream of unborn spirits rising from the brown brick office building.

She gave her name to a speaker box and electronic eye in a heavy door. A buzzer buzzed and a lock clicked open. A guard ran a metal detector over her and Biddy and searched their bags before he let them through another heavy door to the waiting room. They asked her name and took her back to have her blood drawn. When she returned, she sat beside her mother and pretended to read a magazine while she studied the other people in the room. A pair of girls in sweatpants. A middle-aged couple reading the classifieds together. An elderly Asian man and a very young girl whom Livia hoped was his granddaughter. The man stood up, stretched his arms up in the air, and rocked his torso from side to side. He kept standing there, gazing vacantly down at the coffee table with its colorful fans of magazines until the guard told him to sit down. Livia's name was called.

The room was like an ordinary doctor's office except for a rolling table against one wall that held an apparatus the size and shape of a small water cooler covered with a quilted, strawberry-printed sort of tea cozy. Was there some booth at a craft fair that sold cheerful, handmade accessories for abortionists? A nurse told her to take off all her clothes except her bra and her socks and put on a gown patterned with daisies. Another nurse covered her lap with a sheet, pulled up her gown, and squirted cold blue jelly onto Livia's stomach. Briskly, all business, she ran the curved mouth of an ultrasound through the jelly. 'I see it,' she said, snapping the screen shut. Livia had wanted to ask to see it, too – simple curiosity, not a desire to punish herself or a fear that she would see something human in the pulsating wedge of her womb – but she thought asking would be morbid and weird. She also wanted to see the thing under the cloth cover, the machine, but could not ask. She would seem like a tourist. Her interest should be in moving forward, not in the procedure itself. After all, she had chosen to be put completely under. Some chose twilight anesthesia, the woman who scheduled her on the phone had said. Others chose no anesthesia at all, but that was not recommended. Who would do that, Livia wondered, staring up at a mobile of yellow and blue circles revolving near the ceiling tiles in the breeze from the air-conditioning. Who would choose to know so much?

'Just a little pinch now,' said the nurse, sliding a needle into her arm. The doctor and the anesthesiologist, both women, came in.

'You'll only be out for five minutes or so,' the doctor said, businesslike, sliding on a rolling chair to the end of the table and positioning Livia's feet on metal stirrups. 'Scoot down. All the way to the end. Here we go.' Livia felt the cold pressure of a speculum.

The anesthesiologist snapped a line into her IV and fit a plastic mask over her face. 'You might experience a metallic taste,' she said. 'And a tingling in your fingers.' The mobile revolved slowly. Livia would go to the gates, but she would not see inside. 'Count backward from a hundred.' She tasted aluminum. She thought of the number ninety-nine and ninety-eight and then nothing.

Winn, leaving a gray flap of fish skin behind on his plate, escaped from the flickering, wind-rattled room and made his way to the bathroom. He stood at the urinal and then washed his hands, watching himself in the mirror. He had the impression of large eyes, a vague face. Everything seemed slow and indistinct. There was a pulse of air as the door swung open, and Jack Fenn's reflection appeared, his shaggy red eyebrows lifting.

'Hello again,' Winn said.

'Winn,' said Fenn. 'Fee said you were here. Enjoying your dinner?'

At the table, Winn had barely been able to hold still and eat, electrified as he was by animal agitation. Glass after glass of wine disappeared down his gullet, enough that the smiling, portly man of indeterminate Duff origins seated across from him had joshingly asked if he was the one getting cold feet. Over the salad, he had caught Agatha's eye and given her his wink and a small nod. He thought she had understood. 'Yes,' he said to Fenn. 'I think the new chef is all right. You?'

'No complaints.'

Fenn faced a urinal and assumed the stance. Winn dried his hands and listened to the other man pissing. 'Say,' he said, 'while I've got you here, there was something I wanted to mention.'

'Fee told me about the incident with—'

'I was just thinking today,' Winn interrupted, 'when I was waiting to get my leg sewn up, about the Pequod and how much I'm looking forward to being a member.' Fenn did not say anything, nor did he break stream. Winn blundered on. 'I was also thinking how unfortunate it would be if something from the past, our past, was getting in the way. This is my third summer on the wait list, as you know, and that's starting to seem like an awfully long time, long enough that I'm starting to wonder if the holdup isn't something personal, and I'd like to know everything *uncomfortable* has

386

been put behind us. Especially after this business with the caddy.'

'Hmm.' The last of Fenn's piss drip-dropped onto the porcelain. He zipped and flushed. 'I'm not sure what you mean, Winn,' he said, pumping soap into his hands and scrubbing them under the tap. 'I'd hate to think you'd try to leverage this accident with Otis to your advantage. My advice to you – knowing the club the way I do – would be to let that alone. The accident will be noted, but you won't do yourself any favors by harping on it. As for the rest, I'd hate to think you're alluding to what happened between our children. Teddy's had a hard time, and I'd guess, from what he's told me, that Livia's had hers, too. I'd hate to think you'd think I'd keep you out of a golf club because . . . because why, exactly? To punish you? Or to show solidarity with my son? Teddy doesn't have hard feelings toward you or Livia. He wishes Livia all the best.' He tugged a paper towel from a dispenser and leaned against the counter, drying his hands.

Winn was taken aback. 'No, I didn't mean Livia and Teddy.'

'What then?'

'Maybe for how I treated Fee?' he posited.

'Fee? Winn, let me tell you, she's over it. We're both glad you let her go. She wouldn't have married you anyway.'

'I'm fairly sure she would have, Fenn.'

The other man only smiled tolerantly.

'Well,' Winn said, irritated, 'I guess I meant the Ophidian, too.'

'The Ophidian?' Fenn was still smiling.

The door opened and a young man came in. He sidestepped between Winn and Fenn to the urinals.

'Look,' Winn said, glancing askance at the interloper's back, 'I'm sorry you didn't get in, but that was more than thirty years ago, and I think it's time to let go of the grudge. You were going to Vietnam anyway. You wouldn't even have been around to enjoy the club. Yes, some of the guys thought we should take you anyway because of the legacy, and I admit I opposed that, but I hardly think I can be held accountable.'

Fenn, usually so placidly affable, looked astonished. 'Hang on, there. You think I've made it my personal mission to keep you out of the Pequod because thirty years ago I didn't get into the Ophidian?'

'You've always disliked me because I kept you out of the club.'

The boy at the urinal hurriedly finished up and, eyes lowered, left without washing his hands.

'Winn, I never cared about the club.'

'Of course you did.'

Fenn shook his head, almost mournfully. 'I never cared about the club.'

'That's convenient, since you didn't get in.'

'I didn't want to get in.'

'What? But you punched. You wanted to join. Everyone wants to join.'

388

'No. I wanted to please my father, but when I didn't get in, it turned out he didn't give a shit either.'

'He didn't?'

'No, he didn't. The Ophidian wanted the Fenns; the Fenns were happy to oblige. The Fenns wore the special ties and sang the songs and sent back swords and snakes because the Fenns love a good time. And I'm sure the Ophidian *is* a good time. Part of me was sorry to miss out, but Winn, the thing you've never understood about the Ophidian is that it doesn't matter.'

'You've got a lot of nerve, Fenn.' Winn's hand with its admonishing finger rose feebly and then fell back to his side. His heart wasn't in it. 'Why,' he began, struggling to put all the pieces together, 'why, if you didn't care about the Ophidian, and Fee didn't want to marry me, then why aren't you letting me join the Pequod? I don't understand it.'

Fenn tossed his balled-up paper towel in the trash and put a paternal hand on Winn's shoulder. 'Listen,' he said, 'you might as well have some peace of mind. I don't think your chances of joining the Pequod are very good. I think you should let go of the idea.'

'What do you mean?' Winn said.

'It's just not in the cards.'

'Why not?'

'Tough to say. Chalk it up to bad luck.'

'No,' Winn said. 'There's no luck involved. This isn't a raffle.'

Fenn hesitated. 'Look, if you really want to know, the committee doesn't think you'd be a good fit, socially. I put in a good word, but this is out of my hands.'

'I don't understand.' Sluggishly, his mind trailed after Fenn's words, but nothing added up.

'No one can be universally popular,' Fenn said. 'Don't take it personally. The Pequod's stuffy anyway. Play on the municipal course. You've got a great family, you know, lots to be thankful for.'

'The municipal course?' Winn demanded, incredulous.

Fenn held his eye. He gave Winn's shoulder a farewell squeeze. 'Say hello to Biddy for me. And Livia,' he said, slipping out the door.

On his way back to the table, Winn encountered Mopsy standing in the bar and turning in a slow, suspicious circle. 'I'm trying to find the manager,' she said. 'It's so cold in this restaurant. I don't know why you chose it.'

'I didn't choose it,' Winn said. 'Dicky and Maude did.'

'They wouldn't have. They know I don't care for the cold.'

'Maybe,' Winn offered, 'you're feeling the chill of approaching death.'

She gave him a long, gloomy squint. 'This family is falling into the middle class,' she said.

He left her there and went back to the party, catching a glimpse of the Fenns at their table, everyone except for Fee with that ostentatious red hair, the bunch of them looking so pleased with themselves even though Fee was having to lean over and cut Meg's food for her. 'What's wrong?' Biddy whispered when he returned to the table, but he just frowned at her. By the time Mopsy reappeared and Greyson jumped up to pull out her chair, the time had come for toasts. Francis was first to his feet, chiming his butter knife against his wineglass while waitresses hovered around like white moths, filling coffee cups, setting down ramekins of crème brûlée, and pouring the dregs from the wine bottles. 'I would follow my brother into battle,' said Francis, 'and after what I went through today, I have a better idea of what that would be like.'

Laughter. Christ, thought Winn, enough with the whale. Francis said he would follow Daphne anywhere because she was so darn pretty. Winn poured cream into his coffee, and it bloomed up like a white rose. What did Fenn know anyway? Fee had loved him, would have married him, he was certain. He had even felt a *frisson* of attraction when he kissed her cheek in the bar, a gravitation of the scattered iron filings of an old passion. Her body was the same body he had once possessed, and yet it wasn't. Time had wrought its changes, but the difference was not only age. She seemed fundamentally different, transformed by his lack of ownership. He had always thought that when sex was over, everything was over between two people. Nothing was taken or left behind, with the obvious biological exceptions. Two partners disengaged and went their separate ways. No psychic filaments hung between them, stretching through the miles and days that took them farther and farther from their last encounter. If such things existed, the world would be meshed over with them; no one would be able to move; everyone would be held fast, like flies caught in a web. He wanted to think he had taken nothing from Fee and vice versa. But those amorous little filings, that magnetic rust that had responded to her presence might actually be decades-old particles of Ophelia Haviland lodged in his inner workings.

She was pretty, after all his cruelty. Was she prettier than Biddy? He couldn't decide. A memory came to him of her as a young woman: she was sitting in a chair beside the window in her Beacon Hill apartment, her ankles propped up on the sill, rooftops and green leaves outside. She wore a white cotton robe patterned with yellow dragonflies; it was barely closed; he could see the flatness of her sternum, the curve of her breast, her pale thigh. She turned to look at him: green eyes, their slight protuberance suddenly without importance. He had been so silly. She had been good to him; she *was* good. She cut her daughter's food without complaint. He had lectured Sterling on being a gentleman, and yet he himself was someone who would not be welcome at the Pequod, not now and not ever.

Maude followed Francis to give a toast, the words 'lovely' and 'wonderful' punctuating her sentences like cymbal crashes, and he noticed that his leg was feeling better, perhaps thanks to the booze or to Sam Snead's pill. He took a bite of crème brûlée. The burnt sugar ground loudly in his ears. Livia offered something short, witty, and heartfelt, putting on a good show of sororal happiness. Dicky Sr told a story about Oliver Wendell Holmes. Piper wove an endless, tipsy yarn about Daphne's adolescent exploits, ex-boyfriends, clandestine dorm sneakings, and covert drinking until Dominique reached out a long arm and pulled her back down into her chair. Then Dominique stood, her orange dress catching the candlelight. 'Daphne and Greyson,' she said, 'a bouquet of clichés for you. May you be healthy, wealthy, and wise. May the road rise up to meet you. May the wind always be at your back, and may you always have a guest room open for me.' She sat down.

'Hear, hear!' called Dryden from the other table.

Dicky Jr tapped his coffee cup with a spoon and, explaining that he was a newlywed himself, shared a few tired lines about the wife always being right. Mrs Dicky sat stony faced beside him, her fingers drumming the tablecloth, staying limber for her BlackBerry. Next would be Winn's turn. Biddy hated making toasts. One of the long-standing amendments to the constitution of their marriage was that, when a toast needed to be made, Winn would be the one to make it. Usually he enjoyed toasting. He liked the courtliness, the requisite self-possession, the public display of wit and graciousness. Standing over a room of people at the end of a feast, he felt like a real patriarch. But now he was drunk and stoned and had not thought about what he was going to say. Still, when Dicky Jr had at last subsided back down into his seat, he clinked his glass a few times and, pushing so hard on the table that he dragged the tablecloth and all the dishes and glasses a few inches toward himself, got to his feet.

'Well,' he said. The upturned faces waited. He looked down at the cracked shell of his crème brûlée and searched for something to say. Nothing came. He cleared his throat. 'Well.'

He sat back down. And then he was up again at once, not because he had thought of something to say but because during his descent he had seen a look of hurt bewilderment come over Daphne's face. 'You'll have to forgive me,' he said. 'Francis isn't the only one who had a misadventure today. I'm a little woozy. I feel . . . a little foggy. But . . . I wanted to say . . . I wanted to say . . . congratulations to Daphne and Greyson. What a fine match this is. I couldn't be more pleased that these two fine young people have found each other. I don't claim to be an authority on love, but I've been married for almost thirty years, almost half my life.' He paused. He thought someone might applaud, but no one did. 'And I will say to Daphne and Greyson that marriage is difficult, perhaps the most difficult thing you can ever do, besides being a parent, which you're also about to learn something about, but I think these two fine young people are up to the challenge. Here are two steady, responsible people who, I believe, understand the dire commitment they are about to make and will choose to keep that commitment. Because it turns out to be a choice, commitment – not some done deal. When you leave the altar tomorrow, there will still be a lifetime of choice and temptation and doubt and uncertainty in front of you. I didn't know that at my wedding. Getting married doesn't change you. Marriage changes you, though. Imperceptibly. Over time. You don't notice the change until you are changed. I don't know who that person is, back there. I mean the person I was before I got married. I thought I've stayed the same all along, but I'm beginning to think I've turned into someone else. Or maybe just everything around me has changed.

'That's neither here nor there. What I want, all I want, is for my daughter to be happy, and I think happiness comes from realistic expectations. It seems to me that what people want from romantic love is perfect understanding and infinite forgiveness. But if you want that, you should probably ask God for it. That's what people used to do, isn't it? I guess some people still do. People place demands on their husbands or wives that no human can meet. We're not divine. We're human. In my experience, we should be grateful for constancy and continuity and companionship. Let's call them the three C's – you heard it here first. Because we are the kind of people who get married. What else is there to do? You can't date forever. We don't want to be alone. We marry, and we live out our lives. Then . . . well, marriage, even a happy marriage like my own and like I'm sure yours will be, Daphne, is a precursor to death. If you never leave your partner and you're faithful, marriage has the same kind of finality. There is nothing else.'

He sat, took up his spoon, and tapped at his crème brûlée, breaking what was left of the sugar into brown shards. The result was gritty and creamy in his mouth, sweet with a faint, burnt acridness. The room seemed very quiet and, beside him, Biddy was very still, but he did not look up until he heard the chiming of a glass.

'Well,' said Greyson, standing, 'thank you, Winn. For those of you who haven't heard, Winn was knocked off his bicycle today and sustained some injuries for which I think he's probably been given some painkillers. Hopefully he has enough to share with us all. Getting back on track, Daphne and I wanted to thank you all for making the trip out to the island and for being here tonight. We're very excited about our marriage, which, incidentally, we hope will be nothing like death, and about the new baby.' He paused. Daphne was staring at her lap. Greyson rested his hand on the back of her neck, and she looked up at him. He raised his eyebrows, and she gave a timorous nod. 'We were planning to wait and surprise you all,' he said, 'but we decided this afternoon that we wanted you to know the baby is a girl.'

A pleased murmur raced along the tables, and then Dicky Sr burst into applause, standing and clapping and grinning, thrilled to have a change from all those boys. Cheers and whoops rose from the relatives and bridesmaids. Daphne was beaming again and twisting in her chair to take in all her well-wishers, offering each one the chance to bask with her in the beautiful idea of a baby girl. Winn half rose from his seat, wanting to kiss her, to touch her hand, but as her eyes passed over him, he felt her anger push him away, exiling him from her joy.

CHAPTER 16

A WEATHER VANE

As Winn drove, hunched forward and staring with bleary intensity through the windshield, the road tilted from side to side. For a tantalizing moment it balanced on the level before pitching over in the other direction as though trying to tip him off the earth. The world was alive and unstable. The upraised branches of the trees waved like drowning arms; orange tails of mist swept down through the streetlamps and up into the low maroon sky; a cacophony of wind chimes jangled from porches and balconies. Beside him, Agatha rode in silence. The dinner was only fifteen minutes behind them, but Winn pushed at it, trying to drive it farther into the anesthetized ward of his memory. He had told everyone he was taking her to get her finger X-rayed, and when first Dominique and then Greyson pointed out that he might not be in tip-top driving condition, he had blustered and reassured and argued that he should be the one to take her because he wanted someone to check on his leg and it didn't make sense for a whole crowd of them to go back to the hospital. To prove his point, he had hoisted up his trouser leg and again displayed the dark blossom of blood seeping through the bandage. Wordlessly, Biddy had handed him the keys.

Of course, he thought as they escaped from the shingled labyrinth of town onto longer, darker roads, of course Daphne's baby was a girl. Of course, of course. What else could it be? He would have a granddaughter named Duff. Hearing his name and hers said together, no one would be able to tell they had anything to do with each other. She was the green shoot, the furled purple rocket of a crocus, and he was one of the withered leaves she would have to fight her way past.

'I don't think we're really going to the hospital,' Agatha said, looking out the window.

'No.'

'Very naughty.' She shifted, crossing her legs. The hem of her dress rode up, and he dared to put one shaky hand on her warm thigh. 'That was some toast,' she said. 'I thought Maude Duff was going to drop dead. Did you see her face?'

'No.' While he was talking, he had focused on odd, arbitrary things: the edges of the table irises that were beginning to bruise and furl, the round spot on Dicky Jr's head where his scalp gleamed like a worn patch on the elbow of an old coat, the chipped edge of a coffee cup. Mostly he had stared at the black panes of the windows as they pulsed in the wind, seeming to bow inward into the room.

'Maybe if you had said that marriage was like death but was also *lovely* and *wonderful,* she wouldn't have minded so much. I'm with you, though. I'm never getting married. It's a crock.'

She uncrossed her legs, parting them. Uncertainly, he inched his hand up until it brushed the edge of her dress. 'In the bar,' he ventured, 'when you said you were only kidding, what did you mean?'

'I thought I should give us both an out.'

'Oh.'

'I'm not some kind of predator,' she said. 'I'm not a home wrecker.'

But she was. She had to be, or else why was he doing this? She had brought them here; she had made an offer he couldn't refuse, no man could. Sterling must think he was either the biggest hypocrite who had ever lived or else a lunatic. Winn wasn't sure which he preferred, but he was with Agatha now and Sterling wasn't.

'Anyway,' Agatha said, 'I really get what you were saying, about marriage being like death. That's probably why you're here with me. What else could be so fucking boring, you know? The same person, the same conversations with that person, the same conversations *about* that person. The same body. No, not for me. Not ever.'

'Is that what I said?' he asked. He couldn't quite remember. He had meant more that he could not have remained single, that there was a cultural imperative for him to marry. Indeed, he had wanted to become A Husband and Father, but he had never felt the raptures that were supposed to come to husbands and fathers, nor did he feel any less alone than before he married. But what else could he have done? Remaining a bachelor forever would have been unseemly, and he had no evidence that a solitary life would have been more satisfying than what he had. Still, he felt, beyond the edges of his life, the presence of some unidentifiable dark matter, some fate or path he had not seen, still could not see, but that would have led him somewhere better.

No lights marked the driveway to Jack Fenn's house, and Winn passed the gap in the hedges and had to stop and reverse, the shell driveway blazing up under the headlights. Billows of aubergine sky hid the peaks and gables of the roof. Brazenly, he parked as near as he could to the front door. When he turned off the car, the night became very dark.

'Whose house is this?' Agatha asked.

'It belongs to a friend of mine.'

'Are we going inside?'

'Yes.'

'Why don't we stay in here? In the back? Or we could find somewhere at your house?'

'Where? The garage?'

She didn't reply. Decisively, he patted her knee and then opened the glove compartment to retrieve the flashlight he kept there. Leaving the keys in the Land Rover's ignition, he got out and walked around to open Agatha's door. A clanking came from the flagpole, toggles on the rope rapping against the metal. Agatha took his hand and stepped down onto the shells.

The front door was locked, but a nearby window slid easily upward. 'After you,' he said, aiming the flashlight through the void.

'If you say so.' She grasped the sill and thrust one leg into the house, bending to follow it, disappearing inside with a flash of lavender underthings and the scuffed underside of a high heel.

Livia sat alone outside on the deck, in the same chair she had occupied during cocktail hour, gripping the arms so hard that pain radiated up her wrists. Wind whistled around her, working her hair loose from its braids. Squeezing something felt good, felt right, just like it had when she had decided to squeeze Agatha's finger. If she could have the day back, probably she would not choose to break it again, but the sensation of another person's skeleton cracking under her grip had been darkly electrifying. The bone had broken so easily, almost as easily as a turkey wishbone, except Agatha kept both halves: the good luck and the bad luck, the wish and the dud.

Her father had not understood – how could he? Crimes of passion could not possibly make sense to him. He lived in a baffled, stilted world; he had said so himself in that toast, in front of everyone. He had known only to be angry with her for disrupting the day, and she found she pitied him for his limitations. As a young child, while out on a sailboat belonging to family friends, she had glimpsed the curving gray flash of a dorsal fin. 'A

402

dolphin!' she had cried, pinching her nose closed with two fingers before leaping overboard. In the years since, she had come to doubt that she had actually managed to touch the animal, but at the time she would have sworn she felt its rubbery flank slip by beneath her reaching fingers. That was why she had not heard the splash of her father diving into the water after her: she was too busy yelling, 'I touched it! I touched it!' through mouthfuls of seawater. Even when he had one arm around her and was holding her against his chest and the small, hard buttons of his shirt, she kept trumpeting her jubilation. 'I touched it! I touched it!'

'Shut *up*, Livia.' His lips were close against her ear. 'That was a *stupid* thing to do. Look what you've gotten us into.' Livia looked and saw the tall white sails heel over as the distant boat began to come around. 'You've inconvenienced everyone. You could have drowned.'

'But there was a dolphin,' she had said, startled that he didn't understand.

Her father had not replied, and Livia felt his body start to shake. The day was warm, and the top layer of water was cold but not intolerable. She wasn't shaking. He was treading water with short, jerky kicks, sometimes catching her with a pointed knee, breathing too fast. But she knew he could swim. She had seen him swim lap after lap in his red swim trunks at the racquet club, his perfectly regular strokes punctuated by flashes of raggedy hair under the overarching arm, each lap terminating in a tidy flip turn. The knowledge that he was afraid came in a burst of intuition. He was afraid of the ocean, of the darkness below their feet, of drowning. It had never occurred to Livia that he *could* drown. It was terrible to know her parents were going to die but worse to know they were afraid to die.

'Don't worry,' she told him, craning back to see his face. 'I'm here.'

Without taking his eyes off the approaching sailboat, he had said, 'Don't patronize me, Livia.'

In Waskeke Harbor, a few red and green running lights bobbed up and down with the chop, and the yellow glow of town rippled across the water. Far away, toward the distant end of the harbor where she had thrown the lobster to its fate, lights from scattered houses winked behind waving tree branches. Everyone had scattered after dinner. Daphne said she was tired and needed to go home; some of the others had gone to a bar; her father had insisted on taking Agatha to get the infamous finger looked at. But Livia had not wanted to leave. She did not want to make small talk over drinks with the Duffs – she had more than enough drinks in her already – nor did she want to go home and rattle around the house with her mother and sister. She knew Teddy was in the restaurant. Dryden had let the cat out of the bag, and then she had glimpsed him for herself on her way to the bathroom, held his eye from across the room.

She would not stoop to seeking Teddy out, but she saw no prudence in rushing away. Her gut told her he would find her. She gripped the arms of her chair even more tightly. A door opened behind her.

'Livia?' Teddy said, coming to crouch beside her chair.

Winn followed Agatha through the window, pulling it shut behind him. The roar of the wind dropped to a low murmur, interrupted by the creaking of the house timbers and unidentifiable rattles.

'Good windows,' he said. 'Nice and tight.'

Agatha's arms encircled his waist. 'Like me,' she said.

Jesus *Christ*, he thought, both aroused and appalled. He kissed her briefly and stepped away, casting the light around. 'Let's take a look at this place.'

The room they were in was tall and square with a skeletal staircase curving up one side and bundles of wiring growing like anemones from the walls and ceiling. Sawdust filtered through the flashlight's beam like plankton. Agatha appeared and disappeared, a pale wraith. The floors were coated with sawdust and sand, and their footsteps made sliding rasps. A long great room took up most of the ocean side. It had a vaulted ceiling and tall windows that, in the daytime, would be full of blue but now revealed only blackness and the white traveling star of the flashlight, their dim silhouettes lurking behind it. Boards perforated with notches and peg holes, future bookshelves, were stacked beside a table saw, but besides those and a fieldstone fireplace only halfway grouted, the room was empty.

'This is a ridiculous house,' he said.

'Why?'

'It's too damn big. They don't need this much space. The size is downright silly. Everything's for show. Make the house big and splashy so everyone will know how much money you have, but your roof still leaks.'

'The roof leaks?'

'Look at this,' he said, training the beam on the cathedral heights of the ceiling. 'Absurd.'

'Maybe for some people size does matter.'

He shined the light into her face, but she didn't wince. 'Does everything always have to be about sex?' he said.

'Isn't that why you brought me here?'

'You could tone down the innuendo.'

'I'm just playing around.'

'I don't know how to play around.'

'I like that about you.'

He smiled but realized she couldn't see him behind the light. 'That's fine, then,' he said.

In the kitchen, the cabinets had no doors; there were no counters; the empty spaces where the appliances would go gave the room a vacant, gap-toothed look. For a year, all the way from Connecticut, he had sensed this house rising up, plank by plank, shingle by shingle, and now here it was, almost complete, an enemy fortress on his island.

'What now?' Agatha said. She raised one hand to shield her eyes from the light. In the presence of so much darkness and all the spooky maracas and tambourines played by the wind, she seemed young and uncertain.

'Let's keep going.'

Beyond the kitchen, through a narrow door, was a tiled, spigoted space that looked like it would be a mudroom. A narrow back staircase of bare plywood disappeared up into the second floor. Winn sent Agatha up first, lighting her way as best he could. She climbed bent over, her thighs making a lancet arch through which he watched her hands find each step. The light bobbled over the exposed lower curves of her ass, and though he did look and though now, more than any other time, he was free simply to grasp her by the ankles and reach up and push aside that purple scrap under her skirt, his desire had unaccountably slackened. Maybe he was too old for all this debauchery, the sex and drugs and trespassing. Maybe, but he wasn't ready to admit defeat.

Upstairs, she let him pass and then grasped the back of his belt, tethering herself to him as he wandered through another set of abyssal rooms like a diver on a wreck. The floor was a mess, crowded with coiled wire, folded assemblages of cardboard, tubes of caulk, pleats of clear plastic sheeting. A bathroom mirror, propped against a blank wall, surprised them with its sudden flash. They came to another staircase and climbed to the third floor, up under the eaves, its ceiling the inverted twin of the roof's complicated geometry. The dormer windows rattled more in their frames than the downstairs windows had – maybe Fenn was trying to save a buck – and Winn could hear the waves rolling in from Waskeke Sound. With Agatha still hanging from his belt like a dinghy, he was moving toward another staircase, more like a ladder, built into the far wall when something hard and heavy caught him across the shins. He pitched forward with a shout, carrying Agatha down with him. They landed in a tangle, him on his stomach with her sprawled across his back. Gasping, he rolled out from under her, pushed his glasses back into place, and cast the flashlight around accusingly. The culprit was a toilet, white and gleaming, sitting alone in the middle of the empty plywood floor. Pain erupted in his leg. 'Jesus!' he said. 'My leg!'

'Fuck!' Agatha said. 'My finger!' He trained the light on her. She was lying on her side, holding her white-taped hand in front of her face. For a moment, he fought the urge to laugh, every muscle clenched, until intense, vibrating need overwhelmed him, and he curled into himself, undone, letting the flashlight roll out of his grasp, covering his face with his hands as tears rolled down his cheeks. The feeling was vertiginous, euphoric,

408

hysterical – like he was traveling at a wild speed, braced against the sensation, his stomach dropping, bright lights flowing through his veins. Agatha had caught the bug. She threw her arm over him, and he felt her breasts shuddering low on his stomach. This was not her usual laugh. There were no husky *ha ha*'s, just gasps and quivering.

The pain in his leg had disappeared. He was flying. He grasped her twitching shoulders and rolled onto her, finding the stickiness of her tear-streaked cheeks before he found the wetness of her mouth. For a moment, she continued to laugh, but then she latched on with the determination of a suckling foal. The flashlight had come to rest at a short distance, illuminating a strip of floor and a disc of wall. Her hair, spread out above them in a tangle, caught some of the light in its yellow ends. As his fingers strayed from her breast to her ribs to her crotch, he felt a thrill of foreboding that she might be dry again, but this time she was in working order. He let a cry of relief out into her mouth.

'What?' she said, angling her head away.

'Nothing. Everything's fine.'

'Are you sure?'

'Yes.'

'Really?'

'Why?'

'Well. You're not hard.'

It was true, he realized. He wasn't. All the signs

of arousal had been fizzing away in his brain, but apparently the message had been waylaid somewhere on its way to his groin, washed away in a flood of booze. 'God,' he said. 'I didn't even notice.'

She struggled to shift underneath him. He became aware that he was resting his full weight on her, an inert sack. He propped himself onto an elbow. His face was still spasming with the aftershocks of his laughing jag.

'Maybe you just weren't meant to be unfaithful,' she said.

'It's a little late for that.'

'Then, here.' In one deft movement she insinuated her hand between them and undid his belt. He had never before allowed her to touch him – he had only touched *her* – and now, when it finally happened, her fingers tugging on his limp dick felt deeply inappropriate, humiliating, even grotesque. He was a married man approaching his sixtieth birthday, lying on the floor of an unfinished beach house belonging to his imagined nemesis, being jerked off by a school friend of his daughter's. He let out a kind of sob.

'Yeah?' Agatha said, misunderstanding. 'Yeah?'

'No,' he said.

She yanked her hand away. 'What is it?'

'I need some air.' He scooped up the flashlight and made a break for the ladder he had seen before he tripped over the toilet. The rungs smelled of resin and the saw blade. He hadn't seen a widow's walk from the front of the house, but there could be no other explanation, and, indeed, he found that they led to a metal hatch. He needed to be out of this room, this place where someday Meg Fenn would wander with her open mouth and her pigeon toes, where Ophelia Haviland would make up beds for her guests, where Livia might have chased after his grandchild. He threw open the hatch, and a gust of wind bloomed into the attic, an inverted parachute of air. Angling the light down, he saw sawdust whirling around Agatha, who was still sitting beside the toilet, braced on one arm and squinting up at him. The hand with the broken finger rested in her lap. He pointed the light up, out through the hatch, a searchlight against the clouds, and then followed it up into the bluster. The widow's walk was on the beach side of the house, hidden from the driveway by shingled peaks and outcroppings. He heard a squeaking sound from above and cast the beam over the three masts and proud copper sails of Jack Fenn's weather vane.

Behind a thin veil of cloud, the moon was a pale smudge, and then, when the wind tore a hole, it emerged as a perfect round marble of light, its mountains and craters making a stricken face. In the white light, the ocean was a confusion of foam, and the shell driveway, of which he could see only the outermost curve, shone briefly like a path to heaven, white and broad and gleaming. But the clouds knit themselves back together, and the moon was bundled off again, leaving darkness and the sound of surf. The wind abraded his cheeks. He closed his eyes. How unfair to fail even at adultery. That he had not been able to consummate his crime was a meaningless technicality. His guilt was in no way lessened, only his pleasure, and, clinging to his desolate, wind-blasted aerie, he could not imagine that he would ever find relief. The weather vane squeaked. He trained the beam on it again. Slowly, it turned half a revolution before jerking to a stop and inching back the other way. Without thinking, he swung one leg over the railing onto a curve of roof and began to climb.

The whale, since Livia had last seen it, had ceased to be a whale and become a grisly, ruined *thing*. The beach was lit from above by two generators on a low dune, out of reach of the tide, their blinding bulbs set in chrome bowls atop tall metal stalks. The whale's ribs shone white with black, meaty valleys between them. The jawbone was gone and most of the blubber, trucked off somewhere to rot. A few men waded around the corpse in rubber overalls, their hoods drawn against the wind and blowing spray.

She and Teddy were standing behind the generators, sheltered from the men's attention. Flying sand stung her face and bare legs. She had only brought a light cardigan to dinner, and she hugged herself, gripping her arms. A wave washed around the whale, and the whole mess of bone and flesh rocked and fishtailed. The sea was trying to take it back. A hooded man, sitting astride one of the ribs and braced against the wind, dropped his flensing knife. When the wave receded, another man passed the knife back up. The lights rode the turbulent water in an imitation of moonlight. 'See?' she said to Teddy, shouting over the wind and surf and growling generators.

'I see,' he shouted back.

She felt a rush of gratification. She had known he would understand. The whale would *mean* something to him, the way it meant something to her. What exactly it meant, she wasn't sure, but she could feel its importance in her chest, straining her ribs, the way she had felt when she dove off the sailboat after the dolphin all those years ago. She was in a moment around which her life would take shape. 'I wanted to come find you so you wouldn't think I was avoiding you,' he had said on the deck at the restaurant. 'I heard you were here.' It wasn't exactly a declaration of renewed love, but he had taken her inside and bought her a drink and listened to her talk about her father's terrible toast, speculating with her on what could possibly have gotten into him. He'd been interested in the whale; she hadn't had to work too hard to convince him to drive her out for another look.

She turned to him, squinting against the gale. 'Isn't it amazing?'

He was silent. Then he said loudly, leaning close to her ear, 'It really smells.'

She laughed, giddy with nerves. 'But you get it, don't you?'

'Get what?'

She threw out an arm as though the whale were a room she was ushering him into. 'That!'

'What is there to get?'

Another wave caught the whale and pushed it a few feet up the beach. Uncertainty crept through Livia. 'I can't explain it,' she said.

He looked at the whale and then back at her. 'It's just a big, dead fish!'

Despair caught her, almost crushing her. 'It's a mammal!' she cried. He shrugged. He was so familiar and yet such a stranger. The shadows sapped him of color. His brilliant hair looked dark and ordinary. In the car, she had reached out to touch his hair, remarking that she had thought it would be buzzed, but he had ducked his head away and said the army would cut it for him. 'I thought you would understand,' she said. 'That's what I miss most about you – I miss being understood.'

The whale was sliding up and down with every wave. 'What?' Teddy said, cupping one hand around his ear. The man on top of the whale, who had been clinging on like a bull rider, slid down and landed with a splash.

'I miss being understood! You always understood me!'

He drew back, shaking his head, and then leaned close, making his hands into a bullhorn. 'I never understood you!' he yelled into her ear.

'Yes, you did!'

'No, I really didn't! That was the whole problem!'

'You did! You do!'

Firm as a schoolteacher, he shook his head.

'You loved me!' she insisted.

He took her hand, and the gentleness of the touch made her want to hit him. He said something she couldn't hear.

'What?'

'I said,' he yelled, 'not enough.'

The conversation was a familiar one, their paths through it well worn, but the pain of his words took her breath away even though she had invited it. 'It's enough for me,' she said.

He looked at her sadly before leaning close to her ear. 'Livia, I don't have a moral obligation to spend my life with you. This is better. You'll see eventually.'

She chewed her lip and willed her chin to stop dimpling. She watched the whale. The waves were getting bigger. Finally she shouted, 'Promise not to die!'

It was the impossible, universal request of the lover. He laughed. 'I'll do my best!'

The whale was afloat. It skidded up the sand on a wave and then was drawn back out. The men splashed after it, trying to hold on to the exposed bones of its head, but the sea was determined. The whale rolled over, half submerged. A wave foamed up around it. Stripped of blubber and cut full of holes, the whale was sliding into deeper water, sinking back to rest its bones on the ocean floor. One of the men was knocked down by a wave. Livia could barely make out his head among the shadows and white water. 'They have to let it go,' she shouted into the wind, not caring whether Teddy heard her. 'Just let it go!'

Agatha, no stranger to being left in dark rooms by men, waited in the attic, still propped up on one hand, until her palm began to itch from tiny curls of sawdust sticking into her skin. She eased around, leaning back on the rogue toilet with her legs straight out in front of her. Above, the hatch where Winn had disappeared was a dim purple rectangle. Stray gusts of wind fell down into the attic, stirring up dust and raising goose bumps on her bare arms. She hugged herself. Where was he? Pressing with her good hand on the toilet, she got to her feet and made her way toward the ladder, arms stretched out in the darkness.

Coming up through the hatch, she could see the widow's walk was empty, and, with a horrified thrill, she thought he must have jumped. She leaned over the railing, peering down. She couldn't see the ground, not clearly, anyway. She saw shapes that might have been sacks of cement or piles of flagstones but might also be a body.

'Winn!' she called. 'Winn!' Then she saw it, moving slowly along a ridge of the roof: an illuminated disc of shingles and, behind it, a long, dark, creeping shape.

He heard her shouting for him, but he could not reply because his mouth was plugged with the flashlight's rubber handle. If he had one thing to be grateful for, it was that these clouds had not yet brought any rain. They seemed to hang only inches above him, a billowing purple canopy. If he could have risked loosening his grip, he might have reached up and touched them. Since his first trip on an airplane as a child, he had always wanted to touch a cloud, to really *feel* the substance of one, and though he had come to understand the impossibility, the desire had not left him. Pinching the roof between his knees, his jaw and leg aching, he inched along Jack Fenn's abrasive and unyielding shingles. Finally his fingers hit brick – a chimney. All he had to do was squeeze around it, ascend a short crag of a gable, traverse another ridge, and then he would reach the pretentious little cupola that supported the weather vane.

With the care of a mountaineer approaching the summit of Everest, he pulled himself to his feet, his fingers inching up the bricks until they found a grip on an upper ledge. He embraced the chimney as though it were a dance partner. A particularly strong gust buffeted him, bringing with it the first few drops of rain, and he clung to his handhold so hard that his fingernails burned. *One, two, three.* A swooping pivot around the chimney, a rapid uphill scramble, and, after a panicked leap, he found himself belly-down atop the apex of Jack Fenn's house. He had to scrabble with both hands and both feet to keep his purchase, and the flashlight slipped from his mouth and rolled away down the sloping shingles, its beam streaked with rain as it described sickening arcs and turns until it bounced off a gutter with a clang and fell silently into the dark.

Without the light, the weather vane was a black splotch hovering in the near distance. Almost blind behind his droplet-speckled glasses, he wormed his way along the ridge like a sailor on a spar. The shingles had torn open his pants, letting in a thousand splinters and sandpapering away his skin. Still he continued, crawling through the rain, full of grim certainty that the weather vane was an opponent he must face, even though, when he reached it, it proved to be nothing more than a cold assemblage of copper bits, larger than it looked from the ground and squeaking loudly as it tacked the few inches to starboard and back to port. The pointlessness of his mission had, by then, begun to dawn on him, soaking through at the same rate that the rain saturated his clothes, but he had started this, and, by God, he would finish it. He felt around the weather vane's base on top of the little cupola. His fingers discovered three small bolts, three frigid and slippery hexagons securing Fenn's ridiculous finial to his ridiculous house. One bolt was loose, and he twisted it out of its socket and sent it the way of the flashlight. The other two would not budge. He twisted at the wet metal until his fingers were raw. The time had come for the final push, the last great effort. Standing bowlegged, his feet curved into either side of the roof, his shredded pants whipping in the wind, he grasped the weather vane by its hull and pushed against the cold, smooth metal. The solder gave, just a fraction of an inch, but still it gave. The ship listed at an angle. Even the proud nautical crown of this sham of a house was tacked on with spit and a prayer. Triumphant, Winn found a better handhold, weaving his fingers through the stiff wire rigging, and inched around until he was balanced atop the ridge. Agatha had stopped shouting for him. 'You're not hard,' he heard her say with her voice full of disdain, and he winced, his concentration wavering at the precise moment a gust of wind struck him square in the chest. He tipped backward and then, clinging to the weather vane with an awkward, sideways grip, he overcorrected forward and found himself with his chest against the cupola, his feet running in place on the wet slope of shingles. A metallic pop. He slid backward as the weather vane pitched forward, its masts going horizontal as its prow aimed down into the deep. But the welding held, and Winn, grappling painfully with the slippery sails and piano-wire rigging, made a last-ditch attempt for a better handhold. Disengaging his right hand, he swung his arm around and pushed with his toes, propelling himself far enough back up the roof to grasp the ship's smooth hull. He hooked his arm over it. For a moment, he was safe. Then there was another pop and a wrenching, and the ship pulled loose. Winn found himself cradling it in his arms, a sharp copper baby, as he took his first roll and slide down the roof.

He heard himself bellowing. When he struck the first dormer and went slipping down at a new angle, he managed to thrust the weather vane away, tossing it out into space. It vanished as though it had never existed. Clawing at the shingles, he managed to slow himself down, and for a miraculous moment he paused atop a gambreled curve. But exhaustion loosened his grip with merciless quickness and sent him down, down, until, after an even briefer dangle from a drainpipe, he fell.

CHAPTER 17

THE MAIMED KING

aphne was still crying. Dominique sat beside her on the bed, watching her pregnant belly quake each time she drew a breath. Piper was perched on a sea chest by the window, her arms wrapped around her knees. 'Why are you crying?' she asked for the third time, her voice small.

'I don't know,' Daphne said, also for the third time. She took a deep breath. 'Everything just caught up with me all at once.'

'It's okay,' said Dominique. 'You can cry.'

'No,' said Daphne, 'I have to stop or my eyes will be all puffy tomorrow, and I won't be able to look at the pictures without remembering that I'd been crying.'

Piper pulled her knees in closer and rested her chin on them. 'When my sister was pregnant, she cried all the time. Her skin looked amazing, though. Your skin looks really good, too. You'll look good in the pictures.'

'I can't remember the last time I cried like this.' Daphne gazed at the ceiling, awed by her own tears.

'You've been under a lot of stress,' Piper said. 'I say just let it all out.'

'They're not back yet,' Daphne said to Dominique.

'Who?' Piper asked.

Dominique held Daphne's gaze. She gave her friend a sad smile and reached out to smooth her hair off her forehead. Daphne looked afraid. In a crisis of faith, Dominique thought, two ways lie open. Daphne could push aside her doubts, sing loudly to drown them out, and go on marching toward the luminous cloudburst she now saw to be a cardboard prop hung from the rafters. Or she could embrace her knowledge, look through a dark lens, and face a truth.

'No one,' Daphne said to the ceiling. Tears ran down into her hair. A few puddled in the curl of her ear like raindrops in the turnings of a flower.

Piper cupped her hands against the window and peered out. 'Someone's home,' she said.

In a few minutes, there was a soft knock on the door, and Livia came in. She looked like she had been pulled from the sea again. Her black dress clung to her in wet wrinkles, and her hair dripped around her face. She, too, had been crying, but she looked beautiful, vital, new. Without a word, she went and lay down on the bed beside her sister, draping an arm over her.

'What happened?' Daphne asked.

'I saw Teddy.'

'God.'

'No, it's okay. I realized that I don't know him anymore.' Livia propped herself up on an elbow and tentatively placed a hand on Daphne's belly. 'A niece,' she said.

Daphne guided her sister's hand around her side. Dominique knew Livia had never felt the baby kick; Daphne had told her so. 'Do you feel her?' Daphne asked.

'I think so. Yes!'

'Someone else is here,' Piper said, looking out the window again.

Winn opened the screen door for Agatha and eased it shut without a slam. She did not speak or touch him but made directly for the stairs, carrying her shoes in one hand. He stepped out of his loafers and set them side by side against the baseboard. He had lost his glasses in the fall, and so the house was a dim cave; the floor swallowed up his shoes. He rested a hand against the cool wall, steadying himself. Down the hallway, light spilled from the living room. He walked, conscious of the unevenness of his steps, toward it.

A woman was on the sofa under a blaze of lamplight. He thought it was Biddy but feared it might be Celeste.

'You should go up to bed.' Biddy. The sound of a page turning, and he discerned an open book in her lap. He lowered himself into an armchair. 'God,' she said, her tense voice opening up with surprise. 'What happened to you? Where are your glasses?'

'Gone,' he said, stretching out his bad leg and propping it on the coffee table. He wondered if a worker would find them caught in a gutter or half buried in a mulched flower bed. It was mulch that had saved him, an earthy-smelling mountain of it. He had landed on it and rolled down, coming to rest against the side of Fenn's house. What if his glasses were found near the downed weather vane, a clue too convenient even for the Hardy Boys? Leaning close, he examined his raw flesh through the ripped knee of his pants, studded with dark crumbs of dried blood. 'I fell off Jack Fenn's roof. I tore down his weather vane.'

'His weather vane?'

'Sort of a clipper ship thing.'

'Why?'

He rubbed his naked face. 'I don't know,' he said honestly. 'Temporary insanity?'

'Is it temporary?' Biddy asked.

'I hope so.' He smiled at her blurry shape. He felt strange: happy to be alive, full of shame, bound on his edges by a ringing sound, and filled, at his core, with love for his wife.

Biddy opened up the red plastic box that held the family first aid kit and unpeeled what was left of Winn's bandage from his leg. His torn stitches stood up like eyelashes along the edges of his wound.

'If Sam Snead were here,' she said, 'she'd get a needle and thread and sew you up herself.'

'She'd use a fishhook,' Winn said. 'And catgut.'

She held up a spray bottle of antiseptic. 'Ready?'

He gritted his teeth while she sprayed him. 'I blame her, you know. She gave me pills before dinner.'

'What kind of pills?'

'I don't know. Something to take the edge off.'

'But she wasn't the one who took them.'

'I only took one.'

'And,' Biddy continued, 'she wasn't the one who chased a pill with a couple of bottles of wine. Or who suggested marriage is a form of death. Or who vandalized a house when he said he was taking a girl to the ER.' She peeled paper from the back of a butterfly bandage and, holding his wound together as best she could, stuck it to his skin. 'I would send you back to the hospital tonight and make sure you actually got there, but I think it's best at this point if we just go to sleep. You'll have to go in the morning or between the ceremony and the reception. You'll survive. Your scar might be uglier, but that's your own fault.' She added another butterfly bandage and then ran a roll of gauze around his leg and secured the whole mess with tape. She had been sitting on the couch for hours thinking about what to say. She snipped the tape and sat back. 'Part of the reason I married you was that I thought you wouldn't do anything to surprise me. I have to say, I'm not happy you've decided to become a loose cannon after all these years. I didn't sign up for this. I never expected you to be perfect, but I expected you to be, I don't know, steady in your imperfections. I'm a realist. I've always been a realist.'

'Biddy.' He leaned close, and at first she thought he was trying to kiss her, but then she realized he was only trying to get a read on her expression. Without his glasses he was moleishly nearsighted.

She turned away, repacking the first aid kit. 'To bed.'

'Biddy,' he said with reluctance, 'I have to tell you something.'

She snapped the kit closed. 'I don't want to hear it,' she said firmly. 'Wait until after the wedding. Or never. Tell me never, Winn. I don't want to move to the village of the truth tellers. I don't want to know about tonight. I don't want to know about the past. Nothing. This has never been something I wanted to know about. Like I said, I'm a realist.'

He frowned and shook his head, looking muddled. She wondered if he had a concussion from his fall or if he was still working through the booze and pills or what. She thought she had been clear enough. 'Biddy,' he said. He reached for her chin and brought his face so close to hers that their noses were almost touching.

'No,' she said, pulling away. 'I'll look the other way, Winn, but you have to give me some time.'

'Look the other way?'

She spoke slowly, wishing he had not chosen this particular moment to hash all this out. She wanted to enjoy Daphne's wedding, for them all to have a nice day. 'You said you were going to the hospital. But, instead, you took Agatha to a construction site. I'm not asking you why. What would you have done if I had just gone off with some man?'

'You would never do that.'

'I know – you can't even conceive of it. I made up my mind about these things a long time ago. Of all people, I don't think *I* placed unreasonable demands on you. I don't think I asked things that – how did you phrase it? – could only be expected from God. But that doesn't mean I want to talk about it. I want you to go to bed.'

He leaned back, and something appeared to dawn on him. 'You think I was cheating on you?' he said, looking astonished. 'All these years?'

'Well,' she said, 'you didn't seem to be in love with me or to want me very much, and you were gone so often. Obviously, you must have had opportunities. I just assumed . . . I thought . . . well, people need more than what you wanted from me.'

'They do?'

'Don't they?'

They stared at each other. He went slightly cross-eyed in his effort to bring her face into focus. 'Did you,' he asked, 'ever need more?'

She had been faithful to him, always, but she had also always been prepared to imply the opposite if only to level the playing field. 'Does it matter?' she said after a pause.

★　　★　　★

Biddy was wearing a white sweater, and to Winn's exhausted, uncorrected eyes, she looked angelic, soft and insubstantial, floating beneath the painful fireball that was the lamp. He had no answer to her question, and she seemed to expect none. He wanted to stop talking about these things, these hard things, to stop thinking about them. He couldn't tell her that he'd never felt more bound to her, that they had become too elaborately and permanently tangled for any sins to extricate them. We are included in all of our days, he thought. And he would be in all of Biddy's days, and she in his. They sat in silence. Winn remembered he had a spare pair of glasses in his desk and heaved himself up from the armchair to retrieve them, following an awkward, tentative path to his study and fumbling through the drawers. When he returned, sighted, to the living room, he sat beside his wife and patted her feet through the blanket. The ship's clock atop the bookshelves still said it was four thirty. 'I'm never going to get into the Pequod,' he said in a conversational tone, beginning the arduous task of hauling them back to normality. 'Jack Fenn told me. I ran into him in the bathroom.'

'Really?' she said. 'Did he say why not?'

'Apparently, they just don't like me.'

She nodded. The clock ticked, but its hands remained in place. After a minute, she said, 'You smell like manure.'

He tented his shirt over his nose and breathed in. Yes, it was there, earthy and pungent over the sourness of his armpits and the faintest trace of Agatha's musk. 'I landed on a pile of mulch.'

'You really could have died.'

'I think so. I fell a long way.'

'Were you afraid?'

'I think I was lonely.'

After Livia had been in bed for ten or fifteen minutes, the door opened and Celeste came in. Where she had been all this time, Livia had no idea. Probably she had fallen asleep somewhere else, then woken and trailed upstairs like a sleepy child. Celeste went into the bathroom and turned on the light, leaving the door ajar, and once the sound of peeing had ceased and the toilet flushed, Livia watched through slitted eyes as Celeste stood at the sink in her underwear, leaning close to the mirror and then stepping back from it, turning to one side and then the other to appraise the flatness of her belly and the height of her fake breasts in their white lace bra, craning back over her shoulder to scrutinize her butt. Her legs were tanned to the color of Peking duck, and although she was thin as a whippet, her skin hung slack in places – at the junction of ass and thigh, on the inside of the knee – in tiny, pleated wrinkles.

Celeste clambered onto the other bed, pulled up the covers, and began her night's snoring. Livia's thoughts drifted toward. Teddy, but she pushed them away, sending them, like a toy boat drawn to treacherous rapids, gliding toward

Sterling. She nudged them again, and they seemed to float toward her father but settled instead on the tumulus of Daphne's belly, on the girl inside it, the feeling of the tiny foot pressing against Daphne's flesh. The whale was on the ocean floor, and the crabs and fish and worms were feasting. After a while, she heard her parents come up the stairs and go down the hall into their room, first the light, rapid steps of her mother and then the heavier, uneven tread of her father. Their door shut behind them, and she heard the murmur of their voices, the unknowable language they spoke only to each other.

SATURDAY

CHAPTER 18

THE OUROBOROS

The ceremony was *lovely* and *wonderful*. Everyone said so. The rain had stopped in the early morning, and the island seemed new and green, the ocean replenished. Winn had escorted Daphne down the aisle without bothering to disguise his limp. He was the walking wounded, after all, his riven leg held together only by a flimsy panacea of gauze and tape applied by his wife. He had remembered to kiss Daphne when they reached the altar, leaning into the airy, pale space beneath her veil and touching his lips to her powdery cheek.

Under a white tent on a bluff overlooking the Atlantic, the guests sat on gilt chairs at round tables. The sky purpled and then blackened, and the moon, lopsided and waning, drew a gleaming white shell driveway on the water, showing the way to Spain. Sam Snead was in his ear: time for the father-of-the bride and the bride to dance. He faced Daphne on the parquet. The music began, and he entwined his fingers with hers. The bones and tendons of her hand seemed like the exquisite rendering of some mechanically perfect puppet. He was aware of the hardness of her small fingers between his own, the movement of blood through her veins. His other hand rested on her back, and her white-shrouded belly filled the space between them. While the band played the opening measures and the singer in a white dinner jacket pulled the microphone from its cradle, Winn did not move but stood looking over Daphne's shoulder at the faces of the people at the tables, a wall of expectant ovals punctuated here and there by the glitter of jewelry and candle flames. Then the bandleader was singing and Daphne was stepping backward and pulling him with her, tipping him into the familiar steps. As they danced, Daphne stared over his shoulder. He turned them so he could see what she was looking at, but there was nothing. Only tables and faces. She was still looking at the same spot, now on the other side of the room, her face calm but wistful, like someone watching a receding shoreline. He turned her again. He wanted to see it, too, what she was looking at, but he saw only tables, only faces.

Maude and Greyson joined them, then Biddy with Dicky Sr. Francis had Agatha under his grasping hands, and Dryden expertly propelled a twirling Dominique. Livia pivoted by in the arms of Charlie the groomsman. Winn spun Daphne out, and she returned obediently, her hand on his shoulder. The flowers, the candles, the easy swing of the music, his daughter's perfectly made-up face, her artfully arranged hair, the swell of her pregnancy – it all cried out for love, for pride, for fatherly tenderness, even if Daphne would not look at him, even if she had walled herself up with her happiness and left him outside. He did not know how to make her forgive him. He would have to wait. But, in the meantime, he knew how to dance, had danced this same dance as a little boy in cotillion, had danced it with Ophelia Haviland on New Year's Eve at the Vespasian Club and as a bridegroom on a spring evening in Maine and a thousand other times.

The song ended and another began. Greyson came to claim Daphne, and Winn stood alone among the dancers before he found himself holding Livia in her green dress. At first she looked over his shoulder as Daphne had, but then her eyes met his. For the first time, he wondered what she thought of him, really thought, and the question was enough to make him dizzy, to spin the faces and candles and flowers around him, her eyes the still point at the center of it all. For an instant he felt with nauseating clarity what it was like to breathe through his daughter's lungs, to peer out from inside her skull, to be animated by a life that was just like his but also nothing like it. He had to look away, up at the underbelly of the tent, before he could fall back into himself.

Dancing demanded no thought, only habit, but her presence in his arms had become a burden, a reminder of a vastness he could not contemplate. Finally, when he could bear no more, he lifted his arm and spun her away. When her revolution was complete and they were separated by the length of their arms, joined only by their fingertips, he let go, releasing her into a life of her own making.